Library of Congress Cataloging-in-Publication Data

Drake, Monica.
Clown Girl : a novel / by Monica Drake. —1st ed.
p. cm.
ISBN 0-9766311-5-6

1. Clowns—Fiction.
2. Women performance artists—Fiction.

I. Title.

PS3604.R354C55 2007

813'.54—DC22

2006020248

Hawthorne Books
& Literary Arts

9 1221 SW 10th Avenue
8 Suite 408
7 Portland, OR 97205
6 hawthornebooks.com
5 *Form*:
4 Pinch, Portland, OR
3
2 Printed in China through Print Vision

Set in Paperback.

First Edition.
Second printing, February 2007.

For Kass and for Mavis

TO WRITE THIS BOOK, OR ANY BOOK, WOULD HAVE BEEN impossible without the love and support of so many people. In gratitude, I thank:

Kassten Alonso, who understood this novel from its inception, who's not afraid to laugh at a clown, drink red wine and say *What if, what if, what if?*; Alex Behr, for her generosity and attention to detail; Tom Spanbauer, who taught me the urgency of storytelling, the value of voice; all the writers in our workshop, particularly Chuck Palahniuk, Stevan Allred, Suzy Vitello, Greg Netzer and Erin Leonard; Cherryl Janisse; Nirel; Cynthia Chimienti, gorgeous comedienne, keeper of costumes and ritual; Mickey Lindsay, with her brilliance, who knows why ducks are funny; Shelley Reese; A.B. Paulson; Larry Bowlden, who asked *How's the writing?* even before I started writing; Rhonda Hughes; Kate Sage; my parents and family, Barbara Drake, Bud Drake, Moss Drake and Bellen Drake; Charles Mudede; Karalynn Ott; Haley Carrolhach; Kevin Canty; Pete Rock; Elizabeth Evans; Carolyn Holzman, who taught me to defy gravity, or at least keep on trying; and for Candy Mulligan, in memory. —M.D.

Clown Girl

A Novel
Monica Drake

HAWTHORNE BOOKS & LITERARY ARTS
Portland, Oregon | MMVI

Introduction

WELCOME TO THE BOOK OF MY ARCH ENEMY. "RIVAL"
would be a nicer word, but let's be honest.

In 1991, in Tom Spanbauer's kitchen, where our whole workshop of beginning writers still fit around his dinky kitchen table,
every week Monica Drake was the star. The stories she read to
us ... about sitting all night locked inside the Portland Art Museum,
alone to guard the ancient mummy of a Chinese empress, staring
at a dish filled with the preserved contents of the mummy's
stomach—mostly ancient pumpkin seeds. As Monica talked about
being locked behind steel gates and barred doors and bulletproof Plexiglas, the rest of Tom's students, we'd forget to breathe.

Every Thursday night, Monica told about hunting for cash
register receipts in supermarket parking lots, even begging
shoppers for their receipts as they loaded bags of food into their
cars, all because the store sold eggs for twenty-five cents per
dozen if you could present receipts totaling twenty-five dollars.
Monica wrote about a world where characters ate nothing
but cheap eggs, getting stinkier and stinkier in apartments where
everything had been broken at least one time. Wire or glue held
together every cracked lamp and dish or splintered chair. Poverty
and violence haunted every situation. People bought and sold
food stamps for enough profit so they could drink NyQuil all day
and stagger the streets with a permanent green mustache. Her
characters, like the best characters, Monica based on real people
in her life.

To make Thursday nights even worse, Monica's stories made everyone in Tom's workshop laugh. Laughter so loud and honest that to people passing on the sidewalk, in the dark, we might have been apes hooting, or dogs barking.

No matter what you'd bring to read, Monica would write something better, funnier, more surprising, and sexy. Every week, Monica Drake showed us how good stories could be. Tom taught us craft, but Monica taught us freedom. Courage. If my writing improved, it's because her work was always better. If a story of mine got laughs, hers were always funnier. Monica moved away from Portland to study with Amy Hempel and Joy Williams, and now she has a first novel. *Clown Girl*. And all over again, Monica's showing us just how funny and nuts and sad storytelling can be.

Writing this introduction, I'm not doing an old friend a favor—I'm paying a decade-old debt. This isn't charity or flattery— this is honesty.

Writers are nothing if not rivals, but competition as good as Monica Drake is a blessing.

Clown Girl is more than a great book. *Clown Girl* is its own reality.

We should all have an arch enemy this brilliant.

CHUCK PALAHNIUK
Author of *Fight Club*

CLOWN GIRL

People will do anything, no matter how absurd, to avoid facing their own souls.

CARL JUNG

In a theater it happened that a fire started offstage. The clown came out to tell the audience. They thought it was a joke and applauded. He told them again, and they became still more hilarious. This is the way, I suppose, that the world will be destroyed—amid the universal hilarity of wits and wags who think it is all a joke.

SØREN KIERKEGAARD

1.

The Clown Falls Down; or, Sniffles Stumbles

BALLOON TYING FOR CHRIST WAS THE CHEAPEST BALLOON manual I could find. The day I bought it, it was hidden on the lowest rung of a dusty spinner rack down at Callan's Novelties, snuggled alongside shopworn how-to guides: *Travel Europe by Clown Circuit!*, *Rubber Vomit Skits for Beginners*, and *Latex: The Beauty of Cuts, Bruises, Scars, and Contusions.*

Want to tie the Virgin Mary? Start with a light blue balloon. For Jesus, use Easter green. There are tips on tying a crucifix, a lamb, even a Sacred Heart in two sizes, big or small. Ooo la la! These tricks are simple but smart. The grand finale is the *pietà*, Mary with a grown Jesus sprawled across her lap in a four-balloon extravaganza like a tangled link of sausages, or a Japanese bondage trick. The *pietà* or bondage, sacred and profane; in balloon art the two are that close together, one thin twist.

I studied all twenty pages of the flimsy, hand-stapled booklet. And so, ta da! By the chance of cheap pricing I'd come to specialize in religious tricks, clown iconography and chicanery extraordinaire! Most people, though, looked at my balloon art and saw what they wanted to see instead. It was Interpretive Art, abstract and expressionistic. The big plan? I had one. Someday I'd be able to tie all the great works, starting with da Vinci's *Madonna of the Rocks* complete with Baby Jesus, John the Baptist, and a little balloon-twisted angel clustered together on a rocky perch. Already I'd invented my own version of the Sistine Chapel,

Michelangelo's image of God giving breath to Adam. Two balloons linked formed their famous outstretched fingers.

Saturday afternoon, in the thick of a street crowd, I tied a crown of thorns and handed the crown to a tiny girl in a fake leopard sundress. She put the crown on her head as a tiara. "Lovely, lovely," the girl's mother murmured, and tapped the crown with one jeweled hand.

Pure princess, in a crown meant for a martyr.

The mother pulled her tiny daughter away from the spill of day care overflow, five-year-olds out to celebrate the King's Row street fair. The pack surged forward. My makeup was sweating off and my feet hit flat and hard against the cement in cheap, oversized shoes. The summer sun was hotter than I'd ever welcome in the city even on a Saturday. Unused balloons clumped together in the hothouse of my pink vinyl shoulder bag alongside juggling balls, a sleek silver gun, and the gentle rub of a rubber chicken. I pulled out a handful of balloons like gummed spaghetti.

It is easier for a camel to go through the eye of a needle, than for a rich man to enter into the kingdom of God ... That's the biblical quote, but in the world of balloon art the old Camel Through the Eye of a Needle trick is easier than it sounds. Start with one balloon, underinflated. Make the camel really small. Twist a long balloon around the camel's back—that's the needle—and cinch it like a girdle.

I passed the camel and the needle to the dirty fist of the highest bidder, an anonymous reaching hand with a five-dollar tip crushed in it. Bingo! A five-year-old with a five-spot was rich enough for the temporary kingdom of balloon heaven on earth. I shoved the cash in the sleeve of my striped shirt, pulled out another balloon.

Once balloon tying starts you can't get away. There's always a river of kids. I was hired as a *roving* clown, but no way could I rove. Kids had me corralled, pushed to the side of the Do-Your-Own ceramics place, what used to be the Wishy Washy Laundry with all-day breakfast and off-track betting. Next door was the Pawn and

Preen, our little local hockshop salon, but the P and P had been
turned into a dog biscuit bakery, and for this King's Row celebrated.
Street fair vendors filled the air with the grease of Wiggly Fries.
I whistled, *tra la la*, and tried to sidle. Kids blocked my path like
little sentries, hands up, demanding balloons.

Matey and Crack were team-juggling. Crack balanced on a
fire hydrant. I waved a hand. *Ah, yoo-hoo!* I pulled an automated
plastic wolf whistle from the sleeve of my shirt and gave it a go.
With the press of a button, the whistle let loose the loud up-and-
down bars of a sexy call.

They looked my way. I waved again.

They stopped juggling and froze. Matey drew fast from her
old Creative Incompetence routine; she turned to Crack, looked
over her shoulder, past the purple stuffed parrot sewn there, and
made herself comic-style confused, head tipped, one hand
scratching. Crack leaned back and shook a long, striped, stocking-
covered leg at me, a floozy on the fire hydrant in her version of
a high-wire act. They mirrored each other's shoulder shrugs and
went back to juggling.

I was on my own. There was no room for sidling, running,
sneaking off. No way out but on with the show. To tie a wise man,
start with yellow, a knot at his neck like a collapsed artery, head
like an engorged penis. Yellow is all about wisdom. It doesn't say
that in the Christian book, but Buddha was yellow, every good
Buddhist knows it, and in the nineteenth century some big psychic
seer announced that a wise person's aura is mostly yellow too.
The Hopi Indians, they believe in the wisdom of yellow clowns. I
tied a skinny sheep for a greasy-haired kid and another took his
spot like water rushing in.

With the tip of the toe on my oversized shoe, I pantomimed
a line on the sidewalk, a place not to cross, and the kids crossed it.

Hands to my hips, balloons in a fist, I drew the line again.
One kid pushed three others over the line, and they laughed.
I squirted the squirting daisy pinned to my frayed lapel. A spit of

water hit a child's face. "Hey!" he said, and wiped a hand down his cheek. Another kid pushed him forward.

I squirted again, still smiling.

Those kids, the beasts, vigorous in their balloon lust, were God's constant audience, according to *Balloon Tying for Christ*. But for the moment they were my audience, my bread and butter, and they grabbed my clown pants, my shoulder bag, my hot, limp balloons.

The rubber chicken fell out of my prop bag. I dove for the chicken, chased off a pudgy dumpling of a child, got up and fast pantomimed the line again.

The problem was, by my own self-imposed rules I couldn't speak. I couldn't yell. I don't believe there is a good clown voice except maybe a helium breather or some loud, fake Italian braying. Any human voice spoken from a clown face ruins the illusion. My kind of clown says nothing. If we were the Marx brothers— Matey, Crack, and me, I'd be Harpo. If we were in mime gear, what I do might look like mime. The result? Kids don't listen, but on the up-side—I've never been asked on so many dates in my life.

I tied another sheep and broke a clown rule by making two of the same animal in a row. While I tied the sheep and drew the line on the ground to hold back the pack of tiny, sticky hands, a man passed me his business card. *Who are you?* he'd written on the back. *Can I get your number?*

He was an architect, the card said. A Spatial Use and Planning Consultant.

A clown fetishist. A coulrophile. I put the card in my bag and gave a fresh balloon a quick, professional snap. Blowing up balloons made me dizzy, but it was only a passing moment of dizziness. Learning to blow a long, tight, and skinny balloon is a trick in itself—it's all diaphragm, no cheek action. Maybe that's what the fetishists like, the lip work. I smiled at the architect sweating in his summer suit. His face was flushed. His hands ended in a row of rubbery pink fingers like underinflated balloon art.

A second man gave me the dancing-eyebrow leer, flashed

a rack of polished teeth. He was tall, with a head of white-blond hair like a dandelion gone to seed.

I winked back. Gave him a quick wolf call with the whistle now hidden in my pocket. He stepped forward in an amateur clown walk, all bent knees and low to the ground in a long stride like an old R. Crumb "Keep on Trucking" poster. *Nice try.* I squirted my squirting daisy. A silver thread of water arced through the short space between us and rained down against the dandelion man's khaki-clad crotch. Ta da! He stepped back, half-laughed, stepped forward again.

Fetishists don't give up.

I squirted a second warning shot, fluttered my eyes over a fresh balloon, doubled over, then reared back and blew the balloon up like playing a wailing saxophone. I turned to the kids. The balloon grew larger and tauter until it was long and arched as an eager cock. A cock that I'd twist into a religious trick, maybe a Sacred Heart, one of the Shepherd's flock, an angel or cross.

Baby Jesus in a crèche is a quick trick, fast in pale pink. But kids never get it. Some fly it like a bumblebee, others hold it against their knuckles like a swollen hand, a vaginal cluster of plump pink rolls.

Then the crown-of-thorns girl came back, the princess in her leopard sundress. She pushed her way past kids and coulrophiles, mom in tow. The girl was screaming, crying, her free hand full of damp, split rubber.

Such a big voice from such a tiny girl.

"It's O K, baby. The clown'll make you a new one," the mother said, and signed me up like she didn't see the pack of kids already waiting.

I had to move fast. Once kids start cycling back through the line, balloon tying is a losing battle. Sheep boy would be next, his sheep-styled balloon popped in the heat, swollen with the day's sun, twisted into final submission and gone to the big balloon party in the sky.

Nothing lasts forever, right?

It was time to rove. Get lost in the crowd. The kids had me trapped, as Our Lady of the Perpetual Poppers. I tied a third sheep and let the leopard sundress cry. I held up a finger, pointed to another child. Clown sign language for *wait your turn*. I meant to start making anything else—Jesus on the Cross, a wise man, one of the lowing cattle, or even a good old nondenominational, interfaith duck, balloon loon, or common quacker—but all my hands could tie was another sheep. The kids screamed, *No*.

I did a little polka with my sheep, then passed it to a quiet-seeming girl. She tucked her hands under her armpits. "A flower," she said. "I want a flower."

All I could tie was sheep! I couldn't think. This had never happened before. It was like some kind of a stroke, my brain shutting down. The screaming and laughing and crying of children was a wall of white noise that severed my body from my brain. Sheep and sheep and sheep. Light blue, I tied a sheep. Green, more sheep. Even yellow—a wise sheep.

Fake leopard sundress howled and clung to her mother. I waved good-bye, clown sign language for *go away*. The fetishist architect hovered in the near distance. The other, the dandelion-headed dandy with the high-buck smile, he was gone.

I started to tie a replacement crown of thorns but it turned into another sheep. Sheep piled at my feet with all the same twists, the same fat bubbles. The hot force of the sun was like a hand traveling its ninety million or billion or kazillion, however many miles to press against my skin and melt the polyester of my striped Goodwill pants, the ad-libbed clown suit. The sun, the kids, the screams—I felt faint, empty, small as an insect sliding underfoot. The world was onstage. I was the lone audience slouched in the cheap seats.

This wasn't the clown I set out to be.

Once my plan in clowndom was to defeat physics and defy gravity by using sheer strength to balance in positions seemingly impossible in the Newtonian world. I choreographed a silent adaptation of Kafka's "The Metamorphosis," costumed and lit as a live equivalent of black- and-white film. The show was glorious in its melancholy, physical beauty!

"The Metamorphosis"—the story of a man turned into an insect—was the story of all humanity! *When Gregor Samsa woke up one morning from unsettling dreams, he found himself changed in his bed into a monstrous vermin.* Self-expression was the antidote to verminville; I practiced and practiced until I was Kafka's tale incarnate.

But productions are expensive. I needed cash. A software company came out of nowhere and hit me in my sore spot. They offered big cash for a few hours of work, a few tricks. A party. Corporations don't care about bodies defying gravity, human teeter-totters, and translated literature. Kafka? No. They want silly walks, balloons, and juggling. The money's there.

What a grueling job I've picked, Kafka wrote. *Day in, day out...*

I bought my first bag of balloons and the flimsy paperback *Balloon Tying for Christ* as a sure way to fill contracted time. Next thing I knew, I was a corporate clown. I worked for an international cookie company, a burger chain, a mortgage investment bank. I met Matey and Crack on the job. Crack had an agent. She waggled a finger, flashed a few paychecks, and at her side I turned full-on commercial clown as a temporary deal. For the street fair gig, she hooked us up with the Neighborhood Business Association.

I twisted another sheep head, another pillowed body; the kids screamed. My arms were heavy. The world moved closer, noises louder and colors glaring migraine bright. I fell to my knees, fell on my flock of sheep. Balloons squeaked and squirted out from beneath my weight and danced into the air. They shifted, drifting around me. The kids laughed. Of course they laughed! The rubber chicken poked a leg out of my bag as the bag slipped from my shoulder.

Tiny hands brushed against my clothes. Their voices were as one, the cackle of an amplified gag gift, a screeching giggle box. They pressed the squirting daisy, pulled the pom-poms used as hair. One kid took the chicken and swung it over his head. I reached, but could barely breathe in a claustrophobic cloud of peanut butter, grape jam, and soft, sour milk breath. I looked around for the architect, my fan. Any coulrophile would do.

When I caught the eye of a passing stranger, I tipped an invisible glass to my lips. Water. I needed water. The guy kept going. Another looked. I pointed my thumb to my mouth, hand in a fist, pinkie cocked. A drink. I needed a drink.

Clown games.

Nobody would hold my gaze. No adults anyway. They looked in the window over my head, at ceramics, coffee cups, and baby clothes. Where were the fetishists when I needed one? There's no easier way to be invisible than through the embarrassment of clown gear mixed with a plea for audience involvement. Finally, as I curled on my drifting bed of sheep, a man slipped me his card. The card fell into my hand. *Call me*, he'd written, with his number.

A golf course designer. A golf course *spatial use and planning consultant.*

I grabbed his wrist and broke my clown rule—I spoke. "A drink," I whispered.

He smiled. "A drink. Sounds good. Let me know when."

I held on. My fingers pressed tighter around the metal accordion of his watchband. I whispered, "No, I need a drink now. Water…" I said, "I'm sick."

He reached for his card back and shook his wrist free. So long to the dream date! The fetish was broken, the fantasy gone; I was only a sick girl in makeshift clown clothes. He said, "Hey," out loud to nobody, and backed away. His silver watch flashed in the sun. "The clown's sick."

No Florence Nightingale, this clown-stalking links designer.

Matey and Crack turned. The stuffed purple parrot swung on Matey's pirate-clown shoulder and the world receded into a wash of soft colors. The wail of the girl in her fake leopard sundress grew dim. There was a hum that wouldn't stop. I closed my eyes, cheek pressed into the hot hard gravel of the sidewalk. It was coming for me—the short, meaningless life of an insect. Sheep bodies touched my skin lightly, carefully, like a priest's last rites, like gentle kisses. Swimming or drowning, there's not much difference. I was flooded with grease-laden festival air, the bodies, the heat, the weight of air itself. I drifted toward balloon heaven. I was that transitory thing, an underinflated sheep, an empty carcass not meant to last.

W. C. Fields wandered across my mind's eye. He shook a stogie, and in his slow, drunken drawl said, "Hey, don't worry about your heart…it'll last as long as you live." He took a swig off a flask, turned away, and disappeared.

"My heart!" I said out loud, suddenly worried.

"You'll be O K," somebody else said, a real-world voice.

Rex Galore? My clown mate, my savior. A word from Rex and I'd revive; Rex had found me on the street. He was back in town. A hand brushed my face, trailed by the bite of cinnamon.

"Relax," he said. "Take a deep breath. You'll make it."

I wanted to believe his words, to be the truth of the story he told.

I opened my eyes to the blue of a shirt sleeve, a hand reaching out. It wasn't Rex. It was a cop. A cop had cleared the kids back.

House Rule Number One where I lived: Don't talk to cops.

But the cop put his fingers to my pulse. My head was woozy. The cop gave me water. It was a magic trick, the way he pulled the paper cup pulled from the crowd; the cup was suddenly in the cop's hand, then in mine. "Help is on the way," he said and wrapped his fingers around my fingers to hold the cup. A magical cop. Hair on the back of his fingers was sparse, golden as jewelry. His eyes were pale blue. With his second hand he propped up my head. I rested against his palm like a pillow. "Can you tell me your name?" he asked.

Anonymity. It's in the Clown Code of Ethics: *I will always try to remain anonymous while in makeup and costume, though there may be times when it is not reasonably possible to do so*. These were my promises: I wouldn't talk to cops and I wouldn't speak in costume.

I opened my mouth and said, "Nita."

He said, "You need a ... ?"

"Nita," I whispered again, with all the energy I had. The only thing holding the cup in my hand was the cop's hand around mine. Between our two hands our skin grew hot, sweat mingled. He leaned in close. He smelled like cinnamon streusel, apple pancakes. Delicious.

"What do you need?"

His hand, and his help, made me both sad and happy at the same time, and I couldn't hold on to the mix; I felt something inside lift. I was still on the ground while a heat in my body struggled to climb up. The feeling caught in my throat and closed down there, like a sob. Clotted. I couldn't speak if I wanted to.

He squinted, teetered, then caught his balance poised in a crouch. His breath brushed my skin. Ah! Too much. I took another deep, cinnamon-streusel breath. The cop was so close I could've kissed him. For one minute I didn't see him as a cop but as a man, concerned, all sweet skin and golden hair. The cop's eyes narrowed as he waited and listened. Patient. I asked, "Do I know you?"

He was young enough, but still when he narrowed his eyes his skin there turned into a weathered, radiant arc of wrinkles. He shook his head. "No," he said. "We've never met." I saw the blue of the uniform again. He was a cop, doing his job. I was a citizen in trouble.

Rex Galore was what I needed. My Clown Prince. That strong giant, Rex, darling shaman and showman; a touch of his hand would make everything right. Rex was far away. All I had was a cop, a flatfoot, an outsider to our outsider lifestyle.

"Bleeding?" I asked, and my voice cracked as it climbed past that knot of throated sadness mixed with hope. One word, mumbled. Then two: "Am I?"

He said, "You're not bleeding. "Do you have I D?"

My Clown Union card was tucked in my polka-dot bra. I didn't move for it.

The cop took the cup from my hand—from our hands—and set the cup on the ground. Where he peeled his hand from mine, the air was suddenly cool in the empty space that had been our sweaty warmth. I wanted him to hold my hand again, to say that I'd be okay, to anchor me in the world. Instead he reached in the loose pocket of my saggy polyester high-waters, the clown clothes, and his cinnamon smell surrounded me. His cop fingers brushed my thigh through the thin cloth of the pocket lining. He pulled out a handkerchief tied to a handkerchief tied to a handkerchief tied to another handkerchief, never ending.

The kids were a silent pack, watching. Adults looked too now because cop action is the adult entertainment version of a clown show and holds everyone's attention. He pushed the clothesline of pastel handkerchiefs back into my pocket. The sun was a gilded halo around his head, his forehead lined and anxious. He hit the wolf whistle in my pocket, and the whistle screamed out its two notes, one up, one down. The sexy call.

The crowd roared. I felt sick. I lay back against the cop's arm.

"Her name?" he asked again, and looked around.

"Does anybody know her name?" A juggling ball rolled out of my pink prop bag into the feet of the crowd. A kid went after it, chasing the ball the way a dog would.

"Sniffles?"

A voice in the crowd. It was Matey. Matey speaking up. Matey, my co-worker, who didn't even know my real name.

2.

My Chicken, My Child!; or, Clown Bashing Lite

AT THE HOSPITAL DON'T SHOW UP IN CLOWN GEAR, PAINTED with the lush designs of clown face, because if you do, even clean underwear and an ambulance ride won't win your credibility back. They brought me in on a gurney. Somebody said, "She looks a little pale. Ha ha!" He thought I was passed out. I saw him through my eyelashes, hoped he wasn't my doctor.

Don't tell them you've lost your rubber chicken—don't let on that the rubber chicken matters, even if that chicken was half your act, your only child, love made manifest.

I told the EMTs about the rubber chicken on the ride over. "Somebody has to find it," I pleaded. "I can't lose my chicken." They didn't blink.

In the hospital, the EMTs unbuckled the gurney seat belt straps. I half-sat up, sick and limp, then climbed onto an ER cot and closed my eyes again. My mouth was dry, clouded with words I wouldn't say.

"Another clown bashing?" a triage nurse asked. She lifted my arm and slid on the blood pressure cuff. There'd been a string of clown bashings in town. Hate crimes. Meringue pies full of scrap iron, fire extinguishers at full blast. Gary Lewis and his pack of Playboys, they had it wrong—not everybody loves a clown. The crimes were never prosecuted; clowns didn't come forward. What do you say? *Officer, a joke's a joke, but only when it's consensual!*

The blood pressure cuff squeezed my bicep tight as a fist, like a dime-store security guard with a shoplifter. The black balloon of the armband throbbed against my pulse. A second nurse shook his head. "Self-destructed, this one." With a sharp bite, he slid a needle in the back of my hand to hook up a saline drip.

Some people hate clowns, others are afraid, though hate and fear are really one and the same. Those coulrophobics, with their Fear of One Who Walks on Stilts. Fear of one with special skills, clown skills. My only skills.

Nobody cared about my chicken, my child.

The blood pressure cuff dropped away in the release of a deep exhale. The first nurse swabbed my makeup off. She hit me with a damp cotton ball in fast jabs. My face was reflected in the chrome of instruments. The jabbing swabber left white streaks along my chin and blue-black rings that seeped into the creases around my eyes. My lips were still pomegranate red, more like a tweaking hooker than a clown. The intake nurse said, "Rest quietly. Breathe. Let yourself hydrate."

I sipped the air-conditioned air of the hospital like water, in tiny breaths. My heart knocked against my chest like a bird against a window.

She said, "Do you have ID?"

I sat up, fished a hand around inside my sun-hot bra, and pulled out two curled photos. The first photo was of a couple standing on the end of a pier, far away and blurred. Unrecognizable. It was a photo of my parents, so young they weren't even my parents yet, so young they were still in black and white. So young they were still alive, hadn't met their fate on a winding California highway. This was the only picture I had of them and I kept it against my skin, close to my heart. The second photo was of Rex Galore in full costume and full color, breathing fire, and when I saw the photo all over again it was as though he were the one who made me warm that day, not the sun at all but Rex's breath against my skin, his fire act. I dropped the photos on the cot and fished in my bra again until I found my Clown Union card plastered to the sweat of my lower left boob. It came up stuck to my prize patron saint trading card, St. Julian. There was ink on my skin where the card stuck, transferred and reversed into a tattoo by the heat.

The union card lay damp and ragged in the nurse's clean palm. She put it on the counter.

"I don't leave home without it," I said.

The nurse didn't say "crazy" but she did say "social worker." She patted my leg. "Let's get someone for you to talk to, all right?"

"Talk to?" Talk therapy was clown treatment. I could barely hear over the knock and flutter of my own pounding heart, the buzz in my head. I needed a doctor. I gathered my wheezy breath. "Do most people take a fast ride here in the Blood Mobile just for the conversation?"

If I had a broken bone, a concussion, or was in shock, they wouldn't sign me up with their social worker. What if I were an old man, overweight, near the end of a life of beef and sherry? That'd show a history of self-induced statistics toward cardiac arrest— slow suicide. But still, that man would get more than a layman's priest.

I was a clown and got clown treatment: placating voices, a lack of concern. It was Clown Bashing Lite. I said, "If I were a sacred yellow Hopi clown, my people wouldn't treat me like this."

The face swabber came at me again with her damp cotton ball. "Treat you like what, dear?"

Dear?

"That's exactly what I mean!" I pointed at her. I couldn't explain. She wouldn't understand, and nothing would change anyway. But if I were a Hopi clown, it might be said that I looked into the grave and climbed back out, traversed a fine tightrope and made it back for an encore. I'd earn a place of honor.

Instead, the male nurse told the swabber, "She fainted on the street. Fell down." He made an arm gesture, like a tree falling, from elbow to palm. "Maybe hit her head."

The fall was a symptom, not the cause. I said, "I didn't hit my head."

My left arm pulsed and buzzed, my head hummed; my heart

beat against my breastbone like a fist throwing a punch. I caught my breath and said, "How about a doctor? Could I talk to a doctor?"

The triage nurse said, "Do you have family we could call?"

The photos lay curled on the cot. I had all the family I needed in Rex Galore. Better than a phone call, they could bring Rex home, fly him up from San Francisco, steal him away from his interview with Clown College. Then I'd be cured.

When Rex was in town, I'd tell him about the baby we lost. I'd look into his painted face, his brown eyes circled with blue. I'd tell him about the rubber chicken, our pet Plucky, our only child, now gone. After I told him, I'd sleep.

I hadn't slept in a week.

I needed to lie down with the solidness of Rex's bony knuckles, his knobby knees next to mine, his skinny butt and wide acrobat's shoulders and the length of him stretched out on the bed beside me. His arm would be an awkward rock of a pillow below my head. My chest was tight and my hands were numb. With clumsy hands, I scrawled Rex's name and a phone number, the number for a clown hostel. I'd seen the hostel once, where it sat on a field of green and overlooked the blue of the San Francisco Bay.

The nurse said, "Long distance?" Like she expected instead a whole family nearby, maybe packed into a tiny Studebaker idling in the hospital parking lot.

"He's the only family I've got," I said.

The second photo, my parents? That was ancient, ancient history.

A doctor listened to my chest. Only then did they hook me to an EKG. The EKG spit out a code of dancing lights. On the electrocardiogram, I watched my heart like a muted mouth open wide; it screamed one silent word repeatedly. The emergency room doctor read my heart's code, and made the translation: *Ni-tro, Ni-tro, Ni-tro*.

That was the word, my heart's demand, the blood pump's room service order.

Abnormal Sinus Rhythm, the doctor said. Too little blood

pressure in the chambers. "We'll set you up with a cardiologist," he said. "Get a second opinion."

They gave me nitroglycerin. They gave me potassium. Eensy weensy pills to do a big, big job. I would've liked nitroglycerin first thing—that tiny tab of a pill under my tongue was better than breathing, better than food. In seconds it brought my arms into circulation, put my head on my spine, made my spine calm again down my back, my chest at ease.

Somebody said what I had was a Heart Attack. Cardiac arrest.

I lay covered with a thin hospital blanket, shivering under the cooling water of the IV drip. In ICU, instead of heart attack, they said *Wait for the cardiologist. Wait for his diagnosis*. Then my condition became a heart problem, an episode, a bad spell. Anxiety.

The staff said it was a flutter, palpitations, a murmur. That bird against the window. With each passing minute the need for potassium and nitroglycerin drifted into the faded corners of collective memory, off to intermission, a perpetual smoke break in the cafeteria of the False Alarm Wing.

It happened, but nobody believed it.

Don't tell doctors your dreams, ever. Don't tell them your menstrual cycle. Don't say you felt anything *in your head*, or that you *might've known*. If they ask about street drugs, which they will, say no, no matter what. If you say, *I feel anxious all the time*, you'll get Valium. Otherwise, you'll get what they call "mood equalizers," daily doses of who knows what, a gambler's crapshoot in tinctures of chemicals.

As a clown on the street, I had to keep my wits. I couldn't take their chemicals.

Don't tell doctors anything.

A woman came to my room and asked, "Are you a certified latex-free clown? I run activities in the children's wing, and we're always looking. So many kids have allergies these days—"

I reached for my bag and pulled out a handful of balloons. She jumped back, like I'd released biological warfare, and left just as fast.

The intake nurse found me in ICU. She dropped my torn slip of paper on the nightstand. "Mr. Galore is unavailable. We've tried a dozen times."

Worst of all—and what I did—don't cry even when they don't help you, even when they only want a urine sample to charge you for a drug test you don't need, even when the third or fourth doctor asks you politely, again, about the cocaine you already told them all you don't use.

Clowns and coke, clowns as junkies and drunks—doctors can't see it any other way, but I was an artist. The junkie drunk clown thing wasn't in my bag of tricks.

THE NEXT MORNING, THE HOSPITAL CURTAIN WAS PULLED back from around my bed with a sharp scrape of metal rings on a metal bar. "Breakfast," a man sang. He put a tray on a tiny table across my waist and powered up the bed until I was sitting. "Wake up. Let's get some lights on."

I said, "I like it dim." The room was a quiet cave, a hiding place, time immaterial.

He snapped on a light as though he hadn't heard me, then said, "Or maybe this one, over here," and flicked on another beaming fluorescent.

"Off is good," I said.

"Or maybe a reading lamp," and he turned on a third, out of my reach. Soon the whole room was blasting bright, and it was clear who ran the show.

A dietician's note on the side of the breakfast tray read, "Low fat, low sodium, no caffeine." I saw between the lines, into their code: *Low patience, low humor, no tolerance. Clown.*

The man pulled open the blinds with a clatter. My view was an alley. He left me in the glow of every light, my own electric sun.

I stabbed a plastic spork into the sponge of pancake, lifted it, and the heavy dough fell off the stubby tines. I tried again. Halfway to my mouth, pancake dropped to the front of my robe in a sticky smooch. I picked the food up with my fingers, syrup trailing, and licked the empty spork; the grease slick of margarine on the back of the rounded plastic was a non-food I hadn't tasted in years.

Mid-lick of the spork, a cardiologist ducked into my room. He reached to shake my hand, and blew into the steam on a Styrofoam cup of coffee held in his other hand. I reached back with sticky fingers, breakfast rocking like a raft on the ocean of my lap.

"Well, yes," the cardiologist said, and drew his hand away. "Nice to meet you." He searched for a place to set his coffee on the bedside table, then reached for my thin paper napkin and wiped his fingers. Napkin stuck to his fingers in shredded tufts like an old man's ear hair. He sat on the edge of my bed and puzzled over my chart like it was the Sunday *Times*.

"Don't take it personally," he said, finally. "The long delay yesterday, the difficulty with diagnosis. We go by statistics, judge by likelihood. Thin women, young as you are, generally don't have heart trouble." He slid a pen from his front pocket. Made a note.

Thin women. Clown women. Skinny girls like me.

Not heart attacks, no. Skinny women have other problems. They double over, pelvis in knots, and drop stillborn babies in public places—bloody, tiny, and blue. Women have anxiety attacks, not heart attacks; they worry too much, burst into tears, faint. Ta da!

Crazy.

"It seems your mitral valve wasn't closing properly," he said, and made a hand gesture like a quacking duck. His thumb snapped against his fingers. His pen, still in hand, pointed up through the duck's beak like an oversized cigar. "That made your aortal valve work overtime. Maybe a lack of potassium. Do you eat regularly?" The duck flattened, and swirled down to my plate of pancakes.

I shrugged.

He said, "What'd you have for lunch yesterday?"

"I worked through lunch. A gig," I said. "I had a latex ham sandwich. It makes pig sounds, squeals under pressure."

He didn't laugh but only nodded, made a note, then tugged

at an invisible beard on the tip of his chin. I said "It's a prop, right? For the joke: *how's a ham sandwich like a stoolie?*"

"What else, what else?" He waved a hand in circles, like a traffic cop asking me to pull forward.

"Exploding bonbons, smoking gum. A self-refilling pitcher of white fake milk. That's a sight gag that wins every time. I'm trying to cut back on the fake milk, but it's hard. Audiences love it, Doc. I can't give it up."

He made another note. Without looking at me, he said, "What about real food?"

Real food made me want to vomit. For weeks, I had no interest. My pelvis was an empty room, food an unwelcome guest. Instead of answering, I asked, "You think caffeine could've brought this on?" It read *decaf only* all over the dietician's card on the side of my breakfast tray.

The cardiologist looked up from the notes he was writing. "You know, that'd be an interesting experiment. We could get you all jacked up on caffeine, see what happens. But for now, try to eat a little more. Start with your breakfast." He tapped my tray. "It's good stuff."

He had the sort of personality that would let a body live a long time—inquisitive, delighted, and unconscionable. He was money and science, old skin and thinning hair and rings worn into grooves below his knuckles like metal around wood. He cleared his throat and said, "Your chart shows you were admitted through the ER not too long back."

I didn't answer.

"What's this about a miscarriage?" he asked. He smoothed a frazzled eyebrow with the side of his thumb.

Miscarriage! The word made it sound like I dropped my juggling pins or fumbled a football instead of floundered my way through the blood and cramps of lost life. I said, "Let's talk about the exploding bonbons again. I've got this great act. I call it the Girl Scout Shuffle."

"D&C performed," he read. "It's been…" he counted out the days. "Almost two weeks. Are you still bleeding?"

"What do you think, it was twins? Died a week apart?"

"I assure you, it doesn't work that way." Then he asked again, "Tell me, are you bleeding?"

"You tell me—when are my fluids no longer your business?" I was barely bleeding. Nothing to mention. There was no dead baby cradled between my hips. Not anymore.

He said, "Dear, we're in the body-fluid business. You don't have a fever…cramps?"

I said, "I came in for help a while back, and that's over now. I'm here again, sure, but it's a new show. Act One." I didn't even want to think about the last round in the E R : pregnant, then not pregnant, and the drama was over. Curtains closed. There would be no tiny Mr. Galore. No miniature Rex. No granddaughter to my lost mother, grandson to my once-present dad, our tightly pruned bonsai of a family tree.

Soon enough I'd tell Rex about the trip to the E R , but I'd tell him when he came home. And until I told Rex, why tell anyone else? I was two months pregnant when the blood started. Rex was one week out of town.

The cardiologist nodded and wrote on his chart. "Any pain now? Bloating?"

I shook my head, a slow side to side.

"In a miscarriage, you can lose a lot of blood. Become anemic, have complications. Maybe we should get someone in here to do a pelvic."

I said, "It was my heart this time, right? A whole different issue, different tissue." I didn't have claws digging into my sciatic nerve or the wrenching in my gut. I wasn't sifting through blood clots brown and gelatinous as chicken liver, looking for the blue tint of the birth sac. "You can't reach my heart through my hoo-ha— and you're not the first man I've warned that way."

"Your hoo-ha?"

"No pelvic," I said. I looked around for a balloon to tie, a way to ease my nerves. "Can I have one of those rubber gloves?" I'd make the five fingers into a tiny *Madonna of the Rocks*.

The cardiologist nodded, a meaningless gesture, and didn't hand me a glove. He said, "OK, well. There is one more test I'd like your help with." He lifted my sticky hand, looked at my fingernails. Each nail was painted a different color, like a box of crayons.

"For clowning," I said.

He put my hand back on the bedspread carefully, as though my hand were breakable. "We'd like to check your adrenals." He patted the back of my hand. His own hand was laced with a rope of veins, like rivers drawn on a map.

A nurse came in with a paper bag. She said, "Excuse me. Your friends brought this."

"Friends?" I repeated, hopeful, and took the bag from her. Rex was my friend. He topped the list, my only friend at times.

Inside the bag was one juggling ball and an envelope of twenties. No rubber chicken. In blue pen, on the outside of the envelope, it said, *They docked you for leav'n early. Otherwise, it's all here. —Crack.*

Matey and Crack. They were co-workers, not friends. I put the bag beside the bed.

The doctor wrote a note on a prescription pad. "The adrenal test is simple. And it's precise. But we need you to collect twenty-four hours of urine." He gave me the note. "Take this down to the lab, they'll explain the process. You're heart seems OK. Today's EKG looks good."

Still, I could point to a place in the front of my skull where my head was full of the hum of bees, an incessant and displacing rattle that moved in over thoughts I might've had. If this were a clown act, I'd hold a hand to one ear. Bees would fly out the other side.

I asked the cardiologist why an electrocardiogram was called an EKG, instead of an ECG.

He said, "Nazis. Nazis invented the machine."

After he left, I found a napkin on my breakfast tray and wrote that down: EKG = *Nazis*.

3.

Hide and Seek; or, Love in the Ruins

I WALKED HOME FROM THE HOSPITAL DRESSED IN THE mismatched stripes of yesterday's sweaty news. The squirting daisy was pinned to my lapel. The wolf whistle rattled in my pocket. I carried the pink vinyl bag of tricks over my shoulder, and the hospital had added a few new props: an empty jug and a urine collection tray. The jug was orange plastic, as though ready to hold a quart of generic orange juice. The urine tray was white, shaped like a giant lucky horseshoe, meant to fit over a toilet seat. The middle of the horseshoe formed the actual tray, marked with measurements, ounces and cubic centimeters, and plenty of 'em! It was pointed on one edge, like the mouth of a pitcher, for easy pouring—fresh-squeezed urine right from bladder to tray to jug. Voilà! I tucked it under my arm.

The jug and the tray were a pair, a duo, a working team like Matey, Crack and me. Together they made up my new urine collection kit and waited for that third player, the piss itself.

The world was brilliant, gleaming and hard, bathed in sun. It was a welcome-home party after the death rattle of the hospital. But my head hummed and my skin was fragile; I needed the world to be gentle. Rather than brilliant, bumbling and soft would do. I needed a feather bed, a velvet curtain, a high-wire net. Luxury. Mostly, I needed the ℞ of Rex, a prescription dose of his fine love act.

I still felt the buzzing inside my skull, that swarm of bees, the drone of insects lodged between me and clear thoughts. But I didn't feel faint. I swung my empty urine collection jug and it was light as a balloon. The first tinkle of the morning, according to the lab man's plan, would be free to swim its way from the toilet to the ocean. The rest of the day, all the piss I could piddle would go in the jug, up until the first round of the second morning. The jug had to be kept cold, on ice or in the fridge, from the first collection until it came back to the lab. It sounded so simple! Deceptively simple. I tucked the tray over my shoulder, gave the jug a toss. The jug blocked the sun as it twirled in the air, then I caught it between the clap of my palms.

The neighborhood that only one day before was the King's Row Street Fair was now nearly empty, sidewalks still bright with broken balloons and trampled confetti. A woman with a cloud of pale blue hair carried a miniature terrier, bows in the dog's fur. Her turquoise and pink makeup told the rest of the story: no way was I the only clown on the block.

I stopped at a juice cart. The drinks were pricey. When it was my turn, I said, "Green Drink. The biggest you've got. For the health of it."

The juice guy said, "Toilet seat part of the act?" A raspberry was caught in his goatee. His lips glowed orange from an overdose of carrot juice.

Now who was head clown?

"It's not a toilet seat." I adjusted the urine tray over my shoulder.

"Looks like a toilet seat," he said. "What's your shtick?"

I took a straw, tapped it against my hat. "Urine. My shtick is urinating. Right now, I'm a little light on inspiration."

He gave me three-fifty worth of fresh-squeezed Green Drink. I kept walking.

The hanging flowerpots, nylon street flags, and painted bus stops of King's Row district gave way to a narrow band of neighborhood where the streets were a river of orange and black lettering: *For Sale, For Rent, Will Build to Suit*. Every car, house,

building, and bicycle. A wheelbarrow, *For Sale*. A stack of tires.
Even dahlias, cut from the yard, *For Sale*.

For-Salesville marked the hopeful margin between amped-
up gentrification and the economic downslide of my stomping
grounds: Baloneytown. That's what they called my neck of the woods,
where baloney was all the steak anybody could afford.

Between For-Salesville and Baloneytown there were two city
blocks, and on those blocks were two sprawling, gutted ware-
houses. One building was in pieces—a lone storefront, the old
Mor4Les Variety, now tied to no store but just all joists and rebar
and bricks in piles. The other building had a broken-out wall
in front, nothing but dust and darkness inside. Both ruins were
marked *For Sale*, *Keep Out*, with a giant fine for trespassing.
Graffiti on the brick and plaster walls showed how many hadn't
kept out, had risked the fine instead.

I'd risked the fine a few times myself.

The empty lot was its own back stage, the outdoor air a wilderness hidden from the street between open walls. I came to
those two buildings now like old friends.

The Ruins—they were the ruins of our courtship, the blos-
soming, Rex Galore and me. One night, in the middle of the Perseid
meteor shower, he and I lay on a blanket on a cement slab there
and watched stars fall. Meteors marked the sky like sequins on
a cheap dress hitting the dance floor. Rex whispered, "Let's go on
a crime spree. Break the rules, shake things up." His breath was
soft with wine.

"You're my crime spree," I whispered back. "You're enough.
My bad habit, my finest act." I ran a hand over the sweaty muscles
of his shoulder.

Now, with nobody around, I sipped Green Drink and walked
through the Ruins and it was like walking through the Parthenon,
the Acropolis, Stonehenge, or the Pyramids. It was another
country, an ancient place. Stray fire bricks sat in a chipped pile,
red and fat and softly rounded. A midden. A kitchen. An old

faucet handle rested in the dirt, a piece of cast metal now out of work. I was an archaeologist in the kicked-up dust.

A flight of cement stairs led to the narrow platform of an old loading dock. Graffiti danced over a broad stretch of the wall. The words were stylized and unreadable, a jagged and foreign alphabet. I sat on the loading dock with my legs dangling, drinking Green Drink in the sun. A strand of morning glory made its way up through a crack and curled into ringlets. Heaven. When Rex came home, we'd picnic in the Ruins again.

Beside the gap of a framed-in window on the next wall over, the faded paint of an old card-room advertisement was a ghost image, the trace of a sign with nothing left to sell, now shy as the Virgin Mary on a tortilla. Left alone, even graffiti would weather to this same soft glow, like gang members growing old.

Spray-paint cans lay scattered, the remains of an unsanctioned street fair, an aerosol-fueled Dionysian bash. I picked up a can of spray paint, shook the can and felt the ball inside rattle back and forth. I pushed the button. A spit of blood red paint disappeared into the air.

"Hey there," a voice called, behind me. I turned. Saw the blue uniform, a heavy step on the uneven ground. A cop lumbered toward me, weighted down with his belt of tools, his bulletproof shoes.

I threw the can on the ground. Red paint marked my finger.

I was caught red-handed, red-fingered in a debauch of paint cans, evidence against me documented in the swirl of graffiti. Who would believe a clown? Time to disappear. I swung my bag over my shoulder, grabbed the orange jug and Green Drink, and jumped off the loading dock to the worn ground below. Green Drink spilled out the straw of my lidded plastic cup; ten cents worth hit the ground.

I ran.

One hand was a fist where I gripped the orange jug handle, and my fist pumped out in front, then back, elbows in close. The bigger-than-big shoes caught in the rubble; it was like running in slow motion, in soft sand. Green Drink sloshed another twenty cents on the ground. Then thirty cents, and more with each swing of the arm. My head buzzed with the hum of bees, my heart pounded but my sweat was cold. The hospital—I didn't want to end up there again. Trespassing fines, vandalism fines—more bills I couldn't pay! I ran faster, a dollar's worth of Green Drink lying in my wake.

"Wait up," the cop said.

No way.

His breathing was heavy, his belt jangled. He said, "I want to talk to you."

Right. I'd heard that before. I turned a corner, behind a pillar, then went down into a window well that ran the length of the building, a sort of culvert lined with corrugated aluminum. I ducked low, below ground level. This was the closest I could find to offstage. Finally. Bent over double, I gasped for air. When I looked up over the edge the cop was standing still, turned the other way. I waited for my chance, then climbed out the far end of the window well and went around the next corner.

I listened for the cop's breath. His belt. Footsteps. Nothing. I jogged a slow jog back to the front of the building, hugged the wall, and peered around the corner. No cop. Over my shoulder, the street was empty. I leaned against the wall to catch my breath. My hands hummed, far away, one wrapped around the Green Drink cup, the other with the urine jug. I edged along the wall, bricks rough against my clothes, and looked back through the empty hole of a window. There he was. The cop, in the Ruins, kicked a paint can. Examined evidence.

Hidden behind the wall, I looked out through the glassless window. The cop put a hand to his head, ruffled his hair. The sun caught his hair in a golden shimmer. My heart was so loud, I felt nearly deaf.

"Sniffles?" the cop called. He turned a slow waltz in the empty lot. His voice was lost on the wind, lost behind my heartbeat.

He took one step forward, then two. Said it again.

Sniffles? Had he really called my clown name? He bent and picked something up.

Then I recognized him. It was the same blue-eyed cop from the day before, the cop who held my hand and called the ambulance. I recognized his shoulders and the earnest squint. A cop, on my tail. Getting closer. He was cute. Handsome even. But still, a cop, a man, not Rex. Off-limits. I stayed hidden. Nervous, I trembled like a kid playing hide-and-seek. The cop did a lonely waltz, called my name as though I were his unwilling dance partner, then stood in the rubble holding the plastic form of a toilet seat, my urine-collection funnel an impromptu corsage for a date that wouldn't show.

4.

Chance Pays the Karmic Bill; or, Give Chance Some Peace!

I WATCHED THE COP THROUGH THE RAGGED EDGE OF THE glassless window. Guilty or innocent, I couldn't talk to a cop. Even when I knew that up close he'd smell like cinnamon, when his hair was a halo in the sun with pale streaks gleaming and golden as a wise man's aura. Rex Galore wouldn't talk to cops.

Herman, ex-boyfriend-turned-landlord, he'd say House Rule: No cops. Herman had long since lost his license for too many DUIS, and was busted for possession once. Low profile was Herman's goal. In Herman's house, I followed his rules.

The cop spun the urine-collection funnel on two fingers. He whistled the first bars of "Happy Trails." Another spin and the funnel whirled off the ends of his fingers, whizzed past his face and over his shoulder. "Whoa!" he said. The funnel landed like a Frisbee in the dust. Good thing it wasn't his gun—Happy Trails indeed. The dry ground of the empty lot made dust storms on the heel of each step as he walked, picked up the funnel, and kept going. His pants were too long. The cuffs dragged at the back of his shoes. He was probably single.

I needed that funnel.

I followed the cop for a block, creeping close along the wall. He swung the funnel loosely, like a briefcase. I willed him to toss it into a Dumpster or leave it alongside a recycling bin, but he didn't stop until he reached his cop car.

He opened the door and put the funnel in the backseat. He dropped into the front seat, heavy and hot. When he pulled away from the curb, I gave up—what else?—and walked my own direction toward Baloneytown, to my room in Herman's house. That urine funnel lasted in my hands for less than half a day.

REX GALORE'S USED AMBULANCE WAITED IN FRONT OF Herman's house like a faithful dog for Rex to come home. The ambulance waited the way I waited—stalled out and nearly abandoned some would say, though I tried to see it otherwise: the ambulance and I, we waited with patience.

It was an old style retro Travellall ambulance, bought cheap at the county auction. Long and low, it was the same design as a hearse only two-tone, red and white instead of black, a hearse of another color. The side windows were sandblasted with a pebbled fog in white stripes. Crosses marked the windows closer to the front. Gray plastic shades, meant to shelter a patient, were pulled now to hide piles of costumes, props, and gag tricks. That ambulance was our own little *chapiteau*, Rex's and mine, our collapsible, expandable mobile circus. I patted a swiveling chrome mirror, then made my way up the side yard.

Baloneyville Co op it said, on a wooden sign over Herman's front door. My room was the mudroom, off the kitchen in back. I opened the back door, heard a screech. The first thing I saw was the muscled, nearly naked body of Herman's new girlfriend—Natalia, Nadia, or Italia, whatever her name was. She was doubled over and laughing, knees pressed together, ready to piss her miniskirt.

Nadia-Italia, obviously wasted, snorted and stamped a booted foot. Her thighs were thick, her laugh loud. Below the thin string of knotted halter top, her bare back was the blue cascade of a tattoo, the peacock swirl of a geisha in a kimono at a waterfall. Muscles flexed under the tattoo, under her skin, over her ribs, like shifting glaciers. The weight of her foot shook the floor, the house, my nerves.

My little black dog, Chance, ran full speed in circles around Nadia-Italia. It was a scene torn from a circus poster: The Strong

Lady and the Dancing Cub! Chance scooted under the kitchen table and back out, hind legs tucked in tight for speed. Gadzooks! She slid through a pile of newspapers, knocked over her water dish, and kept running.

I said, "What's up?" I put the plastic jug and what was left of my Green Drink on the counter. "What's wrong with Chance?"

Nadia-Italia straightened, eyes wet with tears, she laughed that hard. She snorted again, then tossed her head like a horse. "Look who's home. Little Miss Clown Girl, everybody's favorite tramp." Her hair stood up in three tufts of bleached pigtails, each pigtail tied with yellow yarn. "Our own Shirley Temple for the next Great Depression." She kicked a juggling ball into the wall and the ball ricocheted. Chance ran at the ball, fell, slid, bounced off the wall like a juggling ball herself.

Herman sauntered in from the living room. "Your dog's O K, just wasted. It's my stash that's down. I ought to charge you for the loss."

I said, "You fed my dog pot? You'll make her brain damaged!"

"We didn't brain damage your dog," Italia said. She rolled her eyes and caught her breath, one hand still tugging on the pigtail. "You're catastrophizing, chick."

Herman tapped the ash off a smoke into a dirty coffee cup on the kitchen counter. His skin was the amber glow of whiskey, eyes tobacco brown. Everything about him was calm. Usually, I liked his calmness. His calmness was the reason we still lived together, technically speaking.

I lunged as Chance scrambled past. I said, "Settle." Then, "Ettle-say." She was half-fluent in pig latin, but apparently not that half. With a second swing, I caught her. In a crouch, I held Chance by the loose skin on the back of her neck, and she went limp as roadkill. She panted like mad, her mouth split in a wide dog grin, a Hieronymus Bosch creature. "She's fried—Herman, you let her feed my dog pot? I'm gone for one night, and my dog's a lab experiment?"

Herman rolled a honeydew melon along the counter. He

found a carving knife. "It was an accident, OK? The dog was hungry, found a bag I'd been counting out. Only a gram, two at most." He rested his smoke on his lower lip, pushed aside old papers and empty cups on the cluttered counter, and, with a squinted eye, used both hands to push the knife through the melon. "If you'd been around to feed her, she wouldn't have eaten the stuff," he said.

The melon fell in two pale green halves.

I cradled my dog. "A couple grams?" When I stood, my head was last to find its way, spinning and bloodless. I put a hand to the wall for balance, propped Chance against my hip like a sack of dog food, a clown-and-canine *pietà*. I said, "This dog is twenty-two pounds. Enough pot, you'll kill her."

That dog was my sidekick, a showstopper in training. My big Chance. I couldn't have a clown dog that drooled and stumbled, and not on command, canine mind blown, in diapers, handicapped by the herb. Her only trick then would be the famous egg-in-a-frying-pan routine, that omelet dance of a brain on drugs. I reached for the phone, hit three buttons for local information.

Herman grabbed for the phone, but I swung Chance to one side and jammed the phone against my stomach. He wrapped his arms around me and the dog, came from both directions, pressed the button on the receiver down with one big thumb. "That dog found the pot," he said. "On her own. I'm not going to lose my income over a dog's ganja habit."

I wheezed under Herman's hug. My head crackled, vision narrowed. "Poison Control isn't the cops. It's for health stuff. They want people to call."

"Sure, to turn themselves in." Herman's breath was smoky, close to my face. His heavy breathing and sweat were all too familiar, from the old days when we were a couple, as were his hands, sticky now with the summer sweetness of honeydew melon. I dropped to my knees and made a tight ball around the phone. Under one arm I still held the drooling, zoned-out throw rug of Chance.

"Let go," I said. "I have a right to call."

His ponytail fell forward, over my shoulder. "Give me the phone, Nita."

I was under a tent of Herman, breath, body, and smell. Our history. Then he let go. Stepped away. I dialed.

"Jesus," he said and unplugged the phone at the wall. He tossed the cord. "No calls to Poison Control. And no cops. Not while you live here." *In my house.* That's what he wanted to say.

Herman had no idea how close I'd come to the cops. That gilded, golden officer, with his glass of water. "Poison Control doesn't report to the cops," I said again.

Out of breath, Herman reached for his cigarette and took a drag like the smoke would settle his breathing. As he exhaled with a B-flat wheeze, he said, "I'll tell you what. We'll fix her up." He took another drag. "In the bathroom. There's a brown bottle." He waved a hand toward the hall. "Hydrogen peroxide. Two tablespoons and your Chance'll be good as new."

Natalia-Italia, behind him, cranked open the top on a can of sardines. She held one fish up by its tiny tail and slid the fish into her mouth. Comfort food.

Dog drool ran in a thin line over my arm to the floor. "Really?"

He nodded, and smoked like his lungs were starved, like he'd gone too long without, as though smoke were scarce and necessary. In a cloud of smoke he said, "First she'll vomit, then she'll be good as new. Trust me. I know how to detox, right? She just ate the stuff, like minutes ago."

"You've done this before?"

He said, "My old dog ate drugs all the time. I fixed her up."

I ran my hand over Chance's dark hair. "Where's that dog now?"

Natalia slid another headless, glistening bristling sardine between her lips. She leaned against Herman's sweaty shoulder. Herman said, "She lived a long life, OK? Now go, before your dog digests the stuff. It won't work digested—time's wasting." He shook Italia off.

I took Chance down the long, dark hall. Herman kept our

house dark. That's how they catch pot growers, he said, by the high electricity bills. He knew things like that, like how to do drugs and how to clean up, how to pass a urine test and how to walk a straight line. Maybe how to detox a dog.

I tripped on one of Italia's barbells and banged an elbow and Chance against the wall. The dog didn't flinch. Since Italia moved in, the house was crowded with free weights, sweaty spandex, and dirty towels. Instead of our old couch, her weight bench sprawled in front of the TV.

I sat Chance on the bathroom counter and tipped her head back. Her eyes rolled and showed a sliver of white at the edge like new moons. I poured hydrogen peroxide down her open throat. In seconds she arched her back, opened her mouth, and curled her long tongue. She made a prehurl urp-noise, eyes big now. "Put her in the tub," Herman yelled from the kitchen. "Once you give her the stuff, put her in the tub."

I picked her up like a child and carried her to the tub, her mouth working over a silent stammer. I sat on the side of the tub and ran my hand through her fur. My lovely, silky Chance, sweet dark-eyed stray. "You're OK, baby," I said, and hoped it was true. Her legs went stiff as a seizure; her nails trembled against the porcelain. She slid into a skittering dog dance. I steadied her with a hand to her belly.

When she opened her mouth again and heaved, her stomach grew small and her ribs barreled out, tight under the fur. What came from her mouth wasn't liquid but white foam thick as shaving cream, dense as Fix-A-Flat, flecked with the earthy green bits of Herman's harvest.

Between the gargle of vomit, she chomped her mouth open and closed, open and closed. The whole show was ripe for a ventriloquist act: *A clown and a poodle walk into a hash bar...*

Herman came from the dark hall and leaned against the bathroom door. He flipped the overhead lights off, turned a small night-light on. "That's the way," he said. "That'll bring a dog down." He took a bite from a slice of honeydew in one hand, and held a fresh cigarette in the other. Melon juice dripped off his fingers. The honeydew melon and the cigarette, the clean taste of fruit spoiled by ashes—that was exactly the way Herman had always been, why we once got together and why I broke us up; he was all contradictions.

Chance filled the tub with pot-spiked meringue, her stoner snowdrifts. I ran a hand over her shivering back. "Hang in there, sweets," I said, quietly.

"So, Nita," Herman said. "Where you been, anyway? Looking a little ravished." He took a drag on his smoke, his best friend and pacifier.

I kept my eyes on shivering Chance. "I'm sure you mean ravishing." It wasn't Herman's business where I slept, even when I slept at the hospital.

"Yeah, that's right. Clown date?" Herman said.

Nadia came up behind him in the doorway, a barbell in one hand, a half-eaten banana in the other.

"Funny, I could ask you the same thing," I said. I turned on the water to wash away white drifts of vomit. Chance scrambled to the far end of the tub. She slipped. I caught her.

A gentle world. Nice. A safety net, that's what my baby dog and I needed.

Instead, Chance was a Christmas tree flocked in her own fake snow. Behind Herman, Nadia-Italia raised the barbell with one hand and looked over his shoulder. "Ought to save that stuff. Recycle the drugs, right?" she said.

If I had Italia's muscles, I'd be a clown extraordinaire. I'd defeat physics by defying gravity, no doubt. Italia only used her muscles to build more muscles, until she was made of knotted lumps of stone.

My plan was to get out of there.

The clown money was my ticket out of Herman's house and down to San Francisco, to Rex. I'd leave Baloneytown in the dust. Maybe I'd go to Clown College too. Then I'd sleep in the master bedroom, not the mudroom, right? Ta da!

House Rules would be our rules, Rex's and mine. I'd have my own family again, not a makeshift sideshow.

When Chance slowed her vomit production to nil, I wrapped her in a towel and carried her against my shoulder like a colicky baby. On the way to my room, I stopped to plug the phone back into the wall.

"Hey—who're you calling?" Herman said. "The dog's good as new."

She was droopy and wild-eyed, hardly *new*. "Rex," I said. "Or is Clown College one more joint in the long arm of the law?" Like, the long rubber arm. I pushed past Herman and closed the mudroom door. The phone cord fell easily underneath.

The room was hot and humid, musky with dog hair and breath; Chance panted in the summer sun. Along with the wet-dog smell, the room was ripe with the dizzying whiff of turpentine and the heavy linseed oil scent of paint that drifted from brushes kept in plastic bags.

Two of the walls in the mudroom were made of small squares of glass, floor to ceiling windows, and magnified the heat. The sun came in from behind a tree and made a shadow-puppet show of leaves and branches against the wall. I put the Green Drink and orange plastic jug on a shelf, where I had my own little altar to St. Julian the Hospitaller, patron saint of clowns, fiddlers, murderers, and pilgrims. As a part of the altar I stacked change from my pockets. I piled business cards of the men who asked me out, my audience and fan club.

In clown clothes you walk a thin tightrope, teetering between lust and fear, coulrophiles and coulrophobes. In that narrow band what I aimed for was the laughter of children. O K, more recently what I aimed for was a quick paycheck, a ticket out of Baloneytown. But I wasn't in it for the groupies.

On the next shelf down there was a stack of library books. *Your Baby, Your Body: Watch It Grow!* These were books I didn't need anymore: my body, my baby. Both had stopped growing. The

books were overdue, and the library books were the only thing
with a due date now.

I'd write my own book of miscarriage: *What to Expect When
You Expected to be Expecting, Until It All Went South*. I unclipped
the squirting daisy from my shirt and put the daisy on the shelf,
next to the plastic jug.

Below the shelves, on the floor, was a collection of bowling
shoes, loafers, painted Keds, and curled wing tips, everything
in a size eleven or larger, specially chosen for clowning. And then
there was one pair of Rex's old tennis shoes, absolute boats, his
real size. Rex's shoes bent and crinkled where his toe knuckles had
worn against the seam, as though Rex still stood there, invisible,
feet in the shoes.

The room overflowed with drawings of Rex in charcoal on
paper, in pen and ink, and in pencil. A red clay bust stared
down at me from the top shelf of my doorless closet. "Honey, I'm
home," I said to the clay bust. Rex. The bust didn't blink. Every
image I made of him—drawings, paintings, and sculptures—they
all had the same faint smile, like the *Mona Lisa*, Rex's sly secret.
I said, "Don't be mad, I still love you," then lifted the head, turned
it upside down, pulled a sock from under the neck and tucked a
day's wages inside.

I turned on a radio to block the murmur of Herman and Italia,
and sat on the edge of the bed. Chance crowded against my ribs.

I dialed the number for the clown hostel in San Francisco,
where nobody ever answered.

"Yello, yello, yello, kiddos!" the answering machine sang.
"We're off to the races, but if you leave your name and number,
we'll make sure your birthday party's a smash to remember. Ha,
ha! Don't tell the folks!" A horn honked three times, followed by
the beep.

"Rex, it's Nita," I said into the answering machine. "Are you
there? I need to hear your voice. Call me, OK?" I started to hang
up, then put the phone back to my ear and added, "I've been in the
hospital, Rex." He'd want to know.

I picked up one of Rex's velvet shirts, ran the fabric across my neck, and smelled the smoke of old fire tricks. Clown College was one way to move ahead, but there were others. We could join *Clowns Sans Frontières*—Clowns Without Borders—sworn to cheer the children in war-torn countries, practice tricks around land mines, juggle in food and medical supplies. I didn't plan to do corporate gigs forever. No, I wanted to make a difference in the world: another clown for peace. I unbuttoned my shirt. The satin slipped from my shoulders, a silky caress. I unfastened the polka-dot bra. The flurry of photos and cards fell out: St. Julian, my Clown Union card, my parents, and Rex. Family past and future.

In the early days after Rex left, when I was still pregnant, sometimes I'd imagine that he never came back and there was a romance to the idea of abandonment, the loss of a great love. At least it was familiar terrain—I'd lost my parents young, knew the way things went. But this time, I'd raise Rex's child. Later the kid would ask, "Mom, what was Daddy like?" I'd tap a circus poster glued to a crumbling city wall or unfold a worn program. "He was the strongest man I've ever met," I'd say. "He was gorgeous, and could make me laugh ... " I'd tell stories of Rex Galore until Rex was mythic.

But instead, it seemed, I'd tell Rex the story of how the baby abandoned us.

Herman and Italia laughed together in the kitchen, and the sound was like two mismatched dancers. I turned up my radio, then eased out of the striped pants, the sweaty polyester.

When we met, Rex was a model. I was a student, late for drawing class. He was already naked on a pedestal, posed on a draped white sheet. He had the knotted biceps of a gymnast, the rock-solid terrain of a dancer's thighs. It was winter. He was pale except for a blue lined tattoo of fish that swam around one arm.

Ta da! Magic.

We were a silent movie, Rex and me, that first day, in a class full of students. His eyes shifted toward me, then away, then back. I looked down as I set up my easel. I started to draw, and looked up. Our eyes met. I dropped my charcoal and stepped forward to pick the charcoal up—stepped closer to the pedestal where Rex stood, naked. He watched as I stepped in. I looked up and at the same time bent down, and with one hand groped for the charcoal stick on the floor. Then Rex was a whole geography that loomed over me, the lines of his muscles, shape of his bones, curls in his hair, and I wanted to move to that country, that continent. He was the Man in the Moon, the Eiffel Tower, Apollo, Dionysus. I didn't have to put Rex on a pedestal, because he was already there. Posed.

My face was hot. Something inside me tickled.

He knew I looked with more than an interest in light and shadow, contour and planes. When it was break, Rex reached for his robe. We, students, were the audience, he was the show. He pulled the belt of his robe around his hips, ran a hand over his dark hair, stepped off the pedestal, and turned to me.

Then I was part of his show. Other students pretended not to watch. I brushed charcoal from my hands. My hands were hot, and the coal stuck in a black dust.

Rex walked around the edge of my drawing board to look at my charcoal drawing of him naked—Yikes! There it was: penis, dick, cock, peter, willy, wanker, forced meats, soda jerk. Call it what you want, but it's the hardest part of a naked man to sketch. A penis always looks too big or too fat, except for when it looks too small. Too oceanographic, a sea creature. I know, I've worked at it long and hard, and working at drafting a dick only makes it worse; too much study and the organ is like something from the Art of the Insane, pure fixation. Carefully done, the lines of a penis grow overly detailed, painful in their stiffness, until you've drawn the penis like a second figure alongside the larger body. It's a tiny man, to stand for all men. A dick.

Hidden or blurred, it's as though the artist is afraid of seeing something clearly, afraid to look straight on, to take the bull by the horn, as they say. I'm sure Michelangelo gave his famous David sculpture those massive, oversized hands not so much to convey the power of God working through David, but more to distract from the meager proportions of David's sculpted dick.

Rex was tall, and more than proportionate. The first time I drew him I worked to make his penis look real: a dark cluster of charcoal lines, curling hairs, deep shadows. Obsessive. Inspired. I didn't expect the model to step from his pedestal and see that my eyes had traced every line, curve, and fold. He nodded. Maybe he liked the way I handled his dick. Who knows? He broke through the silent movie then and said, "Take your break outside?" He pulled a pack of cigarettes from his bathrobe pocket.

I didn't smoke, but said, "Sure, OK." He pulled on unlaced, paint-stained work boots, no socks. I followed him into the hall, downstairs, and out of the building. It was raining out and we stood under the building's overhang, apart from other smokers. Rex stood in his bathrobe, naked underneath, as though that was normal.

"Those your pins?" he asked.

I folded my hands over my chest, felt myself blush.

He nodded toward the building, the classroom. Ah, pins! Of course. My juggling pins were in a backpack. They were too long for the pack and the silver, black, and white ends poked out the top as three round knobs.

"You juggle?" His breath was a white trail of smoke, teeth yellowed and perfectly square.

"A little. Just learning pins." I was nervous. Pins are harder than balls—the narrow side of each pin'll slap your wrist with every catch. I held out my arm and pulled back one striped sleeve to show where my arm was decorated with blooming black, red, and blue flowers. Each bruise marked the hit of a juggling pin.

Rex laughed. "Battle scars." He said, "I'd be into team juggling, if you're up for it. Fastest way to learn is with a partner."

A date. He asked me on a juggling date! That's when he told me his name: Rex Galore. Rex, the Clown Prince! The Princely Clown of the After-hours Club Circuit, a movement artist. Of course I'd seen the posters for his shows. Rex had the best graphics in town. He was a different breed of clown—no kids' parties, no Food

Fairs. No smiling, kowtowing, apple-polishing slapstick; Rex said slap was dead. Instead of the fool, Rex was an acrobat. He could juggle toasters and blenders, live kittens even. He could walk on stilts and ride a unicycle.

I rolled down my sleeve. "That'd be nice," I said. "I'm Nita."

"I know," he said.

Did he really, or was it all bluster? It didn't matter. By then, I was already the clown groupie, the fetishist: love.

The Buddhists say if you meet somebody and your heart pounds, your hands shake, your knees go weak, that's not the one. When you meet your soul mate you'll feel calm. No anxiety, no agitation. I say, the Buddhists don't have a clue. When I met Rex I was awash in nerves, because, why not? He was everything I believed in and he came right to me. He asked me out. Why settle for less?

Back in the classroom he stepped out of the boots, ran his fingers through the length of his hair, shook off the robe, and there was his body again: all muscle. He climbed on his pedestal. My statue, my date, the sexiest man in town. An older woman student leaned over and whispered, "That's the way to pick 'em. With a preview. Now you know what you're getting."

As though anything were ever that easy or true.

In the mudroom, the afternoon sun came in through the windows and warmed the floor and the wall behind the bed. The room was a terrarium of dog breath, turpentine, and sweat. I sang something I'd been working on, part of a skit:

Beef Brisket
what is it?
Oh, wouldn't you like to know…

Still naked, I unzipped the suitcase Rex used to hold costumes and let clothes spill out. *Beef brisket, just ee-ee-t it…* I ran my hands through his clothes, pressed fabric to my skin. Turpentine was as good as Rex's cologne because it was the scent of the classroom where we met. I touched a dab of turpentine to the fabric, then lay on my bed with the costumes beside me like a warm body.

That cop? He was helpful, sure. And he was handsome. But a man like that was white bread next to the richness of art, and love. Rex. Chance drew close against my shoulder from the other side and for a moment, in the smell of turpentine, it was as though Rex, Chance, and I were together again, the three of us. Family.

Until Herman knocked on the door. "Hey," he said, his voice sharp. "I smell turp from the kitchen. Clean it up, ventilate, or you're out of here." He pushed an unpaid phone bill under the locked door. The envelope came toward me with a shimmy and a hiss, all warning and demand.

5.

Plucky, Come Home!

IN THE BACK OF REX'S PROP-ROOM AMBULANCE, I GATH-
ered pens and paper and made a sign: *Missing: Rubber Chicken.*
I sketched the chicken's long rubber neck, her fallen-over comb,
dangling legs, and splayed toes. I inked in the black lines of a heart
on her chest, her defining characteristic, like a birthmark or a scar.

The ambulance's two back doors hung open to let a breeze
in. Outside a mechanical xylophone blasted the hard notes
of "Home on the Range," as One-Night Stan the Ice-Cream Man
trawled nearby. I perched on a pile of costumes with the shades
pulled, wearing a sun hat with a big brim and a cluster of silk
flowers in front. The only thing wrong with the hat was two holes
cut in the top meant to accommodate rabbit ears back when the
hat was part of a show.

Below the rubber chicken picture, on my sign, I wrote, *Name:
Plucky. Height: 15″. Value: Sentimental.* Then I wrote: *Reward: $$$.*

I tore off the part about a reward. What could I offer? If the
rubber-chicken thief were a King's Row kid, my reward would
be a bad joke next to the punk's allowance. I crunched the scrap
in my hand.

But I wanted Plucky back. Plucky belonged with Rex and me.
We'd had good times together. I wrote it again, in the space that
was left: *Reward.* Then crossed it off. I couldn't give money away.

But who would return a rubber chicken without incentive?
Plucky would end up tossed in an entryway, left in a backyard, or
given to charity. I wrote it one more time, above the black cross-

off mark: *Reward*, followed by only one dollar sign. I'd pay for that chicken's safe return because she was mine, ours, the first and now the only child of our union, the memento of sex, evidence of sex, Rex Galore.

Rex and me, our second date wasn't a date so much as it was a show. He invited me for a night onstage. We were juggling together, pins in the air, moving hand to hand with a good rhythm going, when he invited me to work with him, to be a moving table, a prop stand in his fire-juggling act. *Put fire in the show, audiences love it.* That's what Rex always said: *Burn shit up.* I was wary. It was so much, so soon, I said, "You don't think we're rushing things?"

He said, "I'm ready."

With the way the pins spun smoothly between us, six in the air, I knew I was ready too. I saw my future: if the date were an audition, I'd nail it.

The night of his show I wore a legless tabletop strapped to my back, in a nightclub, and underneath that board I swayed to Rex's dance. The crowd was sauced. Somebody yelled, "Prestidigiate!" An empty plastic pitcher flew onto the stage. The pitcher spun, beer speckled my face, and I laughed out loud. The energy was nothing like the hollow garages of art gigs, the scream of birthday parties, or the dead air in the corporate scene.

Rex rapped on my tabletop and the sound amplified in my ears. Rex was amplified, bigger than life, his name chanted by strangers, his soundtrack a crazy mess of Ska, tribal, and Cambodian pop. His feet were bare and strong, legs muscled. That was all I could see from down low. His hands hit the floor between his feet and his legs scissored up and out of view. His curly hair dropped to the stage, damp with sweat. Dionysus, Pan. Bacchus, Shazam. My Wonder Twin. He was a god, a gymnast, a laugh riot, a dream.

Rex piled bottles on the table of my back. He balanced fire wands on the bottles and the flames reflected in mirrors at the edges of the stage. I was in the middle of a bonfire, a forest fire, a burning building. Magic. Everyone looked at the flaming pyramid of bottles on my back. My knees rubbed hard against the uneven floor of the stage. Rex rode a unicycle. His single wheel circled as I shuffled.

If Rex asked me to eat glass, I would've done it.

Later, in the quiet of the dressing room, he closed the door. I stood. My legs trembled, knees stiff with exertion, exhilaration, and nerves. Rex said, "You're a natural." He unstrapped the table, lifted it from my back, and set it aside.

"It was all you," I said.

"Not at all!" His big hands reached forward to massage my shoulders. I closed my eyes and groaned. "Tough work, isn't it?" He let his hands slide down my shoulders to the collar of my black catsuit, lowered the zipper in back. The cloth peeled away, cool air brushed my skin and my shoulders stretched larger, free of the fabric. "Goosebumps," Rex said and ran a finger down my spine, his voice a quiet growl. His skin smelled hot, flammable as white gas. He touched a calloused finger to my collarbone, then ran his finger down over my breast and pushed the suit lower. Bottles rolled over the floor between smoking batons. Sweat-marked Lycra clung tight as hands against my thighs, my hips.

We dropped onto a sagging couch buried in costumes, and around us the costumes smelled like every show there'd ever been, every date, every human body: smoke, perfume, and cologne layered over the musty mix of Goodwill and basement mildew, cat piss, the hot animal ripeness of nerves and sweat. This was our opening night. Rex was on top of me, his weight and smell, and the clothes underneath us were like a hundred people there, a bed of empty arms and torn pant legs.

My clown makeup smeared across the white spaces of Rex's clown face and made a print on his skin.

I pushed him back an inch, said, "Your lipstick's smeared, dahlink."

When he smiled, his cracked makeup deepened the creases in his face until he was a marionette, a dusty doll, an outdated mannequin.

He leaned forward, bit my belly. With gentle bites he moved along my ribs, up, until he found the white of my breasts, until I was covered in patches of red, smeared chalk white, and blue-black like bruises. Rex Galore and I blended, designs merged and morphed. Forget P.T. Barnum—sex was the greatest show on earth, and Rex and me, we were a tangle and I was lost in the perfume of white gas, smoke, and sweat. I couldn't breathe. I was buried alive. Did I care? Only for an encore.

Rex undid his fly. The catsuit was a pile of darkness on the floor.

I whispered, "Do you have a rubber?"

He laughed, hushed, a laughing whisper, as though his parents were in the next room, and reached one arm past my head to a nightstand there. "A rubber chicken." He shook the dancing chicken in the air. "Will that do?"

I laughed back, ran a finger along the bumps of the fake chicken skin. "Ribbed and beaked for her pleasure, even. Want me to leave you two alone?"

He threw the chicken on the floor and bit my neck and I giggled and he said, "Never," and he was everywhere then. The couch was a sinking place and I disappeared into the orgy of costumes, the smell of nervous strangers, makeup, and smoke, my naked body buried in the perfume of human need.

I took the rubber chicken home. Plucky was my mascot, the souvenir of our date. Later, much later, there was the conception of our child. And now the miscarriage, unexpected, though I should've expected it because, why not?—family slid through my fingers the same as the old silicone banana-peel trick. After the D&C, after the suctioning away of our tiny fetus, I drew the black heart on Plucky's rubber breast in the place where a chicken might have a heart, over the ridges of implied feathers. Indelible ink.

Now she'd been nabbed by a kid too young to know what love means, what a chicken might mean. Too young to know that a rubber chicken can carry all of love in one indelible ink heart.

On my sign, I wrote *Missing: One Rubber Chicken, One Lover,*

One Unborn Child. Missing: my whole life. I tore the ragged sheet in half, picked up another and started again. Swollen Sacred Hearts, shrunken wise men, and bloated angels bobbed at my feet, the fruits of my labor. On the shopworn dedication page of *Balloon Tying for Christ* it said, "With appreciation and gratitude for my wife and six lovely children who have borne with me through twelve long years of deprivations while completing this work." Such martyrs! *Balloon Tying for Christ* was maybe all of seventeen pages long, with one blank page at the end. The tricks inside, by corporate accounting, were worth hundreds of dollars. Matey, Crack, and me, that's what we earned when high-end work came in. But work didn't always come. We had to promote, and deliver. That book was my cash cow.

One-Night Stan's ice-cream truck, the neighborhood drug mobile, still played nearby. Drugs, ice cream, balloon toys and prayer—these are the things you sell when there's nothing else left.

Over the sound of the ice-cream song, a loud rattle out in the street grew louder. I looked out the ambulance's back doors. There was a man down the block walking a loping shuffle to the music of his own loose-wheeled lawn mower. I pulled a green balloon from my pocket. In Herman's yard, Chance circled, dazed and restless. Sunlight rippled on her fur. I blew up the balloon with a new kind of dizziness after the hospital, and tied a knot at the stem too soon, leaving a long stretch of uninflated balloon tail. I twisted one section for a head to make Jesus-on-the-Cross in Easter green, massaged the rubber to minimize the tail, and twisted dangling balloon legs into place.

Just as I found my focus, concentrated on my work, there was a rap against the ambulance. I jumped, startled, and knocked my hat half-off. A man grinned in at me. The man with the lawn mower. "Patient going to make it, Doc?" He was missing two front teeth. I tipped my sun hat back to look at him. He wore a tank top, dripped sweat, and had that red turkey neck from being out in the sun too long. Chance ate grass at the side of the road, eyes on the man. His lawn mower was rusted.

"What's up?" I said, and stretched a new balloon.

"I'm good, I'm quick, I'll do the whole lawn, front and back, for eight bucks." He raised his voice to talk over the ice-cream truck's song.

We eyed each other through the open back doors. I didn't mind the grass long; it had a richness to it. A ribbon of tiny white flowers bloomed along a sunken channel where water, or maybe sewer, ran below. Speck-sized insects swarmed above the weeds like a burst of tiny bubbles. I tipped my sun hat down again. The silk flowers made the light scritch-scratch of tiny toenails against the straw like the mice that roamed Herman's kitchen drawers.

"What makes you think I live in that house?" I said.

"Oh, I seen you 'round. You're the clown girl. I seen you out here in the overgrowed grass, with your little dog and that hula hoop you got."

I moved in my own newly slowed time, behind the buzz in my head, my after-hospital pace. The sky, through my sunglasses, was a cherry-tinted blue. I took out a yellow balloon for the cross. Gave it a snap, blew it up. The man had a boil on his lip that was lighter than his skin, a swollen flash of white. He said, "What is that 'Baloneyville Coop' anyways?" He pointed at the wooden sign over Herman's door.

I tied the knot at the end of the balloon. "It's a Co-op," I said. "There's a space break in there."

He let his head bounce in a nod, then said, "OK, whatever. That's y'all's business. Mine is mowin', and I'd say your coop needs a little trim." He laughed, like it was some kind of big joke. But he was right. Herman only had a push mower, a rusted reel of dull blade. Our backyard was as overgrown and choked as the front, with an aging apple tree in the center and a blackberry thicket along the fence line. It'd been my turn to mow Herman's lawn for weeks—I was the bottleneck, the hold up. The grass grew longer every day. After the hospital, I needed to rest.

"Everybody needs a little trim, now and again," the lawn mower man said with a grin.

I could pay this man to do my work, or pay for the return of Plucky. One or the other. I said, "I don't own the house. Can't hire you without asking." I doubled the yellow balloon over, twisted the green Jesus around it.

The man drank from a plastic cup carried in a cup holder taped to the lawn mower's handle. He ran a hand over his sweaty face. "OK, seven bucks. Can't go lower," he said.

Baloneytown was the neighborhood dealers, hookers, scamsters, and gangbangers came home to. It was where they grew up. Every corner was marked with a brick wall broken by a driver too strung out, trashed, or craving to stay on the road. Half the houses were red-tagged—windows plastered with red *Condemned* stickers—and the red-tagged houses were still lived in. You couldn't trust anybody.

I picked up *Balloon Tying for Christ* and slid off the pile of clothes and out of the sauna of an ambulance. Costumes clung to my legs, a sea of velvet, satin, and Lycra. Standing up fast in the heat meant more of the swimming in my head, the warm hum of bees swarming, the blood resting around my lungs, around my stomach, nowhere near my brain. I saw a flash of blue against the inside of my eyes, felt faint, and caught the side of the ambulance for balance. I pressed my wrist against a cool, shaded bit of steel.

BALLOON JESUS BOBBED IN THE ROAD, ADRIFT ON HIS cross. In my dizziness, Jesus was a million miles away and still at my feet, a supplicant. My feet were miles away. I pressed my wrist to a new spot of shaded metal, hoping for anything cool.

In the middle of a wrist's suicide slash-line, below the layered skin and above the pulse, there's an acupuncture point that says, *Get back to who you were meant to be.* This is the heart spot, the center. Your whole life the skin on that place will stay closest to being a baby's skin, as close as you can get anymore to the way you started, the way you once thought you'd always be. I pressed my baby-heart-spot center into the shaded metal's coolness, the pulse in my wrist talking to my whole body, to the hum in my head and the blue behind my eyes, saying *don't faint now.*

The lawn mower man wiped his face with one sweaty arm. He said, "I do the lawn next door, and done this one, last time with a push mower. Now I got my own. Got an edger now too, and can come back with that tomorrow. I charge three bucks to edge her. Ten bucks total."

I'd never seen him do anybody's lawn, but when he said he did our lawn with a push mower that sounded about right. Whose turn was that? Herman's? I bent for the fallen balloon Jesus. Lofted him, cross and all, into the ambulance.

"My old lady's at Bess Kaiser Hospital. We need money to have a carbuncle lanced off her breast." He ran his tongue over the boil, then patted his pockets like he was looking for a business card.

A cop car turned the corner, came our way. Quick as Keno, Mr. Lawn Mower took his loping stride off to somewhere behind the ambulance. I bent, looked in the cop car window, and caught a glimpse of light hair cut short, the blue uniform. My heart knocked, lurched. Was it my cop—and when did he become *my* cop? The cop with my urine funnel. With no time to hide—I held my big straw hat in front of my face and looked through the rabbit-ear holes in the hat's crown.

It wasn't my cop. It was somebody younger, weasel-faced. Nobody. The nobody cop gave a thumbs-up and a smirk, then passed on by. Only then did my blood start to move again, heart still beating.

The lawn mower man came out to collect his mower. Maybe I gave something away, a shift in my face, a green tinge of guilt, because to me, joking or not, he said, "That cop looking for you, Clown Girl?" Ha! It didn't come across as a joke. We were each in our own private cold sweat. That's the problem—a cop is a loaded question. Let one cop in, and the rest of the picture is a whole new story.

AT HERMAN'S, I TRIED TO CALL REX AGAIN FROM THE phone in the kitchen. Italia stopped licking peanut butter off a knife long enough to say, "Herman wants to know when you're going to get on with your chores." Her skirt barely covered her ass. She dropped the knife in the sink.

"He asked you to ask me, or what?" I said.

"Look, Herman can be an easy touch, and you're a sad case. But that yard's gone to weeds waiting for you to make a move."

With one ear to the phone, I put a finger to my other ear.

"You heard me, clown." She looked in the fridge and showed me her back, that cascade of ink, the geisha and blue waterfall. It looked as though a smaller, more demure woman in a tiny landscape stood in our kitchen.

I picked up a dead fly from the windowsill. When Italia's back was turned, I floated the fly on her coffee. The oldest joke in the book: *Waiter, what's this fly doing in my soup? Looks like the backstroke, Miss.* Nyah, nyah, nyah.

I took the phone to my room and called again. The machine picked up: "Yello, yello, yello! We're off to the races, kiddos…" I lay on our mattress while the sun dropped lower outside my backyard windows, and I said an incantation: *Call me, call me, call me.*

The third time I called, a man answered. He didn't sound like a clown. There was no fun in the rasp of his voice. "Ain't here," the man said. "He's out."

Rex was always out. "Could you ask him to call Nita?"

"Will do." Before I could get in another word, with a click the line went dead.

Then I heard Italia sputter and cough in the other room. "Jesus Christ. Clown Girl!" She kicked my bedroom door open with one muscled leg. A canvas of Rex fell from where it leaned against the wall and hit the ground with a smack. I started coloring on the Missing Rubber Chicken poster again, fast.

"What?"

She said, "Don't mess with my food."

I said it again, "What? I didn't do anything."

She even had knotted muscles in her face, her cheeks. She said, "Look—mess with my food, and I'll kill you. No joke."

6.

We're All Chaplin Here

"IT'S FOR YOU, NITA," HERMAN CALLED.

Ta da! Rex! It was about time. I ran for the phone; my bare feet slapped against the worn floorboards of Herman's old house. "At last," I said, breathless, into the receiver.

"Now that's a reception," Crack coughed back, her voice in my ear. "Listen up. I've got a chief gig, a big check here. They want the three of us. A package deal, see? If one falls through, we're all sunk. So go to Goodwill, get yourself an undersized suit coat—smallest one you can get your bones in—and a pair of baggy pants. Black. They've got a pile of 'em. Meet us in the lobby of the Chesterfield, 6:30 tonight. Got it?"

"Got it," I said.

She said, "What's a matter? I hook you up with a sweet deal, you sound like I stepped in your birthday puddin'."

I said, "No, no, I'm glad. I just thought..."

"Ah, you're missing your man, is that it?" Her voice was a finger jabbing me in the ribs. "Well, the bigger the dog, the longer the leash. Let him roam," she said. "Listen, here's the lemonade to the story, right? With Rex out of the way, we can run this town. Take over the whole King's Row. By the time you see his mug again, we'll be flashing the cash. He'll love you for that, see?"

Right. I said, "Thank you. Thanks for bringing me along." Before I met Crack, I advertised with an index card on a corkboard at the old Pawn and Preen, and got maybe one job a month.

"No balloons this time," Crack said. "No tricks, and no excuses. Leave the chicken, the popgun, and the exploding gum at home."

The chicken. Plucky. I wished Plucky were home.

"This is the big bucks, Sweets, the real deal. I'll set you up with a hat and a cane."

I said yes to all of it.

I'd been out of the hospital three days, was still on the dizzy side, head buzzing, but could move without feeling faint, could walk at almost normal speed. The orange plastic jug sat empty in my mudroom waiting for a day I could devote to collecting urine. Twenty-four hours of contiguous urine is a tougher trick than it seems. One pee away from the orange jug on ice, and the whole day's urine file is shot.

ON THE WAY TO THE GIG, I STOPPED AND COPIED MISSING Rubber Chicken posters. The poster had a drawing of Plucky, my name, Herman's address, and a dancing money sign as promise of a reward. I stapled flyers to phone poles, one eye out for cops, always ready to silly-walk away fast in my oversized wing tips. Posting flyers on phone poles is illegal, but how else to tell the neighborhood?

To keep my chin up, I recited the Clown's Prayer: "As I stumble through this life … May every pratfall pay the bills. May every tumble lighten strife, all the aches be cured with pills."

I MET UP WITH CRACK AND MATEY IN A HOTEL LOBBY. The lobby was wide and lush, with a thicket of plants in the middle. Prom night. Girls dressed like faded flowers lingered with acne-faced dates outside the hotel restaurant. Skinny kids danced through the lobby like they were on vacation, rustling and laughing, calling out names.

Matey, all in black and white, was perched on the back of a couch, feet on the cushions and her cane across her knees. She leaned forward, elbows on the cane. Her shoulder blades stuck up under her white T-shirt like wings over her thin back and took the place of her trademark fake parrot for the night. Crack paced back and forth in front of the couch. She had on a dark wig, a tidy men's hairpiece, black and shiny as shoe polish.

Matey saw me first, and nodded. "Here she is, Boss."

Crack looked up. She said, "Christ, could you be any later? When I said 6:30, I meant sharp, like on the dot, like the point on your head, see?" She moved fast and bumped into a short girl dressed like an after-dinner mint, all white with red piping. Crack didn't look at the girl even after she ran into her.

"What is this?" She pulled the flyers from my hand. "Missing Chicken. Plucky. Aw, real sweet. Now forget about it." She threw the flyers on the couch and slapped a party-store bowler hat and a bamboo cane against my chest. The hat was made of plastic covered in a thin spray of fuzz like faux felted wool. "Got your suit, sister?"

I had on the big wool pants, and my thighs were sweaty from walking in the summer evening. The air-conditioned hotel was cold as a walk-in fridge. I shivered in my own cooling sweat. I already had on a pair of men's wing tips, one black, one brown, both size massive. The suit coat was compressed, tight in my shoulder bag. I pulled the coat out of the bag and shook it.

"Right," Crack said. "Put it on."

I rested the cane against my leg, pulled on the coat. The shoulders pinched and the sleeves ended half a foot before my arms did.

"Perfect," Crack said.

The coat had the Goodwill seal of hobo authenticity in mingled cigar smoke and rancid sweat. I could barely move my arms as I collected my flyers, shoved them in the pink bag. If I moved too fast, the coat would rip in two. I said, "All this for a prom gig? That's a little small-time for what you said. The big bucks." Prom was teenagers, once a year at best.

"If prom was our gig, I'd shoot myself," Crack said. "Then again, why shoot myself when I've got you two?" She turned on her heel and waved a hand, speaking clown sign language, directing Matey and me to follow.

In the ladies' room there was a counter of sinks a mile long lined with a mirror on one side and prom girls on the other. Every prom girl was cloned across that counter, all of them in pastels, with big hair and bigger plans. They leaned in close, as though to kiss themselves as they painted their eyes and lips with tiny brushes. The air was a sickening war between the bathroom's sanitizer and an army of cheap perfume. Crack, in her black suit and white shirt, pushed dresses aside and wedged her way into the line. Prom girls cackled and fluttered, hens in a henhouse.

"Hey," a hen girl clucked. She had lipstick on her top lip but not yet on the bottom, one bright red lip, the other dry and pale. "You can't be in here. This is the women's room."

Crack tipped her hairpiece. "You must be the housemother, yes?" She grabbed her own boobs through her oversized, rumpled men's dress shirt. "Want to go over my credentials, cupcake?"

Matey moved in behind the girl, hands flat on her flat chest. She stuck her tongue out to one side and let her eyes roll. "Me next, me next!" She pressed up behind the prom queen.

The girl backed off, wobbly in high heels, and found a place between her friends, body guards in tulle and crepe. Matey and I wedged into the girl's spot. I tipped my plastic bowler and smiled, clown sign language for *Sorry*. To say, *We're all friends here*.

To Crack I hissed, "What is this, *West Side Story*? You give these birds reason to hate us."

Crack said, "Aw, you're going soft." She snapped open her hot pink shoulder bag. The shoulder bags were the matching part of our costumes, bought at Ross to look like a team and to hold props while we worked. She poured trays of makeup on the counter, along with triangular sponge applicators, makeup pencils, tampons, a kazoo, and a washcloth. Our makeup came in kits like grade school watercolors. Each color was a small round cake. A paintbrush snapped in place to the side.

Crack spread white makeup on her cheek. She said, "Chaplin. Hop to it," and she looked at me. "Well, step on it, Sniff. Get your Chaplin on, girl."

"All of us?" I asked. "So, we're all the same?"

Matey nodded, twisted sideways and crowded in beside me in the mirror. "We're all Chaplin."

I said, "We're all Chaplin. Bejesus. That's so redundant. Like three Mickey Mouses in the Macy's parade, or three promotional Snow Whites at the same video store."

"Or ten prom queens in the same john," Matey said, loud. Painted eyes flickered our way and glared in the mirror.

"What's redundancy got to do with the price of eggs?" Crack said. "Fetishism is the key. Tap into a fetish, we'll make a fortune, see?" Her face was white now, with no color at all: Lips, white. Eyebrows dusted white. Only her brown eyes, moving fast, were still dark against her face. Her eyes sized me up in the mirror. "If you're not interested in cash, let me know." She looked at me in the mirror, then at herself, then at Matey, then at me again. "If you're keen on small potatoes and Food Fairs, that's your trip. Fine. I'll find another clown girl, read me?"

I twisted my hair into a high topknot. "'Greed has poisoned men's souls,'" I said, and slid a bobby pin in.

"*Hell–o*?" Crack said. "Say what?"

"…has goose-stepped us into misery and bloodshed."

Crack painted on her tiny Chaplin mustache. "Look, I'm not exactly taking it out of your hide. I don't know what you're getting at, but I'm here to make a buck…"

I said, "Just quoting Chaplin. I've sure you've seen *The Great Dictator*." I tucked in more hairpins to keep my hair off my face and flat under the bowler.

Matey piped up: "Like, how do you quote a silent flick? Riddle me that one."

I finished pinning my hair and said, "You're doing that on purpose, I hope."

"Don't count on it," Crack said. With her tiny mustache and the slick hairpiece, Crack looked halfway to her own dictatorship.

I said, "So, what kind of fetishes are we selling tonight? Chaplin and hairbrush spankings, for the prom crowd?" I pulled my makeup palette from the bag and found a sponge in a plastic Baggie. I ran the sponge under cool tap water. I touched one edge of the sponge to the white cake of base.

Crack said, "Again, Miss High Artiste, it's not about prom, see? It's corporate stuff. Call it a logo, branding, whatever they want to call it, but underneath, it's a fetish. A fetish, by any other name, is still the big bucks." She closed one eye and used a long paintbrush to circle her eye with black. "Matey knows about fetishes, right, Mate?"

Matey said, "Hey, fetish? Me? Nah, these clothes were fresh this morning." She bent one foot up, hopped in a circle, and tried to sniff her shoe. Her face was white, her hair pulled back by a dozen tiny bands. She grabbed the counter and swung herself back up to face the mirror, stuck her bowler on her head, and offered a nightmare smile.

"Cover the bruises," Crack said. She smacked Matey on one bruised forearm. "These corporate yahoos ponied up for their own style fetish, not S&M, you read me? A little wear and tear takes the shine off the illusion."

Matey dug in her bag and came up with Flesh Tones Cream, shade: sallow. She dropped the tube on the counter. Farther down the wall of mirrors, a prom girl ran a line of silver eye shadow over her eyes, same movements as me and Crack and Matey, different color was all. Crack drew on eyebrows. "They want Chaplin, we'll be Chaplin, see? If they want their mamas, I say play mama for enough cash. If we give 'em what they want, they'll find a reason to have us back. High demand, high demand. That's us. Mark my words, ladies."

I touched up the white makeup along my chin.

Matey drew a heavy, black, straight line over her thin, arched eyebrows. Her arms were like sticks, her elbows sharp. The white insides of her arms were marked with thumbprint bruises. I wondered if the rumors were true, that Matey was an S&M clown for hire, into the degradation, catering to coulrophiles.

"Juggling pins lately?" I asked, hopeful. Pins caused those kinds of bruises. Sometimes.

Matey glanced at me, didn't bother to answer. Her makeup cracked around her eyes; her eyes were puffy. I felt a flicker of sadness, but the sadness wasn't really about Matey. It was bigger than that. I leaned into the mirror, drew on my own lips, and joined every last prom queen in line doing almost the same. We were a sad parade of longing, those lip painters and me, humans trying our hardest. Mostly, I felt the missing life of my tiny baby, my tiny Rexie, who never even made it into this crappy world.

Baby Rexie never had a chance to be a sucker, a chump, a prince, an S&M clown. Whatever he or she might've been. And then I thought of my parents, who also died too young, but far older than baby Rex. I was the center, the hinge pin of a family not made to last.

"You guys go to prom?" Matey asked.

One mirror down, a round girl in a baby-blue dress plucked a fine hair from her brow. Her chin already sagged. I could see her as an old lady. How had any of us made it this far?

Crack said, "Prom? Ba! But this one, our Vassar girl, she probably went."

Me. Vassar? Prom? I shook my head and looked down, away from the mirror. I organized my makeup stack, to give myself a moment.

"Me neither," Matey said. "I was shooting up, prom night. Learning bad habits." She knocked on the bathroom counter like knocking on wood for luck.

I said, "Is there luck in Formica?" I gave a knock myself. Blinked damp lashes.

The girl in blue packed up her tiny purse: lipstick, lip liner, eye shadow, perfume, keys, tampons, chewing gum, and little slips of packaged condoms.

Matey said, "Hey, that's a better trick than clowns in a tiny car. Give us your secret, Cheesecake."

Crack said, "You must be one-eighth clown, maybe a grandma on the Cherokee side? You got the clown nose." Behind Crack, Matey pretended to squeeze her own nose, as though it were bulbous, and said, "Honk, honk!"

The prom queen took her tiny purse, cut a wide arc around us, and skedaddled toward the door.

We three Chaplins looked back into the mirror. I finished with the thin, pale Chaplin lips, then drew on the famous mustache. Wide eyebrows and a mustache—that's enough to change a whole face. One clown training manual says, *These particular three dots of color alone will divert the eye from the normal visage and render the individual almost unidentifiable.*

"I worked as a fry cook prom night. Flat broke. Minimum wage was its own bad habit."

That made Crack bark out a single-note laugh in appreciation. She liked money jokes. What I didn't say was that I was already an emancipated minor—emancipated by the state and by an accident on the old California Highway One, before that highway crumbled, where it curved through the redwoods in tight hairpin turns along the edge of the ocean's rocky cliffs. I ran a circle of black around my eyes and said, "Every real job I ever had, I wore a polyester suit."

"Shit, don't I know it," Crack said. "Either a polyester suit or a thong and platforms."

None of us worked for minimum wage anymore. As clowns, as long as work came in, we were paid in stacks of twenties. Cash on the spot was Crack's rule. After another night's pay, I'd be that much closer to Rex again, that much closer to building, or rebuilding, the family I didn't have.

Our assignment was to wait huddled in a narrow white hallway, outside some corporate office cocktail party, until we heard the antique stylings of "The Entertainer," electronically remixed.

At least it wasn't "Send in the Clowns," impossible to dance to. We dropped our pink bags in a corner.

"When the player piano starts, that's our cue, see?" Crack said. "Matey, you'll go first. Bust out your best Chaplin waddle. We'll be right behind you. One at a time we all fall down, get up, circle back, and exit. Strike fast, no garnish, got it?"

"Got it, Boss," Matey said, and crouched near the door. She was good at falls. Before the clown gigs she worked grocery stores for insurance money, pulling what they call Slip and Falls in damp aisles, taking out injury claims.

"Walk and fall? That's it?" I said.

Crack pulled a cigar from her suit-coat pocket. Twirled it in her fingers. "Listen, Sniff, let's keep this one simple as our clientele. They get what they asked for."

We came between appetizers and the entrée as an elaborate dinner bell, a fancy signal to corporate employee-guests: move from drinks to the dining hall. Soon enough, the music started, then a strobe light cut in. Crack didn't say there'd be a strobe light. Anybody can do Chaplin in a strobe, but the things make me sick.

Matey took off, feet splayed and cane swinging. Crack followed Matey, with me a ways behind. We waddled like penguins while the flickering strobe made us into a stop-action film.

More than that, the strobe made me queasy. It was like being hit in the head.

Matey smacked into the back of a chair and stepped on the crossbar. The chair flipped backward under her foot. Matey sailed forward over the top. She was in the air, diving, cane flailing out to the side. On the way down she rolled into a somersault, all in the agitated, panicked heartbeat of the strobe. In that light the world was a fragmented place—a hand to a mouth, a spilled drink, a turned head—everyone diced into bits of existence.

Crack hit the chair next, shin against its side. She fell into Matey and sent them both into a tumble.

I saw the chair and was almost there, knew I had to step on the chair, trip, find a way to make it look both real and cartoon.

But as I penguin-walked in the strobe, the chair flashed off and on, and the light was disorienting—was the chair underfoot, or a mile away? My own body looked wrong in that light; my hand wrapped around the cane was a monkey's paw. I was dizzy, my head sang with the hum of bees, and the party-store bowler was a tourniquet. My cane swung like a broken windshield wiper.

I couldn't think, couldn't decide whether to go over the top of the chair or send myself backward. I put my right foot on the back of the chair to go over the top, but the chair slid and I slid too in my slick, mismatched wing tips. My legs splayed. I went down hard, a hot snap, a rubber band breaking. My left knee twisted and I sat on the floor—no rolls, just a grimace and the splits.

Somersaults are funny. Tumbling is funny. Pratfalls, straight back, are pure comedy. But the forward splits? I was a cheerleader. A Chaplin cheerleader.

I had to get up funny. Could I even get up?

Crack and Matey circled toward the exit, then disappeared out the swinging door. Guests followed behind me, gawky and excited in the disco lights, pasty-faced,tipsy and tired. A woman tripped on my splayed leg. Goldfish fell from her hand, swimming out of her mouth as she laughed. I worked my wing tip through the chair railing and tried to stand. I wanted the chair to throw me into a somersault, but then my oversized flatfoot really was stuck, and the chair was a ski on ice, no traction on the hotel carpet.

I tried to stand, went down again, and caught myself on one knee. The chair was a cage on my foot. I wrestled the chair, and both armpits ripped in my undersized coat. The handle of my cane caught my ankle. I tugged on the cane, jerked it loose, and knocked a tray of salmon rings from a caterer's hand. *Voilà*! Salmon-ring confetti. The caterer's face was ugly in the strobe, his mouth a stuttering gash. I slid toward the exit, waved my cane at the party, felt the sweat hot on my palms as I pushed myself forward with my free hand and scooted along like a jalopy in strobe headlights, the cane a dragging muffler.

A drunk woman in a clinging dress doubled over and wiped

her eyes, cramped with laughter lost under the music. A man patted her back, face contorted with his own party laugh. I hit the stretch of linoleum between the carpet and the swinging exit door and the ski of a chair slid fast out in front. I pushed the door open with the chair on my foot, and got out.

Matey and Crack were in the hall, where the walls, ceiling, and floor were all painted primer white, gleaming and bright as heaven. Matey had her jacket off, a cigarette in her mouth.

I groaned and said, "Kept 'em in stitches. And speaking of stitches, think I need a few." Behind me the music was loud, then muffled, then loud, then muffled, as the door swung open and closed and open again, riding its own momentum.

Matey said, "After that dance you'll wake up with a sore bum in the morning, and I don't mean the man of the hour."

Crack glowered. "What was all that?" She said, "When I said no garnish, I meant don't blow it and don't waste time."

I threw the cane aside, bent my leg, and reached through the chair to pull off my shoe, free my foot. The torn pits of my coat tore again. A dishwasher leaned against the wall, apron soaked. He watched me where I sat on the floor massaging my thigh.

I said, "Show's over, friend. Nothing to see."

He lifted one tattooed arm, pressed his thumb and index finger to his lips, took a shadow toke, then raised his eyebrows and nodded, Yes?

A date? No way. My groin had the hot burn of a torn ligament, not lust. But I remembered my pledge to the Clown Code. I was still in costume. My head spun, face hot, and the dishwasher wanted a show. I fake-smiled back, winked, and shook my head in a demure deferral, clown style.

He made a sad face, mouth drawn down, then had another idea. He held his hands around his mouth and breathed between them, an invitation to sniff glue. When I shook my head again, he pulled a card from his pocket and handed it to me: *Jack. Dishwasher*. Two words and a phone number.

The swinging doors cut open, the music blared loud again,

and a tall man stepped into the hallway. He straightened his lapel. "Excellent, excellent work," he said. "Bravo," and he gave a little clap and a bow. His smile was the high gloss of newly whitened teeth. When he bowed toward me, he put out his hand. "I don't believe I've had the pleasure."

Still on the floor, I reached up. The man's handshake was quick and tight.

"That's Sniffles," Crack said. "Our latest joke."

"Fantabulous," he said. His hair was a sea of blond waves.

The dishwasher wiped a hand on his greasy apron, then held his hand out. I hesitated before I shook his hand too, like I was doing him a favor. His skin was waterlogged as a kid in the bath.

The man in the tux hitched up his pants and crouched down. "You were really something out there, you know? Perfect comic timing. Need help with that?"

He pointed to my leg, my hands where I massaged my thigh. Before I could answer, he dug strong fingers into the muscles and tendons of my leg. I shivered when he found a tender spot.

"Did that hurt?" he asked.

"In a sort of good way," I said. It hurt like a massage, releasing the muscles.

Matey swung her arms, clapped her hands together, and said, "Hey! That's my girl!"

The dishwasher, uneasy, moved foot to foot, side to side. The man in the tux laughed.

I said, "No, I didn't mean it like that." I tried to brush his hands away.

Crack, behind him, cleared her throat. "Got something for us?" she said. "We don't have time to hobnob unless it's on the clock."

"Ah, yes, yes." He stood up fast, knees crackling, reached into an inside pocket in his jacket, and pulled out an envelope. "Before we wrap this up, tell me, does Sniffles here ever do any, ah, how shall we say? Any personal negotiation. Private parties? One-on-one."

I said, "No."

Crack said, "Depends what you're asking and what's the wages."

"I don't do one-on-one," I said.

Matey chimed in: "I'm here." She put her feet on the two opposite walls of the hallway and took a few steps up, then jumped down, feet smacking the floor. "Let's negotiate."

Mr. Tux turned to me. "I'd make it worth your while." He pulled out a business card.

I said, "I've seen you before, haven't I?"

His smile was a flat line that curled up on one side. His cheeks were high and ruddy. "Maybe you have. Maybe I've been to a few of your shows. Maybe I'm your biggest fan."

That was all I needed to hear. A coulrophile.

"I'm the boss of this gig," Crack said, and cut him short. "I'll talk to her, we'll work something out."

She took the card. He pulled out another. When he held the second card toward me, I took it.

The dishwasher started counting out bills from his pocket. Maybe ten bucks total. Crack tipped her head at him. "Put your bubble gum back in your purse and dangle, Mr. Clean. No doing." She turned her back on him and pointed to the man in the tux. "Pay up on this job, we'll see what comes next."

He laid the envelope in her open hand. "It's all there, plus a little extra." He winked again.

The dishwasher, damp pants sagging, disappeared through a door that let out a cloud of steam.

"Thank you," the man said, to me. "You made my evening." He flashed his teeth, crinkled the sunburned skin on his newly shaven cheeks, then turned and strode back out into what passed for a party in the corporate world.

Crack counted out the cash, dropped a wad of bills at my side. She said, "That's just the way of it. I do all the grunt work, I'm the brains of the operation, and old Valentino goes for the jinx. Go figure."

"The figure is the answer," Matey said. "Which one was Valentino? That dishwasher was hot."

"Hot like a steamin' pile of greasy dishes," Crack said.

I said, "At least the dishwasher's humble. That other guy creeps me out."

"Sure. All high artistes are creeped out by anyone with cash, but that's your neurosis, not mine. And not his." Crack counted her share of the money one more time.

"Not mine!" Matey chimed in, and raised her hand like a prize student.

To me, Crack said, "We know you're the toast of Baloney-town, living the high artiste life, but that don't make you too good for practice."

I said, "I practice all the time. I did a good job with the penguin waddle."

She said, "Do you see me injured? Is Matey on the floor with a pulled crotch?"

"It was that strobe light. They mess with my head ... "

"Listen, Hot Stuff. Ice the leg, then put heat on it. Back and forth like that. And next time, get in a few warm-up stretches." She took off her bowler hat, pulled off the wig, and shook out her short hair. "I'm not just channeling Marcus Welby here. I'm giving you the first aid rap because our next big deal is right around the corner, see? A publicity shot. It costs money. We'll only do it once, so be on time and go all out. And, I already took your share out a your cut."

Behind her, Matey said, "In this racket, you want to be the grand artiste, start with a sex change. No joke."

A fine tip. I said, "That's one act I'm not interested in."

"Well, Grimaldi the Great, then you'll have to work with the boobs, not against 'em. And don't think your sisters here didn't have higher aspirations once too," Crack said. We didn't start as sellouts, money found us. I'm glad it did. See you at the shoot." She headed down the long white hall.

"Pssst," Matey said, in a stage whisper, and knocked a hand

against her head. "Here's a clue: Women wear makeup, right? But a man in face paint, people see aahh-rt. You and me, we top out at birthday gigs, and that hurts more than anything I'm doing now. That's the meat o' the matter." She tipped her Chaplin hat. Was it true? Was there a latex ceiling, a made-up makeup finish line?

She said, "Careful getting home."

"Careful getting up, more like it," I said.

Matey added, "Call the Tux. Easy cash. For reals."

At the end of the hall, Crack picked up one of the pink nylon bags. Matey grabbed hers. Then there was only my bag, far away, against the shine of the bare white linoleum. Rex, my bag, family, fame and Kafka—why was everything so out of reach?

My leg was a torn rubber band. The swarm of bees drifted toward the center of my head. I used the chair to stand, then sat on the chair and rubbed a thumb along the heart meridian on the inside of my wrist, the acupuncture spot, the baby-heart-spot center. That spot that says: Get back to who you were meant to be.

Crack and her jobs—that was my whole plan, the way to get back to who I was meant to be: Rex's girl, me and Rex performing together, delivering art, not commerce.

Matey pushed the exit door open. Crack called, over her shoulder, "Practice up if you want to stay with us, Sniffster. Otherwise, kaputsky. We'll cut you loose, understand?"

7.

Hostility Shoots from the Hip

THE NEXT DAY, I COULDN'T DO A PRATFALL IF MY ASS DE-pended on it. The pulled muscle or tendon or rubber band in my groin from the Chaplin gig had stiffened with pain overnight. When I tried to start my day's urine collection, no way could I sustain a high crouch over the jug and hold the jug over the toilet. I leaned against the wall. Urine ran sideways. Piss on the toilet seat. Piss on my hand. Piss on the whole homework assignment. I gave up, tossed the jug aside, sat on the wet seat, and let the urine flow.

I needed that funnel back from the cop.

I had the phone, on its long cord, in the bathroom with me to call Rex. Instead, I shook piddle flecks off my hand. Dialed.

"Information," a voice said, in a way that hovered between statement and question.

I said, "Hello there, Information. Could you give me the non-emergency cop number? I mean, the police. Baloneytown precinct."

When I got through to the cops another woman answered, and I realized I didn't have a name for the cop I wanted. Not that I *wanted* to talk to a cop at all, but I needed my gear. I said, "I don't know his name."

"Sounds like he a real good friend of yours, right?" she said.

"He's got sort of light brown, golden hair."

"That's a few of 'em around here." I heard her gum crack. "The ones that got hair."

"His pants hang too long?" I offered.

She said, "Well, I guess that might narrow it. I'll keep an eye out. A cop that needs a tailor."

I said, "Listen, he's got something of mine I need to get back. He's not too tall. He has freckles on his arms. He smells like cinnamon and Sunday breakfast." It was all I could come up with.

"Honey, we're not writing personal ads. If you don't got a name or a badge number, I can't help you." *Click.*

GOVERNMENT-SPONSORED ACUPUNCTURE WAS UPSTAIRS in an old house, over a needle exchange, part of a methadone program at the ragged edge of Baloneytown. *DownSide Up: Sharp-Shooters Rehab Day Treatment Center,* a sign said. *Clean Up With Our Services Before We Attend Yours.*

Treatment in the clinic was dirt cheap. "More if you can, free if you can't" was the motto, and as far as I could tell the government didn't even ask what it paid for—that's how little they wanted to know.

I wanted a quick fix for my busted crotch, an easy cure, cheap and fast, that would send me back out ready to hit the pavement and tie balloons, juggle pins, make lots of funny.

The clinic's wooden porch steps were steeped in sun-hot piss. I took a breath, straightened my big straw hat, then started in. Each step up, my inner thigh burned. W. C. Fields, a tiny devil's voice in my ear, slurred, "Suffering sciatica." I pushed my cane against the stairs one at a time, lifted my bum leg, and pulled on the shaky wooden handrail. I wore one regular-sized, black Keds tennis shoe and one size fifteen clown shoe turned orthopedic; it helped my hip to have a wider base so my foot could spread inside. That big shoe made sense out on the flatlands of Baloneytown's sidewalks, but once I reached the clinic, the rubber toe of the clown-sized Keds caught against the lip of every wooden step.

Inside, the needle exchange wasn't open yet. Men and women sat in orange plastic chairs around what had once been a living room. A man with a purple welt on his cheek cleaned his teeth with his driver's license. A pale girl in a black dress tweaked her nose ring. Over her head, a giant sign said, *No Drugs, No Weapons, No Money Exchanged. No Loitering, No Cell Phones, No Beepers. No Alcohol, No Hand Signals, No Whistling. No Profanity, No Name Calling, No Racial Slurs. No Remaining on Premises Once Your Business is Over. If You Are Visibly Under the Influence of Controlled Substances, You Will Be Removed. ABSOLUTELY NO HORSEPLAY WHATSOEVER.*

The waiting room was decorated with flyers of runaways, missing wives, and men who slipped the guard at outpatient centers. *Needs medication,* every flyer claimed. A picture of a red-haired girl said across the bottom, *We love you. We won't lock you up.* Below that, a second hand had scrawled, *Yeah, rite, Suckah.* A few plaques said, *In Loving Memory of.*

There was a stack of pamphlets, *From Here to Paternity: Surviving Early Fatherhood,* and a glossy poster that read, *Be Up-Beat, Not Beat-Up!* with a picture of three happy women, heads tipped back, perfect makeup. *A Friendly Message from BAPP: Baloneytown Abuse Prevention Program.*

I stole a tack from the BAPP poster and added my own cry for help: *Missing, Rubber Chicken. Plucky.*

When I reached the front of the line, the receptionist gave me a clipboard with a form to fill out and a greasy pen dug from a cup on her desk. I sat lightly along the front of an orange chair, bad leg out in front. On the form, where it asked, *Employment,* I put *Clown.* Then I crossed that off. I wrote *Entertainer.* Crossed that off. Wrote *Performing Artist.*

I marked: No *Hepatitis,* No *AIDS,* No *Heavy Bruising.* No *Asthma* or *Glaucoma* or *Diabetes.* No *Jaundice,* No *Needle Sharing.* Heart Trouble? I tailored my answer: *Maybe.*

Pregnant? I marked No. Newly not pregnant. ABSOLUTELY NOT PREGNANT WHATSOEVER.

I handed in the forms and sat back down. I dropped my pink prop bag on the floor, leaned my cane against the wall, put my hands in the loose pockets of my pants, and ran my fingers over clown toys: three miniature juggling balls, a tube of skin-safe glue, a wad of balloons. I pulled an orange balloon from my pocket, gave it a quick stretch, and started to blow. A nervous habit.

I let the orange balloon deflate against my palm in a squeaking fart sound.

"What's that?" the receptionist asked. She pointed at the big sign on the wall: *No whistling*. I tucked the balloon back in my pocket and sat on my hands, palms flat against the sticky orange chair, until the receptionist called my name.

THE ACUPUNCTURIST WAS RAIL THIN. HIS HAIR BRUSHED the sloped ceiling of the attic room. He ran a hand through his hair, then knocked his head against the ceiling and his hair ruffled forward again. "Criminy," he said, under his breath, and adjusted his tiny glasses. He held the papers I'd just filled out downstairs. There was a rice paper screen set up in the middle of the room, where the ceiling was highest. A portable air conditioner hummed. The acupuncturist looked at my papers, frowned, and said, "Tell me, what's the problem, exactly?" His eyes were sad, forehead weathered by concern. He was a bleeding heart ready to save the world, the kind that gravitated to the sad streets of Baloneytown like litter blowing through a parking lot.

I'd written *groin* in the space on the form under "problem." He already had that. I said, "Well, the bigger problem is money; I can't afford treatment and can't afford to miss work."

He had his pen ready, a page blank. He sat on a tall stool, put his right ankle on top of his left knee, and rested his clipboard against his calf. He wore soft leather loafers with comfy brown socks. He looked ready to play a little folk guitar.

I sat on the paper-covered table and grabbed the tendon at the inside of my thigh. "I fell," I said. "I've strained something." I grabbed my thigh again and sucked in my breath.

He said, "Let me see your tongue."

"My tongue?"

He nodded and shook his hair out of his eyes. The logic lost me. I opened my mouth, held my tongue out. The acupuncturist leaned in close, then leaned back and wrote on a blank page. He leaned close again, tipped his head sideways, and peered into my mouth like a spelunker ready to spelunk.

When it'd gone on too long, I ran my tongue over my dry teeth and said, "The problem's in my leg, at my hip."

He furrowed his brow, looked down, and wrote like a man deep in inspiration, a fast flurry of scribbles. "How do you sleep?"

"Little."

"How's your hearing? Do your ears ring at night?"

I said again, "It's a leg muscle bothering me."

"Healing one part of the system involves the system as a whole. Now tell me, do you eat regularly?"

I said, "I don't even like the smell of food. I've been known to faint at the first whiff of Wiggly Fries." My brain started to hum in tune with the drone of the air conditioner.

"Smelling is ingesting, it's all the same." He held a flashlight to my eyes, one at a time, and moved the flashlight back and forth. "Do you know your neighbors? Are you part of a community?"

"I know some neighbors." I knew the Baloneytown criminals, and now had made the acquaintance of a neighborhood cop, that grown-up golden boy. The acupuncturist jiggled one knee, shook his leg and shook the clipboard as he read. "How does it feel to be … "—he looked at the forms—" … a performance artist?"

"A clown," I said. "And it's tops, in fact. I wouldn't do anything else. But lately I can't think. My head is fuzzy. I've been wiped out, like a weak crop in a bad year."

He held my wrist and took my pulse. "You're exhausted." He wrote a note on his chart, then took my pulse again from the same wrist but a different place. "Ah! Interesting." He shifted his fingers back and forth, fretwork on his folk guitar, and counted under his breath. His fingers were warm, finding the beat of my heart.

He wrote more notes and nodded. "Perfect. You have a perfect example of what we call Heart and Kidney out of Balance Syndrome."

"My leg?" I said.

"A person has six pulses. On you, the heart pulse is the strongest. The kidney pulse is almost nonexistent. The heart is fire, the kidneys water. With too much fire," he said, and used one long-fingered hand to gesture like a plant unfolding in fast motion, "and not enough water,"—his other hand made a sort of pooling movement below—"your system will become disrupted. Heart and Kidney out of Balance Syndrome." He held both hands up, as though announcing a beautiful thing. "Your heart and kidneys aren't communicating."

I said, "Well, I do have heart trouble."

He took out a stethoscope and pressed the cold metal disk to the skin of my back. "Your heart sounds OK. Let me see your tongue again."

I opened my mouth, held my tongue out.

"Yes. Exactly!" he said, and pointed with one long pinkie at my tongue. "You have a narrow split down the center." He wrote in his notes, then looked at me. He said, "I do too." He opened his mouth and showed me his tongue and I saw a line down the middle of it but didn't know enough to tell if the line was particularly narrow.

Softly, he said, "People like us, we're genetically predisposed toward stress on the heart." He seemed happy to learn we had something in common, our ailing hearts.

"Well, that's cold comfort. Least I've got genetic relations."

He smiled. "It's not heart disease. Maybe you're lonely."

Lonely? I wasn't lonely. I had Rex. But here it was—another clown fetishist. In a minute he'd hand me a card. Ask me out. Try the old line about acupuncture for a long-playing, extended dance version of the massive orgasm.

I'd heard it before.

"Have you experienced a loss?" He looked into my eyes. "Abandonment issues, perhaps, or childhood trauma?"

Ah, the sensitive shtick. In through the heart pulse. I

wouldn't fall for it. "No." But even as I said it, I touched one hand to the photos tucked in my bra.

His eyes followed my hand, he flushed, wrinkled his nose, and tapped his tiny glasses. "Sometimes, we bury our feelings…" He looked at me like I was a sad clown on worn velvet, then offered his own half smile.

He offered me pity. Did I need his pity? I said, "I'm so far from lonely, it's not even funny," and reached into my pink bag for a pack of exploding gum, the rubber ham sandwich, or any trick to take the focus off me. My hand wrapped around the silver gun. I pulled it out—*voilà!*

The acupuncturist jumped back and threw up his arms. He hiccuped, hit his head against the sloped roof, and tripped into a wastebasket. "Take a deep breath, don't do anything rash, your whole future's ahead of you, let's talk, we're here for you," he said, as though reciting an office training memo on emergency situations.

I pulled the trigger. The acupuncturist gave a yipe. A flag shot out. "Bang," it said on the flag.

He looked at the flag, frowned, and straightened his glasses with one shaking hand. "That," he said, as he eased his way back toward me, "was not even funny. That's the definition of not funny." His glasses were still crooked. His flyaway hair flew.

I twirled the gun to roll the flag, then pushed the flag back into the barrel with the heel of my hand. "It's a muzzle loader."

He rubbed a hand on the back of his skull. "Totally toxic." He put a hand to his heart, reached up to a shelf for a brown bottle, unscrewed the cap, and took a healthy swig.

It was my turn to look with pity.

"Being a little melodramatic, aren't you?" I said. "It doesn't even look like a real gun. Note the 'Made in China' sticker?"

He held a hand out in front of himself, palm flat against the air like a mime marking the hard edge of a box, and his fingers trembled. When he put the bottle down, he reached for the gun. He wrapped trembling fingers around the barrel, took the gun from me gently, and put it on the counter. He leaned in close. "You know, I should call the police," he said quietly.

"The police?" My first thought was a secret one, curious, hopeful, and nervous: *Mr. Cinnamon?*

The acupuncturist's breath was the bite of alcohol, the musk of herbs. "We don't tolerate hostility in the clinic."

I said, "It's a classic joke, old-time clown stuff. You must've never been to the circus."

"I'll let it go this time," he said and took another sip off the bottle. Licked his thin, pale lips. "But you need to find a little help with that. You only alienate yourself." His arms were scrawny, and for a minute I sensed acupuncture needles maybe weren't his only needle friends.

He said, "For now, lay on the table, on your back. Remove your, uh, your other shoe." He stood up, put the clipboard aside. He didn't give me his card, didn't ask me out or offer his phone number. Maybe I'd headed that one off.

I lay back against the loud rattle of the paper sheet. The acupuncturist breathed out deeply as he tapped tiny needles into the crook of my hand, between my thumb and fingers. The needles didn't hurt, but they felt like someone had tapped my funny bone, touched a nerve. It was a warm spread of pain that made me want to laugh and cringe and gag all at once—comedy and tragedy, aligned in every cell. I willed myself not to flinch. The silver gun was a pale glimmer on the shelf, tucked between chrome-topped jars of cotton balls and Band-Aids. An ambulance passed outside. The wail of the ambulance grew loud, then faded, as somebody else's emergency moved into the distance.

The acupuncturist turned off a lamp on my side of the room and said, "I'll leave you to rest for twenty minutes."

Then I was alone, covered in needles, afraid to move. My heart raced. I wanted to sit up or roll over. My mouth was cottony. My heart spoke again in Morse code: *heart trouble, heart trouble, heart trouble ... die or go crazy, die or go crazy ...* The acupuncturist didn't understand. It wasn't loneliness, it was something more.

I had to tell them—yes, I had heart trouble. Real trouble. I hadn't filled out the forms right. Nitroglycerin and potassium! Where was the bottle he drank from? I needed medicines. I needed to relax, wanted a balloon, to stretch and tie an animal, twist balloon knots until I was at ease again.

My body weighed a thousand pounds, I hadn't slept since Rex left town. In the smoke of a warm incense, I tried to quit listening to the story of my own frantic heart. I let go of the noise in the street, sirens and buses. My arms and legs and spine were heavy against the table. I felt then like two bodies, one outer and one inner, one smaller than even my bones, one large and ballooning. I was a balloon sheep, St. Sebastian of the acupuncture needles. The Virgin Mary. Skin was a membrane thin as rubber. I could see the inside of my eyelids, calm and dark, spotted with orange.

"OK, that's it." The acupuncturist snapped on the lamp. I twitched, suddenly awake. He pulled needles from my feet, hands, and head.

"That's it?" I was an inflated balloon in a skin-colored casing, too empty to sit up.

"I've found some medicine that'll help." He handed me a palm-sized red box with a picture of a person's profile on it. "It's Chinese, to boost the system." As he said "boost" he made a gesture like a weight lifter, like Natalia-Italia-Nadia flexing her narcissist muscle—shoulder dropped, one curled fist. He said, "Take ten at a time, up to thirty a day. Great stuff."

I took the box, opened it, and shook out an amber jar with a cork lid sealed under heavy wax. The writing was in Chinese. "This'll fix my leg?"

"Your leg? Ah, that. Ice it and apply heat. Back and forth. While you're watching TV or whatever." It was the same advice as Crack gave. He held my popgun out by the barrel and said, "Lay off the hostility. We store hostility in our hips and joints. It doesn't do any good. Notice when you're alienating yourself. And be glad you're not dying. Earlier, I had a client with walking pneumonia, one collapsed lung. He may not make it. At least you're not him, right?"

This was my prescription: empathy with boundaries, gratitude for what I had. The gun quivered in my hand. I stuck it back in my bag.

ON THE WAY HOME I SAW THE LAWN MOWER MAN PUSHING his lawn mower down the center of the empty road in his long, loping walk. He called over, "Hey, Clown Girl, ready to have your chicken-scratch lawn mowed?"

I adjusted my daisy sunglasses. "Don't think we can do it."

He stopped in the street. I limped forward, slow progress.

"What'd you do? Looks like you got a case of the jake leg coming on." He watched me limp toward him in my oversized shoe, one hand on my hat. "Get the right fit on that shoe, might walk a little easier. Goddamn, how big is that sucker anyway?"

I waved a hand. "I'm fine."

"Well then, how 'bout this. How's about you buy this mower off me. Twenty bucks, and you can mow the lawn yourself as many times as you need. It's a good mower. I use it all day, some days."

I knew then where he came from: For-Salesville. My head still buzzed with the hum of bees, but now I had the jar of Chinese pills deep in the pocket of my striped pants. I took a step, leaned on the cane.

He said, "Got a brand-new blade too. Cuts grass like butter."

I said, "It looks old."

"Sure, from back when they knew how to make a lawn mower. Won't quit on you. Like an old Checker cab, or a Singer sewing machine."

I hung my cane over the lawn mower's handle. Twenty dollars. At least I'd know what I was getting—a simple thing. I didn't care what Herman would say; I'd take my turn at the lawn, but not with the push mower while the weeds were high, while the sun was blasting, with a strained groin and the invisible hand that clutched my heart, squeezed my lungs, kept my breath shallow, and left the buzz in my brain. I pulled a twenty from the envelope stashed inside my pink shoulder bag. Clown money. Rex money.

"Nice hat," the lawn mower man said. "Got some holes in it, though."

I nodded, meaning, *I know*. He put the bill in his pocket and nodded back, meaning *Good-bye*.

The sidewalks were uneven and the tires on the lawn mower hard as tires on a shopping cart. The machine rattled under my hands as I pushed it home. The rattle in my hands was a larger reverberation of the hum in my head. I leaned into the mower like a crutch. The single oversized Keds spanked the asphalt.

When I got to Herman's block, Herman and Nadia-Italia were on the couch on the porch.

Herman saw me, jumped up, and said, "Whoa, whoa, whoa! House rules. No gasoline, no need. We got the push mower." He came toward me, puffing on a smoke.

I'd anticipated the resistance. Ready to negotiate, I called out, across the space between us, "I'll use it once, get things trimmed back."

Herman was halfway across the yard when he ducked his head and made a fast U-turn. He did a stiff-necked walk back up onto his porch.

I won the argument that easily?

The cool shadow of a car pulled up alongside me. With the deep purr of a strong racing motor, a car slowed to match my own bum-leg, rattling-lawn-mower-for-a-crutch crawl. The car's exhaust was hot breath, breathing down my neck.

8.

Cinnamon Buns and the Angel Act

I DIDN'T LOOK AT THE CAR THAT SHADOWED ME. IN BALO-neytown it was better not to look: just keep moving, know where you're going, and keep your ears open. The car rolled along beyond the fringe of my flowered sunglasses. I had my eyes on the house, was almost there. Herman, in quick retreat, made a dive for the porch, then bent to rearrange empty glasses. He consolidated ashtrays fast, like a kid whose folks had just pulled into the driveway back early from vacation. Nadia-Italia snapped into motion, tripped over the arm of the couch, and scrambled on all fours for the front door. The screen door banged closed behind her. I hefted the Snapper mower toward Herman's broken walk.

"Excuse me," a voice said.

The blade guard snagged on the curb. My big shoe stubbed against a stack of empty fried-chicken boxes and forty-ouncers snuggled where the asphalt met the curve of cement. An electric twang cut deep into my bum hip, sent me into a flush of cool sweat. Chance, in the house, barked at the window.

"Ah, St. Julian," I whimpered, leaned into my cane and rubbed my thigh.

"Hello?" It was a man's voice. From the car.

Without looking, I said, "I don't need to buy anything and don't want any trouble. Move on."

The man said, "You all right, Sniffles?"

I held on to my hat and looked up at the sound of my name. This was no ordinary B-town harassment. It was a cop car that shadowed me, close and quiet as a shark. And there he was—the cop, the one who whistled "Happy Trails," who chased me from the empty lot, who cost me most of my Green Drink. Soon as I saw him I wanted to duck and run, or do a duck run, a waddle on out. I was trapped!

But he was also the cop who held my hand on the sidewalk, who saved my life the day I fainted—the day I almost became a show that couldn't go on. Even more, he was the cop with my urine funnel. I needed that funnel.

"Sprained muscle," I said. "Comes with the job."

"I'd give you a ride," he offered from the window of his purring cruiser. Our eyes met, and his were endless, blue as a Slushee, blue as windshield wiper fluid. An unnatural blue.

I looked away fast, kicked the mower's blade cover back into place. "I'm home." I nodded at the overgrown yard, the cluttered porch, Herman's lopsided bungalow and the hand-painted sign nailed over the front door: *Baloneyville Co op*.

Chance kept up her bark against the front window: *Come in, come in, come in!*

Herman was a human sonar machine camouflaged behind a plant, pretending not to listen.

The cop left his car running, got out, and walked over. "Let me help you with that," he said.

"Thanks, but no thanks," I said. "Any clown worth her greasepaint can lift her own lawn mower, sprained groin or not."

The cop held up his hands in surrender. The sun hit his badge, his hair, his gun. I was dizzy, blinded by this man, his gear. I cleared my throat. He cleared his throat. He said, "Well, maybe you've been looking for me."

Chance's bark was a car alarm blasting behind us. Herman squinted from the shadows of the porch. *House rules*, his squint said. *No cops at the co-op*.

The cop said, "Heard a rumor that somebody called the station. Said I had something she needed?"

"Wasn't me," I said, loud enough to broadcast to the whole

neighborhood. I hung my cane over my arm and put both hands on the mower again. "No way, sir."

The cop slid his hands near mine on the mower's chrome push bar. His arm kissed the side of my arm and doubled the heat between us. Together we pushed the rattling mower up the walk, toward the driveway. He giggled. The cop giggled like a boy, at a private joke.

I said, "What's on your mind, officer?"

"This caller, she said I had cinnamon buns."

His cloud of spice sweetened the air as he said it, and I blushed. Sweat was a finger-tickle down my spine, a shiver in the heat. I said, "No, that you *smell* like cinnamon buns. Like cinnamon, I mean. I don't know about your buns—or *the* buns, I mean, whoever's buns."

The cop's left hand brushed my right where our hands wrapped around the mower's handle. No wedding ring. His laugh burst again, and I saw the lines around his eyes like rays drawn around a child's sun. He said, "So you know about the cinnamon, but it wasn't you who called the precinct, huh? Funny, that."

I pushed my hat farther down onto my head. "I just happened to notice the cinnamon. Independently, I mean. Just now."

"Just happened to notice the cinnamon, you did?"

"Not that I *noticed*, noticed." I said. "I mean, not how you make it sound. I..."

His eyes were bright, laughing, looking at me like I was the most important thing on earth. I couldn't help but smile back. Our hands were hot and close. I had to break away.

"I've got it, O K?" I tugged the mower to shake him off. The cop let go, still smiling. I gave it another yank, and stumbled on my big shoe. "Crumb!" I said. My bum leg squawked and with one arm tangled in my pink bag of tricks, I fell. Tall grass rustled around me, a laugh track. I shook the cane off and flailed against the grass, against the laughing, like a clown drowning in a silent joke. The mower righted itself with its own weight like a bowling pin.

The cop offered a hand. "Practicing for the rodeo?"

"I'm not a rodeo clown," I said, with all the dignity I could muster. My sunglasses slid low, my hat sat cocked. I dropped the pink bag. It was no small trick to get up. I fought the tall grass, straightened the hat, and took the copper's hand in mine.

He came forward and pulled me up. He stepped on the rubber toe of my big shoe as I pulled my foot away, and he stumbled back, then pulled me forward with his momentum; the world was a fast blur, all sun and color. My heartbeat doubled. I smacked against his chest, hat knocked askew; the sunglasses smashed into the bridge of my nose and I knocked loose his shoulder mike. "Whoa, Nelly!" he said.

My hands pressed into the grosgrain nylon of the uniform shirt, and I felt the spread of his pecs underneath. His body was hot. He held my arms a moment too long, long enough for me to feel the strength in those hands, like a decision well made. He let go, dropped his hands, reeled his shoulder mike back in by the cord, and reattached it to his chest. "That's quite the big sneaker you've got there."

Herman? The big sneak, who slunk along the porch and peered out between planters?

The cop tapped the empty toe on my mismatched size fifteen with the tip of his heavy cop shoe. "Tricky." He picked up my cane and handed it back to me.

My breath was fast and shallow, the world aswim. The squirting daisy tacked to my hip was crumpled as used tissue, plastic petals bent. Dry grass clung to my clothes and hair. I hoisted my pink bag onto my shoulder. "You like the shoes? If you want to buy a pair, I got another set just like 'em inside. Opposite foot, is all." I pointed and crossed my hands at the wrist to show the switched feet. The joke felt right, familiar terrain in the midst of an unnerving situation.

Herman hissed a quick, "Shit," like I'd given out a family secret.

The cop looked toward the sound of Herman's whisper just as Herman hid behind a narrow, broken bookshelf. He had a couple of shaving nicks on his throat. "Baloneyville Coop," he said, pointing to Herman's sign over the porch.

"That's Co-op," I said.

The cop squinted at the sign. He surveyed the place. Maybe we were a coop, trapped, and this cop was a hawk with an eye for detail. He said, "While we're at it—last I checked this was Baloneytown, not 'ville.'"

He turned back, wiped a hand across his forehead. "I suspected you might be the one looking for me, because as it happens, I do have something of yours."

"Something of mine?" So he still had the urine funnel.

"Your halo," he said, and drew an invisible circle in the air over his head. "You left it at those old buildings."

The Ruins. I said, "Ah! About that, I wasn't ... I didn't spray that spray paint. I found the can and—"

"No worries. You do an angel act?"

My fingers played over the tips of the tall grasses that tapped against my thighs. "Sure, sure." I could do an angel act. "A clown angel." I said. "That's why I need the, ah, halo back. Got it with you, perhaps?" I tapped my fingertips together, hands like spiders. Nervous.

He shook his head. The sun shimmied in his hair as though over a field of wheat. He said, "Didn't expect to see you. But I can bring it by here anytime." He jerked a thumb at the house.

I said a fast, "No no no." No cops at the door. "It's all right, we'll work it out. I'll find you, OK? At the station."

"Or I could give you a ride, we could get it right now." His prowler purred in the road, the door open and ready. The console was a cluttered rack of cop gear. A stack of papers filled the passenger's seat. A shotgun gave a dark smile from another rack bolted to the floor. Heat waves rose off the white hood like fumes off gasoline. His office.

I couldn't get in that office with Herman watching. I said, "Let me give you my card. "We'll work something out later." I turned away and reached a hand into the sweat of my bra.

"Funny place for an angel to keep her résumé," the cop said.

I found the worn edge of one damp clown card and pulled it out, stuck to St Julian, that old Hospitaller. I tucked St. Julian back in my bra, turned and leaned in close to hand the cop the card. Should I turn myself in, as the one who'd noticed his cinnamon smell?

I paused, debated. Weighed the options: *Eenie meenie miney moe* ... Quietly as possible, I said, "Actually... O K. Maybe I was the one looking for you."

"I knew it was you!" He said it loud, and busted into an easy laugh.

I jumped, gave a glance at Herman, at the street, then at the cop again. *If he hollers let him go.* "Listen, it's been nice talking, but I've got work to do." I pushed the mower. A stiff wheel caught on a sharp stick, a tangle of weeds in the overgrown lawn. It rolled with a stutter. I used both hands.

"Let me help," he said. He kicked away the weeds, and reached for the mower to guide it back out on the sidewalk. "You starting it up, or putting it in the garage?"

What he called a garage was a wooden shed that leaned against the fence alongside the driveway. The shed was triple-pad-locked. Inside were items that might, to a cop, call for an explanation, if only because they needed no explanation. Herman-of-the-porch sucked in his breath, and froze.

With all four of our hands and the cane together on the chrome bar, the cop helped me push the mower up the drive to the shed. He said, "Peace officers aren't just about crime. We're here to make the neighborhood a friendlier place."

I watched his jaw move. He said, "In lots of ways."

I asked, "Anybody ever say you look like Steve McQueen?"

His blue eyes turned to me. His skin shifted into the lines of a smile. "The ears?" He nodded. "I've got McQueen's ears."

"More than that," I said. "The eyes, that color. The upper lip. The hair..."

"Like in *Bullitt*?" he said, hopeful, and gave a McQueen eyebrow raise, a crease to his forehead.

I said, "More like in *Love with the Proper Stranger*."

"Ah! I was hoping for *Bullitt*." And he laughed his loud, boyish laugh again. His laugh made me laugh. "I'm Jerrod." He held out his hand. I shook it. His skin was rough, his palm warm. Safe. We were side by side on the lawn mower handle, and as we shook we jostled into each other, and again I felt dizzy. It was all so close, I had to get out of there. On King's Row, this cop's hand had been the only thing between me and panic, me and despair. Back then, I'd been ready to tell him anything.

Our neighbor came out of his house across the street, in a faded blue bathrobe, and called over, "Make sure he read you your rights."

"What are my rights?" I whispered.

"You got the right to sleep it off, Willie," Jerrod hollered back.

"I got my rights to watch too, Jerry. You know that much." The neighbor, William, sat on the porch, spectator to our spectacle.

"Jerry?" I said, "You know him?"

Jerrod nodded. "Like a flu I can't shake. Sat side by side in second grade." More quietly he said, "Now a petty criminal. I know 'em all. This part of town, they watch like I'm on TV."

"I know the feeling," I said.

"Yeah, I bet you do. Look," he said. "Every window."

A glance at the houses showed what he meant: In every front window the curtain was pulled away from the edge, or parted at the center. Some blinds were wide open with a face looking out. Others were closed, with a telltale gap.

"Let me give you this," he said. He handed me his card. Officer Jerrod Evans, DPSST # 502210, North Precinct. "Listen, whenever you want to pick up your halo, just give a call. Maybe, if you wanted, we could get a bite to eat, or a cup of coffee? You could tell me about your life onstage, the Baloneyville Co-op."

Behind me, Chance still spoke in her furious dog language:

Fuck, fuck, fuck. What are you doing? I took the card, and slid the card up my sleeve.

"I could show you a few tricks of my own," he said.

Herman, behind Jerrod, gave me the slit-throat signal, the curtain call. A finger drawn across his Adam's apple, eyes big and bulging: *Cut. Scene's over. Now.* Herman and our neighbor William—big men, tough guys, rendered powerless by Jerrod's creased uniform, the badge and gun.

I was in the spotlight, sharing it with Jerrod. Did I like standing next to that kind of power? I wasn't sure. But the power was there. Who else could leave a good car idling in Baloney-town? Nobody but a high-ranking gangster or a cop. Jerrod had the keys. The position.

He ignored the neighbors, the whole street of peepers, and asked, "You got a key for that garage? We could put this thing away."

And get us put away, the whole house, sent up for Herman's operation.

"I'd need to a...to..." I tried to imagine whatever script Herman would want me to follow. "To see a search warrant," I said.

"Sheesh! Nobody trusts an officer anymore."

"I trust you," I said. "I just trust that you might be working."

Herman cursed again, under his breath. Apparently, I had the script wrong. With a rattle and crash, he dove over the side railing, ponytail flying. Jerrod whipped his head around, reached for his gun.

I touched his sleeve. "A cat. Spooked by my dog." Chance beat against the glass. A flowerpot spun and fell over the rail into weeds.

"Sounded like a pretty big cat." He looked down the block.

"I better go look for him. Herman gets testy when he hasn't been fed. Listen, we keep the mower out here, in the yard." I pushed the mower to the side of the shed. "Right here. It's done."

Jerrod looked at me. "Leave it outside, it'll get stolen. Even an old lawn mower. I had a call the other day, about two blocks down from here, somebody had their lawn mower…stolen…part of a big break-in…"

He said, "As a matter of fact," and he crouched down. He took the side of the lawn mower in his hands and tipped it up. His mouth tightened. His eyes shifted in that quiet way, narrowed into a new sadness.

I said, "We never have any trouble. Been keeping it out here for ages—"

"How long have you had this?"

I said, "Oh, since, at least…"

Before I could finish my own short lie he said, "You couldn't have had this mower more than a day, Sniffles. Look, right here." He tipped the lawn mower over on the grass to show me a metal tag. "Robertson," it said on the tag. Below that was a row of numbers freehand etched into the metal.

"Sniff Robertson," I said. "Part of the clan?"

He cut me off: "I filled out the incident report myself."

I stepped back and said, "I bought that lawn mower today, used. About ten minutes ago. Right before you showed up. It wasn't mine before today." How fake and weak the truth sounded! Nervous, I asked, "I bought stolen goods?"

He rose, brushed grass from his knees. He took a tiny notebook from a pocket. "And from whom did you say you bought this mower?"

Ah! The syntax, the notebook—my heart jumped. The bees buzzed against my brain. "A man, on the street. I didn't get a name."

"Have you seen him in the vicinity prior?"

"Sure. Maybe a week ago? He had…a different mower with him then. Shit. He wanted to mow my yard."

"Can you give me a description?" His pen was poised.

"About my height," I started. "Sweaty, with a boil on his lip. Soaked."

"A sweaty man with a boil…" Jerrod moved slowly as he put his notebook away. He pulled out my clown card and read the card again, like the card might hold a clue. He cleared his throat.

Across the way, on his porch, our neighbor sipped a Yoo-Hoo. Jerrod looked at me, his eyes pale blue, quiet and sad. He said, "I hate to do this to you, Sniffles."

"What?"

"I wish I had another option."

"What?"

He said, "It's policy. It's got to be enforced. It's not my place to make selective decisions."

"Let's not be indiscriminate," I said. "Policy?"

He said, "I need you to take a little ride, with me."

That ride again! "Later, OK? Another time." I was ready to run, to limp off. But where to go when I was already home?

"Those numbers on the side of your mower?" he said. "That's probable cause. Stolen goods."

"What?" I said, "I'm being arrested?" I tugged on my sun hat, straightened my glasses.

He didn't look me in the eye. He said, "Unfortunately, you're our only suspect to date in a burglary. As an officer, it's my job to maintain the safety of people and property in the area. In short, yes. I need to take you down to the station, take your fingerprints and file a statement."

I said, "A statement? Do I even have a statement? Everything's coming out a question?" The bees doubled the size of their hive in my brain. I cleared my throat. "I don't know anything about this mower. It's barely mine, I just got it, you can see the yard. Does this look like we've owned a lawn mower?" I waved a hand over the crop of weeds and the tiny, fizzy bugs that danced like the spray on new champagne.

I said, "I don't want to go to the station, I can't do that. My heart." I wouldn't last a minute in the slammer!

Jerrod said, "Sniffles, I can't make autonomous decisions... We have to treat all situations equally. You have the right to remain silent," he said.

My rights! A clown doesn't have any rights. Silent? Ha. That's already the lay of the land in clown work. The bees were frantic;

my sight collapsed around itself. My heart thumped. Chance barked at the window. I covered my ears.

"I don't have to handcuff you," he said. "If you'll just get in the car, we'll go down to the precinct and get this cleared up."

Cuffs? I dropped my hands to my sides and whispered, "Handcuff me. Please. It'll look better."

"Really?"

"Please. Cuffs on," I said. I turned around, threw myself against the shed, and slapped my hands together. The shed shook under my weight, the boards loose. Something crashed inside.

"Hey! No rough stuff," the neighbor, William, said. He waved the Yoo-Hoo bottle and rose up from his plastic chair. "I'm witness here."

I waited for the cuffs. When nothing happened, I turned my head to one side and looked at Jerrod. Jerrod turned his Steve McQueen blue eyes to the neighbor in a glare. Muscles rippled along his jaw.

"Citizen review," the neighbor mumbled, dropped back into his chair, then fumbled around like he'd lost his Yoo-Hoo cap.

Jerrod reached a hand to my shoulder and walked me to the car; I stayed out ahead of him. "Cuffs," I whispered. "Please. This looks a little too friendly."

"OK, OK. Whatever you want. I'm sorry about this," he said, and he snapped the handcuffs on. Two silver bracelets. Tiny teeth inside. Even in the heat, the metal felt cold. Final.

"Is that too tight?" Jerrod's breath tickled the side of my ear.

"Just fine," I said.

He helped me settle in the backseat. Then he walked up the driveway, got the lawn mower, and pushed the mower back down to the car. The car bounced as he popped the trunk and struggled to bungee-cord the Snapper in.

Jerrod threw my cane in back with me, then closed the door again. Through the grill that separated us, I could see the back of his neck and the short hair there. I searched for his eyes in the rearview.

"I didn't steal it," I said, one more time, "for the record."

We drove in silence past Baloneytown's lineup of hookers and johns. Every other hooker leaned forward to get a better look into the cop car, to see who was in the crook's seat. I stared into lipsticked lips and open rabbit-fur coats too hot for the weather. Every one was in costume—high heels and tiny shorts, old dresses and tall hair. I caught my reflection in the window: a sorry old sun hat, Elton John shades. My costume. I wanted to laugh and cry and most of all just keep breathing. We drove past cars marked *For Sale*, and bicycles, mattresses, couches, cardboard boxes all *For Sale*. There were even a few optimistic realtor signs, like anyone ever bought into the burg.

I said, "Out of all the deals in For-Salesville, I had to pick a hot one."

Jerrod mumbled, "Tell me about it."

"What's that mean?" Any conversation would be better than none.

He didn't answer.

We passed the same girl twice, on the side of the road in her greasy silver dress. Then we passed the same stack of tires for sale. The same worn-out old house with a dog chained to the realtor's post. Finally Jerrod took a right where before he'd gone left. We headed down Bleak Street, then Bleaker Street, then Bleakest, toward the Ruins.

He turned onto Joad, then the short, unpaved stretch of Prosper, then onto Bleakest again, in a circle.

I said, "What, you're paid by the mileage?"

After too long, Jerrod pulled over in back of the buildings. He sat there with the car idling. Voices squawked on the radio. He cracked his knuckles.

I was handcuffed in the back of a cop car, where the doors didn't open. We were in a deserted part of town. I barely knew the guy. He was a cop with a boy's laugh and a man's gun. He had all the cards. The guns, the asps, the keys. I watched the back of his neck, and wondered if Jerrod had ever beaten anybody up.

Maybe he'd clubbed a man with his nightstick. That's what the
tools were for, right? Could he have pepper-sprayed protestors,
cracked a head with an asp, shocked a perp, maybe even shot
somebody with his gun? For all I knew, Jerrod was a murderer. But
he was a man who laughed like a boy.

He got out and opened the back door. He held a ring of keys
in his hand. "Get out. And turn around."

I did. Turned in the empty lot. My legs were weak.

His voice was steady. "The thing is, the lawn mower's part of
a bigger break-in. There's a procedure I have to follow and not
following it could cost me my job. What I'm doing right now, it's a
punishable offense in my line of work." He unlocked the handcuffs.
I heard the key in the lock, felt the cuffs drop away.

He said, "What I should do is follow the path of probable
cause. I should read you your rights, search your person, cut
the locks on that garage, go into the coop and search it top to bottom. I could corral your boyfriend there hiding on the porch
and check out his story. Whoever else you've got living in the coop.
Chances are, they'd be in the car, riding along beside you now.
Those are all things I should do. But I won't."

I shook out my wrists. Like air rising in a balloon, blood
coursed hot back into the acupuncture points, the baby-heart-spot
center in the middle of the inside of my wrists. The suicide slash
place.

"Sniffles, I'm letting you off. I don't think you stole this
lawn mower, though I don't have evidence to the contrary. I don't
think you're the thief. I'd be wasting my time if I took you in, wrote
you up."

He said, " I'll save you from a record. This time."

I wanted to pee, needed my jug. The sun was so bright it
was an insult, a slap against the walls of the Ruins. I said, "I don't
know anything about where that lawn mower came from…"

He held up a hand, like a traffic cop directing me to stop.
"Listen. I don't want trouble. I'm going to say I found the mower in
an alley. Easy enough." He said, " Now do me a favor. Lay low for

a while. Pretend like I took you in. Can you do that?" He said, "What with everybody watching back there, I had no choice but to arrest you. I've arrested your neighbor for less, plenty often."

I stretched my arms over my head to feel my own freedom. My breathing grew deeper. The Ruins were mine. "How can I thank you?"

He said, "Just don't let on that I let you go. Hang out here for a reasonable length of time. Tell anybody you can that I took your fingerprints, your statement, and that I might be in touch."

"Will do," I said. My shoulders ached. I stretched one, then the other.

"I mean it. You could get me fired. And don't buy goods off the street." He got back in the car, then tossed me the bamboo cane. I picked it up out of the dust.

"One thing," I said as I straightened.

He waited.

"That guy on the porch? He's not my boyfriend. For what it matters."

Jerrod looked at me without answering.

"That's all," I said.

He put the car in gear. The car rocked and lurched as he drove over broken cement. The tires of his cruiser kicked up a cloud of the dry ground.

"Hey, wait." I ran behind the car, with my limp and my bum-leg lope. Jerrod kept going, across the empty lot. He stopped before he pulled into the road and looked both ways twice, even though it was an empty side street. A law abider. I caught up to him and tapped on his window. He pushed a button inside. The window slid down.

"How long?" I asked. "How long is a reasonable length of time?"

He watched me with those sad, discouraged Steve McQueen baby blues. "A movie and a cup of coffee," he said. He shook his head. "About that long. No longer." Then he powered up the window and pulled away.

9.

Lost Chance

EARLY EVENING, I LIMPED HOME FROM THE RUINS. THE air was golden and dusty, the sun an orange balloon floating over the peeling, patched roofs of Baloneytown. A pack of Krumpers on a corner lot gave me a nod, like I was a distant relation. It was a generous move, because I could barely walk, while they were dancing their hip-hop hearts out.

At the co-op, Herman met me at the door. "Inside." He nodded a tight nod toward the dark room behind him.

"Like that isn't where I'm already going?" I leaned into my circus cane and limped up the porch stairs. The wooden steps shook and tipped under the weight. Herman closed the front door fast behind me, as though to keep a wily dog in—or to keep prying eyes out. The living room was dark behind heavy orange curtains.

I dropped the cane and pink bag of tricks on the couch, kicked off the sweaty clown shoes, and took off the sunglasses. My face was tight with sunburn. I reached for a light switch.

Herman caught my hand.

"No lights," he said.

I said, "Sorry, I forgot." That house rule—to keep the electricity bill low so Herman could run the grow lights.

He said, "Nice act, Clown Girl. "

"Huh?"

"The cop and the talking clown, two birds on a lawn mower, the full production for the whole neighborhood. In front of my customers." He raised an eyebrow.

I sighed and sank into the dog hair–matted couch. "How was I supposed to know the lawn mower was stolen?"

Herman frowned. "What—you thought that dirtbag you bought it from was a Costco representative?"

I said, "It doesn't mean it's stolen just because—"

"And you know I don't want a gas mower around anyway. House rules." He lifted a curtain and peered out. Herman's ponytail slinked left and right along his back as his head jerked side to side. Herman, my lovely ex, once with the soul of a poet, now was an unwitting advertisement for the evils of pot. If I were to sketch him as he stood, I'd call the piece *Pure Paranoia*. Talking to the window, he said, "So, you're dating cops. Tell me that isn't true."

"Dating?" Revise the title: I'd call the piece *Deluge of Delusion*.

A slim shaft of setting sun cut into the room when he lifted the curtain. My eyes adjusted. Across the room Nadia-Italia sat curled on an overstuffed chair in one dark corner. She unfurled her big legs and heavy arms, stood, and padded toward Herman. "Hermes—," she started to say.

"Why on earth would you call that dating? I don't usually get arrested on a first date."

In a falsely high voice, meant to be mine, Herman said, "Did anyone ever say you look like Charles Bronson?" He let the curtain fall back into place.

Nadia-Italia laughed and rubbed Herman's arm. "It's the kisser, right, baby?" she joined in, her voice dropped lower than usual—but not much lower.

"Steve McQueen," I said. "Not Bronson. You guys work all afternoon on that act? Maybe it's time to take it on the road."

"I know who needs to hit the road," Italia said. With one finger she flicked a crumb off the phone table, and the crumb disappeared into the dark, dust, and dog hair.

In the room's dim light, with shadows along each curve of muscle, their arms summer-brown and tank tops loose, Herman and Nadia looked like a charcoal drawing, all soft edges, perfectly sketchable. Herman's black ponytail rested along his neck and outlined the curve of his skin as it found its way to the muscles of his back. Nadia-Italia was an overfed, Egyptian-eyed cat. The two were a pair of sleek leopards appraising a babe in the woods. It was almost lovely, almost funny. But Herman's voice was sharp, his eyes narrow. And I was the fool babe.

"Hermes, she stole a *lawn mower*," Italia said. She yawned as she said it. "How lame is that? Now she's hanging with the sheriff of Baloneytown. You saw her." She rolled her foot over a free weight on the floor. The weight made the boards creak. "Kick her out."

I said, "Look, I can try to follow your nutso-facto deductions, but really, I barely know the guy. The cop. We're not dating, no way. I've seen him around, is all."

"Sounded like he knows you," Herman said. He reached a hand and tugged a nylon thread that hung from my—from Rex's—shirt. He tugged the thread like a leash. In a silky whisper he said, "What would Mr. King Clown say about you slinking around with a cop?"

I pulled the leash out of his hand. "He's the Clown Prince. And I'm not slinking. It was an arrest, for Christ's sake."

"Like that's any better?" Herman said. Even if Herman had let go of the frayed bit of my shirt, I was still hanging by a thread.

"We can't trust her, Hermes." Italia stretched, and came to rest against Herman's shoulder. "Just end it."

"Sugar, stay out of this." He shook Italia off.

She rolled her eyes, turned away. "Gladly. Let's both stay out of it, Hermes. Pack her bags." She waved a hand over her head, bye-bye, and went into the kitchen.

Herman inched closer. "What's the business card for? The phone number?" His eyes were red-rimmed. He was fried. "Relaxed," he called it. I smelled the smoke of his breath as it left his lungs.

The business card was only another card in my stack of cards—the golf course designers, the spatial use and planning consultants, the dishwasher and the rich dandy in the tux from the Chaplin gig back hall. Now a cop was in the mix. Jerrod. Steve McQueen. Mr. Cinnamon Buns. "He's a neighborhood cop, doing his job."

Herman stood over me, pressed a fist into the arm of the couch, and leaned into it. Where the muscle of his forearm began to rise, that sinewy hill up from his wrist, he had the blue lines of an old tattoo. In the near dark the tattoo was blurry, but I knew what it said: *NITA*, my name, carved there back when it didn't matter that a tattoo was forever. The night Herman wrote it he laughed because my name was all straight lines, razor thin. "Easy," he'd said. Now he said, "Your other man called. While you were on your cop date."

"Rex?" I asked. "What'd he say? What did you tell him?"

"That you'd been picked up by a cop..."

"Picked up. Great. Thanks a lot." I said, "You do that on purpose."

"...and that I'd pass along his message. He said, 'Don't worry, I'll try you back in a few.' Or maybe he said he'd *be* back in a few..."

Agh! I wanted to scream. I said, "Well, which is it?"

He said, "Don't know. That's all I've got, message delivered."

"So, then, in a few what?"

"What?" Herman looked dazed, either for real or as an act.

"He'll try back, or be back, in few what? Minutes, days? Beers?" I spoke fast; my heart beat faster.

Herman shrugged. "Sounds like you two need to iron out a few communication problems, 'cause that's a serious rela-tionship breaker." He took my hat off and dropped the hat on the couch.

I said, "Very funny." His fingers brushed my hair. I jerked my head away. "Don't."

"You look tired." He lifted my hair behind my neck, gave the nape of my neck a squeeze. He ran his thumb in a small circle, just below my hairline. "Relax a little." His hands smelled like tobacco. He said, "Thought Rex'd be back by now. What's the hold-up?"

I shrugged, said, "He's got things going on. A few shows. Still waiting for the Clown College interview." As though Herman had asked me to explain, I said, "They keep rescheduling. Soon as he gets it worked out, he'll be back. For me."

Herman dropped his hand lower and pressed his thumb into the muscles behind my shoulder blades, a tiny massage. "Three weeks of rescheduling, huh? And you still think he's coming back."

"Of course he's coming back." I closed my eyes. With my eyes closed, Herman's hand on my back could have been Rex's hand. A little friendly massage. I gave in to it. "I'm here, his ambulance is here…his unicycle…He said…he'd…be back. Gone a few days, then back…"

Herman's fingers crept down to my bra line. My muscles warmed.

He said, "Is all this suffering for your art really necessary?"

I said, "Comes with the terrain."

"Or is it suffering for Rex? 'Cause I think you could do better, if that's what it's about." He put a second hand on my other shoulder. Leaned down. He lifted his fingers through my hair, and each hair tingled my scalp, my spine, my nerve endings. "You've done better before."

I had to laugh. "You?" I asked. "Ha!"

He said, "I'll work on that sore thigh, if you want." His breath was thick with smoke, sweet with the residue of pot and bitter under cigarettes.

"Bad idea." I sat back and twisted to push his hand away.

He said, "Why get uptight? I've done it before."

"Rex and me, we're a team. It's not just about suffering, it's love."

Herman straightened up, rubbed his face. He said, "Hey, I'm not trying to bust up your monogamy, just being friendly. You look shot, I give you support and there you go reading into it."

"Read into this—Rex is what I need. That's it."

"OK, OK. Keep up the Mary Tyler Moore act, all the way, huh?"

"Whatever that means." I shifted on the couch and reached for my hat.

"It means, you should watch yourself. You might appreciate a little generosity now and then." He nodded toward the banging sounds in the kitchen. "She's ready to put you on the street, but it's my place. I say you can stay until Galore gets back. It's a favor, because I like you, and you could recognize it. But bottom line, Nita, if you bring cops around, you're out."

Out?

"The favors wear thin," he said.

Like Crack, Herman was ready to cut me loose that easily: Practice the pratfalls, or I'm out. Stay away from cops, or I'm out. I needed the clown work for cash to move from Herman's house, and needed Herman's cheap rent to save money until then.

I needed to stay away from the cop, for all reasons.

I was only a name cut in Herman's arm, a needy tenant, a friend who kept coming back. I was four letters of straight lines. *Nita*, that meaningless blur of tattoo. Italia-Natalia-Nadia, banging pans in the kitchen, had a better answer with the mystery of her ever-shifting name, the way she disappeared sometimes. When she was gone, Herman always wanted her to come back.

I'd rather she disappeared.

"Thin ice," Herman said. "Skating on cracks."

"So's your brain," I said. "That cop has his own beat. I didn't bring him around."

And then there was a knock on the door. Herman and I, we both jumped. Italia clattered pans in the kitchen. Herman looked at the door like he'd never seen the door before. I didn't move. Italia didn't come out.

Herman asked, "Who is it?"

Like I could see through walls. I whispered, "Maybe it's for you."

The knock sounded again.

God help me if it was Jerrod. *Thin ice, thin ice, thin ice.*

Herman inched closer, looked through the peephole. He took his time. I stood behind him, afraid to breathe. He opened the door.

A high, scratchy voice said, "We gots your rubber chicken." I couldn't see past Herman's shoulders. "Pluu-ucky?" the voice said. "We gots Plucky here."

Plucky! How my heart leapt at the name!

Herman said, "I don't know what you're peddling, but we don't need any plucky shit, and we don't want any rubber chickens." He started to close the door. I ducked in and put a hand out to keep the door open. A short woman in worn sweatpants held a faded rubber chicken by the neck. She shook the chicken as though tantalizing. Her tongue showed at the side of her smile. Half her teeth were gone. One rubber foot was gone from the chicken too. The other rubber chicken foot was pale, a bleached and weathered pink.

"Ree-ward?" she said. Then she hacked, turned away, coughed again, and stomped a foot. The chicken in her outstretched hand danced a gimpy jig to the rhythm of her cough. "Where's the ree-ward?" she choked out again.

I said, "That's not my chicken."

I tried to close the door. The woman threw herself in the way. She said, "What do you mean? It's a rubber chicken, just like in the pitcher. Reward, it says, right here." She shoved the chicken between her knees and used both hands to check the front pocket on her hoodie. When she pulled it out, the flyer was matted and stained with something I'd like to think was a spilled decaf soy double latte, but probably not. Probably it was blood. She held the flyer toward us with one hand and retrieved the chicken from between her knees. She was barely four feet tall.

"I know what it says, but you've got the wrong bird." I tried to close the door. Herman stopped me this round.

"You know about this?" He took the flyer. I wouldn't've touched it.

The woman said, "This here's your Plucky. This Plucky bird's jus' been out in the alley for a while. Maybe you don't recognize your Plucky, hmm? Maybe your Plucky hit some rough times, and now you won't take her back in."

I said, "I'd know my own rubber chicken."

Herman squinted at the flyer. He said, "What the hell?"

"Maybe your Plucky jus' fell in with the wrong crowd, maybe she was looking for love and thought she'd found it...but you can't trust nobody round here, that's what Plucky knows now. Uh huh." The woman's eyes were flat and dull. She'd quit looking at me. "Plucky maybe learned a few things, and you say, 'No way, no second chances,' and jus' like that, man, turn her ass back out on the street."

I said, "Who are we talking about here?"

The woman swayed on the porch. She said, "Plucky don't look so good now, but she's got the same old heart she had back when you held her close."

Herman slammed the door. Muffled, the woman's voice came back. "Maybe spare some change? At least."

"How many of these are out there?" Herman said. He shook the wrinkled flyer. A cigarette butt fell from one creased corner.

I gave a shrug. "It's not like it's got any big information."

He said, "Cops and drug addicts. Do I need that combo at the door? You're offering a friggin' cash reward." He snapped a finger against the paper.

"I'll take care of it," I said, though I wasn't the only one bringing around drug users. The difference was, Herman's were customers.

"*Thin ice,*" he said again. "This is about the breaker."

"I'll pull the flyers down."

"Sheesh." Herman fell back against the couch.

I limped into the kitchen. My cane tapped against the chipped linoleum.

"Injured in the line of duty?" Italia asked. She sucked ice cream from a spoon, with a carton in her hand, her knuckles big. "They must a treated you pretty bad down there. You look like crap."

I shifted the bag on my shoulder. "Down where?"

She stuck her spoon in the ice cream again. "At the station, like? Am I wrong, or didn't you just get arrested?"

My face was reflected in patches of glowing gray-white in the window over the kitchen sink. An overgrown laurel hedge kept that window dark all day. In the blurred shadows of the hedge, my eyes looked big and sunken like a skeleton head, holes in a mask. I set my pink bag and sunglasses on the counter, ran warm tap water, and cupped my hands to rinse the dust of the Ruins from my face.

Chance's dish, on the kitchen floor, was still half full of kibble. She never left her dish half full. I called her name. She didn't answer. Nadia-Italia put her palms on the counter and hoisted herself up backward to sit.

"Chance?" I called again. I opened the mudroom door. The room was empty, no dog. I tossed my bag and cane on the bed. "Where's my dog?" I said.

"Lost your only Chance?" Italia smiled. I swear she smiled.

I said, "It's not funny. She was here when I left. What'd you do with her?" I opened the basement door and called Chance, down the dark stairs.

"You lost your Chance and you're trying to blame it on others." Italia sat on her hands, her big knuckles under her thighs, on the counter. She shook her head at me. "Maybe the little yapper joined the circus."

I said, "Tell me—where's Chance? No joking." My heart picked up its pace again. My hands felt weak.

"No clowning, Clown Girl?" Italia still smiled. "I'm not your dog's keeper. It's not our job to watch that rat terrier."

"She's a schipperke, not a terrier. Herman!" I called. My voice cracked with panic. I looked in the backyard, stood on the back steps, and called for Chance again. Nothing. I called Herman's name again. Then Chance's. Then Herman's, until finally Herman came out behind me.

He said, "What up with the noise?" He pulled a pouch of tobacco from his pocket.

I said, "Where's Chance?"

Herman took rolling papers from the side of his tobacco pouch.

"She was here when I left," I said. "At the window." I went into the yard and called her again. Herman followed. I kicked at the weeds.

First Rex, then the chicken, and now Chance was gone? First my folks, and ever since then, my life. Nothing came together. I picked up an empty clay planter and threw it into the grass. The planter broke into pieces. I couldn't take it anymore. I called for Chance and kicked my way through the broken shards.

"Hey, easy, easy," Herman said. He sat on the back stairs. "Listen—the dog was going insane. Barking at the windows, scratching at the door. We opened the door, that's all. She's a dog, right? She'll be back."

He balanced his tobacco on one leg, sprinkled a line in the paper, and rolled it between his fingers. I called for my dog, and my voice sailed out into the neighborhood.

"You want a chance with me, girl?" somebody called back.

Herman said, "Remember when you were a kid? Maybe you had a family dog, you let it out, and it came back."

"Chance is not that kind of a dog," I said. "She's a puppy. She's a schipperke. She's high-strung."

Herman licked the edge of the rolling papers. He said, "The whole world's high-strung, clowns included, it seems. Chill. The dog'll come home."

The thought of searching the neighborhood on my bum leg made me feel weak. I had no help. Where was Rex? If Rex were home, Rex would get Chance back. Rex would stand up to Italia, and Chance wouldn't be gone in the first place.

I sat on the steps and folded my hands over my calves. I put my forehead on my knees. I had to shut down before I exploded.

Herman ran a hand over my back. He rubbed my shoulder.

He said, "Remember how it was back when you had plans, and ambition? The whole art thing."

I half-turned to look at him from the corner of my eye, his hand still rubbing my back. "I have ambition now. More than ever. I'm working on a plan." I had Kafka, a vision, a message and a massage. The muscles at the back of my neck gave in to the warmth of his hand.

He said, "I mean artistic ambition, not just financial."

"I have artistic ambition. I won't stay a corporate clown for long."

Herman rubbed my left shoulder. "You sure? Money sucks in the best of the best."

The best of the best. That was Rex, in my book. And money hadn't gotten to him yet. Not at all! In fact, he didn't earn enough to cover the cost of his own face paints. The door clattered open behind us. Herman's hand fell away from my back fast.

Italia said, "What're you doing?"

I sat up. Herman looked at me. I looked at Italia. She looked from him to me.

I smiled, put a hand on Herman's thigh, and said, "Like old times." Easy buttons to push, I couldn't resist. OK, it was a bitter moment—I was bitter. I was a bitter clown on the precipice of corporate wasteland. I baited Italia because she let my dog out when that dog was all I had. In a soft voice I murmured, "You've always had such strong hands."

Herman said, "Drop it, Nita."

Italia said, "Herman?"

He said, "Look, don't worry. What do you need?"

She ran her nails over the screen of the screen door, with a sharp scritch of sound. "There's like, some kind of family at the front door, with a rubber chicken..." she said, and made the scritch again.

Herman flicked loose tobacco from his tongue. "Christ." He nodded his head at me. "They're yours. Get rid of the bounty hunters, I'm serious, or you're out on your ear."

10.

Our Kodak Moment; or, Rexless Behavior

ALL NIGHT I LIMPED THROUGH BALONEYTOWN. I CHECKED every piece of worn tire rubber, pile of old clothes, and cascade of trash, anything that looked like a possible curled dog-body in the dark. As the sun rose I sat on the sagging couch on Herman's front porch and made a sign: *Find My Lost Chance! No tail, no collar. All Black. Knows Tricks. Left-handed, half-trained, full-blooded schipperke. Reward: $$.* I drew a picture of Chance sitting up and begging, her two paws in a prayer pose, as though she prayed to come home.

I was stretched out on the porch couch when Herman opened the front door. He rubbed his head, his sleepy hair. "You're up early. What gives?"

I flipped the poster over to hide it. "Work. Clown gig."

"Crying doesn't become you. Makes your eyes puffy." He ran the end of his thumb along the side of my face. I knocked his hand away. Unruffled, he asked, "Where you working today?"

"Photo shoot. Publicity."

Herman laughed. "Oh shit. Bad day for that one, 'cause you're looking like hell. But that old paint and spackle covers pretty well?"

I tucked the flyer close to my hip and went back to the mud-room, where I stood on the mattress Rex and I called our bed and checked out my face in the shard of green-tinted mirror duct-taped to the wall. Herman was right. My nose was sunburned and my skin was a map of red patches. My eyes were bloodshot, puffy, and shadowed. My lips were cracked. Every mirror asked the old existential clown question: If that's me in the mirror, then who am I? I was a wreck. I could still hear Crack issue her order: *Go all out. Show up looking good. Photos cost a lot of cabbage; we'll do it once, that's it. You read me?*

Ah! Bless St. Julian for whiteface and war paint. I faced the mirror again and got to work. The room was quiet without Chance's rapid, summer-hot panting, her sudden fits of scratching her toenails against the wooden floor. My stomach was an empty pit, my heart a pounding fist.

Go all out, see? In my book that meant call on High Clown style: big hair in a cloud of fried red plastic curls fluffed with a pick, two waxed spit curls tight over my ears. I'd wear a river of blue tinsel clipped in my wig. Big red lips, black arched brows, and of course I'd break out my best red rubber nose: classic.

I snapped the seal on the acupuncturist's amber jar of Chinese pills, pulled the cork, and shook half a dozen of the white pills, smaller than BBs, into my palm. I swallowed three with a drink from a dusty glass of dog hair linted water beside the bed. I took another pill and let it rest on my tongue, where it melted fast as candy. When I didn't feel anything, I popped three more. They rattled against my teeth. I bit down without breaking them, like biting on ball bearings, and rolled the pills under my tongue, where they melted into nothing.

A naked Rex watched from a scratchy ink drawing on the wall, with his ever-present secret smile. He peered in miniature as a sculpture on top of the bookshelf. He turned his back in a pencil sketch, showed an ear in oil paint, and held a hand open to the sky. I sat on the bed, the phone on my pillow.

I slid another pill on my tongue.

Rex was everywhere, but I couldn't get him on the phone. I called one more time, and said into the clown hostel answering machine, "Rex? It's Nita. There's some trouble with Chance...she's gone, Rex. She disappeared. Rex? Are you there?"

I slid on a pair of his striped pants, to keep Rex with me

through the clown shoot. I needed the luck. They were Lycra acrobat pants, snug on Rex but loose on me and brushed my thighs in a band of wide stripes. I rolled a fat cuff at the hem and tied a pink scarf at the waist. Ta da! I put on my best ruffled collar with blue piping at the edges, over a striped satin shirt.

Stripes are key to clowning. That was a line from our edifying routine, Clowns in the Schools. The Clowns in the Schools shtick started in black leotards and plain face. Then Rex and I, we'd dress in front of the kids. Rex would pull on his skintight pants and say, "Stripes are the cloth of the outcast, the proud flag of clowns, prisoners, and artists." He'd give a toothy smile.

"The dress of scalawags, rapscallions, and reprobates," I'd chime in, as I stepped into a big striped tent of a dress. We'd rehearsed a hundred times.

We'd team juggle disks of face paint as Rex recited, "The best clown gear finds its place in tradition. History. It's sacred in some communities, prized in many cultures. Should a clown wear whiteface or go natural? Be a German country bumpkin, the Auguste clown, or a Native American ethereal spirit?"

"Jester, juggler, acrobat, Pierrot, or Harlequin," I'd say, and cock an eyebrow. Clowns in the Schools was government-sponsored for about ten minutes. Then we lost our funding. Still, we practiced.

"Getting dressed is all about calling on the other world— the underworld—to find a spiritual patron, an inspiration," I said out loud, to myself now.

Rex Galore was my inspiration.

Maybe he wasn't in the underworld, but he was a long ways away, even as his spirit surrounded me. I kissed the tip of my index finger and touched my finger to the lips of the red clay head, where it hovered in the closet. My bank, my love, my heart. My future.

There was only one detail left: my nose.

I lifted a barrel-shaped wooden clown doll from a shelf. With a twist, the clown fell in two halves, and a smaller clown fell out. I gave the second clown a twist and an even smaller clown fell out. When I turned the third, one more appeared. A final twist, and there it was. My prized red rubber nose, lovingly made at the Red Rubber Nose Factory.

Those Clowns Sans Frontières ran the factory. So noble! Every penny of income from the Nose Factory went to kids in war-ravaged countries. Kids without limbs, without homes, without rubber noses. Once, Rex and I talked about starting up a chapter of Clowns Without Borders right in Baloneytown, a neighborhood bad as any other.

Bottom line, though—I wasn't a red nose clown. For the photos, my rubber nose was a talisman.

I slid on my big-frame, squirting, daisy-rimmed sunglasses, dropped the jar of Chinese pills in my bag, chose my best hand-painted Keds, and grabbed the staple gun.

My orange hospital jug was a glowing harvest moon that looked down from the top of the bookshelf. *Harvest*, the moon of a jug said. *Harvest that urine!*

I still had no urine in the urine bank. I had no urine funnel.

Now, after a night of looking for Chance, I was completely confused. When was the first piss of the morning in a night without sleep? When was the last piss of the night?

I put down my pink bag and carried the orange jug into the bathroom. I slid down Rex's striped acrobat pants, held the jug above the toilet, bent my knees, and hovered. My groin muscles burned. I could barely sustain the pose. I gathered up my shirt, held it out of the way. A sloppy stream ran toward the narrow jug opening; urine ran warm over my hand. It ran fast. A mess. I cut the flow, then let it go again. My ripped groin shook. A cold sweat cut across my forehead. Tiny yellow lakes decorated the toilet lid and the worn white linoleum floor.

But I had piss in the jug. Bingo! I was on my way to a urine harvest. Finally.

I screwed the lid on the jug and wiped the outside off with toilet paper. When I gave it a shake, the jug had new weight to it.

The bottom of the jug was warm from urine inside. Time to get it on ice.

My designated shelf in the fridge was a narrow middle space, second down from the top. The jug was too tall for my shelf, though. It fit instead on the shelf in the door, a shared area crowded with soy cartons, white wine, weight lifter's shakes, and organic juice.

I closed the fridge and wiped my hands down my striped-clad thighs, satisfied.

ON THE WAY TO THE PHOTO SHOOT, I COPIED MISSING Chance posters. I copied Missing Plucky posters too. To hell with Herman and house rules; Plucky, Chance, Rex—I needed them all to come home.

"Cha-ance," I called as I walked. "Here, Chance! Here, girl!"

"Nope," some joker with a nasal whine called out an apartment window. "Not a chance, baby." He giggled, coughed. Then giggled again.

A group of kids hung out on a porch. "A clown!" one kid said. As a mass, they tumbled off the porch, arms and legs in full swing.

Already late, I waved the kids back with one big blue glove. "I'm off work, kids. Not a clown." I showed them the palm of my open hand. In my other hand I waggled the heavy-duty staple gun. I kept walking and called again. "Chaaa-a-ance. Here, girl. Here, puppy-puppy-pup!"

The kids danced alongside me as I walked, all whispers and giggles. I was breaking the Clown Code of Ethics, on the street in costume but not performing. All I had to do was tie one balloon animal, toss an invisible ball, trip on a bump or even a bum on the sidewalk. Squirt the sunglasses, and I'd be up to code.

I didn't have it in me.

"Do a trick!" a kid with a crusty nose shouted. He was right beside me. "A joke!"

"No need to shout." I stopped at a phone pole, slammed six staples in around the edge of a Missing Plucky poster, then drove another six staples home for Chance. "Say, kids, have you seen this chicken?" I held out a flyer.

The boy chipped at the snot. His arm was scarred and thin. He said, "I got one—listen. What did the vampire say to the clown?"

By all rights, I should've given this refugee of a kid a free red rubber nose.

Another kid cut in and answered. He said, "Something tastes funny! Get it? Tastes funny."

Crusty Nose made to bite my arm. I jerked my hand away and said, "Nice joke, kids. Now, have you seen this dog?" I held out a second flyer.

The boy laughed, teeth jagged and flashing. A second kid pulled on my shirt tail. The taller kids squinted. One girl reached for the flyer. I let it go into her dirty fingers, pulled out another flyer, held it against the pole, and punched staples in around the edge, each time with the loud pop of the staple gun.

"What you doing out there?" A mom's voice drifted through the screen door. "Get in here now," she said, and held the door open. The biggest girl turned away first, let the Missing Chance flyer fall to the ground, and the others followed her back to the porch; the snot-nosed kid walked backward, waving.

I yelled, "There's money in it, if you find her."

The older boy poked his head out. "How much?" A hand grabbed his shoulder. Then he was gone, and the screen door clattered.

On a side street, a yellow rubber nub poked up out of a garbage can. A rubber chicken–colored yellow nub! Plucky? I pulled on the nub, and it grew bigger, kept going, growing longer and stretched out—something held it from below—and then it snapped and slapped against my hand. It wasn't Plucky at all, but rather was the tip of an old rubber glove covered in motor oil stuffed under a stack of catalogs mixed with porn. I wiped my hand on the ground, over gravel, bottle caps, and new grass.

THE PHOTO SHOOT WAS IN THE BASEMENT OF THE BALO-
neytown Lucky Strike bowling alley, *Featuring the World-Renowned
Strike and Rake Lounge!* A photographer Crack knew was doing
the photos for a cut rate, some kind of favor. I didn't want to know
what kind. I stapled flyers to a nearby pole. Out the open doors
of the Lucky Strike, already I heard the smash and clatter of pins.

Inside, a cluster of drunks in the Strike and Rake Lounge
started rubbernecking, like I was the freak on the scene. They were
bar refugees hiding from sobriety.

"Well, bowl me over with a rubber nose," one called out.
His skin was green, his eyes red, and his hair a thin collection of
well-greased strands. He gave a big tongue wag. Ghouls.

"You must be the Rake," I said, and kept going. I followed
Crack's directions, *through the lounge and past the cigarette
machine* ... I headed toward a narrow set of dimly lit, industrial-
green cement stairs.

At the bottom of the stairs, the basement was dark. I crossed a storage space. One light was on in the far back, and in that
light I saw a handwritten sign taped to a nearly hidden door: *Pssst!
Sniff and Matey—In Here!*

I pushed that door open, stepped in.

Inside the room glared bright; it was a nest of draped white
sheets and photographer's lights, full of smoke and with empty
bottles on the floor. An old toilet was hooked up in the back corner,
no stall. Crack sat on a chipped office table and puffed on a Swisher
Sweet. A man swiveled in a swivel chair. His eyes were hidden
under folds of skin, drooping lids, and dark circles, like an old sea
turtle. He had a camera, two or three lenses, and rolls of film
scattered in front of him. The man ran his fingers over his skinny
mustache again and again.

From above came the rhythmic rumble and smash of the
bowling alley: *Th-th-th-th-ump! Kaboom!*

Crack took the stogie out of her mouth. Her jaw fell open.
She said, "What the hell is this?" She came at me fast, put the

Swisher Sweet back in her mouth, unbuttoned my collar, and roughed up my clown hair. "You look like Bozo."

"Bozo!" I said. "It's the cloth of the trade!" I flinched when her hand came at me. "You said go all out. This is my best stuff. High Clown."

"High on something, all right! Now let's fix it up." The cigarillo jumped between her lips. She tugged on my wig. The wig was pinned on with bobby pins and the pins clawed my skull. She squeezed one long-lashed eye against the smoke of her own cigar. "This is *way* too Ronald McDonald."

I tried to pull away. "We're clowns! This is all-out clown stuff." I pressed my hair back into a round poof. "I'm dressed to find my spirit leader."

"Well, ain't that a fine kettle of fish," Crack said. "Plan to do kids' gigs forever?" Crack was dressed like a hooker Harlequin, in a dark wig, loud fuchsia lips, a fake fur-trimmed polka-dot dress, and fishnets sturdy enough to catch a marlin. One glance at the photographer, and it looked like she'd caught a shark.

"'All-out' as in, like, let's sell ourselves, right? Not all-out jokers." She had a cobalt blue heart drawn below her right eye. Her nose was big, but that was her real nose, nothing she could do about it. Her wig was a bouquet of tight curls.

She patted me down, then reached up and pulled the red rubber nose from my face. She tossed the nose over her shoulder.

"Hey," I said. "That's bad luck."

In a halo of smoke, Crack said, "No, it's tough luck."

The nose rolled across the table and fell off the far side. She reached for my ruffled collar and gave it a shake. "Slut it up a little, you got it? Think audience."

I pulled away from her, climbed under the table, over the white sheets.

Crack crouched down beside the table and said, "Ask yourself—who do you want to engage? Who's got the cash? Who's going to pay your way, see?"

My nose was a red sun setting on the horizon of the sheets,

guarded by the photographer's tapping foot. "Parents? They cut the check." A guess. I grabbed the nose. As I stood, my head knocked on the edge of the table. I slid the nose in my pocket and reeled back, a hand to the knot on my skull. The bees took up their swarm in the distance. A strike crashed in the alley above.

Crack dropped her stogie and ground it out under the heel of one Mary Jane. "You want to throw strikes, or you going to throw balsa at them pins the rest of your life?" She unbuttoned two buttons on my striped satin shirt. "Got anything like a push-up bra?" She dug in my pink bag. Missing Plucky posters fluttered to the floor. "Maybe a couple balloons. Blow these up." She shoved two balloons at me.

"Those are banana style," I said. "Twisters, long as my legs."

The photographer gave an eyebrow raise that lifted the folds of his puffy eyes; a stirred sea turtle, he murmured, "There's a thought..." He checked his watch. "When's the other skirt getting here?" His voice was gravel, like he drank whiskey out of an ashtray. He dropped a pack of smokes, hands shaking.

It was hard to think of Matey, all bones and fists of muscle, as a "skirt."

Crack said, "Matey'll be here any minute." She turned to the photographer, pulled me by the shoulder and said, "Now you tell me. Would you pay for this?" She pointed to me like I was merchandise, straight out of For-Salesville.

He stuck a bent cigarette between his teeth, shrugged, and smiled out of half his mouth—a smile I didn't like at all. He ran the back of his thumb over his bottom lip, hand trembling, and swiveled in his chair. "She's a real trouser-crease eraser," he said. His moustache jerked under the words. "I just might."

"Oh, lovely," I said. "You two are a fine pair." Over the crash of pins and a cheer upstairs, I said, "I'm a good clown. This is a good clown look. It's classic." I took the balloons back and put them in my pink bag. "I'm not trying to be a glamour girl."

"As boss of this rig, I say it's time to start. Do the glam-clown thing, a big-ticket item. You read me?"

"Glam clown?" I said. "No, no I don't read you. Glamour and comedy, they're opposite sides of the same coin. Sexy or absurd. One or the other. It's not the stripper doing pratfalls, the clown with the pasties."

"Look," Crack said. "I'll give you a clue: we're in this for money."

I nodded.

"Show her the graphics, Pete." She snapped her fingers.

The photographer lifted a shaky hand and unrolled a poster on the table: *For a Good Time, Call Trixie, Twinkie, and Bubbles!* Crack's cell phone number was printed at the bottom. In between was room for a photo.

I said, "Who's Trixie, Twinkie, and Bubbles?" I'd never heard of these clowns, not in our neighborhood.

Crack and the turtle traded a shifty glance. The photographer smirked and Crack laughed out loud, a single note: "Ha! Could be anyone. That's the whole deal of it—fantasy. Where the skirts are short and the party's long," she said. She tapped a finger to the poster as she said it, as though adding the words.

"Oh shit," I said. "Us, Crack?"

She pulled a bottle from her pink prop bag and sprayed my red wig with a candy-smelling hair gel. "Look, grown-ups have money. They spend it. And they don't care about rubber noses." She combed her fingers through the fake hair, twisted the front of the wig, pulled the curls away from my face, and slid a bobby pin in to set a hank of the wig in one little pin curl. The knot on the back of my skull was hot and throbbing under her hands. "Corporate parties can't hire strippers anymore, but they can hire clowns. Got it?" She said, "Can't have a lady in a cake, but they can have heavily made-up chicks in Lycra paid to do anything."

My head jerked each time she ran her fingers through the tangles of the plastic wig.

"That's where we cut in. Opportunity. Trixie, Twinkie, and Bubbles! We'll make a killing, I tell you—a killing!"

She stuffed Kleenex in my bra and pinned Rex's acrobat

pants back to make them snug over my thighs. I let her work, and thought about the stack of business cards on my shelf at home, the endless string of suggestions, dates, and phone numbers. The architect. Those spatial use and planning consultants. The dishwasher. So where were clowns on the titillation continuum? Somewhere between sex with a nun in full habit and a stripper, I'd guess, made-up and covered up. Not what I wanted to be.

"I don't know about this, Crack. It doesn't feel right. Doesn't feel like art to me."

"Art?" she said. "You're joking? It's the oldest art in the book. And listen, I know your best interest—you're looking to make enough lettuce to hook up with Mr. Sexy Rex. Plan to do that by tying knots into a balloon Jesus?"

Christ.

I glanced down at Rex's acrobat pants. The stripes of the cloth outlined the muscle of my thighs and made a tight V at my crotch, an arrow to my Mound of Venus. Stripes aren't just for clowns and cons; stripes are also for prostitutes, all the way back to Leviticus. The mark of the sinner: striped stockings, striped cloaks. Indulgence and punishment.

Crack was right—I needed the cash. I was stuck. Trapped. Rexless. This was Rexless behavior I was caught up in.

She brushed my tangled wig and her fingers clawed their way through the synthetic strands. My neck was in a kink the way she held my head. I looked at Crack over my shoulder. Her eyes were circled in black. Her lips were brilliant red, her neck was marked with the creases of new wrinkles, age finding her already. "Got a problem with strippers?"

I said, "It's not what I'm trying to be." My voice was thin; the words fell apart, breaking as I spoke.

"You've already got a client," she said, like this was a good thing. "We ain't even started this joint venture yet, and already Lover Boy, from the Chaplin gig? He left a message on my cell—says he wants a private show, you and him. How's that grab you?"

"Exactly—I don't want him grabbing me! Crack, I don't think it's my thing—"

"What, to be a breadwinner? I've been a stripper, a hairdresser, and I managed a bank. There's no difference."
The cobalt heart high up on her cheek danced as she spoke. "But trust me, I'll make you some cash. That, I know."

It was true; Crack was the only reason I could lend Rex cash to travel to Clown College.

She leaned in closer. "What's on your face, motor oil?"

I put a hand to my skin. My fingers came away black and oily. The trash can, the rubber glove. The greasy reminder of porn in a Baloneytown alley.

She pulled my head back, looked into my eyes, and asked, "You OK in there? You're pale as a ghost." Crack and the photographer laughed. She let go of my hair, smacked me in the butt. "It'll work out. Don't worry so much. Now go freshen up before Matey gets here. You look like you been crying all night."

It still showed? I took my bag back to the mirror on the wall beside the toilet.

"Make it pretty," she said. "Sexy. Like the ad says, a good time, right? A party. Put a little heart, like this one." She pointed to the heart on her cheek, bit the edge of her fingernail, and spit it on the floor.

The photographer pointed his camera at me. *Flash.* "Sad clown on the way to the john," he said, through yellow teeth. Did he mean the toilet or a hooker's john? In the mirror's chipped reflection my orange wig, parted far to the left, now was decorated with a row of twisted curls in Crack's design.

"One thing," she called over. "I've got a job for us day after tomorrow. Noon. Supereasy. Clown clothes, clown face. All you have to do is show up, but it's a high-buck gig; I promised 'em three girls."

Three girls. I wiped white pancake off my blotchy skin. I opened my kit and began again. In the mirror I watched Crack sit

on the photographer's lap. She ran her tongue over her deep
fuchsia lips.

The door swung open. "Ta da!" Matey flung herself into the
room and slid on the nest of the photographer's white sheets mixed
with empty beer bottles and ashes. "Whoa!" She caught herself
from falling. Her pink bag swung on her shoulder. "Badaboom!"

"Ah," Crack said, and jumped up again to clap her hands.
"Our favorite S&M clown."

Matey took a fast bow. Her hair was slicked up onto her head
and decorated with Christmas ribbon. Her dress was tight, cut
low, and her fishnets snagged. "Thanks, but don't flatter me," she
said. "Every clown's an S&M clown, even the ones that don't
know it yet." She dumped her pink bag upside down on the floor
near the slice of mirror where I worked on my face.

"I'm not," I said. I feathered in a heavy, cobalt blue line of
eyeliner.

Matey dug through her things until she found a cake of
white paint. She looked up, rolled her eyes, and said, "And then the
other ones that don't know it yet." Her wrists were freshly
bruised, her arms tough and knotted. Her dress fit like a plastic bag
around a pack of carrot sticks.

Crack put her hands on my shoulders, gave me a backslap.
"Sniff here's the high artiste." She winked. "Remember? Riding our
sorry gravy train until the local Shakespeare troop comes along."

Matey bit down the end of a fat covered brush and pulled the
cover off with her mouth. "Can't separate it out," she said. "Every
clown's a bottom and every bottom's a fool, and there's money in
taking the underdog role."

I leaned in toward the mirror, didn't say anything. That
wasn't how I saw it. Sure, a clown's an underdog, but that didn't
make every clown a fool. It was an art, in my book, to take on the
role of the oppressed. We spoke up for those without a voice. We
were those without a voice—voluntarily relinquishing speech—
and we illuminated the plight of the impoverished through every

act. I let it go. Instead, I changed the subject. "Which one am I?" I drew my left eyebrow in a high, puzzled arch.

"Which what?" Crack reached for her makeup kit. "Bottom or fool?" She pulled out a tiny mirror and put another layer of mascara on her giant fake lashes. She used a special oversized mascara brush for her oversized lashes, carried in a big tube.

"No. Trixie, Twinkie, or Bubbles?" I asked. "Who, in the show?"

She shrugged. "What ever you want, Sugar. Makes no diff to me. A name's just another kind of package. Marketing. Starts the day you're born."

11.

The Tidy Side of Hell; or, Tonics, Soporifics, and Palliatives

ONE LONE LOBSTER BEAT A CLAW AGAINST THE GLASS wall of a small tank. The lobster's narrow, empty world was perched over a frozen sea; blue Styrofoam tray after tray of Dungeness crab, leggy purple squid, and bundled smelt rested on chipped ice below. *Tick, tick.* The lobster knocked, as though to flag down help. Across the aisle what had once been a herd of grass-fed cattle now lay silent in bloody pools of iced New York strip steak, flank steak, ribs, tongues, and burger. Edible flowers bloomed on a small green stand, a miniature field ready for harvest. *Tap tap. Tap. Tap tap.* A lobster s o s. *Get me out of this dead heaven.* I knew the feeling.

Luxury FoodSmart was a warehouse-sized nightmare of money just beyond the borders of Baloneytown, where gentrification spilled over from King's Row. The building used to house the YMCA. Now, at Luxury FoodSmart, even a two-pack of hard-boiled eggs cost half my day's spending allowance. I kept my big-frame squirting sunglasses on as a shield against overly enthusiastic fluorescent lights and wore my wig riding low. I tapped my cane against the polished linoleum, sucked on Chinese BBs like a PEZ addict, and slunk farther into the store.

Leonardo da Vinci said water was the most destructive force on the planet. Water corrodes metal and eats through rock. But da Vinci forgot about the corrosive power of cash; when money came into a neighborhood, the old buildings toppled. Even people disappeared.

I headed fast for the corner marked *Holistic Pharmacy Lounge*. There, beyond the organic loofahs and prescription bubble bath, one wall was lined with amber and blue vials that glistened like jewels. Tinctures. Cures.

After four hours of Crack's photo shoot, I needed any cure I could find. My nerves were rattled. My mouth tasted like metal. The fear that Chance would never come back tugged at my throat like I wanted to cry. The Chinese pills wouldn't last forever. I couldn't afford to end up back in the hospital, and I'd already blown the day's urine collection—hadn't been able to hold my piss until I got back home. I needed a panacea, a remedy for the ache in my gut, in my heart, in my head. There had to be a cure for the broken heart of a lost dog, a miscarriage, and a missing rubber chicken. The cure for a life where family slid away, where nobody stayed and nobody lived long enough. The family tree was a hedge, a shrub, a lone weed. The only cure I knew was Rex, but Rex wasn't around. I needed a cure for that more than anything.

The first tincture I picked up, Go-To Formula Forty-Nine, promised to cure depression, mania, indigestion, indecisiveness, stubbornness, weak circulation, confusion, and skin abrasions. Sounded good to me. Without thinking twice, I slid the vial into the wide sleeve of my clown shirt. Ta da! Magic; the vial disappeared. I'd fight the neighborhood's financial erosion. My own little battle was an economic cure: shoplifting.

Clowns have an edge as shoplifters. Coulrophobia, the fear of clowns, works in our favor; people don't look when they don't want to be involved, to be burdened with invisible objects, imitated in public, or made to hold a clown's leg, a slippery fish, an exploding hat.

It was completely against the Clown Code of Ethics to use performance as a weapon: *I will use my art only for the greater good, to create happiness, never to inflict harm.* But yes, I did it. In clown gear, I stole.

There were liver cleansers, colon cleansers, and gallstone removers. Valerian, passionflower, and hops promised to relax muscles, heart muscle included. I slid a vial of valerian into my other sleeve.

My heart beat faster with each tincture. A cashier read a magazine behind a shiny Courtesy Counter. She licked a finger, turned a page. I reached for a vial of Chaste Tree Berry tonic.

A low voice said, "Find everything you need?"

I whipped my head around and looked up from under the off-kilter wig. A man in a cream-of-chicken-yellow button-down oxford swung his hands. *Tim*, his name tag said. *How may I help you?*

I put a hand to my brow and turned to survey the wall of tinctures, *from the Pacific aaawll the way to the Atlantic.* I whistled long and loud, and turned back to Tim. I wiped the back of my hand across my brow and nodded. *Yes. Yes, I found everything I needed, and then some!* I gave the A-OK sign, thumb to forefinger, but Tim didn't run. Instead, Tim's eyes turned to my pink bag. I wrapped my hands around the handle of an imaginary shopping cart and lurched off, down the tincture row. Tim stood there a moment longer, watched my act, straightened a Miracle Cream display, and moved on.

I slid a vial of licorice concentrate in my bag.

Even with Tim gone, the tincture aisle was getting hot. I had to work fast. No time to research. Pau D'Arco was for blood; I liked the name—Brazilian, maybe. Where in this country would we say D'Arco? Cleavers was a good name too. I slid a vial of each into my bag and could hardly breathe, loaded down with tiny tinctures, stolen promises. I reached toward a winking golden bottle.

A hand tapped my shoulder. *Tim?* The blue cuff of a uniform, golden hair on the wrist. The cops! Lightning danced at the edge of my vision; the ceiling fell and my heart squeezed. Arrested? Again, so soon! When I turned and saw his face, for a minute I was relieved—at least it was the cop I knew, Mr. Magic, charming and helpful. But still, it was a cop! I was glad to see him, but didn't want him to see me. Distance.

"You shop in your clown costume?" Jerrod asked. I could barely hear his words over the knock of my heart, the brain buzz.

He held a banana pointed at me like a gun. In his other hand he had a plastic bag with two kiwis inside. It was the law enforcement weaponry of some peace-loving island paradise.

"It's a free country." I spoke too fast: "You shop in your cop costume." I shouldn't've said *cop*. Police. That's the word. I shouldn't've said anything. I felt the weight of stolen valerian slide inside my big sleeve. I added, "Right?" and smiled harder, wider. "How are you?"

"I'm all right. Thanks for asking. And no. First of all, it's a uniform, not a costume, and I don't usually shop in my uniform. I'm supposed to be off duty, actually, but said I'd answer this one last call. Heard over the car radio they needed somebody to diffuse a potential situation." He waved the banana toward the front door.

"A situation?" I looked around. The place was calm. No alarms, no gunmen. Only the racket of my beating heart. "What's going on?" My heartbeat confessed to thievery: *he knows, he knows, he knows...*

He shrugged. A tendon in his neck flickered to the surface, then disappeared again. "Let's just say, I'll give you a police escort out this time, Sniffles."

"Me?" I reached for an empty shopping cart as though to prove my good intentions, to tether myself to the world of shoppers. The cart slid away, I slipped, and the world was untethered, off-kilter.

"The call said there was a clown scaring customers... I thought it might be you."

I righted myself, grabbed the cart again, and reined it in. "They called on me? Who did?" My heart murmured, *Run, run, run away*.

"This is a family place. The clown getup makes people nervous."

"Family? What do you mean—clowns are family fun."

Jerrod gave me a doubtful eye. He scratched his head with the banana and took a deep breath. I took a breath too, and felt the walls expand for a moment, giving me precious room to breathe. He said, "I'll tell you the deal—it's more the whole John Wayne Gacy thing." He slid the banana in the plastic bag alongside the two kiwis.

Shit. Gacy. "That guy ruined the gig for a lot of clowns. His act fostered the whole prejudice … If one Asian woman commits a crime, does that bar Asian women from grocery stores?"

Jerrod said, "Well, save that question for debate team. Here, they just don't want kids to see it."

I said, "Gacy was more of an ice-cream man with a clown suit for the holidays—"

Jerrod cut in: "You can finish the shopping if it's fast, I'll escort you, then we need to move on."

The shopping. Stealing, more like it. Stealing and tapping into a collective coulrophobia, using the worst of the clown for personal gain. I threw a box of Mediterranean Bath Salts in the basket, to look like I was shopping. *Mineralized Tension Relief Mined from the Gaza Strip.* If I left with Jerrod, would he arrest me outside?

"You don't live far from here. I could give you a ride home."

That cop car again. No way could I pull up in a cop car. The vial in my sleeve was cool against my skin where it leaned against my pulse point and spoke to the beat of my heart. My heartbeat whispered, *Stolen lawn mower, stolen tinctures … save yourself.*

I had to keep the upper hand.

"Nice package." I pointed. He looked down at his yellow banana in the plastic bag. The two soft, hairy kiwis rolled to either side like wrinkled testicles.

"What?" he said. "It's a snack." But he blushed, a quick red flush along his jawline. A shy cop.

I had him off guard and kept my advantage. I said, "I've seen bigger bananas."

He said, "Listen, Sniffles, enough. You're lucky I heard the call. Somebody else might not be so nice about the whole setup. Now let's go. I'm doing this as a favor, and I've had a long day."

Another favor. His second favor for me.

"And because you've got a good heart," he said. He smiled then, and pointed to his own cheek.

I mirrored his move, touched my face. My fingers came away tinted with red and white paint. It was the heart drawn in makeup, from the photo shoot. I said, "Thanks. I forgot about that."

"It's very becoming. But it's not O K to wear the face paint in a place like this. It's like wearing a mask in a bank, makes people worry."

I followed him to the front of the store. At the checkout line, he threw his fruit on the scale. My chest was tight, my throat a knot. The cashier rang Jerrod's fruit up. Jerrod peeled dollars from a wallet. I pushed my cart into an aisle.

"You buying that stuff?" he asked.

"Gaza Strip Bubble Bath?" I shook my head. "I'm not that kind of girl—not a Gaza Stripper," I said. The valerian rattled in my sleeve.

On our way out, we passed Tim, the clerk. Tim stacked boxes of organic pesto-laced mac 'n' cheese. Two boxes for ten bucks. Talk about robbery! He said a fast, "Thanks, officer."

Jerrod tipped his head back, a quick nod. The electric doors slid open.

Outside I said, "I'll take it from here." I couldn't get in his car again.

On the outer wall of Luxury FoodSmart they had a public billboard. *Wellness and Community Building*, it said across the top. I pulled a Missing Chance flyer from my pink bag, then pulled out the heavy weight of the staple gun. Jerrod waited, watched. I hung the flyer.

"This isn't illegal, is it?" I said. "I'm sure you've got bigger prison fish to fry."

He said, "You lost your dog? Shoot, Sniff. When did that happen?"

"Well, actually, it was when you sentenced me to an afternoon in the Ruins. While I was busy pretending to be booked at the station, after you arrested me." I said, " My roommates let her out."

"Jeez, sorry to hear it." He sounded sincere. He leaned in over my shoulder, and his cinnamon scent wrapped around me. He studied the drawing. "You know, I think I saw her. Right around here ... I saw a little black dog, earlier today, that made me think of you."

"You saw her?" I turned, fast. My cane spun out and knocked into his shin. My big clown sneakers kissed the toes of his shoes, our feet tangled. "Where? When? You sure?"

"Just a couple blocks down," he said. "I'm not sure it was her, but maybe."

It was a possible sign anyway that she was alive. My dog, my little clown pup in training! I followed Jerrod's lead, though stayed a few steps behind, and as we walked I let the valerian slide down my sleeve into my palm. I shook the gotu kola down the other side and dropped it into my deep pants pocket.

Clink. The gotu kola hit another vial, already in my pocket, and the clink was to me the sound of a tiny jail cell door falling closed. *Clink! You're a thief!* We passed Jerrod's parked prowler.

Jerrod said, "It's walking distance. She ran when I came near her. Just like somebody else I know, now that I think about it." He turned to me. I palmed a vial fast.

Up ahead was the blue sign of Hoagies and Stogies, a cigar bar sub shop. It was no kind of place to eat, because the meat and cheese and bread all tasted like stale cigar smoke. But they sold cheap beer.

He said, "It's hard to arrest a dog."

"Arrest?" The last thing I needed was to pay bail on my dog. "What sort of charges?"

"Vagrancy," he said without hesitation. Then he looked at me. "It's a joke."

A cop joke. I didn't even know cops made jokes.

Hoagies and Stogies had dark, smoked glass in the windows and tiny purple lights strung up above. Anybody could be in there and could look out those dark windows and see me with Jerrod, sauntering alongside an officer. I took a few steps to the left.

Jerrod veered in close, stayed at my side. I pulled nylon hair in front of my face.

He said, "Just another block. Down an alley."

The whole thing made me jumpy. Anticipation, nerves, the unknown of it. I tapped my cane along the ground, then balanced it over one shoulder. Jerrod's eyes were on an empty lot. I unscrewed the lid on the valerian vial and kept my hand down low.

"Right about here," he said. The lot was the backside of a few weather-beaten, world-weary houses. I called Chance's name. Jerrod cupped a hand around his mouth, called and scanned the empty lots. The banana and kiwis, sweating in their plastic bag, swung from his other hand at his hip. While Jerrod wasn't looking I hid under the tent of my own fake hair and shook drops of valerian onto the end of my tongue.

Valerian tastes like the earth, like dirt, a bittersweet promise mixed in alcohol. It was early evening. The air was soft and skin temperature, with a quiet wind gentle as kisses, a peach sky striped with hazy blue.

"You can see OK, in those glasses?" he asked.

"Of course." The huge sunglasses, ringed with plastic flowers. I smiled, reached up and pressed behind the earpiece. Water shot from the center in a wide arc. "Keeps people away."

He didn't laugh, but only nodded. "Is that the goal?" he asked. "What?"

"To keep people away?"

I nodded, and said, "Just what the eye doctor ordered." I pressed the back of the glasses again, but this time, instead of a wide arc, the water trailed into a trickle and hit my cheek. I said, "Really, there's no goal. It's a job. I'm a clown."

He called for Chance again and kept walking. I did the same. There was no sign of her. Finally, I had to ask, "Was my dog really even out here? I mean, did you see a dog at all?"

"Of course she was here," he said. "What do you think, I'd lie about it?"

Through my glasses, his skin was tinted soft blue in the even-

ing light. "Maybe, to get me out of the store? So I'd follow you."
I watched his face for a sign, a way to know if he'd made the story up.

"You're funny," he said. He didn't smile.

"I'm supposed to be funny." But I wasn't joking.

"Not that kind of funny," he said. "You're funny because you
don't trust me. You act like I'm the Green River Killer or something.
If I wanted you out of the store, I have other tools. Things we
learn in the academy, right? Not subterfuge." He said, "I let you off
easy the other day, over the lawn mower thing. I did everything
wrong just to let you off on that one. I walked you out nicely today,
no big scene. Now I'm out here calling for your lost dog. Is anybody
else helping you out?"

In the empty lot, a Styrofoam cup caught in the wind bumped
along the rough ground.

He said, "We got a call today that clowns were congregating
in the basement of the Lucky Strike. Suspicious activity. That
whole place is bad news. All I could think was that maybe you were
there."

I said, "It was our publicity—"

"Stop! Don't tell me." He put his hands up fast, as though to
shield himself from my bad ideas. "I took the report but didn't
follow up because I don't want to know. I keep seeing you in all the
wrong places. I like to see you—but not that way, not there,
because I'm paid to be in the wrong places and I don't know what
you're doing there, I just hope you're not paid."

He said, "You know, I've got a good feeling about you, but
maybe I've been wrong the whole time. Maybe you stole that
lawn mower. Maybe you crashed on that sidewalk high on drugs.
Maybe you're just like everyone else in Baloneytown. For all
I know, you steal lawn mowers to support a habit."

A habit. The tinctures clinked in my bag and in my pockets.
I winced and ran my fingers over vials like prayer beads.

He said, "I grew up in Baloneytown. My folks are still here.
My old grade school friends. I've seen it—I've got plenty of reasons
to be cynical, if that's what I wanted."

He was right. I didn't look at him. After a minute I said, "So, why are you out here?"

"Well, when you say you lost your dog, I want to help find her. That's my job, and it's the way I'm made." He gestured, with a swing of the bag of kiwis and the banana, at the rubble of the lot. The sun had started to sink toward the roof of a house with a blue tarp tied to it. The tarp flapped in the breeze.

"I've never turned my back on Baloneytown yet. There's good people here, and some troubled folks too, but I'd like to help out, you and everybody else." He said, "Mostly, I'd like to see that my instincts are right, that you're someone I can respect, not suspect—that there's at least one good clown in this burg."

I turned to look at him. He blinked, as though he had dust in his eyes. His eyes seemed more clear blue than ever. When I spoke, my voice came out softly. I said, "You look tired."

"I am. It's been a long day. A lot of hassles. Mostly, I'm tired of being treated like I'm the criminal." His pant legs were dusty. There was a sweetness to him, and to his exasperation. He was right, I was unappreciative. What clown wouldn't want a cop on her side? He was there to help me find Chance, my charmer, that left-handed half trained schipperke.

The blue light of Hoagies and Stogies flashed down the block. "Listen," I said, "if you're off work, would you let me buy you a beer?"

He swallowed. His Adam's apple made a quick duck and bob. "Shouldn't we keep looking for Chance?"

I said, "I'll keep looking. I looked all last night, and put up posters all day. But I want to buy you a drink."

He nodded, and looked out over the rubble of the lot, then said, "I appreciate it, but I don't usually drink in uniform."

"Ah, right. I don't drink in uniform either," I said. "It's against the Clown Code of Ethical Conduct." I straightened my wig. I wanted him to know we had a Code of Ethical Conduct, because now I felt like a bigger heel than ever, suggesting to a cop that we break the rules. "It was just an idea." I said, " I shouldn't even talk in costume."

He said, "I shouldn't wear mine once I'm off work."

"Me neither," I said. "It's against code."

He said, "Once in a while, though, in Baloneytown, I might drop in someplace. I wouldn't do it in over King's Row, but here. They usually like it. Helps with community policing." He said, "Sometimes a few of us in the precinct'll have a beer together, just to be seen on the premises, maybe at a place that's having trouble."

I asked, "Really? Well, we could just have one, right? We could stay here in Baloneytown, walk over to Hoagies and Stogies. They can always use a little policing." *Tap tap*. I felt like the lobster in its aquarium, tapping against the edge of my small world. A beer with a cop—that wasn't the way I saw my life. It was risky. I'd take the risk. I wanted him to say yes. "I'll drink in costume if you will," I said.

"I don't know," he said. "Contributing to the delinquency of a vaudevillian…sounds punishable." He still looked tired, but he smiled. I was glad to see the smile.

When Jerrod turned and walked back the way we came, I followed him, then caught up by his side. We stopped in front of the bar. He pulled the door open and held it, waiting for me to go in. The smoke and spilled beer of tavern air laced its way out the open door, dank but welcoming, an invisible hostess. The smell of the tavern was exactly the same as every tavern anywhere, and in that way it was the scent of all the times Rex and I sipped beer, played pool, and ate free popcorn while we worked on acts. It was the comforting, familiar smell of smoke, mildew, and hops, that herb for relaxing muscles, heart muscle included.

I asked, "Think they'll call the cops on a clown?"

"Here they don't mind, as long as you're dressed. Besides, I am the cops." Jerrod reached for his cuffs and gave the cuffs a friendly jangle. "If anything happens, we'll say you're in custody."

12.

Drinks on Me; or,
Oddball, Corner Pocket

WE STEPPED INTO THE SMOKY DARK OF HOAGIES AND
Stogies, and through my sunglasses all I could see was one heavy-
set man on a barstool and the scattered stars of cigarette glow.
Other faces floated like weathered moons farther back, in the
shadows. I leaned on my cane, tipped the sunglasses up to look
for an open table, and, as my eyes adjusted, saw the place was
crowded with huddled drinkers. I stopped fast, surveyed; Jerrod,
behind me, bumped into the back of my thigh.

"Oh!" I swung my hips forward. "Don't bruise that big
banana."

He said, "Banana? I'm just happy to be seen with you."

I smiled, but inside winced—I couldn't be seen with Jerrod,
a cop, courting disaster.

A man at the bar pointed his stogie at me and in a loud
drawl said, "Well, if it ain't my ex-wife, Petaluma. Dressed to the
nines, too. Makes me want to propose all over again."

I stepped behind Jerrod. His badge glinted in the red beer
light. The place went quiet. Eyes on the cop.

"Want to see a Baloneytown dance recital?" Jerrod whispered. In a louder voice, the voice of authority, he said, "If anyone
here's on probation, you've got about two seconds to get out.
Then the clown and I start checking ID."

The air in the room tightened. Nobody moved. After a moment, eight, ten, or maybe twelve shadowy figures rose from
their tables and stools. They turned and bumped into each other.

A chair spun and fell. The drunk at the bar held on to his straw hat and threw back a shot like the tail end of a cup of tea, pinkie finger in the air. The back door flashed open and closed, open and closed, and the room was cut with a wedge of daylight just long enough to show the tangled silhouette of drunks in a scramble. The man in the hat swiveled left and right as others stumbled around him; he rumpled his tie in fat fingers. "Forgive me my peccadilloes," he slurred, to nobody or everybody.

"And you thought only clowns could work a crowd," Jerrod said. He waved a hand toward a table. "Looks like a spot just opened up."

I said, "Ta da! Nice work." I dropped my sunglasses back on my nose. Jerrod stepped forward. As I walked in his wake I tripped against a bump in the carpet, grabbed Jerrod's elbow, tap-tapped at the floor with my cane, then stumbled into the back of a chair.

"Careful," he said. He led me around a skewed, fake-wood table that was nearly invisible in the darkness. "And watch out. They've got an extension cord taped to the floor here." Jerrod's hand was pale against the blackness as he pointed. Duct tape flashed at my feet; it crisscrossed the carpet like silver scars. "It's a fire-trap. I should issue a citation."

"Remember, we're off duty," I said. "No need to put the costumes to work."

"So a cop and a blind clown walk into a baaahr!" the drunk in the straw hat called out, too loud. He gave a tug on his necktie.

From behind my dark glasses, I made out the man's red honk of a nose, jowly cheeks and small slit mouth. Beside him sat a tiny sliver of a human with oversized hands and an oversized beer mug.

The sliver hissed, "Lay off, Duke. You'll land us all in the stir."

"What's the problem, Silvo m'boy?" the first man said, in his drawn-out drawl. "A man can still talk in this land of bilk and rummy, can't he? Everything else I do is either illegal, immoral, or fattening."

Jerrod dropped his banana and two kiwis on a sticky table near the front window. Eighties Motor City rock rattled from a speaker fastened overhead. Jerrod stacked used pint glasses, picked up an empty pitcher, and set the dishes on the next table over. I leaned my cane against the wall. Jerrod pulled out a chair, and I pulled out a second chair, but then saw Jerrod meant his chair to be for me. Chivalry.

I pushed my chair back in, a hair's-breadth too late; Jerrod had changed direction too and sat in the chair he pulled out. He got up again fast when he saw that I'd pushed my chair back, but just as he got up, I pulled my chair out again. His knee knocked against the table hard enough to tip the saltshaker over. With one hand, Jerrod caught the rolling salt. We both stood then, cop and clown.

He said, "Hey—I thought we were off duty. What's with the routine?" He pulled out a chair one more time, waved a hand over it, and as though to a suspect said, "Sit."

I sat in the chair he offered. He went to the counter to order.

While Jerrod had his back turned I fished the tincture of valerian out of one deep pocket, dripped valerian onto my palm, and licked it off. I ran my tongue over my lifeline, an eye on the cop, my new friend, antithesis to the life I'd been living in Herman's house, with Rex Galore. They'd freak. For good measure and calm hands, I shook more valerian onto my tongue.

Over the bar, a handwritten sign said: NO DRUGS, NO WEPONS, NO FIGTING. I dug in my pink bag for Chinese BBs, ate them like breath mints, and all the while scanned the room for my neighbors, Herman, or anyone who'd care if I had a drink with a cop.

A second sign read: GAMBLING ALOUD IN GAMBLING CORNER ON STATE SPONSERED GAMBLING MACHENES ONLY.

The drunk in the straw hat called out, "Say, Addie, m'dear, was I in here last night? And did I spend a twenty-dollar bill?"

The bartender was a skinny old woman in a long black wig. A cigarillo dangled from her thin, painted lips. She set a pitcher up to pour, then put two frosty glasses in front of Jerrod. Over her shoulder, she said, "Yep. That's right. Twenty at least. And no tip."

The man took off his hat. He wiped a handkerchief across his forehead. "Boy, what a load that is off my mind," he said. "Thought I'd lost it."

"What I'd like to know is where you found it," Jerrod said.

The drunk said, "Don't worry. I don't keep any secrets from you I don't keep from myself. I'll tell you when I remember."

Jerrod asked, "Addie, is it still happy hour?"

The bartender leveled her eyes at him. Her mouth, around the cigarillo, was a thin-lipped scowl. "Just look at the happiness," she said, with a smoker's rasp, and tipped her chin at the sorry crew who lined the bar. She put one long, pale hand out.

Jerrod dropped a few bills in her palm, then came back to our table with the pitcher and two cold glasses. Frost on the glasses was wiped clear where the heat of his hands had been. He poured the beer and raised his glass to clink against mine. "We'll find Chance."

A hollow spot in my heart gave a squeeze as he said her name. My dear Chance. I bit on Chinese BBs squirreled away in my mouth and washed the dust of the pills down with beer.

That easily, I broke another rule in the Clown Code: Drinking in costume. Weak-willed. Clowns Sans Frontières, those altruistic jokers, they wouldn't drink in costume. But the beer was good, cool and thin, and I gave in to its charms. My red lips marked the edge of the glass in a heavy clown smooch. "It was supposed to be my treat."

"Next time," Jerrod said, confident there'd be a next time. He looked at his hand on the table, at the base of his glass. The dim tavern light left shadows near his eyes that made him look older, and mysterious. He cleared his throat. Took a drink of his beer. Showed his shy smile.

"Tell me," I started. "What made you want to be a police officer?" I took care to say "police officer" this time, not "cop."

He nodded and said, "It's a good job. Hard work. I like being

someone who can make a difference. I guess in some ways it was
either this or my brother-in-law could get me a job driving a
bread truck. Union work. Being an officer is more meaningful,
community-wise."

Make a difference. I knew the feeling—Clowns Sans Frontières was my big plan to help the planet. But I acted cool.
"A difference, huh?" I said. "How long've you been working at it?"

He ducked his head, sipped his beer, and shrugged. "Near
eight years."

I said, "You get to know just about everyone in the neighborhood, I'd guess, in your work." He probably talked to everyone—
not just to me. I wasn't special. And the beer we drank together, it
wasn't a date.

Jerrod said, "Most of these people I've known since I was a
kid. Nobody's gone too far. That bartender, Addie Mulligan—
they call her Mad Addie—she used to be our playground monitor,
back when I fell off the Kiddie Coaster and cracked my head."
He rubbed the back of his head as though it were still bruised.

"Why do they call her Mad Addie?" I asked.

"Stick around, you'll find out." The smallest fleck of beer
foam rested on his upper lip. He touched the fleck with his tongue,
and it was gone. He slid his glass back and forth on the table
from one hand to the next, and looked a little doleful, like Steve
McQueen in a scene from just about every movie McQueen ever
made.

"You don't mind?" I asked. "I mean, arresting people you
knew as a kid?"

He said, "I do what needs to be done, focus on the job, deal
with the embarrassment later on, over—" he swirled the beer
in his glass. "Over a beer. After a while, you get used to it. Besides,
the way I see it, better a patient friend with a badge than an irate
stranger, right?"

I slid my glass back and forth on the table too. "I see what
you mean."

"Heck, I asked to be in this part of town, and they need good police here. Growing up, these people are half the reason I decided to be a cop in the first place."

"So it's about more than just not driving a bread truck," I said. "It's about policing the playground monitor."

He let that go. "Play pool?" The table was open. He stood up, fished change out of his pocket, and put a quarter in the slot. "No money involved, and I'll let you cheat if you want." He pressed the lever. Balls fell inside the table with the crash and roll of celebration, like kids let out of juvie jail early.

"Thanks for the offer, sir, officer." I laughed. "I'll play, but I don't need you to let me cheat." I was good at pool. Physics, I understood. I knew all about vectors. That was my original goal in clowning—to create the illusion of defying physics with muscular comedy. I wanted to be able to stand when it looked like I should fall, to spring up when gravity would pull down, and to balance at impossible angles. I wanted to win, or at least stay on my feet, even when it looked like losing. I grabbed my cane, followed Jerrod to the table, and slid the cane through my fingers as though knocking phantom balls in already. "I'll rack." I nudged him out of the way with my hip, and hung my bamboo circus cane on the table's edge.

Jerrod's break was an all right scattering but the balls stayed too much at the foot. None fell. He ran his hand over the powder spool.

Rex could break to cover the whole table every time. Rex could make a jump shot, run the table, and shoot out. So could I, on a good day. I chalked up the cane's rubber tip. Then I bent my knees, bad hip trembling, and sighted down the wobbly line of the bamboo.

Jerrod said, "Think a cue might help?" He smiled, like I was a cute trick.

I smiled back, still in the crouch. "Take a cue from this," I said, and used the cane to knock the cue ball into the ten. The ten rolled smack into a corner pocket. The cue ball spun like a dancer. "Stripes! My lucky color."

Clown stripes, the outsider's stripes. Hooker's stripes, too.

Jerrod said, "Not bad, though stripes isn't a color, last I checked."

"Where I work, it's the color of money." I moved around the table. Peanut shells crunched underfoot.

He said, "In my profession, I'd say it's the pattern of jail time. A repeating pattern, all too often." He asked, "So, how long've you known those housemates of yours?"

I chalked up. "Didn't meet them all at once." Put the cane behind my back, twisted around with one leg up in the air, tongue to the side of my open mouth, and waggled the cane back and forth. I tapped the far side of the table, then the opposite side, to call a double-bank shot, and knocked the twelve in a fine run to the side pocket without disturbing the rest of the layout.

"A cop and a clown, head to head!" the drunk in the hat yelled, over at the bar. "Haven't seen that since my dear grandmama double-parked my little perambulator."

"You got the DTs," his tiny sliver of a friend said. "You're seeing things."

"You mean to tell me you don't see a cop and a clown shooting the lights out over there?" the first drunk asked. With one pudgy hand he reached for the flat brim of his straw topper.

The sliver nodded. "I mean to say you ain't got a granny. And I got the DTs too." He burped.

"Ah, yes. I see … It's hard to tell where Baloneytown ends and the DTs begin, isn't it, Silvo?" The man in the hat said, "Nurse Addie, time for rounds. For my fellow patient and me, that is." He tapped his empty pitcher, then fumbled and knocked his hat off backward.

Jerrod picked out another cue stick and called to the bartender, "These sticks are crooked."

Mad Addie rolled her eyes. "Show me somethin' in Baloneytown that ain't." The men at the bar ducked low, as though to escape notice.

My third shot, my hip shrieked in a wince of pain. My knee

buckled. I hit too far to the left; the cue ball veered around my mark, kissed a solid, and pushed it closer to a side pocket. Rex never would've fallen like that. Jerrod lined up his shot to take advantage.

"Merry Christmas," I said.

He asked, "Where'd you live before this?"

I smiled, leaned into the pool table. "Why're you asking?"

He shrugged. The two ball went in without scratching. No spin on the cue ball, though, just angled enough to hit the bumper. No leave. His second shot hit too lightly. The ball rolled, gentle and tired, across the green felt. It rested at the edge of the pocket at the foot of the table, where a breath could've sunk it. The cue nestled in at the far end.

"What kind of cop shot is that?" I asked.

"Strategy," he said. "Patience. Now the cue ball's trapped. You haven't got a shot." He chalked up, like chalk would help.

"Ah, strategy. I see. And to think, I underestimated the play." I twirled my cane like a gunslinger, caught it in front. "Nine ball, far and away," I said, then took a gamble on a jump shot. The cue jumped a solid, hit the nine to a corner pocket, and stopped fast on impact. No wasted motion. Nice and clean.

Mad Addie scowled and tapped a sign on the wall: NO JUMP SHOTS, NO MASSÉ, NO BALLS ON THE FLOOR. Her finger was skeletal, her voice hoarse. She said, "Jerry, you two better be playing with your own balls."

Jerrod flushed, embarrassed, nodded a silent OK, ma'am.

I ducked back down to the table. "Time to take a little ride, fifteen and eleven. Across town and downtown." The cue ball hit the fifteen in the left side pocket, veered right, and hit the eleven in the corner. "And the solids rest easy. Untouched." Somebody in a far corner cheered. A hand clapped against the bar.

I was a clown hero, beating the cops: Anarchy beats order any day! That was the unspoken message, my gift to the crowd.

"The clown's got the nuts here. Got the nuts," a drunk hollered.

I shot fast—too fast. I barely nicked the edge of the cue ball. The other end of my cane scraped the felt.

The drunk in the hat stood, and leaned forward over the bar to look; beer cascaded from his tipped hand. "Call out the coast guard!" he said, and straightened. He sloshed the other way, spilled beer on his gut.

Jerrod hit the one ball in a side pocket, and said, "This is why Baloneytown stays the way it is." A little louder he added, "I have no sympathy for a man who's intoxicated all the time."

"That's all right," the drunk said. "A man who's intoxicated all the time doesn't need sympathy. He needs a stenographer." He pulled on the end of his wrinkled, beer-soaked necktie.

Jerrod bent low in a way that made creases in the pants of his uniform and those creases were like arrows to his crotch. My eyes followed the arrows. He aimed for the glowing red of the three ball and said, "Your boyfriend's had that house for a long time."

"Herman?" I leaned into my cane. "I told you, he's not my boyfriend."

Jerrod, warmed up now, on a run, said, "Who is your boyfriend?"

"What makes you think I have one?"

"You're a pretty girl. Anyone ever tell you that? What's a pretty girl like you doing in Baloneytown anyway?" He turned his head only, and kept his hands steady. He said, "You have perfect lips."

Clown lips. Hooker's lips, always plain except when they were painted too much, when I was working. Now they were drawn in dark red, thin but curvy, for Crack's photo shoot. The lips of Trixie, Twinkie, and Bubbles. He said something else then I couldn't hear because "Sweet Jane" was too loud on the jukebox behind us. I stepped in closer, leaned over the table too, nearer to Jerrod, and asked, "Ever have to shoot anybody?"

He didn't flinch. He watched my lips. "Side pocket." He tapped the table with his cue stick, leaving a fine blue dust.

"It's not as common as it looks on TV, you know. Shooting people." He missed the shot.

"I don't have a TV. But I've seen a few cops pull their guns in our neighborhood anyhow." It was my turn. I chalked up, and said, "Time to clean house. North and east." I pointed my cane at the corresponding corners. One shot sent the thirteen and the fourteen home. The eight stood alone. I knocked the eight ball in. A scattering of solids lay like random stars in a night sky. "Rack 'em." I gave my cane a friendly swing.

Jerrod said, "Think I got taken." He dropped another quarter and shoved in the lever. The balls fell with a loud rush, chipping and clicking as they found their way into a line on the ledge underneath. "With most people, showing a gun is enough. I spend more time calling the drunk wagon on folks like Dukenfield over there." He pointed to the drunk in the hat. "Enforcing restraining orders, listening to talk about dog litter on the wrong lawn."

I liked the way he said dog "litter," like dogs dropped crumpled cigarette packs and used Big Gulp cups.

He said, "In this neighborhood, growing up, the choice was cop or criminal. I chose cop. That's all, end of story." He laid the triangle on the table and dropped the balls in. He looked serious as he racked. His eyes were in shadow, and his jaw muscle tightened, then relaxed, then tightened again, the same way as when he called for Chance or when he caught me with the stolen mower. Like maybe even fun took work and worry. He clicked the balls together in the rack, held his fingers between the balls and the plastic racking triangle with his thumbs outstretched, then lifted the triangle gently off the racked balls. He gave the triangle a spin, and tucked it away.

I used my full body force in the break. My cane bent and flexed with the impact. The balls scattered. A lone solid wandered toward a pocket, teetered, then fell. I walked around to the other side of the table. The table was crowded, solids clustered alongside stripes. "The old umbrella." I tapped my cane on the far three corners. "Side pocket."

I hit the cue ball at an angle, down and against the opposite far rail to the left. It bounced off the side rail and headed for the foot. It bounced off that bumper, came back at a new angle, and hit my mark into the rail, table's side right. That ball ricocheted across the table again and into the left side pocket, as called. A perfect box step.

"Going for the easy ones, I see," Jerrod said.

"Watch this!" I pulled out the big plans. Yes, I have a weakness for audience, wanted to put on a show, give the drunks something to watch. Maybe I was showing off for Jerrod too. "Flying trapeze," I said, and hoisted one hip up on the table's edge with the other foot on the ground. I'd shoot low on the cue ball for maximum backspin. A little draw.

I ran the cane through my fingers. I visualized the vectors, aimed to defeat gravity. The one and the four balls nuzzled each other at the head of the table. Hit the balls just right, with the right speed, a smidge of English, it'd send one to each corner pocket, then launch the cue ball back my way. I said, "I call this one Cash on the Barrelhead. Any wagers?"

Nobody made a bet, but a few yodeled, hollered, guzzled. I hoisted my hip on the table again. Leaned in low. Sighted. Took a deep breath, let the crowd fall away and the eighties rock fade. Moved into my zone. I pulled back, cocked the cane, and followed through. The cue ball raced the length of the table, a bullet that struck the one and the four and sent them packing. The cue ball hit the far bumper. It caught air! It flew back at us, in a beautiful clown arc—but it didn't arc. A line drive! It whipped right at me. I ducked.

The cue ball sailed past like a flying fist. Jerrod ducked. The cue broke the window with a crash. The beer light swung and sent shadows dancing. Our table wobbled, the pitcher spilled.

I said, "Shit."

Mad Addie barked, "Hey, hey! That's enough. I'll call the cops. Happy Hour's over."

Jerrod put his hands to his chest, to his badge and uniform, as though to check if he still was the cops. Somebody knocked over another table, a round of beers on the floor. Mad Addie spat out a stream of curses: "Cocksuckersbustingupmyjointaintthe-firsttimeIputupwiththisshit—" She pushed me aside and made her way to check out the damage. Her face was a shar-pei of scowl lines.

Like a kid in trouble, Jerrod leaned down fast to pick up broken glass. "It's not as bad as it looks," he said. "One window, that's all."

Behind him the tavern door opened and the light shifted to show a silhouette. When the door closed again, I saw her: Italia. She lifted one hand, looked around the room, and gave a toss. The cue ball! She caught the ball again softly, in her palm.

Shit. I ducked behind the pool table.

Mad Addie, midsentence, said, "Dimwitsandassholes, who'dafuckingstoppedtothinkthe motherfuckerscould'vekilledsome pieceofshitonthestreet...where'dthatgetme, yabastards—" She chewed the back end of her cigarillo like a horse chomping an apple. "One a yous get a garbage bag." She clapped her hands. Nobody moved. "Get! You lazyassssonsofbitches—an' I mean it," she said, and clapped again. "Or the joint's closed, no last call."

The Sliver, a grifter, and Dukenfield made a tangled dive behind the bar. They came up with six hands on the same plastic bag, a stumbling rush toward Jerrod.

I peered over the edge of the table. Jerrod was on his hands and knees picking up broken glass. Addie loomed over him and pointed out glass shards with the chomped cigarillo, curses falling like ash from her mouth, a bar towel over her shoulder.

When Nadia-Italia flashed the renegade pool ball, some-one yelled, "The clown did it!"

"The clown?" Nadia-Italia said. She tossed the cue ball in the air again and surveyed the bar, cool as a Little League champ ready to cream the other team.

I was the other team. Gulp. I ducked down again.

Jerrod turned to throw a handful of glass in the garbage

bag and saw me cowering. "Sniff, what're you doing?" He rocked back on his heels and reached a hand to my arm. "So you broke a window. We'll fix it up."

I held a finger to my lips to shush him, tried to brush his hand away. Too late. Italia's big shoulders moved in like an eclipse. She came around the table. She reached down, knuckles near my face, fingernails a deep purple, and dropped the white cue ball.

I caught it, a reflex.

"Your shot, Clown Girl?" Her lips parted in the shine of plum lipstick.

"Hand it over." Mad Addie clawed the cue ball out of my open palm.

A date. Nadia-Italia would tell Herman I was there on a date. A date with a cop would get me kicked out of the house—exactly what Italia wanted. It would save her the trouble of "breaking that bitch in half."

I could barely hear over the sound of my heartbeat, the ocean in my ears. All I could see was Italia. The world narrowed. My pink prop bag rested far away, the strap looped over the back of a chair.

My heart, ready to burst, spoke in the fast Morse code of biology: *you'll die or go crazy, die or go crazy, die or go crazy, die or go crazy* … I had seconds to live. My heart was too big for my chest, my head hummed. I couldn't move fast enough, had to get out of there.

Italia moved between the pool table and the wall, blocking my way. "Where you going?" she said, in a singsong. "Herman's on his way, and he'd lo-o-ove to meet your friends."

Jerrod stood, pants soaked with spilled beer at the knees.

Mad Addie grabbed Jerrod by the belt loops. "Get another goddamn bar towel, son. Pronto," she croaked out.

I took a chug of beer, tossed the half-full glass to Nadia-Italia, put my hands on the side of the pool table, and lifted my feet to the ledge like a gymnast mounting the horse. The ache in my groin was a nagging pain now, dimmed by time and drink. Like a quick and loud prayer, I hollered, "Double or nothing—Clown Girl, corner pocket." I ducked my head and turned a speedball somersault across the table.

My red wig was the rustle of dry grass around my ears; the plastic flowers on the sunglasses pushed against my face, and I felt the lumps of Crack's hairdo, each pin she'd used to tack down the curls, as my head pressed into the felt tabletop. Beer raced up the back of my nose. A vial slid out of my pocket. I rolled again. Another vial slipped.

"Hey," Addie hollered, and snapped her dirty rag at me with a spray of crumbs and stale beer. "That's new felt." The stream of curses fell from her mouth again: "Goddampoolplaying sonsofmotherlovingcashsuckingwhydIeverbuythisdumpJesus..." She dropped into a mutter.

Vials and tinctures fell from my pocket, tangled in balloons. But I came up with the sunglasses still on. When I hit the other side, I rolled off the edge to the floor and reached for my bag. It was far down a tunnel; my arm stretched, and I reached all the way, that long distance across the gap, in slow motion. My hand closed around pink vinyl.

Mad Addie yelled, "That'll get you kicked out a here. That's the first and last time, you know it."

I threw myself in a run toward the back door. My heart beat in my head, arms, neck.

I saw the flash of duct tape just as I tripped on the extension cord taped to the floor; the beer-mildewed, peanut-strewn carpet came up fast under my palms. The pink prop bag slapped open on impact. Juggling balls, tins of paint, and my silver gun skittered out in front, wrapped in a tangle of green, yellow, and red balloons. Tinctures scattered like jewels.

I grabbed the gun, stood up fast, the business end of my trick pistol trained on the drunk pack.

The bar went quiet except for the rattle of Crap Rock. Everyone stayed back. Only Nadia-Italia took one step closer, away from the throng. "What do you know?" she said. "The clown's packing." The muscles in her shoulders danced. She pulled a strand of hair down from one of her three pigtails, and ran the strand through her teeth.

"Back," I said. "I mean it." I shook the gun at her and picked up my bag. She leaned against the pool table. I edged toward the door. My face was hot, vision tight.

Jerrod took a step in. "Now, hold on there, Sniffles—"

Did I hear a siren outside? Had somebody called? Before Jerrod could finish, I turned fast, slammed a shoulder to the metal door, and ducked out. The door opened into a narrow, blind alley. I looked left, right, then left again. A Dumpster sat to one side. The other direction was blocked with a brick wall.

The door swung open and knocked me in the back. I fell forward. Jerrod, Nadia-Italia, and a flock of drunks came tumbling out in a cloud of tavern air, old smoke, and spilled beer.

From the ground I flashed the gun, the only language that worked with this crew. "Back up," I said. My voice broke and grew faint. A chirp.

"All of you, back up," Jerrod echoed me, only his voice was steady where mine was fragile. He cut through the crowd, his own gun still holstered. He put his hands to Dukenfield's shoulders, turned him around, and said, "It's under control. Everybody, back inside."

They didn't move.

"In!" he barked again. "Or I'll call for more crew, have you all downtown." Then they scrambled. To me, he said, "Sniffles, do it for me. And for yourself. Put the gun on the ground."

We were alone in the closed alley. I dropped the gun. It hit the ground with the light clatter of hollow plastic. Jerrod jumped, like it might go off. I kicked the gun his way; he ducked to the side, then came forward and picked it up. Gave it a shake. BANG! The flag popped out. Jerrod jumped. "What the—?"

"Fake," I said.

He said, "I see that now." He used the heel of his palm to

push the red BANG! flag back in the muzzle. When he offered a hand, I took it. I let him lead me past the Dumpster.

I put my other hand to my forehead. The beer was wearing off, the Chinese pills. The tinctures. "This is why a clown shouldn't drink in costume. It goes right to our wig-wearing heads," I said.

The alley opened up to the street. I took a breath. We stopped walking. Jerrod shoved the plastic pistol in his tight front pocket and put his hands on my arms. He looked at my face, into the scratched lenses of my daisy-rimmed sunglasses, and said, "This isn't the circus."

I said, "I know. I'm not a circus clown. I'm a people's clown. A clown without borders."

Jerrod said, "I'm serious. What're you thinking?" His face was close to the red wig of my hair. He drew me into his cloud of cinnamon spice. "You could've gotten yourself killed. Mad Addie, she's got her own weapons, you know? A shotgun behind the bar."

The night air was soft. "Killed? Jesus." I put a hand to my heart. Shook off Jerrod and leaned against the wall. "Shotgun?" Adrenaline beat against my body from inside. "I'm going to faint. I've got heart trouble. I'm sick, I need to sit down."

"Take it easy. Just breathe," Jerrod said. He held my hand as I slid down the wall. He checked my pulse.

"I feel sick. I'm not kidding." The wall was my support, my world, and all I had to hold off *death or insanity, death or insanity,* the two immediate options.

"Some holdup artist—this is all a little on the self-destruct- ive side." Jerrod massaged my hand.

"I left my cane in there."

"Don't worry about your cane. I'll get it later. And what is all this stuff?" He dropped a fistful of the spilled vials, like a handful of raw amber.

"Medicine." I felt like I'd had the wind knocked out of me. I slid the rest of the way down, sat on the sidewalk with my back against the wall. "Valerian." I held my hand out. Snapped my fingers, opened the palm again. "I need it."

"Valerian?" He read the labels and sounded each word out carefully. "Go-tu kola, Pip-siss-iwa ... It's overpriced snake oil, Sniffles." He slid the silver gun back in my bag. With the tinctures piled in one hand, he put his other hand on my back. "You're O K. But you're wasting your money on this stuff."

My money. I didn't have extra money. The tonics were hot, stolen.

He sat beside me. I'd never seen a cop in uniform sit on the sidewalk before. "So what's the gun a cure for?" He dropped most of the vials to the ground. Two of them he shook in his hand like a gambler's dice, and said, "Same prescription as the sunglasses—to keep people away?"

"It wasn't even real ... it's a prop gun." I picked through the vials on the sidewalk until I found the valerian, unscrewed the top, and poured drops into my mouth. My hands shook. My bones shook.

"I know it's a prop, Sniff—now—but those drunks in there, they don't know. Flashing a gun is the fast track to trouble." He ran a hand over my wig. The wig rustled against my ears like leaves in the wind. "Let's take this off."

"No, don't." I pulled my head away, put a hand to the wig to keep it in place. The evening sky was heavy with low clouds. My glasses dimmed the world further, a sweet dusky blue. I said, "Jerrod—you should get up. You need to go." I didn't want him to go. His hand on my back was a warm reassurance. Under his hand, the knot of a fist around my heart loosened. The pounding in my ears eased. Maybe I wouldn't die or go crazy, not just yet. I said, "You can't be seen on the street, outside a tavern, in uniform, on the ground."

He ran his hand in circles over my back. "Don't worry about me. Just breathe. You're O K."

I was a cat, under Jerrod's hand. A stray cat, left out in the cold too long. And the solution was the cause again, like stealing the tinctures, getting away with something. "You know," I said, "I can't be out with you, can't be seen with you."

His hand stopped circling. "You can't be seen with me?"

I looked up at him, past stray strands of the red wig. I said, "It's not you."

"What's wrong with me?" He took his hand away. Where his hand had rested seconds before, I still felt the warmth and weight, and held on to the warmth of it, to keep my heart calm, my bones at ease. Consolation.

"It's the cop suit. I can't be seen with a cop."

"So you're judging me because I'm an officer. My job. You're worried what your friends'll think?"

"It's not what they'll think, but what they'll do. They'll kick me out of the house." I said, "You have to understand—it's like the fear of clowns. Like those families, back at the grocery store. Only it's a fear of cops. Is there a word for that, fear of cops?"

He took a deep breath, stood and brushed off his pants. "Paranoia, poor socialization, that's what that is," he said. "I'm the good guy here. And you don't need those herbs." The vials lay in a cluster on the walk. He tapped the bottles with the toe of his shoe. "What you need is to stop hiding, stop being afraid of everybody, and take care of yourself. Stop with the sunglasses and the pistol routine—"

"I'm not the only one carrying a pistol, or the only one in costume. Maybe you're a little afraid of something yourself, officer?" When I stood, my blood was slow to follow, head dizzy, and for a moment the world narrowed again. In panic, I reached for Jerrod's hand. He held my hand, and gave it a squeeze. Quieter, I said, "They'll think we're on a date."

Jerrod brushed a strand of my clown wig behind one ear. He ran his palm over the makeup on my face. "Well, that's one thing I'm not afraid of," he said. The white dusty powder of dried water-based makeup clung to his skin. When he lifted the sunglasses off my nose the world became a lighter place again, as though he'd bought me a few more evening hours. "Maybe this is a date," he said. "Would it be so bad?"

In the new light of my evening's reprieve, his face was soft, earnest as the moon.

I said, "Well, no. Not so bad. Not to me, but really, they'd kick me out of the house. I'm not kidding. You saw my friend the weight lifter, right?" I nodded back toward Hoagies and Stogies. "She's looking for a way to do me in. Sink my ship. Herman doesn't want cops around, I mean police, and he thinks I'm a cop magnet now and Italia's his right hand—"

Jerrod leaned over, and he kissed me.

I kissed him back. I did. I leaned toward him and pressed my lips to Jerrod's and his mouth was sweet with beer. My pink clown bag slid forward on my arm. Tricks and props and cures spilled onto the sidewalk and rained down around our feet.

Ooo la la! That kiss was fine, and it was full of all the words I didn't need to say. It was an experiment, empirical, a single moment of unearthing the archaeology of emotion—Jerrod's were the first lips to touch mine in years other than Rex's painted smooch. He was the first body, the first smell to surround me besides Rex's kerosene and sweat. And for the moment of the experiment, in the comfort of Jerrod's sweet cinnamon spice, the luxury of his skin, the press of his mouth, the kiss was a tincture better than a palliative, soporific, or vice. I was calm. Ta da! Calm.

When Jerrod pulled away, it was with a dash of red clown paint across his mouth, and a dot of white where my nose touched his cheek, the press of my skin on his.

"What's so funny?" he asked. Then he kissed me again.

13.

Silence Isn't the Only Thing That's Golden

FOUR IN THE MORNING. THE DEPRESSION HOUR. THE hour of brain chemistry and despair. My mouth was cotton-mouth-beer-drinking dry. I reached for a cup of cold tea on the floor beside the futon. My fingers grazed the dry skin of Chance's sharp nose. Sweet, sleeping Chance. I stretched farther, gave a pat, but there was no soft fur, no silky ears. Just the nose. I fumbled in the dark. Nose? It was no nose, but a blackened banana, caught in the blankets like a fish in a net! I dropped the banana and sat up fast; my other hand hit the coarse hair of a kiwi, smashed against the sheets. It was Jerrod's bruised banana, the one he left on the barroom table, and his smashed kiwi—his fruit in bed beside me!

In the grainy moonlight the blackened banana was unwelcome as a severed horse head. The room was thick with the breath of overripe fruit. This was no accident—it was a threat, either from some unpaid tropical bookie or from someone much closer to home: Italia. She knew I'd been out with a cop.

The second kiwi rolled loose against the sheets in its tiny hair shirt, a fruit martyr doing penance. I'd be the one doing penance if Nadia-Italia had her way.

In the shadows, the Mount Rushmore of Rex as a clay bust perched on the closet shelf stared down at me and the banana. Rex stared from the hard lines of ink drawings and the curve of sculptures, his enigmatic smile caught in the moonlight, that smile turned now from complicit to condemning: I was guilty. I kissed a cop.

But Italia had snuck into my room while I slept. She trespassed.

God—I couldn't stand it! If Rex were in town, nobody would threaten me with a bruised banana. Nobody but Rex would kiss me, and I wouldn't even look at anyone else but Rex, my man, my show, my whole family and all I had.

I threw the banana out of bed and it hit a window with the soft thunk of a broken-necked pigeon. Why had I kissed Jerrod? What was I, crazy? Kissing a cop on the street. I was weak, weak, weak! So much for Clowns Sans Frontieres, those clowns without borders—I was a clown without boundaries. Without even the cheapest of boundaries! With one mistake, my world would crumble, slide away like sand in a tipped sandbox, melted cotton candy, a popped balloon Jesus. Nadia-Italia'd tell Herman. They'd both tell Rex. Maybe that poltroon had already told Herman. But no—more likely she'd drag it out, enjoy the power. I was at her mercy, and it was my own fault.

I was a worthless lump of earth. A clod.

Clown and *clod* came from the same root word: A lump. I shook Chinese BBs from the almost empty jar. I couldn't lose Rex. Why did I give in to Jerrod?

If Rex were home, he and I would take a flashlight, walk the streets, and call Chance until she appeared. Because Chance was gone, I wanted Rex home more than ever, and because Rex was gone, I couldn't stand the thought of losing Chance, losing our rubber chicken, our child, and then failing the urine test because I lost the hospital equipment too.

"Nobody ever lost a dime underestimating the intelligence of the American people." That's what P.T. Barnum said, and he made himself a fortune. If P.T. Barnum could do it, why couldn't I? I had talent. Brains. Maybe even looks. And I had artistic vision— the Kafka sketch, my literary interpretation. I could do more than lose things.

Clown and *clod* were related, but so was the word *cloud*. I couldn't forget that. That's the clown's real job—to stay grounded

on the earth, the clod, but with her head in the clouds. I needed
to keep my head, and keep the clown dream alive.

All I needed was a new plan, or at least a swift variation on
the old one. I'd be a Horatio Alger of the clown circuit, an American success story; I'd pull myself up by my own striped stockings.
A modern, striving Emmett Kelly. I had to cut to the chase, earn
some real moola, and move out gracefully *before* I was thrown out.

If I moved out at will, I wouldn't have to explain. Rex would
have a place to live when he came home—a real place, not a
mudroom, a clod room. A clown room.

When life sucks, throw yourself into art. That was Rex's sur-
vival tactic. *If the audience doesn't like the act, burn shit up. Light
something on fire. They go for fire every time.*

I could earn money as an artist, not just as Crack's unwilling
whore. Not as Trixie, Twinkie, or Bubbles. This would be the last
night I'd spend as fate's stooge.

Just thinking about my round-the-corner success made
me thirsty. That, and the beers I drank with Jerrod. Or maybe
the pills I snacked on like popcorn. Or the tinctures I threw down
by the bottle.

I tiptoed out of my room for water, and when I turned the
corner a wedge of white glare cut through the kitchen.

In the spotlight of the open fridge, Italia held my orange
plastic jug to the shine of her plum-tinted lips. She tipped
her head back, and drank. I whispered a quiet, "No," and sucked
in my breath, but it was too late. Vitamin B–rich urine ran in a
trickle from her mouth. I froze. Yikes—the horror! I was doomed.
Below her half shirt, her abdomen rippled like an earthquake.
She threw herself forward and spit everything out. She spit on the
fridge, on our chores list. She spit on the worn chart that said it
was forever my turn with the lawn.

"What the hell?" The orange jug was marked with her purple
lipstick at the rim. "What is this shit?"

Not shit, but piss, I thought. Maybe hers was a rhetorical
question, thrown out to the darkness. In the slim hope that she

hadn't seen me, I ducked behind the table in the center of the kitchen even as my bum leg screamed, unwilling.

She smacked her lips together. "Is this…Christ…it's piss!" She'd figured it out! Then she dove at me around the table. "You… Clown Girl!"

I straightened up and ran around the table. She doubled back and came at me from the other way. I ducked, reversed direction, almost tripped on a barbell, and jumped to keep from falling. I skidded past Nadia's outstretched hand. She threw the jug at me. Urine rained down, the jug bounced off the stove.

I turned the corner, made it to my room, and slammed the door. Italia's weight-trained fists hit the mudroom door like hammers.

My mouth was sand. My heart was a knot. *Heart trouble, heart trouble …* I needed to stay calm. I couldn't go back to the hospital. I pressed in the lock and pulled on the doorknob. My legs were light and shaky, and so was my head, pumped up on Chinese BBs. "I didn't do anything," I hollered through the door.

Italia hit the door again. Three quick hammers. "And you won't ever again! Open up," she hissed, as though through a clenched jaw.

The lock was only a button pressed into a two-bit knob. I had to work fast. I used a shoulder and all the strength I had to shove the dresser in front of the door. The dresser scraped along the wood floors.

I got on my knees and dug my fingernails into the loose cotton of the futon mattress. I lifted one side. The other half lay as a dead weight, a clumsy dancer. My pillows tumbled off. I folded the mattress over, tried to flop it up on one end. My bad leg ripped anew and my back ached as the mattress and I two-stepped toward the door.

Italia snarled, "I drank your clown piss? What the hell? I'm going to twist you into those balloon knots." The dresser trembled. The knob moved back and forth with a tight jerk and a clicking sound. I hefted the mattress against the chest of drawers.

"I can still taste your piss, you little skank." Italia spit, three times in a row, fast: *Hack-too, hack-too, hack-too...*

Hormones, estrogen, androgen, testosterone—all the working out Italia did, I swear she was making her own Y chromosome. She was nuts. Worse than the "Twinkie defense." She said, "I'll kill you, Clown Girl. If you mess with my food..." *Hack-too.* "Jesus. You knew I'd drink out of that jug."

She'd kill me! She meant it. I yelled, "It was medical. I needed it for medical tests."

"Oh, now you're a freaking urologist... "

I said, "No, a patient! The doctor asked for that urine, for tests—"

"Sick clown piss?" *Hack-too.* She beat on the door again. "So you've got something and I drank it?" Her fists came harder and faster now. She spit as she pounded.

The coins on my shelves rattled. A sketch of Rex fell off the wall.

"Nothing catching. Urine's really clean. I read that. It's acidic." When did my voice get so high?

The door buckled. My vision narrowed. The bees in my brain were buzzing at full tilt. I said, "Women washed their faces in urine, in the old days." My voice broke. There were spilled BBs on the floor. I picked up a few and put them between my teeth. *Calming.* Through a mouthful of BBs I yelled, "Swamis drink it. People live on it."

Italia slammed against the door and everything shook— the door, the floor below us, the house. The futon slumped to the ground, a casualty of our war. I was trapped. Trapped in a room of small glass windows.

"Open the door," Nadia hissed, breathless. The wood made the sound of splintering, giving way. "You put that piss on my shelf on purpose; you set me up."

"It wasn't your shelf," I yelled back. "It was in the side door. Communal!"

She body-slammed the door again. "It was my part of the communal rack. You knew it."

"*Your* part?" Clearly, she was crazy. "We don't designate on the communal side." My voice trembled. "That's what *communal* means."

"I'll kill you, girl. Kill you—" Methodically she slammed into the cracking door.

"You put that banana in my bed," I yelled back. I couldn't run if I tried—my torn ligament was shredded after the sprint in the kitchen. It was the kind of pain that deserves a name, like a special enemy, a military tactic, or a new disease in search of a salable angle: Hip Socket Hell. The Rotator Awareness Plan. I yelled, "It breaks a house rule, coming in my space." I picked up a stretched canvas and swung the hard corner edge at the glass panes of my tiny windows.

"What's going on?" It was Herman now, outside the door. "What're you doing, babe? Stop, you're breaking the door."

"I'm going to kill her," Italia said. "Giving me hep C, the swine flu, whatever's in her piss."

"She put a banana in my bed!" I yelled. "I was asleep. And I don't have hepatitis." I hit the windows again with the wooden edge of the canvas. Glass rained down around my feet.

"She put piss in the fridge in my area—"

I yelled, "It wasn't your area, you know it."

"She was at Hoagies and Stogies—"

"Back off, sweets," Herman said. To me he yelled, "What's going on? What're you breaking?" Then to Italia, he said, "Babe, listen. Back off, for real. Settle, OK?"

Herman was big, but Nadia-Italia was crazy. I said, "Call the cops. Quick!" I swung at a second pane of glass, building my escape route. "Herman, hurry!"

"I'm not calling the cops, Nita. I'm not calling your cop boyfriend on my girl. This isn't a time for jealousy, or whatever feelings you still have going on—"

"Herman! Call any cop you want." I swung again. "And he's not my boyfriend."

"Open the door. What're you breaking?" Then, to Italia, Herman said, "Let me talk to her. Alone."

Two windows were broken out, but the windows were still too small to fit through. I needed at least four cleared. I'd have to smash the thin wood in between. I pulled glass shards from the wooden frames. I ran my hand over the jagged edge, to loosen broken pieces.

Hack too. She was still there, outside.

"Hey, don't spit on the floor, man. Go upstairs," Herman said. "No joke. Wait for me." Then he said, "Nita, calm down. Don't break anything, O K? I'll talk to her. Open the door."

Italia spit again. I held a bloody finger—cut on the shards—to my mouth. "I'm not coming out. Not as long as she's there. Not without the cops."

I waited, still and silent, until I heard them walk away. What if they came around to the outside? Now I had a hole in my windows. I held the canvas like a shield and grabbed a juggling pin, ready to swing for the bleachers.

There was the quiet rattle of a wire inside the door handle, a sound as tiny as mice doing orthodontic work. The door popped open. It swung outward—the dresser and the slumped dead body of the mattress hadn't done a thing by way of a barricade.

Herman's head popped over the top of the dresser, a puppet show, face puffy, his hair in a tangled knot. Puppet Herman said, "Nita, it's four in the morning. Don't you ever take time off?"

I dropped the tools of my trade—the canvas and the juggling pin, shield and weapon—and fell to my knees. Heartsick. Exhausted. "She's a total loose cannon."

"You're bleeding." He reached a hand over the top of the dresser, as though to pet a dog, but couldn't reach me. His arm flapped in the air.

It was true. I was covered in cuts. And then I started to cry.

With one long arm Herman reached over the chest and

pushed on the mattress until the mattress inched down toward the floor. I scurried out of the way.

He said, "Nita, what're you crying for? You'll be O K. Put pressure on it."

"I'm not crying about a few cuts," I said. I flung my hand aside, and blood splattered on my striped pants. I wiped it into a smear. "That doesn't matter." I was tired and sick. My dog was gone. Herman seemed so far away, I barely knew him anymore. I needed a comforting hand, a pat on the back, somebody to smooth my hair. Somebody to kneel beside me and say that everything would be all right. The soft scent of cinnamon, or the bite of sweat. Jerrod, Rex, Herman.

Emancipated minor? I'd been one for years—emancipated, but no longer a minor, and I was ready to have a team, a side, a family. Somebody to back me up. A person shouldn't be emancipated so long.

"She won't bother you," Herman said. "We cut a deal."

He tried to slide the dresser, but instead knocked the dresser over. I scrambled like a hamster in a cage dodging a falling water bottle. A sock drawer slid open on the way down and a silky rainbow of tricks and scarves fell out. Herman climbed over the mess. "Don't worry about the windows. That's easy enough to fix. But what's up, what's with the piss in the fridge?"

I coughed, and choked out, "I wasn't trying to mess with anyone. I have a bad heart." Then I started crying all over again, feeling sorry for myself—sorry for the fist of muscle, that failing, overworked blood pump, the underappreciated overachiever.

Herman said, "Are you sick?"

Upstairs, Italia stamped the floor, stomped the hallway, and threw something that clunked and thudded down the stairs.

"Not sick, really. Not contagious, but there's something wrong…They don't know what yet." I said, "Maybe a heart attack, maybe a panic attack, depending on who you ask."

Herman didn't offer a hand to my shoulder. No curative, restorative pat on the back. He said, "Huh. Well, here's a house rule: no biohazards in the kitchen unless you clear it with me first, OK? But this time, we'll grandfather the piss in. Store all the piss you want, as long as it's clearly marked. *And* medical."

He said, "And get rid of the rubber-chicken dealers. We're still getting about three a day."

I nodded.

He said, "What were you yelling about a banana? What's up with all that?"

Italia coughed, and the cough rattled through my room. She had her head to an air vent upstairs. *Hack-too.* She spit again.

I said, "Nothing."

Herman cocked an eyebrow. He wasn't buying it. Through the vent, Italia coughed again.

He said, "What were you doing at Hoagies last night?"

Ah! So he'd heard that much. "Just shooting a little stick. Practicing trick shots. Clown stuff," I said, and gave a shrug of innocence.

"Bull pucky," Italia said. *Hack-too.* "She's lying." Her voice was far away and tinny, like reception on an old-time radio.

"Sweets," Herman said to the air vent. "Go to bed. I'll be right there."

"She's full of shit," Italia said. A cloud of dust fell from the vent.

I stood up and yelled, "Stay out of it." My bad leg winced, and my hands were still bleeding. I picked up a striped scarf and wrapped the scarf around my cuts.

Italia said, "She was out with a cop." Her voice was small, and sharp. "Cop date," her voice echoed in the vents. "That's a cop's banana." It was like having a tiny, tattling fly on the wall.

"Cop's banana?"

I said, "Herman, she's crazy. Here's the deal—I was out practicing pool shots, clown work. A cop came in the place. I had to run out. She saw me run…"

Herman nudged the smashed banana where it lay near the window. He picked the banana up, held it by the stem, let it dangle. "I don't need to hear the whole story," he said. "I don't think I want to. Just keep the cops away from the house. Don't talk to Italia, and she won't talk to you. We'll be our own little demilitarized zone, OK?"

He stood up and dropped the fruit. "Your room smells like compost, Nita. Clean it up, before we get rats."

I said, "It wasn't a cop date. It wasn't. I ran out—why would I run out on a date?" I turned up, toward the vent. "You saw me run," I yelled.

Italia's tiny tattling fly voice said, "I know what I saw."

What had she seen?

Then the phone rang, and the ring was a new voice in our quarrel. The ring was light and loud and insistent. Herman and I froze. The phone, in the kitchen, rang again.

Herman said, "It's like, past four in the morning. That's probably the cops right now. Shit."

I said, "The cops?"

He said, "Who else?"

The phone rang again. I whispered, "Why would the cops call us?"

"You tell me," Herman said, and flashed a scowl. "Maybe you stood up a cop date. Maybe you ran out." He peered into the dark kitchen.

"I didn't have a cop date." If I said it enough, I'd believe myself. And in the quiet of my unquiet mind I said a fast prayer to St. Julian, that clown-loving Hospitaller, the only one on my side.

"OK, all the noise then," Herman said in a hushed voice. "Breaking glass. Maybe they think it's domestic violence."

The phone rang again. We stood still, frozen. "Wouldn't they just show up?"

Herman inched toward the kitchen. I tried to breathe. Herman picked up the phone with a clatter. "Hello?" He made his voice deeper than usual, as though he'd put on some kind of manly voice costume. Then he lightened up. He said, "Dude, you know what time it is?" He laughed. "Cool. No, no problem. I'll put her on."

Jerrod? Herman wouldn't take that easy tone with Jerrod.

He brought the phone to my room. *Rex*, he mouthed silently. My heart picked up speed. Rex? I took the phone, and everything went into slow motion. Why was Rex calling now? Herman pointed to my little alarm clock and shook his head. I waved him off, and put the phone to my ear.

"Rex?" I said.

Herman stood listening. I turned my back on him.

Rex said, "Nita." His voice was warm and rough and pure music. He said, "What's up? What's the problem? Tell me what's going on."

Shit. "Problem?" Maybe he'd heard already that I'd kissed a cop and was on the verge of eviction—that was a problem. I dabbed at my hand with the scarf; the scarf was soothing and cool. "Who said anything about a problem?" I could hear people in the room with him. A woman laughed, a man said something.

"I've got about twenty messages from you," he said. "One says you've been in the hospital."

"Ah, that," I said, relieved. "Yeah, well…Old news. I'm OK." I was half-sick, arms buzzing, stomach queasy. I leaned against the tipped-over dresser. "What're you doing? Why're you calling so late?"

Behind me Herman said, "We'll talk, Nita. The conversation's not over," and he left the room.

Rex said, "We just got in from a gig. I spaced the time… You sound winded."

I dropped the blood-dabbed scarf, sat on the floor, and collected stray Chinese BBs that lay caught in the floorboards. "We were up," I said. "Everybody. I was talking to Herman. Hey, did you have your interview yet?" At the foot of my bed, a naked Rex in pen and ink stared back at me.

"Not yet," he said. "They changed the date again, but it's coming up."

I said, "It's good to hear your voice." In the background, at the clown hostel everyone talked at once, then there was a noise like a blender, or a power drill.

Rex said, "So, the baby's OK?"

Oh, no. The baby. I couldn't tell him. Not at four in the morning, on the phone, when I was already a mess. I'd end up crying. I said, "Everything's fine. Just hurry back."

I chewed on a few dog hair–dusted Chinese pills, and said, "Rex, I should move down and live with you. I'm tired of Baloneytown, and I hate being apart."

He said, "You get out much, see anybody?"

"See anybody?" What was he hinting at? I said, "I don't do anything. I'm here. All the time. I just want to be with you."

He said, "I mean, what've you been up to?"

"Up to?" I asked. "Absolutely nothing. I'm waiting for you. Say the word, and I'll move down."

"Babe," he said, "we don't have a place to live yet, not even a car to live in. I'm sleeping on a couch. Besides, maybe I won't get into Clown College, then we won't move here."

We. The whole world was in that word: Rex was still making plans for the both of us. So he hadn't heard, he didn't know. My life wasn't ruined, so far.

I said, "You'll get in. You're amazing." I took a deep breath.

"There's a lot of hot clowns in the world, Nita."

Rex was the best I'd seen. "You miss me?"

He said, "Of course, I miss you all the time."

The sculpted head in the closet, the face at the foot of my bed, the pen and ink drawing—they were all Rex, and spoke to me through the voice on the phone. I asked, "Rex?"

"Yeah, Sniff?"

"What's it like when you're modeling, to be up in front of everyone, naked?"

He laughed and said, "Well, it's my job. I tune out. Concentrate on not getting a hard-on. Why're you asking?"

I laughed. "You mean when I'm in the class, or all the time?" I was fishing for a compliment.

He was honest instead. He said, "All the time, pretty much."

All the time. O K. Well, that explained the elusive, enigmatic expression—my mudroom was filled with pictures of my dear Rex Galore trying not to get a hard on. He asked, "Are you doing your art? Painting at all?"

"Sketching, some." The chicken poster. "And working with Crack and Matey."

He said, "Corporate, commercial."

"It's good money."

"That shit'll make you sick," he said. "Selling out, it's no good." I listened to the clown hostel party in the background, a woman's voice getting higher and higher, then a bark of laughter. Art clowns, living it up, oblivious to time or money.

I said, "Rex, if I had a choice I'd rather work with you, do shows. But Crack's work is cash. We need it."

"That's why they call it whoring," he said. "Corporate baby-sitting."

Silence on my end. Then, "It's not whoring. And it paid for your trip."

He said, "Listen, Sniff, just take care of yourself, O K? Do the work that makes you happy. That's all I'm saying. In a few days or so, I'll come back. I'll make you right as rain, fit as a fiddle." He hummed a few lines of the song, *fit as a fiddle and ready for love.* I saw him then, juggling, riding his unicycle. It was all in the whistle. His big hands, his hair, the whole show that was Rex Galore.

He stopped whistling to ask, "How's the ambulance? Anybody break in?"

Our ambulance, our storage room. "It's fine. But hurry back. It can't sit there forever." My Rex. I was ready for him. "And you owe me a few kisses."

"I do?" he asked. "Am I in arrears, my fair clown?"

"Definitely. Kisses in arrears."

"Sounds fair to me." He laughed.

I said, "Rex?" Talking to the phone, to the ink drawing, the sculpted head.

"Yes?"

"When you come back..."

He waited.

I said, "Could we maybe do some of the old stuff? Some of the street shows, like we used to."

"You mean with the hat, the nickels and dimes, all that?"

I said, "Yeah. With the amplifier, the old buck-and-wing. Get Chance in for a few dog tricks."

His voice was quieter. Soft. "There's no money in it, Sniff, and I'm not so big on getting arrested anymore...but whatever you want. When I come back, we'll do it."

Perfect. I didn't need prescriptions, acupuncture, and the Chinese pills. All I needed was for Rex to come home. After we hung up, I sat on the slumped futon and listened to the house creak. Now and again I heard a moan through the heat vent. Maybe it was the normal sounds of an old house, or maybe Nadia-Italia and Herman were getting it on, a tangle of muscles and sweat and skin. I tried not to think about that as I lay awake.

The summer sun rose, orange and pink, and seeped in through the broken windows. Nadia-Italia's voice cut in on the old-time radio of the heat vent overhead: "Sleeping tight, little clown? Well, it's not over. I'll get you," she hissed, her voice coming down from above, the voice of a vengeful god. She said, "Get you like you've never been got before."

14.

Bounty Hunters and Piss Thieves

THREE DAYS LATER I HANDED MY JUG OF URINE TO A giant man squashed into a tiny padded chair behind the hospital lab office desk. It had taken three days since Italia's midnight snack to find a day for collecting urine. The giant gave the jug a shake in one of his thick paws. "You joking? This some kind of act?" His nose was a fat button in the middle of his face. The side of the jug said *Nita's Piss*, in big black Magic Marker, with a hand-drawn Mr. Yuck face, courtesy of Nadia-Italia.

I straightened my daisy sunglasses. "That's what they asked for. Twenty-four hours of contiguous, continuous urine."

He shook the jug again, like a dog shaking a rabbit, then handed the jug back. "No way is that twenty-four hours. Dump that out, give it a rinse, and start again." He said, "If that's all you got in you, you need hydration. That's a easy diagnosis." He went back to his paperwork.

I gave the jug a shake. It was light, with a quiet sloshing inside. It was light even considering how much piss missed the jug when I aimed my own stream, in my funnel-less collection process. I held it up and looked at the bottom of the plastic where a seam came together—no leak. The bottom was dry.

"I swear there was more here," I said.

The giant gave me a side glance, a short grunt. I slapped my way out of the office in my oversized Keds, the jug under my arm.

WHEN I GOT TO HERMAN'S, THERE WERE PEOPLE IN THE front yard and two women up on the porch. A tangle of black dogs swam lazy circles in the overgrown grass.

Herman was at the front door. "Listen up—we don't need any rubber chickens," Herman said, his voice loud. "Take your rubber-chicken playdate and piss off." He tried to push the door closed.

A woman on the porch put her foot in the door, and held out a piece of paper.

"I got the address right here," she said. "And I know I got the chicken."

She slammed the chicken against the door like she was tenderizing it, with its beak open, the rubber comb trembling. She waved the paper in her other hand.

I pushed my way through the people on the steps and said, "It's me you want. Let's see the chicken."

I'd recognize Plucky in a heartbeat. An indelible ink heartbeat, even.

She spun around, and the chicken flung its legs out like a kid on a merry-go-round. The woman was dressed in a pink fake Olympic tracksuit, and had her hair in two thick, matted French braids. Her skin was a mess of scars, like some kind of champion Olympic junkie. Herman let go of the door. The woman fell against Herman, and righted herself fast. A second woman in high heels and a hooker's stained white cocktail dress pulled back against the rattling porch rail. She clutched another rubber chicken to her acne-scarred chest. Was that Plucky, held so close against the woman's weathered skin? Would my Plucky be out with a hooker?

Herman said, "Shit." He rubbed his shoulder.

Two men and another woman in the yard came up the stairs behind me. "I got your chicken right here," one man said. "What's the reward?"

"I was here first," the Olympic user said.

It was a rubber-chicken roundup. They all had rubber

chickens held out like strangled babies. Everywhere I looked I saw Plucky, but it was never really Plucky, only a cheap imitation.

"Nita," Herman shook his head. "It's not getting any better— it's worse. It's been the same story all morning."

A man in the yard called, "Got your dog, right?"

A black mutt on a knotted rope. The dog bent his hind legs and arched his back, moving into the classic squat to leave what Jerrod called, so nicely, "litter," in the long grass of Herman's lawn.

Jerrod. I hadn't talked to Jerrod since the kiss. Each patrol car that passed looked like Jerrod's car, his silhouette inside.

I saw Jerrod everywhere, Plucky in every hand, and Chance in each roaming stray.

"Get the dogs out of here," Herman yelled. "Off the lawn, OK?"

The lawn. The grass was summer brown and waved back and forth as though to say, *Remember me?* Down the block two more people headed our way. Each dangled the buttercup-yellow body of a rubber chicken. A black-and-white pit bull mix loped at one man's heels.

A man stuck a chicken in my face. "So what's the reward?" A price tag danced in the sun, stapled to the chicken's foot. The scent of plastic drifted like the breath of Christmas packages, the wax of birthday candles.

I said, "This chicken is brand-new. You know it's not mine."

"It's better, right? New's always better." The man smiled a chipped toothed, sour beer-breathed salesman's smile. He was a salesman with nothing to sell but the one rubber bird. "Look, I paid three bucks for this thing. You think I need it?"

I shook him off.

"You didn't pay for that," the hooker barked out.

Some others had new chickens; most carried worn-out old hens, the paint faded off the wings and faces. Some weren't even rubber. Some weren't even chickens. And all the dogs were big, old rotties and labs mixed with collies, Danes, and who knew what. The reward seekers may have been dog owners, ready to cash in on man's best friend.

A fine Baloneytown how-do-you-do.

I pushed my way into the house. At the door I turned back. "Everybody," I called out. "My rubber chicken was special. It has distinguishing features."

"Like what?" a woman yelled up.

"When I see it, that's who gets the reward. And my dog is little, with no tail." I slammed the door closed. Turned. Herman stood waiting. He had one hand wrapped around his arm, around the tattoo that seeped into his soft brown skin, the letters that were my name. Flecks of dried blood marked the beginning of where Nadia-Italia had drafted her own lines over the top, a camouflaging peacock as one more way to obliterate me. Somebody knocked on the door. I slid the dead bolt across it.

Herman said, "You're pushing it, Nita. If they're not friends or family, and they're not here to buy herb, we don't need opportunists hanging around."

I leaned against the door to catch my breath. Nadia-Italia was lifting weights in front of the TV. Her breath and my breath, we matched each other, wheezing. She was plotting, I knew it. Every minute—plotting how to make good on her threat.

Herman said, "If you put up a sign offering cash in a neighborhood like this, you're going to get answers."

Nadia-Italia stopped lifting, sat up, took a big slug of water, wiped her mouth with the back of her hand, and said, "So what is this, Take Your Urine to Work Day?" She nodded at the orange jug swinging in my shaky hand.

I said, "Every day seems to be take my piss somewhere day around here—somebody drained my jug!"

Nadia-Italia only laughed, and lay back down on her weight bench. I stepped toward her and shook the jug over her head like some kind of percussion. "You poured this out—"

"Don't talk to her," Herman cut in. "She didn't touch your piss."

Italia turned her head. One eye was squinched where her

face pressed against the weight lifting bench. "Think I want your urine, Clown Girl? Had my fill, thanks and no thanks."

"I think you're messing with me."

"You're breaking a house rule. No talking to me. Now scram," she said, smiled and went back to her bench press.

15.

The Juicy Caboosey Show; or,
Full Flame and Glory!

BURN *SHIT UP*. REX'S STAR PERFORMER'S ADVICE RATTLED
in my head. Ever since talking to Rex on the phone, I was more
agitated than ever. I was desperate and, worse yet, guilty. All else
had failed—especially my willpower when facing down the
lips of the law. Now my only recourse was fire. Burn shit up. No way
could I practice fire tricks in the slim space of my tiny room.
I needed to practice. A new clown skit was the only ticket I held,
the only train I'd ride.

I had skit ideas aplenty: *The Beef-Brisket Dance*, *Two Clowns
in a Shower*, a soft-porn balloon routine called *Who's Hogging the
Water*? I could pull out the old silent version of Kafka for art lovers
in the crowd. And then there was *Everything Sisyphus*, the quintes-
sential clown act, struggle sans redemption. Now I needed a new
routine that was bigger, hotter. On fire. Darkness would transform
Herman's overgrown backyard into a stage.

In a world of clown whores and virgins, I'd cling to the integrity of art.

I waited until after midnight. The house was quiet. I waited
longer. After one o'clock, I mixed a highball of valerian tincture
on the rocks, rolled Chinese pills over my tongue, and braved the
blank canvas of a rehearsal space in the open backyard. From the
yard I looked up to the converted attic room Herman shared with
Nadia-Italia, where the pale blue-white light of a TV flickered
behind the curtain; Herman slept with the TV on, which was
entirely wrong in a Freudian *feng shui* kind of way. Freud said that

for every couple having sex there's always at least six people in the bed, counting both sets of parents. With Herman, there was a whole laugh track, a news report, commercial breaks. There was product placement, right through climax, through dreams, through the morning alarm. There was a focus on ratings, but zero award nominations.

The long grass of the backyard whispered over the satin of my clown pants. A briar clutched my clothes; the valerian highball spilled as I stopped fast, and with one hand pulled the clutching briar away. The thin line of a perfect circle where the dry grass parted was Rex's welded metal wheel hidden in the yard. The grass had grown so long since he left, the long grass seemed a sign that Rex had to come home soon. This couldn't go on forever.

He'd come back to failure: our missing Chance, cops, the urine collection and constant near-eviction.

I lay down in the grass, rested my drink in a nest of its own to one side, and rolled like a deer making a bed in an open field. My weight pressed the grass into a tatami mat of bent stalks. Sticks and rocks pressed into my back, but still I rolled. The edges of the flattened grass would mark the finite reach of my makeshift stage.

OUT FRONT, OUR BATTERED AMBULANCE SLEPT IN THE glowing halo of its own white rusted roof and reflected the buzzing streetlight. I called, "Chance," in a whisper as I walked out to the ambulance. "Here, girl. Come on home."

My hands shook, one wrapped around the valerian highball. A car crawled slowly down the block. Something creaked on a neighbor's porch. I moved fast, swung open the ambulance's back doors, climbed up and let myself fall into the lush pile of props and costumes; the darkness was haunted by the ghost trace of Rex's body, the air filled with sweat and kerosene.

It was warmer in the ambulance than outside. I kicked a foot through loose clothes on the floor until I felt something solid, then reached down into the clothes. It was an empty can, labeled

Canned Laughter. A sight gag. I threw the can back into the pile. Fished again.

Every space inside the ambulance opened into storage. There was storage in the ceiling and floor. The single cot folded open like a trunk. There was a medicine chest attached to the wall and when I opened the latch, face paint, body glue, fake eyelashes, artificial scars, and latex ears tumbled out.

Below the medicine chest was a single backward-facing chair, where an EMT would sit. The chair opened up, like a wooden box with a padded top. None of these compartments had what I needed.

Under the costumes, swimming in the clothes, were beanbags and juggling balls, angel and devil sticks, fake cigar boxes, spinning plates, and rubber rings. I toe-tapped the edge of a diabolo and pulled on a short pink wig. The pink hair had been bunched into fat tufts with dabs of super glue.

I was a toy in a toy box, one plaything among many.

Then my hand, deep in the props, slid across the broad nylon curve of the Pendulous Fake Breast Set. Aha! Rex hadn't used the Pendulous Fake Breast Set in ages, but still I recognized the shape and texture before I pulled its weight to the surface. It was a peach-colored bib, with sand-filled nylon sacks like water balloons that hung in front. I slipped the bib over my neck, on top of my clothes. I gave one boob a squeeze and it let out a duck call. The other side chirped like a dog toy. Voilà!

Those boobs were practically Kevlar, a bulletproof vest. They were the leaden apron a hygienist makes you wear at the dentist, the body armor of the Army Reserve. Safe. That's how I felt behind the Pendulous Fake Breasts—safe, sexy, and funny. What more could a clown want?

Guys aren't the only clowns who can play the Big Girl suit. Why limit myself to fake ears and noses? I got down on my knees in the pile of costumes, new jugs swinging low, and kept up the search. Soon enough, my hand found the curve of the Fabulous Fat Ass. The matching partner, the bottom half of a two-piece ensemble. And just like that, a new idea was born: Hello Juicy Caboosey Show!

It all made sense. I'd be a sassy, busty clown girl juggling fire. Of course—why not? I'd play to crowds high and low. I'd find the fine line between Crack's clown whore and my own comic interpretation, work both sides and move easily from the comedy of burlesque to striptease, slapstick to sexy. I'd graduate from Clown Girl to Clown Woman.

I stood on my knees in the world of costumes, slid down the elastic waist of my striped satin pants, and sang quietly, *I'm every woman...* The Fabulous Fat Ass snapped on in front. If getting dressed as a clown is about tapping into spiritual guides, finding history in the clothes and makeup, well, my spiritual guide for this show was one big girl—sexy, round, and ripe. Who wants to be a skinny, orphaned, emancipated clown bruised by a miscarriage? No, I'd transform myself into a fertility goddess. It was the Venus of Willendorf calling me out.

Other than a little camel toe as I stretched the formerly loose pants back over the Ass, it all came together so easily! I'd invent my own show, self-promote, and move from clown lackey to star performer.

I pulled the valerian vial from my long pocket and shot a few more drops of valerian over the tumbler of melting ice to calm my thrilled nerves, mitigate my fear of success, fear of failure. I could do this. I could bust out in my own newly busty way.

And the key to success was Rex's tip: *Burn shit up. Light anything on fire, audiences love it.* I swung the melons left and right, shimmied my shoulders, and on my knees did the Grand Teton Jiggle Dance.

I'd do a new silent, sexy version of Kafka: Gregor Samsa wakes up, finds he's metamorphosed into a woman with an hourglass figure—where every second counts!—and his world's *on fire*. I'd do a busty Beef-Brisket Dance, *on fire*. Two Clowns in a Shower *on fire*. And *Who's Hogging the Water?*—that'd be mixed genre, soft porn plus fire. Even an ordinary juggling show with a bodacious bod and the pins on fire would be a new show altogether.

I found a tin of face paints in the medicine chest. In the cabinet's mirror, I patted white on my cheeks, drew stars around my eyes, and lined my lips deep red.

A narrow cabinet opposite the cot, near the ambulance's back doors, had once held an oxygen tank and hoses. I crouched down in front of that cabinet and rested on the Ass like it was a beanbag chair. Soon as I opened the slim cabinet door Rex's spare fire-juggling batons, his best maple-and-asbestos-handled torches, fell out—like a sign that I was on the right path, the torches fell right into my new mondo bazookas, right into my ripe casabas, bounced off, and landed in my lushly padded lap.

AS I STOOD IN MY HOMEMADE CROP CIRCLE IN HERMAN'S backyard, I saw the first complication: Juggling with boobs demands a whole new skill set, with a new center of balance and an increased sense of self. In short—the boobs were in the way.

I started with practice tosses. Three balls in the air. My arms smacked the sides of the heavy, swinging nylon sacks. I knocked into one gazonga and missed a catch, first try. The boob barked out its duck call. But the Fabulous Ass kept me grounded and I gave it a shake-shake-shake, like maracas, as I tossed the juggling balls.

I had a small tape player in the backyard, and played Stevie Wonder in a whisper as I warmed up. *When the summer came…* One ball, then two, then three in the air, quick and easy tosses; I grew accustomed to moving with the Pendulous Breasts. It was great to be up and working so early. Shadows moved in the hedges that lined the yard. The tall grass rustled. This was the clown equivalent of farmwork. I tossed two balls up into the night sky as one came down, then reversed the pattern. Two down, one up; two up, one down. *Milking the Cows*, I'd call it.

Simple stuff, child's play.

Juggling is like dancing, and it's a form of self-hypnosis. The balls were my partners, caught in our rhythmic swing. When

I juggle, I can't help but tell a story as I watch the balls move; I individualize and anthropomorphize. The balls touched my hands and flew on their route again as though I had little or nothing to do with their trajectory. And as they bounced, they were kids on the playground, running and jumping. They were little goats, leaves in the wind. A green ball was the leader and two reds followed, in a circle. Or the two reds were friends and green tagged along in opposition. One moved right while the other two swung left. Two kids got along, one was an outcast. Then they all turned around, followed the rebel, the renegade.

I bent my knees and did a booty-swing as I juggled. The Fabulous Ass swung away, then back, and gave my tush a comforting pat-pat-pat.

When I gained grace and quit slapping my arms into the flop of the Pendulous Breasts, I switched to batons. Batons in the night air were pure magic. The ivory sticks lifted into the dark sky, waved to their brothers the stars, and twirled close without touching each other; I barely touched each one. They sprang from my hand. Slivers of the moon.

With my confidence up, I went for the fuel—a can of turpentine from my room, meant for cleaning brushes.

Like pouring drink in a drunk, I poured turpentine down the aluminum throat of the torch, where it would fuel an asbestos wick. The torch was a solid thing, elegant in its slim curves. I filled two more, wiped them down with a rag, tossed the rag in the grass, and set the fueled torches aside unlit.

One thing about juggling fire: keep your fuel in a juggler's fueling bottle with a narrow, EZ-Pour nozzle and a Safe-T-Snap lid. They make the bottles for a reason. I couldn't find Rex's fuel bottle. I used turp straight from the turp can, and rested the can to the side on the long matted grass.

I snapped the lighter, and the familiar *whoosh* told me who was in control: It was in my hands this round. Not Rex. Not some other clown. Me. I swung one burning torch into the air and it was a comet against the sky. Like a well-trained bird, the torch landed back in my open hand.

And I was the Statue of Liberty.

I was the Clown of Liberty, and claimed my freedom with a new show. The yard danced amber and blue in the firelight and the distant edges closed in, darker than ever against the blaze. I was protected from eyes by hedges, protected from the world by my Kevlar ta-tas. I threw back a shot of my own fuel, valerian tincture down my open throat, then lit a second torch from the first.

Two torches crossing in a perfect arc overhead was the dance of white ghosts, leaving tracers. Beautiful! It was hypnotic, the fire shimmering and wild against the tranquil black background of deep night.

Adding a third torch was tricky. I had to manage two in one hand, with the first two already burning furiously their eternal clown flame.

With three torches lit, I adjusted the pink wig, turned up the radio a smidge, and gave the first serious, dangerous toss of my new career. For rhythm, I sang along with Stevie Wonder. *Very superstitious…* I shook my Fabulous Booty. The weight of it was like a conga line, hands against my hips, shaking back. *Wash your face and hands…* I swung the Bodacious Melons… *when you believe in things that you don't understand, and you suffer…*

The batons overhead crossed in their arc like a magician's trained doves, my ghost relatives. There's a power in fire and I had that power harnessed. I was transfixed. Transformed. In my zone. I was an angel lost in a dream in the wilderness of the yard, a conqueror with the whole world ahead of me. The air was soft as water. The moon smiled down. A falling star answered any questions I had and the answer was *Good Luck, Fellow Star!* The message from a kindred spirit, a falling scrap of fire that burned out, light years away.

The torches, those harnessed meteors, danced at my command.

A voice cut through the dark, over Stevie's song: "What're you doing? Shit, is that you, Clown Girl?"

And I flinched, the dream broken.

Nadia-Italia. Her voice came at me from nowhere, from everywhere. I lost the rhythm. One torch fell from the sky like a dead bird. I caught the other two, second and third. The first lay still, a broken-necked dove burning in its own quiet pool of orange and blue flame against the roots of dry, matted grass.

Crap-ola!

I didn't have time to look for Italia, but instead held the two torches in one hand, bent low, and ran fast to collect my fallen friend, my trained pet. The sand-filled sacks of the Pendulous Breasts swung forward as I stooped. The momentum pulled me faster, with the weight of the funbag-sandbags at my shoulders. I kicked a leg to find my balance, but the Fabulous Ass bounced against my own ass and pushed me ahead in my crouch. I couldn't see the radio underfoot below the flopping boob bib; the radio rolled under the swing of a leg, and a muffled Stevie Wonder sang into the dirt. I stumbled. My oversized shoe hit the turp can and knocked the can into the grass. I tried to catch myself, but the weight of the boobs! The oversized shoes! My bad hip called my name, and laughed in a crackle of ligaments. One knee went down, into the damp ground, and the torches in my hand smacked mother earth. I skinned my palm. My pants ripped at the knee.

The first torch down doubled its quiet flame, like an accident victim vomiting blood into the roots of the overgrown yard. The flame seeped and grew, and fast-formed a line fed by the spill of the tipped-over can—then the can of turpentine itself was touched by fire; fire bloomed from the spout like a sight gag, and in a loud whoosh the can swelled. The sides blackened and bent.

"Jee-sus!" Nadia-Italia said, behind me, from the window upstairs.

Grass smoldered under the torches in my hand where they too lay along the ground. The turp rag leapt in its own quick fire.

I picked up the torches, stomped on the flames, and gave

myself a hotfoot. The rubber on my shoes curled and darkened. Still stepping in fire, I reached to straighten the can.

"It's OK," I called. *Burn shit up. Audiences love it.*

"Chick, like, it'll explode!" Italia's voice was a sharp screech, her own ambulance wail. "Herman, wake up!"

Didn't sound like my audience loved it.

"Calm down, calm down," I said, and stomped faster. "No need to tell Pop. Show'll be over in a minute, and panic will get us nowhere." But was she right? Would the can explode? I was shielded only by the false security of the fake boobs.

I took seventh-grade chemistry. "It won't explode until it creates a vacuum," I said. I shoved the unlit ends of the burning torches into loose ground. "It has to burn through the fuel first." I inched forward, one hand out. My voice cracked as I yelled, though I tried to sound confident. My hands shook, and my heart was a rush of blood washing veins, chemicals. Nerves.

"What the hell?" Herman's voice at the window joined Italia's panicked song.

"She set the yard on fire!" Natalia shrilled. "I saw her do it."

"Under control," I said.

Nothing was under control. The yard burned in three places.

I grabbed the can in one fast move, like the can was an animal ready to run. I grabbed it, and caught it. But that can was more than an animal. It was Loki, God of Fire. Unleashed. The sides of the metal can sizzled under my hands. I yelped and flung the can far away from me, into the tall grass of the yard, and a streamer of fire followed the can like a comet. A shimmering line of yellow-white flame fell on the grass like a rope, like the tail of a kite. The flame snapped and hissed and fast grew into a wall.

Then my short pink hair was a flash of flame too, as fire jumped to the nylon strands and dabs of superglue. There was no time to think. I beat my hands against my head, against the burning wig. The world smelled like melting Barbie dolls, the burned breath of a Christmas toy dropped against the Yule log. I pulled the pink hair off and flung it, but too late. My nylon sleeve was in flames.

"Crapola! Crapola!" I ran in a circle and threw myself down. I rolled on the grass where the grass wasn't on fire, but the Pendulous Breasts resisted my momentum, and everywhere I rolled sparks flew. The Pendulous Breasts duck-quacked and chirped a cacophony of party sounds. I was guilty, and now I was on fire. Who would've known hell was so efficient? A few mistakes and hell came to me faster than room service.

Stevie Wonder's voice melted, then ground to a slurry, low halt.

A fist came at my face in scattered blows. I was blinded. No— not a fist. It was a hard blast, a bitter stream, a fire extinguisher beat against me.

"Coulrophobia!" I sputtered. The fire extinguisher gang!

The blast moved from my face down my arm, then was gone. I blinked until my vision cleared.

The first thing I saw was Herman's naked muscled butt, his pants in one hand. He sprayed a white blast of fire extinguisher foam, but the extinguisher was small, and here size definitely mattered; it sent a stream light as piss dancing over the sizzling yard.

"Get the hose!" He yelled. "Spray down the house."

I tried to breathe.

When I didn't move, he yelled again. "You're out, OK? You're out. So help with this shit."

Out? Kicked out? I lay on my back. The Pendulous Breasts sat on my chest like twin demons. The sand was twice as heavy soaked by the fire extinguisher. I was beat up. Spent. "Out of the house?" I asked.

Herman didn't let on if he heard me. He ran for the hose.

Italia came from the house more slowly. Wrapped in a tiny blue bathrobe, legs naked, she sipped a carton of protein drink and leaned away from the smoke. She said, "God, you're self-centered. He means *out*, like you're not on fire, right?" Then she said, "Oh, wait. I see a spark." With one long, muscled and tattooed arm, in slow motion, she poured her drink on me. The protein drink was a pale, lumpy cascading ripple from the dark sky, a thick splash against my open eye, and I jerked away. Nauseous.

She tapped my scorched Big Booty with one foot. "Girl, you've let yourself go. The least you could do is get up."

WHEN THE FIRE DEPARTMENT GOT THERE I WAS STILL ON my back on the ground, wet and cold, trying to breathe and wanting to vomit. The Juicy Caboosey tush put me in some kind of yoga move, with my back arched and head tipped.

My fake boobs were scorched, pocked with melted nylon.

I was sick. The yard was a blackened scar. Herman's face was a dark mask, soot-stained, eyes red and rimmed in white. He was a Clown Prince of his own, or at least a Barenaked Baron. Once the fire was out, he stopped and put his pants on.

The paramedics knelt to check my vitals. "Just relax, OK?" A fresh-faced boy paramedic put a coat under my head to fix the angle made by the Ass.

"It's my heart," I said. I put a hand on the boob suit. "I have a bad heart."

"We'll give it a listen," the fresh-faced paramedic said. "So, what's your name?"

I told the paramedics my name as many times as they asked—maybe five or seven. I told them my real name, Nita, not Juicy Caboosey or Sniffles. I held out my arm for the saline drip; that thin needle under the skin fed saltwater, a hospital-standardized taste of the ocean, to revive the premammalian center, bloodstream like an early memory.

"You'll be OK," a paramedic said. They lifted me, complete with the sandbag weight of the Ass and the Pendulous Demon Twins on my chest, onto their lowered gurney.

Where was Jerrod? My cop, my safety net, that apple dumpling of a uniformed streusel. The EMTs buckled me in. My hands were hot under new burns. Herman brought his soot-streaked face toward mine. Behind him, the sign, *Baloneyville Co op*, was blackened.

He let me hold his hand and followed alongside the gurney. I wanted to squeeze Herman's hand, to transfer heat, to make him my salve.

"Herman. I'm dying." I coughed. My chest was tight. A paramedic shoved an extra blanket under the arch of my back.

Herman rolled his red-rimmed eyes.

"You're not dying," he said. "And you're not getting out this easy. When you come back, house meeting. No fire tricks."

Nadia-Italia yelled, "She threw that can of gas! I saw it hit the shed."

"I didn't throw it at the shed." I coughed again. Perhaps more for Herman's sake than my own. I hacked like I had instant coal miner's lung. I said, "It was on fire, I tried to put it out. Besides, you didn't like that lawn anyway, right?" I coughed again. "At least now we don't have to mow. That's the bright side." His yard was a charcoal pit.

He dropped my hand. I saw what was coming and counted the seconds, like counting between when lightning strikes and the crash of thunder.

By the time I reached three, Herman blew up. He said, "Jesus, Nita. Total disrespect. Same as always. You could've burned the house down. That's dangerous shit." He took a cigarette out of his pocket, started to put it in his mouth but his fingers were clumsy and tense and he broke the smoke in half, threw it on the ground. "They'll investigate. My insurance'll go up, cops'll be over here." He said, "Bottom line, when you come back, I want you gone. Period." His mouth was a damp red gash in his soot-covered face. "Last straw."

I was on my deathbed—my death gurney—and Herman was giving me the bum's rush. I said, "Herman—"

He said, "Forget my stash, you could've killed us in our sleep."

The paramedics lifted my new bed. The gurney creaked

and rocked as the stars grew closer, and it was like riding a wave. "Let's talk about it, when I'm better."

Herman backhanded an invisible foe, shook his head, and folded his arms as though to hold in a rib cage of fury. The paramedics swung my bed into place in the ambulance's tiny room. Herman and Nadia-Italia, united against me, walked arm in arm across the blackened lawn.

16.

A Turn for the Nurse

IN THE BACK OF THE AMBULANCE IT WAS ONLY THE TOUSLE-haired boy paramedic and me. The ambulance rocked and bar-reled into town while the blood in my body swirled as a nauseating eddy in my chest. The siren sang opera to our tragedy. Everything smelled like burnt polyester. My bigger-than-big Keds were black-ened, melted cheese at the rubber toes, dripped and solidified into a Salvador Dali. The back of the ambulance was a crowded vault of supplies, but might as well have been empty for all I cared because it wasn't Rex's ambulance and didn't have the sexy, sweaty comfort of his body, his presence. My cure.

"I can't breathe," I said. The Ass under my hips made my back arch and the fake breasts thrust up. "I feel a knock in my chest. Like a gasp in my heart. Am I dying?" My breath was shallow, the words broken. When I tapped my chest, one Pendulous Breast gave a thin wheeze. Sweat trickled down my temple. Away from the fire, my skin cooled under the sweat like a fever.

"We're going to give it a listen." The paramedic reached as though to unbutton my shirt but stopped short, his hands in the air in front of me.

The Kevlar boobs barred the way. Over the hill of the Pendulous Breasts I saw only the top half of the paramedic's face, his worried eyes and twisted eyebrows. I was at his mercy.

If I could blow up a balloon, tie a few Madonnas, I'd catch my breath and settle my heart. I tried to reach in my pocket. The nylon seat belt cut across my path.

The paramedic touched the curve of the boob suit.

With empty hands I had no props, no balloons, no way to draw attention away from me and toward a trick, a rubber toy, a balloon animal.

I said, "Pass me a latex glove, I'll make you a reenactment of the Annunciation. The whole thing, I promise."

He slid his hand tentatively along the curve of a fake boob. He handled me like I was the prop.

"Hey," I said. I gave a weak smile, called on my clown powers, and tried to summon the fertility goddess meant for that outfit. With my best vaudeville purr, I said, "What are you, a faith healer?" My voice cracked. I fluttered my eyelashes. "That's a fine medicine—you touch me like you know me. I'm better already." I took a deep breath, counted to eight, and didn't feel better at all.

"Just doing my job." He grabbed one mound in each hand and lifted. The left side quacked, and the paramedic jumped. The right boob, victim of the fire, was only a sad hiss in quiet echo.

He was cute, in a Boy Scout kind of way. "Working on your paramedic's badge?"

He dropped the boobs against my chest. The demons hit me with their full sandbag weight. "I've got to get to your heart."

"Sir, you're halfway there. Touch me again and it's all yours." I gave another big clown wink. Really, I wanted to make my exit, to be out of the ambulance, offstage and back in my room. If I could curl up on my bed with Rex's costumes, a valerian tincture, and a bottle of pills, I'd be fine.

He cocked an eyebrow, took a breath, and pulled a radio off his belt. "I'm serious."

"Just the way I like my medical men—serious." Stand-up and one-liners are the clown version of whistling a happy tune. I'd work the crowd even if it was only a crowd of one.

The radio squawked out a rush of static. He held it close and said, "Patient appears to be stable, though there may be…" The last part was muffled as he turned away. "Appears to be in clown clothing…"—his voice dropped even lower—"…delusional…"

Delusional? Did I hear him right? "'Delusional'?" I said.

The paramedic put the radio down and turned back to me. "We're going to give you a little oxygen." He rammed two tubes up my nostrils. He pointed at the boobs. "Show me how this thing works. I need to hear your heart." He unfastened one of the belts that held me to the bed. When he found the snaps at the cleavage, the boobs fell apart willingly and dropped to either side of my chest as two heavy weights.

He put the cold end of a stethoscope to my chest. His breath brushed my neck. I blushed, warm under a mask of greasepaint and soot. The oxygen was cool against my lip. I was scared.

I touched his shirt. W. C. Fields came to the edge of my vision, shook a leg, and said, "Don't look now, but I think you're taking a turn for the nurse."

"Nurse?" I said, and coughed through the soot in my teeth.

"I'm an EMT," the Boy Scout said. "Not a nurse." He put a clip on my finger. "This clip measures your oxygen level." He taped the ends of wires to my skin, hooked me up to a machine. "Now lay back."

I looked to W. C. Fields for guidance, but he was gone. The Boy Scout spoke into his radio: "Seems to have sustained minor burns."

Minor? The oxygen slipped from my nostrils with a cool rush of wind over my face. The scout used one hand to put the hoses back in my nose. "Patient may be in some sort of shock," he murmured into the radio.

I drank in the oxygen. Slowly, I calmed. The pieces of my body came together again: arms, legs, head, heart. Skin, nerves, breath—everything that had been humming and crazed, it quieted. I pressed my weight into the Ass under my hips. By the time we got to the hospital, I was ready to walk in on my own.

DON'T SHOW UP IN THE EMERGENCY ROOM READY TO WALK in on your own. Don't try to sit up, tug at the nylon straps that hold you to the gurney, and tell everyone you recovered real fast on the way over. Don't say the fresh air did you good, or the company on the trip made it worth the ride. If you claim to be fine when you're strapped to a stretcher—that's hospital code for "crazy." The fast track through the ER is chest pain. Say "heart trouble," and you're bumped to the front of the line. I didn't have chest pain by the time we got there. Still, the paramedic told an intake nurse, "The patient complains of heart trouble. Difficulty breathing."

Emphasis on *complains*.

I pressed my elbows into the gurney in an effort to sit up, with the Ass in the way. The straps pulled. The unsnapped boobs hung open like a waterlogged life preserver, heavy as cement, meant to sleep with the fishes.

"I'm OK now. I can breathe again." One elbow slid on the slick industrial sheets and I fell back against the cot fast. My arm was wretched with burns that danced along the inside of my forearm, like a fry cook after a hard night.

The nurse, maybe seventy years old, rolled her eyes like any one of the prom girls in the hotel bathroom on our Charlie Chaplin gig night. It was her own mime routine. "Got it. We'll take care of it," she said. She picked up my arm, looked at the burns, dropped my arm back down, and said, "So, you've got a few burns."

With no novelty to my injuries, I wouldn't make the medical textbooks. She unsnapped the mobile IV of the saline drip from the short piece of tube where it entered under my skin, but left the gear end of the setup in the back of my hand. "In case we have to hook you up again," she said, and turned away.

"Should we get her behind a curtain?" a preteen candy striper asked. The candy striper stretched an Ace bandage like some kind of physical therapy for the flat-chested.

The nurse shook her head, waved a hand. "No hurry at all."

The candy striper nodded, turned and skipped down the hall, her shoes a loud clack and rattle. The nurse brought a wheelchair over, but the wheelchair was routine. She said, "You'll be fine, won't you, honey? Just a little trouble you're in." She gave me a pat on one knee.

Placating clown treatment, all over again.

She unstrapped the belts. I sat up, and slid around on the Ass to swing my legs off the side of the gurney. I said, "Why do I keep coming back to this joint?"

"Some people like it here. They feel safer." The flab on the back of her arm shook like a sad fish. "They like to know help is available, to fend off a late-night fear of death. An existential dread of being alone."

Cheap psychology. "It was a rhetorical question."

"Rhetorical, confessional, fundamental—ask away," she said. "Long as you've got the coverage, I'm here."

"Coverage? I've never felt so exposed. I lost my wig, and now my boobs are flopping out." I gave one dangling boob a shake; smoke and ash drifted from it. Sand fell to the floor. I dropped into the wheelchair.

The nurse sighed, "Insurance coverage."

"Ah." Shit. I didn't. There was nothing light about insurance coverage, no joke there.

The paramedic came back with a consent form on a clipboard. The nurse asked him, "She been like this the whole time?"

He nodded. "Some kind of shock."

I wasn't in shock. I started to say that, but when I opened my mouth I said, "You think this is shock, you ought to see me when I get the bill."

Badaboom.

It was the oldest joke in the book! I was regressing. Why did I say it? Nerves. Maybe I *was* in shock—some kind of brain freeze. They left me parked in the wheelchair with the placebo IV, just the works in my hand, the IV equivalent of a fake cigarette filter, a baby's pacifier.

Rex could breathe on my burns, and they'd turn to comedy.

I got out of the wheelchair. A nurse swung by and took me by the arm. I said, "Just take the IV out. I'm done with this place."

"All in good time." She smiled and led me behind a curtain,

into a tiny room. "Let's have a chat. What drugs do you take, if any, and how often did you take them?"

A standard question.

With nothing to hide, I reached low into my long pocket. My hand came back out through a burn hole. I waggled my fingers, little puppets, then tried a second time. My blistered skin was raw and sore, the pants tight over the Fabulous Hindquarters. On the way back up, I had to hold the pocket down with one hand to keep from turning it inside out. I barely got my hand back out again, full as it was on the way up with the amber bottle. I uncurled stiff fingers and handed the nurse the valerian tincture. I said, "I take a few sips of that, and..."

She glanced at the label, sat the bottle aside.

I reached in my pocket again and this time pulled out the small pot of Chinese pills. "I took ten of these. Or fifteen." I pressed the jar into the nurse's hand. "Maybe twenty." I couldn't remember.

The nurse looked at the jar, put it on a counter next to the valerian.

"I feel great now," I said, and gave what I hoped was a winning smile, though actually I felt weak, ill and alone, small and inconsequential. Reflected in the chrome of a paper-towel dispenser, my face was a soot mask, my hair a fright wig. Except it wasn't a wig. It was my hair. Nobody offered to swab off the mask. I said, "You know, all I need is a hairbrush, a damp cloth, a tray of face paint..." I leaned closer to the paper-towel dispenser and ran a finger through the soot mixed with grease-paint caked on my skin.

The nurse bent to peer at the burns.

"A beauty salon, that'd do the trick. Or a dressing room." I said, "Bad hair day, and all those little lines and wrinkles...Think I'll be going." I made a move.

The nurse stepped between me and the curtain. "And how did you do this?" She pointed with the back of her pen at the burns along my hands and the streaks of blisters forming on the inside of my arms.

"Industrial accident, you might say. Injured in the line of duty. Working on a skit, I lit one too many torches. A little spilled turpentine."

"Turpentine and torches, at four in the morning?" she said. She wrote something down.

"What's time to a torch?" I said. "Besides, they're meant to be lit on fire." I hoped this helped my case.

The doctor came in and the nurse handed the pills to the doctor. "She took these."

The doctor put on his half-frame glasses and looked at the jar, the picture and the words in Chinese. His face was the red of a lifetime of drink, or a bad trip to Cancún. His neck was heavy with folds and wrinkles, and he wheezed like he'd just run a marathon. *Oh doctor, heal thyself!* "Why would you take these?" he asked. "You don't even know what's in here."

I shrugged. "I don't know what's in aspirin, really. I don't know what's in cough syrup, except alcohol."

He looked at me, tugged at a stray nose hair, then looked at the bottle again. "You took this before or after you burned your hands?"

I shrugged. "I took them all week. I can't tell if they're working."

"Habitual," he said, and tapped the nurse's clipboard. She made a note. He said, "What were you trying to cure, with this so-called medicine?"

"My pulse, my heartbeat. It's too strong sometimes. My heart and kidneys don't communicate." I quoted the acupuncturist and his expertise.

"Ah, communicate?" The doctor said, "Communicate with *whom*? Extraterrestrials perhaps?" He smirked.

I said, "Don't be crazy. With each other. They're out of balance."

He said, "Your heart wasn't speaking with your kidneys, so you wanted to cure your pulse. Did I get that right?"

I said, "Sometimes, Doc, I can't stand it. I lie in bed and

feel my heart beat. I feel it in my legs, in my arms, in my back. My chest gets tight, and I can't breathe." The only reason I told the doctor anything was in case he could help.

He nodded. "Cure your heartbeat...Very Edgar Allan Poe. Do you have other, what you'd call, symptoms?"

I said, "I get splitting headaches sometimes, right at the top of my head, mostly when I'm premenstrual."

The doctor nodded. "Probably a little cranial neuralgia."

"Cranial neuralgia?" I said, "What's that? Sounds serious."

He said, "Not at all. It's nerve pain, a sort of pain in the head."

Great. I said, "So you're diagnosing my headaches as pain in the head. How scientific is that?"

The doctor looked at the nurse, then at the clipboard chart. "Anal neuralgia," he said, and tapped the chart again.

"Anal neuralgia?" I said, "Hey, I can do the math. A sort of pain in the ass?"

The doctor smirked again, gave a flirty chuckle. "You're a sharp cookie. Now tell us, how did the fire come in?"

"The fire," I said. "That's another thing entirely. An accident. Juggling."

The doctor wrote in his notes, and said, "You have first-degree burns."

I said, "First degree—is that the worst, or the best? With murder, it's the worst."

"With burns it's the opposite. If this were murder, it'd be third degree." He opened a drawer and took out a small silver hammer.

He tapped my knee. My leg bounced.

I said, "Now you're giving me the third degree?"

He said, "They're first degree. Definitely first."

I said, "Funny thing is, once I was working on my second degree, a master's in Clowning, but they kicked me out of school for drinking the helium."

"You make a habit of taking helium?" He motioned for the nurse to add that to her notes.

"Doc, I thought it would raise my grades—"

This whole conversation was a mistake. But I couldn't stop. I was scared, nervous. Jittery and infected with one-liners, locked in a comic's logorrhea. The jokes were my second mistake, after handing over the pills. They were my third, if you count catching the yard on fire. But my biggest mistake was what came next: I tried for honesty. I said, "Listen, I'm a clown, this is what I do. Skits, and juggling. Sometimes it backfires." I swung aside one melon on the dangling boob suit, reached in my bra for the ever-present union card, and pulled out a small flurry of family photos. My parents on their pier, Rex in full flame. A folded napkin fell to the floor. I reached again, found the union card; it lay tucked close to my heart.

The nurse picked up the napkin. "Is this yours?" She unfolded it and read it out loud: "EKG = Nazis." She turned the napkin over and read, "Christ was a Christian clown. Work on tying Madonna."

"EKG equals Nazis?" the doctor read again. He caught the nurse's eye.

She turned the napkin sideways and read, "Every clown is Christ."

"Ah, the heart of the matter," the doctor said. The matching caterpillars of his eyebrows raised. "A Christ complex. Delusions of grandeur. Persecution." He nodded slowly. Put his reflex hammer back in the drawer. The nurse tucked the napkin in a folder, then turned away and disappeared behind the curtain.

Here's what I know now: never let a misunderstanding go unclarified in a hospital, same as in a school, jail, or prison. Never carry a diary with you, not even a day planner if you write notes in it. Don't say, "Yes, that's mine," to any odd scrap of nothing, to what might have been interesting in the free world.

The hospital, it's a gateway. The path to incarceration.

Your best bet is don't even write anything down. Ever. Most of all, don't go near the hospital unless your problem is obvious as a bullet or a broken leg, and don't go more than once. Otherwise you'll learn about a two-doctor hold, Doctor Two-Hold, a seventy-two-hour detainment—and seventy-two hours can be longer if it's late at night or over a weekend.

Two nurses came to escort me down the hall, one on each side. The Fat Ass clung to my waist like a sinker. The boobs were a yoke around my neck. We came to a set of double doors where a sign said *L-Ward*, in big purple letters above the doors. One nurse pushed a button. With a click the doors swung open. We moved through them. I heard the soft click a second time as the doors locked behind us.

"You're in a safe place," a nurse said.

Another, behind a desk, said, "We've got a little paperwork. Standard admitting procedure." They showed me to a small room with windows on three sides. The windows were blocked with cream-colored blinds. "Have a seat."

There was one chair, the only thing in the room. The Ass barely fit in the curve of the molded orange fiberglass. The admitting nurse handed me a clipboard of paperwork and a purple crayon.

"A crayon?"

"For your own good." She smiled. "No sharp edges."

I balanced the paperwork on my knee, used the back of my arm to hold a flopping boob out of the way, and used the crayon to fill in the date, my name, and social security number. "You start with the easy questions, I see."

The nurse smiled again. "If you need me, press this button." It was a silver knob on the wall. She backed out of the tiny room, pulled the door closed.

The crayon stuck against the blisters on my palms, and the whole writing kit made for big, sloppy letters. Then came the real questions: True or false. *I believe sometimes violence is justified, when a person is asking for it.*

I crayoned in, *Define 'asking'?*

True or false: *The world is against me.*

Sometimes?

A dark shape moved just beyond the windows, outside the room. I reached to part the blinds. My hand hit glass before my fingers reached the blinds, like a mime routine. An invisible box. I spread my fingers over the cool window. The blinds were on the outside? I crouched low and tried to squint through the narrow slats. The Pendulous Breasts swung forward as I leaned. I could only see bits. A security uniform. I went back to the questions:

I believe I am a danger to myself and/or others.

People can hear my thoughts.

Nobody understands me.

I worry about my health—sometimes, always, or never.

At the bottom of the page there was a handwritten prompt: *What does the following mean to you: E K G = Nazis? Please explain.* Also: *Christ is a Clown? Explain.*

"Hey," I said, out loud. "What is this? Who else read my napkin?" I tried the door. The door was locked. I was locked in. I tapped on the window. *Tap, tap, tap.* And again I was the lobster in an aquarium, a prisoner in the tidy side of hell. I hit the chrome knob to call a nurse.

The door swung open, knocked into me, and threw me back, and the sweaty doctor fell fast into the room, backed by a nurse. He said, "You have a right to request a lawyer. Would you like a lawyer at this time?"

I said, "Lawyer? What, am I being sued?"

He said, "We think you should stay here for a while. We'd like to keep an eye on you. We've decided you'll be admitted."

"Admitted?" Like a hospital was a club I'd been hoping to join.

Admitted, detained, arrested. Murmur, palpitate, flutter. Language was a thin line being drawn, the deciding factor, nothing more than a name.

"We'll treat the burns, see that you're O K," he added. "You'll get a few nights rest."

"A *few* nights?"

They didn't care about my burns. Superficial, they called them. Minor. First-degree blisters. But what this new language changed was the name of my ward. Now *E R* became not *I C U*, but *Psych*. *Psych* at the top of my folder. *Psych* on my record. Psych would be the place keeping me from going back to Baloneytown, to the house I'd rather not be living in anyway.

I saw it now: *L-Ward*. Those big purple letters over the doors. *L* stood for Loony Bin. The Mental Motel. *L* was for that barely audible click of somebody else controlling when the doors opened.

In the made-for-TV version of my life this is when I'd start swinging. I'd fling an arm back to push the guard's hand from my shoulder, lift a knee to his crotch as he lunged my way, and run down the hall, robe flapping, slippered feet slick against the shine of the linoleum. I'd kick and scream until Prozac or its next of kin showed me how much I needed the hospital's help.

Instead, I felt tiny. My shoulders were small. My arms were sick with the grip of burns. The IV gear in my hand was only a plastic tube and tape, but it felt like a needle under the skin and that thin line of plastic gave the hospital control.

I said, "No no no. No thank you." I couldn't run if I had to, with the boob suit heavy around my neck. I could only waddle; the Ass slapped my butt with each step.

"It's in your best interest."

"Interest? Lock-up? I have zero interest in being locked up." I said, "A hospital's a terrific institution—"

A nurse said, "I know, I know... and you're not ready to be institutionalized yet. That's what they all say."

Shit. I needed new material. It was a variation on a line from Mae West. "You beat me to the punch."

She said, "Punch?" and made a fast note.

I said, "You beat me to it."

She stepped back. "Beat?" She made another note.

"Rather aggressive language," the doctor said.

"I mean, you stole my lines." I peeled the Pendulous Breasts off my neck and dropped them to my hand. They reached the floor; I bent an elbow and lifted the boobs far enough to dangle.

The doctor and the nurse both jumped back. "Armed," the doctor called out. "She's armed. Security! Somebody call security."

The nurse ducked out the door. The doctor stayed between me and the exit.

"Armed?" I said. "What're you talking about? You're crazy."

The doctor said, "Just stay calm. Stay...calm." He pulled an amber vial from a deep shirt pocket and shook pills into his palm. My Chinese B B s? He swallowed the pills without water, like a bird choking down an unwilling minnow. Security came up behind him. The nurse hid behind Security.

"What's the problem?" the guard asked.

The doctor, suddenly brave with backup, cleared his throat, deepened his voice, and, like a line from a favorite old movie, growled, "Drop the weapon."

"The weapon?" I held one thing. "This?" I swung the boobs. Everyone jumped back. The boobs slapped together like massive numchucks, like a toy a psychiatrist would have on his desk— particularly a Fruedian. They poured grains of sand to the floor as they slapped and swung, and gave off a cloud of scorched polyester.

"We don't want to use force," the doctor said.

"What do you mean, armed? These are boobs. I'm not armed, I'm boobed." Another one-liner, that nervous habit.

"Whatever it is," the doctor said. "Let's not argue. Just drop the, ah, what you'd call boobs."

I let go. The Pendulous Breasts fell to the floor.

The doctor relaxed. His shoulders sagged. "That's a girl. Now we'll just move slowly, O K. We'll take care of your burns, see to your needs. And the fire department has a few questions. Soon as we get you admitted, they need a moment of your time. They're waiting outside." He slid along the wall toward me.

Beyond the door, I saw them: blue uniforms, a line of men. The fire department. I felt a cold sweat on my back, and my palms steamed.

"After you talk to the fire department, we'll give you something to help you sleep. Show's over. The curtain will drop. And it'll all be different when you wake up."

The nurse stepped in, ran an alcohol wipe over the inside of my elbow.

A shot?

"Clean up the burns," the doctor said. "Then prepare the meds." He had a file close to his chest. Written across the top, in large red letters, it said, *Possible danger to self and others.*

The firemen shuffled, impatient.

The nurse bent over her tubes and bandages. She said, "Doctor, there's a fly in this ointment."

One fireman came forward, the smallest of the pack. He moved fast in his blue uniform, and I saw then it wasn't a fireman at all—it was Jerrod. The streaks in his hair were muted under the hospital's lights, but they were still there, gleaming and golden. The lines around his eyes were more weathered than ever. He needed sleep and looked serious, maybe sad. I smelled cinnamon and spice over the antiseptic air, the apple streusel cloud of sweetness. My friend. He flashed a badge.

My only hope.

He reached for me.

"We need her downtown. Right away. She's dangerous."

Dangerous? He grabbed my arm. His grasp wasn't gentle. Shit. He pulled me forward. Something in my neck sprung with the whiplash of his yank. "You'll have time for questions." He waved to the firemen. "You'll all have a chance. She's not going anywhere. We're managing this city's clown problems. The bashing, the improv—we're on it."

"I didn't do anything," I said. "Not on purpose."

He said, "You'll have time to tell your side of the story."

I said, "The boobs! Please."

I couldn't stand to lose another thing. First my chicken, then the dog. First Rex, then our baby. First my parents, then everything else. "Just grab the boobs."

Jerrod jerked to a quick stop, leaned toward me, and whispered, "Grab whose boobs?"

"Mine." And fast as his hands came toward me, ready to comply, I pointed at the two lumps of burnt sandbags on the floor. "Not mine—those. Those are my boobs." The boobs were scorched and crumpled as well-worn paper lunch bags.

"Ah, pyromaniacal evidence," Jerrod said, loud enough for everyone to hear. He darted forward, grabbed the boobs in one hand and held me by the elbow with the other. He held my arm as we marched down the hall. The firemen got out of our way, though not fast enough or far enough to escape the jiggle of the Ass as it jostled side to side. It knocked into firemen as Jerrod pulled me past. The swing of the Ass was like two heavy hands, a gun to my back.

17.

Evidence, One and All; or, Life's Bloody Picnic

SOON AS THE CAR ROLLED I KICKED OFF MY BIG SHOES. The burns on my arms pounded in rhythm to my heartbeat. The one-liners slipped away like a winter coat I didn't need in the spring of being sprung. It's against Clown Code, or at least against my own code, to ride in the back of a cop car—don't even get in a car if the door handles don't work from the inside and the windows won't roll down—but this time the ride was an act: My Big Escape.

I hoped it was an act. I'd barely escaped. "Jerrod?"

He said, "Relax."

OK. A prisoner in custody would ride in back. I got it, that was my role in the shtick. I lay across the seat and rested my head on the scorched Pendulous Breasts, two big, leaking pillows. The seat smelled like the K-9 unit, animal and damp.

"I have a fever," I said.

Jerrod drove through the sprawling acres, the endless prairie, of the hospital's lot. He said, "You'll be fine. I'm taking you over to the evidence room."

What was that? I sat up fast. The bunched Ass held me at a cocked angle. "So now I'm evidence?" I pushed against the iron grating that separated the front and back seats, and tried to right myself. "Thought you'd take me home."

He said, "That too. Maybe. First, we're holding some evidence you'd be interested in."

"Evidence of what?"

Through the metal grating, in the rearview mirror, his lips parted. "It's a surprise."

So he had evidence of my arson effort, my Big Girl Suit, Herman's pot plants in our shed? Maybe he had the juggling torches, the turp can, a melted wig, charred grass. I was a dog on the way to the pound, the perp with the turp. "I don't know if a cop springing evidence on me is the kind of surprise I need." The snaps at the crotch of the Fabulous Ass chafed my sweaty thighs. Ash residue was like minute shards of glass caught in the elastic at my elbows and waist.

Jerrod rolled his window down.

I wanted evidence of my own bed, and a cool shower. I'd been up for a day and a half, through the fire and out again— reborn by fire, a Hopi Indian yellow clown might say. I reached inside my pants with both hands.

"What're you doing back there?"

The IV works in the back of my hand snagged. My throbbing arms were sticky with ointment. Jerrod's eyes darted back and forth in the rearview, between me and the street, me and the street.

"Eyes on the road." I tugged at the crotch snaps on the Fabulous Ass. Jerrod looked at me in the mirror again. I said, "OK, if that's how you want it, watch me pull a rabbit out of a hat. A bra down the sleeve, roast beef from a deli case." I tugged, the snaps gave, and my hands slapped against the inside of my pants. With a wiggle and a shove, I pulled the Fab Ass out past the waistband. "Ta da!" I dropped it on the floor, fluffed the burnt pillow of the Pendulous Breasts, lay across the seat, and closed my eyes.

THE EVIDENCE ROOM WAS A WHOLE CINDER BLOCK WAREhouse behind an abandoned grocery. We drove down the alley and parked in front of an unmarked door.

"This is what they call the Annex. There's Impounded Cars." Jerrod pointed to a narrow, gated parking lot between buildings.

One long white car in front had the windshield broken out and doors pocked by bullets. Walking without the sandbag weight

of the Ass for the first time in hours, I was light as an astronaut.
I made my way toward the car corral barefoot over rocky macadam,
free of the big shoes.

"I'll warn you, the cars get grisly. Baby seats, flattened roofs,
things you don't want to have on your mind." He bent to work his
key in the lock in the shadow of the doorway. "That white sedan
was a high-speed chase. Maybe you saw it on the news."

"I don't watch the news." A silver cross on a piece of yarn
dangled and glinted from the sedan's mirror; the car itself was a
white ghost.

The evidence room was huge and dark until Jerrod flipped
a switch to bring it all into full color. Everything was under plastic,
with yellow tape and orange labels.

"Check this out." He pointed to a plastic-wrapped door
that'd been taken off its hinges. "Bullet holes from both sides." He
lifted the door away from where it leaned against a wall. "A big
drug bust, about six blocks from here. That shoot-out didn't even
make the news." He held the blown-to-bits door in his hands
and dropped the weight back and forth to look at one side, then
the other. "And look at these locks." He ran his hand over
the plastic, over a row of dead bolts and sliders. "They knew somebody'd be coming."

The cement floor was cool and smooth under my bare feet.
I brushed a finger over the door's ragged metal edge, where a
bullet'd cut through. Maybe Jerrod shot one of the bullets. "Were
you there?"

He nodded and shrugged, then leaned the door back against
the shelves. "I was working."

I followed him down an aisle. "So you could've been shot?"

"Had my vest on. But that doesn't protect a guy's head,
I guess. Weed whacker?" He grabbed a plastic-wrapped bundle.

"Ah, now there's a civilized weapon," I said. "The great weed-
whacker massacres."

"You'd be surprised. But think about this stuff. It's the real
deal. People's lives, death. Yard work. Somebody could write a

book about evidence and the stories behind it." He picked up a plastic-wrapped golf club and swung, following through, then looked up toward the fluorescent lights as though watching a ball sail. "Everything turns up here." Under an opaque sheet, there was the gleam of chrome. He pulled the plastic back to show star-shaped hubcaps glossy as the liquid roll of mercury. "Your punk neighbor Willie'd love a set of rims like that."

The burns on my arms hummed with the buzz of the fluorescent lights. I was tired, bleary-eyed, and fevered. I asked, "Don't you have somewhere to be?"

"Not for hours."

We passed racks of stereos, a shelf of TVs, answering machines, and car parts. "California King." He pushed one hand against a mattress that rested against the wall. "Try it out." He dragged the mattress to an open space. The mattress hit the linoleum with a smack that echoed through the warehouse. "Go ahead. You look tired."

"Exhausted, even." I bent, ran a hand along the plastic, and pressed the plastic flat to look through for the rest of the evidence of whatever crime had brought the mattress to that ware-house—bullet holes, blood. All I found were tiny blue flowers embroidered into fabric and an ordinary white tag, the old *Do Not Remove Under Penalty*. "What's a mattress in for?"

"Could be anything," Jerrod said. "It's a pillowtop," like that was an explanation.

The mattress was inviting as a hammock. I'd been up all night. Gravity called, with its own unbreakable law. I stretched out. The mattress was solid and springy, better than a hospital mattress, better than my futon. Still, it was strange to lie flat in a warehouse without a sheet or blanket, with no right place for my hands. It felt like a visit to the acupuncture clinic before the needles started. One hand was stiff, under blisters and the IV gear taped to my skin.

It was strange to lie down in a room, a big room, with a man who wasn't Rex.

Jerrod sat on the mattress and bounced up and down. He said, "Look. You're hardly moving."

"Rock me to sleep." I closed my eyes.

I didn't notice he'd gotten up until his voice came from farther away. He said, "Maybe you need a teddy bear."

Something slapped me gently on the shoulder. I opened my eyes to a flash of yellow. Plucky, the rubber chicken! There she was, in all her glory, with her tattered red comb and the black indelible ink heart on her bumpy yellow chest, unmistakably herself, mine. Ours. I sat up and held Plucky in both hands.

"Where'd you find her?"

He shrugged, looked away, then back. "The first time I met you. On the street. Some kid dropped it, and I picked it up after you left. I tried to tell you, but you ran."

"I never thought I'd see her again." I held the chicken by her slender neck. Her yellow feet dangled, and I swear her rubber beak showed an open smile like a crow on a hot day. "You get the reward."

He waved a hand. Laughed. "Nah. It's nothing. And hang on—"

He headed down an aisle.

I sank into the mattress, curled up with Plucky, and sang her a little chicken song, all clucks and trills.

Plucky, that souvenir, me and Rex, our first real date. Our useless rubber, a shared joke. Between clowns, a shared joke is a shared prayer. Jerrod had given me a little piece of Rex back.

"Behind door number two…" The tools on Jerrod's belt jostled. He jogged down the aisle and pushed a lawn mower. I sat up. He stopped in front of Plucky and me on our raft of a mattress. "Take it home."

"My lawn mower?" I hardly recognized it. "Don't they need it, as evidence?"

"In theory, but nobody's working on the case. It's a dead end."

Herman only had a charred patch for a yard. "Jerrod, I don't want to get you in trouble."

"Sniff, trust me—take the lawn mower now, or the next time

you see it some rookie cop'll be cutting his own grass. This stuff piles up so fast, we can't keep inventory." He waved a hand at the endless shelves, then leaned on the mower like a man finished with a job well-done. The lawn mower tipped back, a bucking pony.

What to confess? "I burned Herman's yard. All the grass. It's gone."

He shrugged and tapped a foot against the blade guard. "Heard a little about that…and…" He pointed at me, my charred clothes and hair. "I'm no farmer, but don't they burn fields sometimes, to get a better crop next season?" He tipped his head sideways, half question, half answer, eyes squinted, both elbows on the mower.

"I won't be around for next season's crop of yard." I ran my blistered hand along Plucky's rubber comb. "I just may be kicked out."

He stopped tapping his foot against the back of the mower. "Kicked out? That's harsh, Sniff. Got a place lined up?"

I shook my head.

He pushed the lawn mower aside and said, "Well, take the mower back to the old Baloneyville Coop anyway. Maybe it'll be your ticket back in. If not, I've got an extra room…"

I shook my head again before he even finished the sentence. No way. I couldn't live with a cop. Rex'd never come back if I roomed with an officer. He wouldn't come within miles.

"OK, well, listen. We're not done yet. This is just like Christmas, right?" He let go of the lawn mower and headed down the aisle again.

"See you later, Santa," I said, and bounced Plucky against my toes. Her yellow legs dangled like wilted flowers. The plastic over the mattress was soot-stained now, and I pressed my blistered fingers into it. Then, from the piles of confiscated goods, there came the tap dance of toenails skittering over linoleum. Chance swam toward me. She ran down the aisle and it was a dream. My dog, in full health, coat glossy and eyes bright! Ka-zoom! She ran into my lap. My little football, she almost knocked me over. She stepped on the rubber chicken, knocked into the IV gear. I put my face to her fur.

Then I had it all again—my firstborn chicken, my baby dog, and the lawn mower. Jerrod came down the aisle with the urine funnel in one hand, like a lucky horseshoe. He put it on his head and crouched into a duckwalk. In the other hand he had a gray metal tackle box, and held the box out as though for balance. When the funnel fell, he picked it up and tossed it Frisbee-style. It skidded across the mattress and hit the end of a shelf that rattled and reverberated like a gong. I laughed out loud for the first time in, what? Decades, ages, eons? The first time since Rex left. There was such luxury in having everything back all at once.

"What more could I want? Thank you. It's crazy, better than Christmas." I ran my hand over Chance's fur. That sweet dog. "You've fattened her up."

Jerrod sat on the mattress behind me. Then we were a family on a Sunday morning in bed—Chance, Jerrod, and I. The mattress shifted. Jerrod lifted my hair away from my neck. I didn't turn, but I wanted to, to put my arms around Jerrod, hold on, and say thank you. How nice it all was! I stayed frozen. Cautious.

Jerrod ran his fingers over the thin, torn cotton of my striped pants. He said, "Give me your hand."

"Is that a proposal?" I turned toward him, safe behind a joke.

"Well, marriage is beyond what I had in mind." He opened his gray tackle box. Band-Aids rustled out. "Give me your arm then. How's that?"

I held out an arm and couldn't help but smile.

"The other one. With the IV in it."

He wrapped his hand around mine, held my hand the way he'd held it on the street the day I fainted. He used three fingers to hold the IV works against my skin and with his other hand gathered a corner of the tape. "Trust me," he said.

"You've done this before?"

He ripped the tape off fast, leaving a burnt feeling, a zap of lightning, the ache of a deep bruise, hot and sudden.

"Shit."

He said, "Now I have."

I smiled. "Just like getting a bikini wax."

"Really?"

I laughed again. "How would I know? I've never had a bikini wax. I'm a clown, not a beauty queen."

Jerrod rubbed my skin until the pain quieted, then slid the IV out. Blood ran, dark and red. He pressed against the spot and blood seeped between his fingers.

I said, "I'm disease-free."

"I believe it." He kept pressure on the back of my hand.

"And why? You barely know me."

With my free hand I helped him pull the backing off a Band-Aid. Between us, blood dripped onto the plastic that covered the mattress and mixed with soot. Evidence. Jerrod put a square of cotton against the back of my hand and drew the Band-Aid over it. He opened the aluminum package of a disposable damp cloth and ran the cloth over my soot-covered arms. The cloth was cool and smelled like baby oil.

"You're a nurse," I said. The Band-Aid tightened when I closed my fist, then relaxed as I opened my hand again.

"Just a little professional development training." He ran the damp cloth down my arm, sent shivers down my spine. "I had the chicken and that white plastic horseshoe all week. Just found Chance yesterday. But I'd been looking forward to this, to returning everything." He said, The best part of my job is when I can make somebody happy, and get it right."

It was true, he'd returned everything. Everything except Rex Galore. And the lost baby, the child I would've had with Rex. Or my parents. Nobody could bring back my family, future or past, because I was the single stalk of a failing family tree. I smelled the future the unborn baby should've had in the clean scent of the waterless wipe Jerrod used on my skin.

He said, "The whole idea behind policing is about making

the world better, but somehow, nine times out of ten it doesn't work that way."

"This is a pretty good start," I said. My voice broke, caught on a sadness that crept in.

"You're lucky the burns aren't worse."

He put ointment on my blisters. His touch was light. He unrolled gauze, started at my wrist, then followed the gauze in circles. Chance followed his hands with her nose. With each turn I felt closer to Jerrod; his hands moved up my arm, and I held my breath. He dressed the wounds, but it felt more like he was undressing me; close enough to unbutton a shirt, unhook a bra, adjust my collar. I wanted to touch his knee, his jaw, his Steve McQueen ears.

I wanted Jerrod as a medicine against the sadness.

He wrapped my arm like a long white glove. His breath on my skin was a shoulder tap, a secret hello. I pulled back to see into his eyes. He held on to the gauze and as I pulled away the wrap tightened against my skin like a Chinese finger trap.

He snipped the gauze with scissors. The tension released against my wrist, but stayed in my chest, my heart; I was waiting, but didn't know what for. He tucked the end of the gauze under another loop and his fingers brushed my skin.

"You're hot," he said.

Sexy? Fevered, more like it. I said, "Jerrod, we should talk."

He looked up then, at me, all blue eyes, and his eyes were so clear, and at the corners, those wrinkles, he was almost laughing. He held my arm, held the gauze, and equally steadily he held my gaze. With the first aid cream and scattered bandages, we were adrift in a medical picnic, the mattress our blanket in a forest of confiscated goods. My blood on the mattress between us was like seeing the back side of my skin, my insides, a secret—Jerrod had seen me inside and out, burned and in the psych ward. And still here he was, beside me. But the blood and the burns were all circumstantial, a string of bad luck, the anomaly. I didn't want to think that was me—a wreck, a mess, a mortal.

I said, "This isn't a date, you know. We still barely know each other. Right?" I added.

He worked a metal clip into the end of the gauze to hold it together, then let go. I pulled my arm back. He said, "I know a few things about you."

"You know where I live, that I have a dog and I'm a clown. That's it."

"And," he said, "I know that you faint in the heat. You juggle. You're pretty good at tying balloon things, animals, and some kind of knotted sculpture."

"Christ figure," I said.

He fit the roll of gauze back in the tin box, and stacked the Band-Aids. "What's that?"

"The one that looks like a knot? It's supposed to be Christ after the deposition." I nodded. "Crumpled on the ground. My own invention." I flexed my arm and felt the muscles shift under the wrap.

He said, "The one that's like a knot, with two balloons worked together?"

"Ah, the knot with two, that's the Ascension. Kind of looks like an octopus. All white?"

"The one I saw was blue and white." The lid of his box wouldn't close. He rearranged tubes of ointment, scissors, and packets.

"That'd be Mary. Mary at her son's feet." I lay back against the mattress.

"With the little thing at the top?" He made a corkscrew movement in the air.

"The angel, at her shoulder? That's the Annunciation. Completely different."

"OK, then. The Annunciation. That's something I know— you tie the Annunciation in blue and white." He muscled the box closed and tried to work the latch.

"Anybody who's seen my show knows that ... Wouldn't they?" I added, "If they get it."

"Could be a big 'if,'" he said. "And I know you love your dog." He moved his arm to give Chance a stroke; his cinnamon apple smell reached me through the cindered bouquet of my own skin. "That shows compassion… And I know you look great in a leotard, up for anything, and equally stunning in a fat suit. Not every woman can pull that off."

So that was how he saw me—as a girl in leotard paid to do anything. Crack's words. I sat up again. He smiled, a slight and boyish smile, and ran a hand over my good arm.

"You've got me wrong if you think I'm a hooker, or a stripper, or a heavily made-up chick in Lycra paid to do anything. I draw a line—I'm not in the clown gigs for the free drugs, or the groupies."

"Whoa, whoa!" he said. "Back up. You see me as a groupie?"

"I don't know… I appreciate you returning my stuff. It's wonderful even, but I have to tell you up front, I'm not looking to date, paid or otherwise."

"Paid?" He got up off the mattress. "Do I have my wallet out?"

He had something out. *Is that a pistol or are you happy to see me?* I held the nervous one-liner back. "Could be you're trying to buy me with favors. All I want to do is clear the air, lay my cards out, right?"

"Maybe you're not used to anyone being nice."

I said, "Nice? I'm used to nice. I'm not an S&M clown, in it for the degradation, if that's what you're getting at."

"That hadn't even crossed my mind! Sniffles, you're making some fast assumptions—"

"Well, that's the world we live in. I know what people think when they see a girl in a clown suit. With me, it doesn't apply; I'm a straight up performer, in it for the show."

"Jeez. I wouldn't think you're a hooker when you're out there tying balloons into the Madonna and Child."

What could I say to that?

"I mean, if you were tying Mary Magdalene, or a flock of sinners, then maybe…" Jerrod sat back down on the mattress. "Sniffles, I see you as a person trying to do meaningful work.

Meaningful to yourself, at least. I like your work ethic. Letting people know you're a clown takes at least as much courage as being a cop."

I looked to see if he was serious. There was no hint of ridicule.

"The way you stand up to the world, despite the clown bashings, the clown flashers..."

"Flashers?"

"The exhibitionists. The stalkers..." he said.

"Stalkers?"

"And the clown identity theft, the big-shoe fetishists... Some say it's a fool's game to wear a clown suit in Baloneytown, but the same folks probably think I'm a patsy to wear a uniform, to be the one sworn to keep this burg together. You're just like this room— everything you do, it's all evidence of who you are. You're a risk taker, wearing your art on your sleeve the way I wear my badge."

"You mean that?"

"Of course I mean it. After all the times I've seen you, and talked to you... But you're right. I don't really know you. I've never once seen you *au naturel*."

"Naked?"

Jerrod said, "You could take yourself more seriously—"

I cut in: "I do! I do! This is serious clowning. Performance."

He tapped the daisy glasses. "I'd say the Elton John shades aren't the way to show it."

"It's a paradox, I know, but I'm a serious clown."

He shook his head. "I get the feeling you're trying to hide..." He said, "This is the first time I've seen your hair. I've never seen your face without makeup."

"Is that so different from other women?"

"I don't know if I could pick you out of a lineup." He opened another packet from the first aid kit, and unfolded the white baby-scented towelette. "So, why're you hiding?" He started to wipe makeup from my cheek.

I ducked, dodged his hand. "I'm not hiding. I'm performing."
I smelled his sweetness, along with baby oil and antiseptic.

"You can't perform all the time." When he leaned in, I let
him. Slowly, carefully, he wiped makeup from under my eyes.
The cloth was cool against my fevered skin. He ran it along my jawline. My throat tightened. My eyes grew warm, like I was going to
cry, and I felt like there was something I meant to say, but couldn't
remember what.

Jerrod said, "Maybe, sometimes, I hide behind the cop
clothes too, in my own way. It's a costume, sure, but what I know
from experience is, you've got to let yourself breathe. Right?
Keep some private time. Give in a little, and relax. I don't even
know your real name."

If that was a question, I didn't answer it. Jerrod ran his
damp cloth down the side of my face.

I said, "I relax in costume." I felt more at ease when I was
close to Rex, and I was closer to Rex when I wore Rex's clothes.
The work was our work, Rex's and mine. With each swipe over my
skin, Jerrod moved me further from clowndom. Further from Rex.
I grabbed his arm. "That's enough. Don't."

The mattress crinkled. *Here it comes*, I thought. The moves,
the fetish. The kiss. I held my breath. The warehouse hummed. The
lights were bright and timeless.

He said, "OK. So show me something then."

I turned, looked at him. What did he mean?

"A trick, a skit, a sketch…" He waved a hand, as though at
an invisible stage, and so called on the Clown Code of Ethics to hold
me accountable: *when in costume, in character*.

"Fair enough." His request wasn't so different from every
kid on the street, every coulrophile and corporation, but this time
it was more than a fair trade for the return of Chance and Plucky.
Besides, I could use the audience feedback. "I've got a little something I'm working on."

I stood and found a spot on the floor in front of Jerrod.
There was an awkward moment of calling up my character, getting

into the swing. I wiped my hands on my thighs. "Don't look at me," I said, and gave a nervous smile.

"Don't look?" With a hand on Chance's back, he said in her ear, "We must have the cheap seats."

I laughed, embarrassed. "Just give me a minute, like the curtains are closed?"

He averted his eyes, hummed, tapped his hand against the mattress. He leaned back against his palms and crossed his feet at the ankles. I looked to the ceiling as though to a guiding star. Then I turned my attention inward, took a long, deep breath, stood up straight, shoulders dropped, and counted backward from ten. Concentrating on each movement, I faced my audience, Jerrod and Chance.

"Here we go." Right away my breathing was wrong but I plunged in. "This will be a brief presentation of the introduction to an interpretative version of Kafka's 'Metamorphosis'! My work in progress."

Jerrod clapped, I gave a little bow, and took another deep breath to ready myself. Then all was silent except for the humming lights. I bent my knees, as though to sit in an invisible chair. My thighs ached, my groin muscle was tight. I straightened up, broke character, shook it out. "I should clarify, it's not a literal rendition, if you know the story."

"No need to explain." He waved a hand, as though drawing me forward.

I said, "Ignore the bandages."

He nodded, settled in, reclined with all the ease of a man eating grapes and wine in the grass on a summer day.

I bent my knees again, relaxed into it, kept my back straight, and sat once more in my invisible chair. I lifted my arms, elbows out, hands poised as though to type on a keyboard. And then I typed—stiff, burned fingers and all. *Click click click click click click . . .* There was no sound, but I heard it. I cocked my head and pretended to read from notes as though transcribing. *Click click click.* The bandaged arm was hard to work with, but I did my best.

It's important to stay with an action long enough for it to sink in.
A novice would move from typing to the next phase too soon. Me?
I typed. Methodically, meticulously, each gesture articulated and
clean. *Click, click.* I leaned toward my imagined notes, squinted
at the pages, and when I reached the end of a line—because, in my
mind, I used an old-fashioned typewriter—I hit the return with a
zing! *Click, click, click!* And after a while, as I typed I slowly, almost
imperceptibly, started to hunch forward. I brought my elbows
up higher, shoulders raised. I bent my knees, swayed my back until
my rear stuck out, crooked my neck, and with the pacing of a bud
turning into a flower on a stop-action film, my typing movements
morphed from poised and efficient to pinched and harried.
I bent forward farther, brought my elbows up level with my ears,
opened my hands a bit, and soon I wasn't a transcriptionist at
all anymore, but was an insect, arms and legs frantically fighting
the air, head rotating. With a swivel, I fell on my back, trapped!
I was a bug on my back, typing or flailing, and it was one and the
same: a menial job turned into a meaningless life, a short life, the
life of an insect.

That's where the story began.

"Ta da! It's just a sample." I stood up, brushed off, and when
Jerrod clapped again I took my second bow. "There's more...but
not today." Then I added, by way of apology or explanation,
"In Kafka's story, of course, it's a man and he isn't at work, but home
in bed. He wakes up and finds out he's been transformed. It's just
more dramatic, I think, to add the action, the job—"

Jerrod said, "I know the story, and I'd say it works, this way."

"You know the story?"

He laughed at my surprise. "You think police officers don't
read."

In truth, I didn't know they read beyond speeding tickets and
incident reports, but I said, "I didn't mean it that way. What'dcha
think?" To perform and not hear how it went over, that's like
walking naked through town, worse than walking in clown clothes
even, fully exposed.

He said, "The one-person production? Pretty smart. Focused."

I never had the luxury of a grown-up audience anymore, except sometimes Rex, and now I nodded, listening, rapt. "So you could tell what was happening? The insect part?"

"Exactly! Very clear," he said. "I had trouble with the story back when I read it, because I didn't get it. I mean, why'd the guy turn into vermin? Whose fault is that? Making it a one-woman show cuts out the other characters. Streamlines."

I made it a one-person show because I had no actors, nobody who was in as deep as I wanted to be with this Kafka thing.

He said, "The way you do it, I'd say it's the character himself or, in your case, herself"—and he pointed, touched my arm—"making choices, turning herself into a cockroach, or a beetle."

Ah! My spirits dropped. Wrong audience. Jerrod wasn't in the swing after all. "But it's *society* turning him into a bug. Society is implied, by the wage slavery..."

He listened, nodded. Tapped a finger to his lips.

I tucked my knees in, leaned toward him, and said, in a rush, "...the social expectation that we hold meaningless jobs, trade time for money, humanity for a paycheck." This was a key point. Was that a grin behind Jerrod's hand? I was on my favorite terrain now, and way too eager for understanding, afraid of being misunderstood. I said, "Like the whole system, capitalism, is one big roach motel and we're all checked in, we're not getting out."

It was definitely a grin behind his fingers. Slowly he said, "Society, huh?" He said, "Well, I like your spirit, but you lose me in the logic."

Drat. Of course he didn't get it, because he was part of society, sworn to uphold society. Because he was, as I suspected, all that and middle-class too. Jerrod didn't live the way Rex and I lived, as renegades, artists on the fringe. Putting the concept in simple terms, I said, "On a deserted island, nobody would be a transcriptionist. It's a socially imposed role based on hierarchy—"

He said, "Sure, Sniff, but look around. There's acres of stuff, right?" He gestured toward shelves of appliances, toys, sports gear, and car parts. The evidence room was practically a Wal-Mart.

"What's stuff got to do with—"

"Everything here was part of a crime. And for every last bit, there's somebody who'll say it was society's fault. I don't buy it. I mean, maybe I'm just a cop, but I make my own choices. 'Society' seems like another word for a whole lot of people trying to shake responsibility…"

Fast, I said, "But not everybody has the same options. Some people are born into money, others are poor, compromised… forced to—"

He laughed then, and stood up. He bent and picked up a handful of golf balls from a bucket. "You're talking to a kid from Baloneytown. If I let society push me around, the society I lived in? I'd've been dead a long time back."

He tossed one golf ball in the air and caught it in the same hand. "I started making my own choices in grade school." He gave a second toss, one ball again. Then two, and three, juggling, and then the first ball went out of bounds, too far in front. Jerrod caught it by a long reach. The second one came down close to his chest. He stepped back, then ducked as the third fell. It was a dance, the way he grabbed out and back, arms akimbo, knees bent, and his holster danced with him; the asp and cuffs jiggled and clanked. Then I was the audience, resting on our mattress. His awkward, heavy cop dance was cute, and out of control, and he missed one ball, then a second bounced against the linoleum.

When I laughed, he said, "See? I'm a clown too—made you laugh." Fallen golf balls disappeared like mice into the plastic-wrapped evidence piles. "I have to warm up, but I can juggle, when I practice."

"I believe it," I said, though for a real juggler warming up doesn't matter. The moves come naturally.

He bounced the last ball hard against the floor. It shot toward the ceiling, came down again, flew up, and was gone to a rattle and crash. He reached a hand, pulled me to my feet, and the two of us, trailed by Chance, started back toward the door. I pushed the lawn mower.

Jerrod said, "I'm kind of a performer myself. I'm not a real big cop, right?" He held his hands to his chest and walked backward a few steps in front of me. He wasn't much taller than I was but he was solid. Strong. "Not half as big as most of the guys I go after. There's an art to being tough, so I keep my act up, same as you."

I said, "Don't forget the gun. That's a pretty good prop with the law on your side." I maneuvered the mower around a spill of electric cables in broken boxes that cluttered the aisle. Jerrod kicked cables out of the way.

"Sure, and the art is to not use the gun. It's a prop, exactly. You know what Chekhov said about guns."

That caught me off guard. "Chekhov? The Russian author?"

"Who else?" He shrugged. "In school, I read all that stuff."

So he'd read Kafka, and now Chekov too, it seemed. "They have you read the Russian classics in cop school?"

He pointed at me and said, "That, right there, is what I mean. People make assumptions. I've got an associate's in English."

I didn't expect that at all.

"Anyway, Chekov said if you plant a gun in the first act, it'd better go off before the show ends. As a cop, that means I'd have to shoot somebody every time I flashed the weapon. And that's probably about the way it goes down; a cop on the scene changes the story."

"Bingo!" I said. "Exactly!" Precisely what Herman was afraid of.

He said, "So I keep the gun holstered."

"You take law-enforcement tips from Chekhov?"

"And," he said, "I read *Crime and Punishment*. I think about Raskolnikov and his moral code when I hit the streets of Baloney-town. I read *Les Misérables*."

He was earnest and generous, and now, with literature, he was in the world of ideas—my favorite world. He held the door. Outside, morning had moved in, bright and hot. Chance blinked

into the glare. I pushed the mower over the bump in the floor
at the doorway and stepped gingerly forward. Under my bare feet
the asphalt was soft, already ripe, rich with the smell of a hot city
summer.

"Sure they won't miss the lawn mower?"

Jerrod said, "If a case comes up, Raskolnikov, I'll know
where to find you. Otherwise, forget about it." He shrugged. His
thigh muscles were tight against the blue of his uniform pants.
Golden hair along his arm glimmered in the morning sun.

I leaned over, let go of the lawn mower handle, and I kissed
him. A quick kiss. His lips were open. His mouth was the taste of a
stranger. I closed my eyes. I liked it. I liked his warmth and breath
and mouth. His hand slid over the burnt polyester of my shirt, he
held me by my arms. I half-opened my eyes, pulled away.

"Was that you, or society?" He grinned.

It was biology! Yikes. I moved out of his grip. "That," I said,
"was a thank-you. And it was nothing." I walked ahead. But
with my face turned, in the moment, tired and happy, I smiled. I
couldn't help but smile, any more than I could help the flush of
heat that crept up my neck.

18.

Death Throes of a Chicken Flock

FLOATING ALONG IN JERROD'S COPMOBILE, IT WAS THE first time I rode in front, like a cop's sidekick, like his girlfriend, like his wife. Chance climbed in back. Grit between my teeth was from soot on my lips. The seats of Jerrod's cruiser were red and soft as a new couch, an expensive bed, a boat on calm water. I tipped my head back, looked out over the long stretch of hood, and breathed coconut air freshener. Through narrowed eyes the world was a dream that tasted of soot. My hands were hot, especially under the gauze. Chance panted, her damp nose pressed to the metal divide.

Jerrod said, "Maybe I'm a cop because I've always wanted to save a damsel in distress. That's a cop's job. And Sniff, you look pretty deep in distress to me."

I opened my eyes, ran one soot-covered hand across my face. "If you're charmed by incompetence, that's just another kind of coulrophilia. Love of the buffoon."

He said, "Coulro-what-ia?"

I looked out the window. Exhausted.

When I didn't answer, he said, "One of these days, Sniff, it'll be time to run away from the circus and find a home."

"I have a home." My home was wherever Rex lived. Our own clown alley. My skin ached, the burns throbbed. But the cop car was so steady, smooth and dreamy. That cop car was like Jerrod, far as I could tell. I held Plucky on my lap. Jerrod steered with one hand. "Speaking of..." Herman's house came into view, complete with a party in full swing in the blackened pit of a yard. Herman was a mad conductor in a wild orchestration, while a swarm of people dodged his flailing arms. William was on his porch. One-Night Stan the Ice-Cream Man had his rig in the street.

In the air-conditioned cop car, the calm broke. I sat up fast. The seat belt snapped and jerked against my shoulder as though to keep me away from an accident. *Danger*.

And that seat belt was right, there was danger up ahead: I'd lose everything if I showed up in a copmobile. A seat belt couldn't save me now.

"Stop here." We moved closer. I tugged at the belt. "Stop!"

Jerrod put his foot on the brakes. The car skidded like a spooked horse on rough gravel. "We're not there yet." He let up on the brake, and the car lurched forward.

I took the seat belt off. "Stop, just stop. I'll walk."

Too late! William, Herman, and One-Night all watched the cop car from down the block, their faces round and shadowed as apple pies.

Jerrod said, "Those guys keep an eye out for police the way kids eyeball clowns."

He was right.

"A cop car couldn't get within miles, and they'd know. If you're trying to hide, I should've let you out across town."

I worked fast to put on my big clown shoes, now with the melted rubber toes. I opened the car door, climbed out, and bent low behind the open door like I was ready for a shoot-out. I swung the Pendulous Breasts over my shoulder. One sandbag boob hit me in the back. Ugh! My lungs spit out my breath, and from the crouch I fell over. I stayed low, caught my balance, and rose up enough to peer through the car window.

"See you later," I whispered, and cradled the Fabulous Fat Ass. Still crouched down, with the front door open as a barricade, I let Chance out of the back of that red flag of a cop car. The dog and I ducked and loped to the shade at the side of the road. I ran like a hunchback, with one Pendulous Breast as my hunch while the other dangled forward as a goiter. I clutched the rubber chicken and the Ass, and huddled over the bundle like I carried a stolen child.

"Sniff, your mower," Jerrod said.

Drat! He left the car running and went to the trunk. I hid near a thin tree until he had the mower out, push bar extended and wing nuts tightened down. He moved gracefully in the sun and brought the mower to the side of the road.

"Can you get all this?"

I piled the scorched Caboosey suit on top of the mower. Nodded.

He said, "If you need help, just call." I nodded again, and waved him off. He gave me a salute good-bye. The melted-cheese shoes did their own shuffle to the lawn mower's music as I moved toward the house. The rubber chicken dangled.

Herman's voice drifted down the hot street: "I don't have the reward. I don't know anything about these chickens. We don't need a dog—"

Then I saw the yellow of chickens in every hand, chicken dealers milling in the burnt yard.

"What's that about?" One-Night called over. "Police, cab service, and yard care all one deal? Some shit like that."

I ignored him.

"And clownin'," he said. "Clownin' around Baloneytown. Clownin' with the cops."

"Get off my lawn," Herman said, and gave his invisible sheet another shake. One woman laughed.

"Ain't no lawn here," a man said, slapped his thigh with a yellow chicken and kicked the blackened ground.

A girl in a polka-dot dress said, "Think we're going to trample the grass?" She had three rubber chickens, all different colors, like an act. Herman's yard was a circus. He swatted chicken dealers off like flies. They circled and settled back where they started.

Herman saw me and pointed. "There's your girl. In the

stripes. Nita, pay somebody and get 'em out of here." He spit on the ground. "It gets worse every day."

But I was a kid just home from the fair. "I've got my chicken back," I said. I held her up by the neck and flashed a smile. What did I think—that they'd cheer?

Somebody groaned. One chicken hit the ground and kicked up a cloud of ash. Then another fell, like an apple off a tree. A man pushed his way out of the group. Another followed, then came two teenage girls with a baby. One girl gave her chicken to the baby, tucked it into the blankets. The crowd dispersed. Chickens dropped to the street, long and yellow and lifeless.

Behind me, One-Night said, "Can I have that?" I turned to see a skinny woman throw a chicken at the open door of the ice-cream truck. But while the chicken venture capitalists wandered away, one man came fast down the road. He was big, in a stained white muscle shirt, and walked like he had some place to be.

Herman turned to go inside. He said, "OK, Nita, the chicken show's over. You manage the stragglers."

The new guy tapped Herman on the shoulder. Herman shook the man off like a gnat. "We don't need a rubber chicken," he said. "And we don't want your stray mutt." He hunched his shoulder, as though to shake away another shoulder tap.

"Rubber chicken, my ass." The man pulled back his fist and swung. Herman turned into it. Fist and face, they met with a crack. Herman's head jerked and his ponytail made a silky leap just as his knees buckled, his mouth opened. He went down. Clocked.

"Shit, man?" Herman tried to crab-walk backward in the ash and dirt. His hands were black, his clothes covered in soot. The red fist painted on his jaw started to swell and he worked his mouth, open and closed. "What's up?"

The man stood in the burnt dirt and waited for Herman to get up again.

I said, "Jesus, should I get the cops?"

One-Night Stan quick-shifted his ice-cream truck into gear, a fast bleat of "Home on the Range," and moseyed.

Herman's eyes went wide. "No cops," he hissed, still on the ground, a hand to his mouth.

"Bad piss." The man pointed one fat finger at Herman. "You sold bad piss. Cost me my job, my girlfriend, weekends with my kid. You think that's a joke?"

Herman, through his slack jaw, said, "Get out of here, Nita. It's not your business."

"Bad piss?" I said.

The guy said, "If I wanted dirty piss, I'd use my own."

"It wasn't dirty, man. I swear." Herman stood up and leaned to one side, then tipped the other way, a sapling in the wind.

"Joke's on me, asshole. Uppers, downers, foreign shit. Rehab, that's what they say now. I'm supposed to go to rehab for drugs I don't even know what the hell they are."

Foreign shit? My Chinese pills, the nearly empty urine jug. I put it together.

The man said, "Know how much that costs? More than drugs, that's how much. More than clean piss."

Herman rubbed his jaw.

"That's a warning, asshole," the guy said. "I won't kill you this time. I'm not looking for life in prison. But mess with me again, your ass is meat."

The man left in a cloud of soot. Chicken dealers watched from the street. The street was littered with chickens, a regular rubber slaughterhouse. I followed Herman as he staggered into the house, went right to the freezer, twisted the ice tray, and dumped ice on the countertop.

"You sold my urine?"

He put the ice in a plastic Baggie. Herman had a lot of plastic Baggies around his house. "Nita, lay off."

I reached past him, into the fridge, grabbed my orange jug, and gave it a shake. The jug was nearly empty. Again? "You gave me a urine test. That's what you did. You gave me a test and made yourself some cash."

"Nita, you're on drugs, and want to blame me for what happens?" Through his swollen jaw, behind the ice pack, he said, "Typical drug addict's lack of accountability."

"Herman, I was collecting that for a reason. For my health."

"Maybe if you'd lay off the drugs, your health'd improve. Tell you, it's the last thing I suspected, you on a bunch of shit... Listen, it doesn't matter whose fault this was. I don't blame you that guy almost killed me—"

"Blame me?" I said.

"—but here's the deal: You can't live here anymore. Find another place. I love you, Nita, but you're bad juju. We can't have it."

"You sell my urine and I'm bad juju?" I had to laugh, a bitter laugh. "You're insane. You're right, I can't live here."

I went into my mudroom. "I'll move out," I yelled. "Right now, even." I bundled up an armful of Rex's costumes and shoved them in my pink vinyl prop bag on top of my balloons, the silver gun, and the makeup. I reached up into the closet and slid down the clay bust of Rex. The sock was still in place as a cork, my savings inside.

Herman was in the kitchen when I cut through. He leaned against the counter, a smoke dangling from his fat split lip. He held the ice pack to the side of his jaw. Water dripped off his elbow and puddled at his feet. "Where you goin'?" His speech was chopped by the smoke between his lips and his frozen, swollen jaw.

I said, "Like I'd tell a urine thief my new address." I went out the side door.

He followed. My big shoes slapped the charred yard. What did I care? I kicked the ground on purpose, walked in a flurry of ash, stomped my way to the ambulance and flung open the double doors.

Herman said, "Listen, Nita. I don't want things to end badly."

The ambulance was hot inside after two days closed up in the sun. I knocked costumes and Goo Glue off the padded, backward-facing chair, and put the bust on the chair, as though that bust of Rex, with his sly smile, were an EMT ready to work.

Herman said, "We can do this in a good way."

I turned around. "You steal my medical homework, clean out my urine till, and throw me out. Think that has an upside?" I started to make a bed for myself on the cot.

He leaned against the open back door, ice pack to his jaw. In the broken voice of his thick and frozen tongue, he said, "You goin' to sleep out here?"

I didn't answer.

He said, "'at's cool."

"Thanks for the blessing, Hermes, but you don't own the street."

"No, sure don't," he said. After a minute, he added, "Nita? Listen—you kin still come in. Use the bat'room, or whatever."

I turned to look at him then. "Are you joking?"

He shook his head. Held his ice pack.

I said, "That's real generous, Herman. But know what? You should pay me to use your toilet, that's what you should do. I'd rather pee in the street."

"Nita, be reas-noble. Y'burned up the yard," he said, with his jaw still swelling further. "Almost burnt the house down. Date cops, bring people around, rubber chickens, stray dogs. I been answerin' the door all day. I got my jaw busted. The least you could do is let the urine thing go. So I sold a li'l piss, so what?"

"I'm not dating cops," I said. As I said the words, the bandage on my arm held me as though Jerrod's hand were still there. A cop. The only cop. I was burned up and scabby, in my worn clown suit, but I had the bandage and I had the memory, a moment of being taken care of. A kiss. A breath. I said, "You'd think I could put aside a little piss and expect it to be there when I got back. That's all I wanted. To keep one measly thing."

19.

Sexy Rex and the Emergency Comforts

IT WAS TIME FOR A NEW SHTICK, THE BIG FISH, THE whole schmeer that would turn my clown career around. The Juicy Caboosey show was on the back burner, literally, with the suit scorched to ruination.

My metamorphosis sketch, the Kafka interpretation—that was a good act. It was an excellent act and close to my heart, but it was complicated, subtle, and moody, not the quick break-out piece for an unknown clown. I needed something simple and fast. I was a sinking ship. The ambulance was a fine campsite but I couldn't call it home.

It was time to go High Concept.

Early morning, I left Chance in Herman's burnt-up yard and went to Hoagies and Stogies. Two bleary-eyed men were schnock-ered at the bar. John Denver sang from the jukebox. I had my toothbrush in one hand, the orange piss jug in the other hand, and my pink bag over my shoulder.

After only one day in my new digs, already I'd lost the urine-collection tray again, either in Herman's house, or perhaps aswim in the sea of costumes in the ambulance. I cut across the tavern's dirty carpet and headed for the bathroom.

Mad Addie, behind the bar, wrapped her knuckles against the counter. "Customers only, customers only," she said. Her voice was like an exotic bird, raspy and sharp. She tapped one finger against a sign on the wall: *Toilets For Customers Only*.

The old men looked up. I went back to the bar and bought a pint.

After I paid, I took the jug to the bathroom. So what if the first piss of the morning was meant to go down the drain? I'd gotten nowhere yet on my urine savings plan, and needed every drop. I crouched in the stall and used all the Kegel muscles I had to direct my piss in a steady stream into the mouth of the jug. I flicked stray piss off my hand, wiped my hand on my thigh. I brushed my teeth, then went back out, sat at the bar two stools down from the drunk geezers, and drank my pint.

"Could you put this on ice?" I asked, held up the jug and gave it a slosh.

"We're not a U-Store-It," Addie said. She tapped another sign. *We're Not a Storage Fasility*, the sign said. She dropped her smokes and cursed.

"How about a few cubes then?"

When she gave me a cupful of ice, I pushed five ice cubes one after the other into the mouth of the jug.

I took my time with the breakfast pint and waited until I had to pee again, to get my money's worth. Beer would fuel my urine factory. Why leave with a full bladder?

The tavern windows were covered with dusty red and white checked curtains. The curtains blocked the world from drinkers and hid drunks from the world. There was just enough space at the top to see the sky beyond the blue-tinted glass. I stared out the windows at the wide-open sky and tried to think big. This was still America. There had to be a way to make a name for myself, maybe get on late-night TV, or at least find a surefire gimmick to shine on the moneyed streets of King's Row.

I'd work with what I had: if religion is the opiate of the masses, religious balloon tricks would be the speedball, the crack cocaine, the glue-sniffing toxic fumes. It was time to call on the greatest of the great masters.

How hard could it be to tie a balloon version of Leonardo da Vinci's prize painting, *The Last Supper*? Everybody loves

The Last Supper. I pulled a balloon from my pocket and gave it a warm-up snap. Mad Addie leaned against the back wall and watched from a distance.

If I did this right, who knew? Maybe I'd be the next place of pilgrimage. The faithful would come from miles to see God and da Vinci work through my balloon-blowing lungs. I'd make it a salon act, for starters, small-scale and personal.

Traditionally, there's been no delicacy to balloon art. That's where I'd revolutionize things. Chiaroscuro, sfumato: I'd find a way to translate da Vinci's painterly tricks into rubber and air.

Maybe I'd pioneer a line of designer balloon colors in da Vinci's palette. Why stop there? I could have a van Gogh line, a Gauguin line, Toulouse-Lautrec and Tintoretto.

I blew the balloon halfway up and left space inside to create the right balance between air and emptiness. What could be more delicate than a composition made of air and a lack of air? Instead of leaning on the big twists—neck, elbow, waist—I'd find the small articulations, the pinkie fingers, the back of the hand, the turn of an ankle. *The Last Supper* is all about gestures.

I sipped my beer, and made the first tiny twist in one end of a yellow balloon.

Da Vinci's *Last Supper* is a tangle of bodies; I worked from memory. There were six disciples on either side, bodies clustered in a knot of infighting, power struggles, and deceit. The clustering part would be easy. Only Jesus, in the middle, stood on his own. After Jesus, I'd tie a sheep and put the sheep on the table.

Maybe da Vinci didn't serve lamb in his painting of the Last Supper, but there was room for interpretation. Jesus himself was the lamb led to the slaughter.

I tied a balloon-sheep Jesus.

Judas had to be handled carefully. I used a green balloon for envy. Art critics would understand. I was so careful with the air; I found the right balance and left room in the balloon to work. I made a tiny twist. That would be Judas's hand, laid on the shoulder of his neighbor.

I tried to remember the lean in his back, the turn of his head. I hunched over my work, and made a hundred tiny twists. The final piece would be a sculpture in the round, without what they call *frontality*—it had to work from all sides.

Where were Judas's hips, his thighs, his cock? I invented the areas that would be covered by the table. Tiny, tiny twists. I'd need more than one balloon. I had the scale wrong. What I made looked like a cluster of grapes. I took out some of the twists and started again. The balloon grew tight, the twists tricky. I wanted his foot to be perfect, full of everything Judas stood for.

And the balloon burst loud as a dropped rack of pint glasses in the morning tavern, zipped out of my hand, and whistled through the room. One old man belched. Mad Addie pushed her way off the wall like a lazy swimmer. She cut through the haze of the tavern air.

She eyeballed me, opened a drawer in the back of the bar, and took out a big black marker. She reached a skinny arm and wrote along the bottom of a cardboard sign taped to the wall: *No Balloon Tricks. No Clowns.*

Then she turned to me and tapped the words.

"Oh, shit," an old man said. His bleary eyes opened wide. "They're on to me."

I said, "No clowns? But that's your whole clientele." The other old man at the bar gave a slow, drunken stare. I said, "I see where this is going—and if fun is outlawed, only outlaws will have fun." I had to restrain myself from hitting the mechanical wolf whistle call in my pocket.

"I'm having a damn good time," Mad Addie croaked, without a smile. "And I'll eighty-six you if you try it again. How's that for an act?" Smoke trickled from her nostrils. "You're lucky to be here at all, after that pool table stunt."

I rubbed two uninflated balloons together between my thumb and first finger. My career was calling, loud and insistent. I sipped the cool, thin beer. My heart beat fast.

I'd hone the da Vinci trick until it was irresistible. Once I had a following, I'd pull out the Kafka interpretation, because that's what it was really all about—resisting a world that wanted to change me into vermin, into a madly typing secretary, all elbows and sweat on the brow. I'd been a secretary back before I found the clown circuit. Kafka was the voice of my resistance, my own religion, my grand opus.

As I stared out the top of the tavern windows, above the red and white curtains, I saw a person, a head, move into view and for a moment block the sun. Long brown curls, a strong jaw. It was a head too high up for any mortal.

Rex Galore!

Who else? Like a vision, a god, he swam along, gliding, high outside the tavern windows. He floated against the sun, turned the whole world into a stage.

I didn't mind being audience to Rex.

I left Jesus the Lamb on the bar, grabbed my urine jug, bag, and toothbrush, and ran to the door. Rex was far down the sidewalk, moving fast on a unicycle with a backpack on his back.

"Rex!" I yelled, and ran after him. The urine in the jug sloshed as I ran and the beer in my gut did the same. I ran and sloshed and ran and sloshed, and yelled again, "Rex!"

He made a tight turn on the nearly empty sidewalk, then pedaled one swipe back, one forward, one back, one forward, to balance in place, and squinted in my direction.

Poor Rex—were his eyes failing? I waved the hand with the toothbrush in it. Finally, he seemed to see me. Again I ran toward him, sloshing inside. He pedaled slowly back my way.

I laughed when we met up, my head tipped up to look up at his face. Rex cast a shadow where I stood, and he was in the glow of the sun, every split end and curl illuminated.

"Get down here," I said. I needed to touch him to know he was real.

He looked down at me and said, "What happened to your hair?"

I laughed again, and shrugged. "Oh, Rex. I burned it up."

I ran my fingers over the singed ends. I couldn't quit laughing. My hair would grow back, but everything inside, it tickled. Luscious. Delightful. My knight on his horse was home. He climbed off the unicycle. I put my orange jug on the ground, threw my arms around him, and pressed my face into the heat of his chest.

"You smell like a tavern," he said, and sniffed my burned hair. "Or a barbecue."

"Hoagies and Stogies," I murmured. The cotton of his T-shirt caught on my lip. I wanted to tear that shirt off, feel his skin. Hold him forever.

He pushed me back to look at my face. "Who're you drinking with this early?"

I smiled up at him. "Don't be jealous. I was by myself." I cuddled against him. He smelled like summer. I said, "Unless you count these two old men," and I giggled again.

"I'm not jealous," he said. "Just, I've never known you to hit the taverns for breakfast. Or solo."

I pulled the toothbrush from my pocket. "I needed a place to brush my teeth."

We walked together toward Herman's. Rex put an arm over my shoulders and steered his unicycle in the other hand. We were a family then, the three of us—me, Rex, and the unicycle, that skinny metallic child.

"Plumbing out at Herman's place?" Rex asked.

"Ah, well," I said. "No, the plumbing's not out. But we are. We're kicked out, Rexie."

He said, "How could I be kicked out? I haven't even been in town all month."

I walked along beside him and cradled the orange jug of pee in one arm. "I lost Chance, for days, but got her back yesterday. Can you believe it?"

He didn't let me change the subject. "Where are you staying, if you're kicked out?"

I said, "And I lost the rubber chicken. But look, *voilà*!" I pulled Plucky from my bag. She came out of the bag squished and folded in half, then found her shape. Resilience was the beauty of a rubber chicken.

Rex stopped walking. He put his hands on my shoulders. "Nita, tell me. Where are you staying that you can't brush your teeth?"

We were close enough to the house. I pointed down the street. Rex squinted again, like he needed glasses. "That's Herman's," he said finally.

"No, the ambulance."

"The prop room?"

I nodded. Our own little *chapiteau*, the mobile circus.

He started walking again, faster this time, without his arm around me. "So you're pregnant, drunk, and living in our car." He looked up at the sky, "It's great to be home." It wasn't the homecoming I'd expected, not at all.

I had to run a few steps to catch up with him. "I'm not drunk," I said. I reached for his arm. He jerked away.

"You act drunk."

I reached again and said, "I'm just happy you're here. I can't believe it." I was shaking, I was that happy. I trailed along behind Rex and tried to snag his arm. He shook me off. "And there's another thing, Rex. I'm not pregnant. There's no baby. I lost it." I imagined I'd look into his eyes and talk about it, not blurt the news out like a bad lunch. But there it was. He stopped. I bumped into him.

He said, "You 'lost' our baby?"

I nodded again. "Two weeks ago."

His eyes, green flecked with brown like a winter pond, were paler in the sun. "But we saw its heartbeat," he said.

That little black-and-white pulse on the ultrasound, the shrimp-curl of a head and body, the heartbeat of Rex and me alive in one creature, our future.

"I know." My eyes grew blurry. I couldn't open my mouth, couldn't speak.

Rex wrapped a big hand around my head and pulled me into

his chest. He petted my hair. I breathed in his skin, his sweat. Rex. We walked without talking. When we got the ambulance, he climbed in alongside me. I rearranged costumes and moved piles to make room.

He said, "Tell me what happened."

I said, "You're the only person I wanted to tell."

When he kissed me, his lips were everything I remembered, all of Rex in that kiss. His eyes were on me. The heat of his hands.

"It was awful. I was working a car-lot opening. Good money," I said, like I had to defend the gig, even though this time Rex didn't even flinch at the kind of clown work. And it would've been good money, if I got through without an ambulance bill.

"I didn't know anything, I've never been pregnant before, but that day I had cramps so bad I had to sit on a curb. Right away, the first second, somebody yelled, 'Hey, the clown's sitting down,' and they called the manager out of his office."

Rex unbuttoned my shirt. I let the satin fall away. The ambulance was golden where light crept in around the shades.

"It was a nightmare, Rex." I leaned into his hands.

"I'm sorry," he whispered. "Sorry you had to go through that."

"It gets worse," I said. "When I stood up, I felt something like a lot of blood, and freaked, thought I was going to faint, made a beeline to the bathroom. I dripped blood on the white showroom floor. I had to get out of this leotard, and my hair was a big pile on my head, and my makeup was a mess."

Rex put his arms around me. I couldn't get enough. "I had a rash, maybe from wearing makeup in the heat, I don't know— but I was sweating and there were all these blood clots, like big lumps of brown Jell-O, and I didn't know what they were. I put them on a paper towel, thought they might be the baby. In the hospital they said they were just big blood clots. Somebody called an ambulance."

"You should've called me," he said.

I had called him, about a hundred times. But now I

shrugged and said, "There was nothing you could do. They gave me what they called a 'procedure.' A 'D & C,' they call it."

Rex didn't even say anything about how we couldn't afford the hospital bill. He leaned his chin against my shoulder. I said, "They kept calling our baby the 'product of conception.' That's what the D & C was for—to get rid of the product of conception." I put my hand in his hand and spread out his fingers. His hands were cracked. He pressed into my bare back. I twisted, and tugged at his T-shirt. "Let me feel your skin," I said.

He pulled the T-shirt over his head.

"Pants too."

We were all elbows and knees as we wiggled out of our clothes. In the street, the ice-cream truck sang, and William called out a "Hello, what's up," while in our tiny house with both of us naked, I held on to Rex's sweaty skin and drank him in, head to toe. I'd been starved.

"You smell like summer." I pressed my nose into his warm sweat.

He laughed, said, "So that's why they call you Sniffles," as he pulled away.

I whispered, "Don't. I like it. Rex Galore Concentrate." Rex-essence in distilled form was better than valerian or pipsissiwa or any other herb. I held his shoulders and put my nose back to the soft skin of his underarm, but he only laughed.

"It's concentrate, all right. Three day's worth, one on the bus." He said, "That tickles."

"You could sell your sweat as an aphrodisiac."

"Only to a crazy girl." He had me wrapped in his arms. "And I wouldn't want anyone else to have it."

William and One-Night were a murmur of voices. A car went by.

"It's like we're in an eggshell. Like we haven't hatched, we're incubating together."

"A double yolk," he said.

Perfect. Another guy wouldn't have a clue what I meant,

would think I was weird for saying we were in an eggshell. Another guy wouldn't get naked on a pile of costumes in an ambulance on the street.

I kissed his sweat. A curled chest hair clung to my lip.

He said, "Nita, just so you know, I'm only here for a few days. I have to go back down."

"Speaking of going down..." I kissed the line of hair along his belly. His cock straightened and pointed, a long, fat finger.

Rex tried to pull me back up toward him, his hands on my shoulders. All business, he said, "For a show. Listen to this, Nita—it's an audition, held at U C Berkeley, a joint deal with Clown College. They're giving out four Emmett Kelly Awards. If I make the audition, I'd be a Community Arts Advancement scholar."

I didn't let him pull me up. "Let's talk work later."

He said, "Hey! Listen. For the application, I need an act."

I tasted all the time I'd lost, apart from Rex; it was a world, an ocean, a story in the smell and hair and skin. His hands relaxed, and he dropped back into the swirl of costumes.

Outside, a baby cried. A woman yelled, "I told you not to stay all the damn day." A second voice said, "I know, I know..."

I straddled Rex, and one of my knees hit the wheel well. The other pressed into the side of the cot. He held my thighs, gave in to me. Sweat ran down my back. We were two lizards, making love in the heat of our terrarium as the sun moved higher into the midday sky. It was nice. Hot. My cure.

Afterward, I fell asleep in that heat and it was as deep as if I'd been drugged. It was the first time in over a month that I relaxed enough to sleep. I couldn't stay awake, had to give in.

Minutes, hours, or years later, through my eyelashes I saw Rex on his knees, jeans halfway on, no underwear. He sat back and pulled the jeans up, then rocked forward onto his knees to zip the zipper.

"You're going out to piss?" I asked.

He said, "Shh, shush. Keep sleeping. You need it."

I said, "With you." I reached for his leg, wrapped my fingers around the denim.

"Come inside, we'll sleep inside," he said.

I said, "I can't. We're kicked out. Remember?"

He pulled his shirt on. "Nita, I don't think Herman'll mind if I crash in the back room. I've been sleeping on a couch for three weeks. Spent twelve hours on the bus to get up here. I can't sleep in a pile of costumes."

Rex was leaving me, again, so soon?

He said, "Don't look like that. I'll be inside. After I get some shut-eye, we can get some food or something. A beer maybe."

I pulled a purple satin cape over my naked body, part of a costume. What if he talked to Herman? What if Nadia-Italia ratted me out?

He said, "You'll sleep better without me. You can stretch out, relax..."

There was a gummy stain on the cape, glow-in-the-dark fake skin that melted off during an act. I picked at the spot like a scab, and said, "Don't go. Please. Just stay." I wanted him with me and I didn't want him mingling and the moment was crucial.

He climbed out the back doors. I rocked forward, onto my knees, following him as though caught in his wake. A kid rode a bike in the street. I pulled the cape around me more tightly, the satin a cool skin. "So what—you'll live inside, and I'll live out here?"

He straightened his shirt and ran a hand through his hair. "It's only for right now, Noodle. We'll get our own place. Here, or in San Fran. Whatever."

I hugged the satin cape, wiggled my toes. "When?"

"When we get the money. After this Berkeley gig, when we hear back from the school, see if I'm in, and if they give me a little scratch. Then we'll know what we have to work with, OK?"

I patted the costumes beneath my bare ass. "Just get in here. Sleeping doesn't take money."

He said, "Nita, I've been on the road all month. I need a bed."

I was out of options. "Well, when you're in there," I said, "avoid Herman. And Nadia-Italia. She's nuts. Totally unreliable." It was all I could do.

"Thanks for the warning." He turned toward the house, saw the yard. "Hey—what happened?" The scorch.

"Don't ask. A real sore spot with Hermes... Nothing you want to bring up, right?"

Rex started to let the doors drop closed. Then I could only hear his voice, see one hand that still held the door. "Are those my maple juggling torches?" he said. "Like, toast?"

I pretended not to hear. I called, "Rex?" He pulled the door open and came back into view in a reprise, the Rex Galore Show. I said, "Can I go with you, when you go to the Berkeley gig?"

He put a hand on my ankle and rubbed my shin. His hand was muscled and strong. "It's expensive, Nita. If you come down for a visit, how're we going to save cash for a real move?"

"Earn it. That's the easy part." I'd been working since I was fourteen.

"We have to take it one step at a time. Think of now as an investment. I'll go down, get the scholarship, and then we'll put the other pieces in place."

One door fell closed. Again I leaned forward and said, "Rex?"

"Yes?" he waited, with the second door half-closed, his fingers curled around the door, part of his face still visible. Behind him a woman parked her car.

I said, "We're doing O K, mostly. Right? Because we're in it together. The clown stuff. We'll get where we want to be."

Rex nodded and squinted in the sun.

I said, "Promise me you won't talk to Herman. And if I need anything, from in the room, I'll come knock on the window. You could pass things out, right?"

"Sure. I'll pass things out." He bent toward me, gave me a kiss, then let the ambulance door swing closed.

20.

Sliding the Slippery Slope

THE AMBULANCE WAS AN EMPTY HULL, A WOMB WITHOUT a baby. I lay naked on the costumes, arms and legs heavy in the heat. I was a body but not the baby in the ambulance's womb; I was fetal tissue, placental residue. The satin of the purple cape draped over my belly, soft and smooth. Voices sang like birds up and down the block. I tried to sleep. After a while, I heard the low cascade of Rex's laugh not far from the ambulance window. He was outside?

I earned a new place in heaven anytime I made Rex laugh like that, low and for real.

So he was coming back to the van? Maybe he was ready to hang out. Ready to let me wrap my leg around his under the table in an air-conditioned diner. I pulled back the shade. Rex was on the porch, his bag at his feet, and the unicycle lay across the walkway like he hadn't even been inside yet. He talked to a skinny little joker in a striped tank top. The guy had his back my way. Rex stood, legs wide, and balanced a single scorched juggling pin upside down on the palm of his hand. Rex's face was open and animated, eyebrows moving. The other guy was in black cutoffs with big boots, white legs and a bowler hat.

But wait a minute—it wasn't a guy. Those were Crack's bandy legs! The bowler was from our Chaplin routine. She and Rex yukked it up on the porch, and Rex leaned against the rail like he had all the time in the world.

I fished around in the costumes on the floor for something

like clothes: a velvet robe, gigantic yellow pants, a chef's hat that wouldn't do at all. I wanted Rex to look at me, but not like that. I kept fishing. Outside, Crack waved an arm down the street, maybe told a story. Her voice moved up and down with muffled words. Rex listened like it mattered.

I found a red sequined clown dress, pure wrinkles, three sizes too big, with sequins missing in a patch on the ass, and an orange ruffle around the neckline, but at least the dress was somewhere on the road to sexy. I slid the dress on and tied the straps together in back with a scarf to make it fit.

I gave myself a hit of powder, a dash of eyeliner, and just as I drew the makeup brush along the curve in my lower lip, almost ready, there was a knock on the ambulance's metal hull in three hard, echoing raps: *Ka-chung, ka-chung, ka-chung.*

The walls reverberated. I jumped! My hand drew a red line across my cheek. Shit.

The knocking started again, *Ka-chung, ka-chung, ka-chung.* I rubbed my cheek with the butt of my palm. The back door swung open. Sunlight cut in, and against the sun was the silhouette of Crack in her bowler.

"Yoo-hoo!" the silhouette said. "My little blessing in disguise. All gussied up?"

"It'd be a whole lot better, next time, if you knock on the glass." I tapped a knuckle against the window to show her how delicate a sound that glass made: *ting, ting, ting.* "Like a door chime."

She slapped the side of the van door again. *Ka-chung.* I wiped red makeup off the side of my face. She said, "You look great, but a day late and a dollar short. Where've you been?"

"Me?" Since when did Crack care where I'd been? I said, "Well, I was at Hoagies and Stogies, and then I ran into Rex...and we were here—"

She cut me off. "One job. A piece of cake." Slowly, annunciating as though I had to read her lips, she said, "All I asked you to do was show up. Is that so hard?"

"One job? Ah, crapsters! I forgot." After the photo shoot, she'd thrown the job at me. Ages ago. "I never wrote it down."

"And whose fault is that? I promised 'em three girls, they got nothing. Except me. I count for, like, maybe half a girl. But I did my best, put on something pretty."

"Matey didn't show?"

"Matey's off the scene for a while. A broken arm. Clown-bashing, she says, if you believe that for a minute."

I said, "I'm sorry, Crack, really."

"Sorry doesn't cut it in a small town." She shook her head. "The clown business runs on reputation. That's one word-of-mouth job that won't come our way again."

"So it's one job…" There was a time, before I met Crack, when one job could be my whole month's income.

"Right, and they tell two people, and let's say those people hire somebody else for their next bash and we lose how many more contacts by not being at that gig? It's about face time, Sniff. Business."

I said, "Look, I'm sorry—"

She cut me off. "Personally, I don't care how you feel. I care how you work. In my circus I need all fools on board, especially until Matey's up and running again. But look, see? I'm done lecturing, ready to deal: here's a way to make it up to me, and make it up to yourself cash-wise at the same time. Two guys, they want a clown date. You and me."

She knew exactly what I'd say. "Crack, I'm not a hooker."

"Could've fooled me." She tugged on my orange dress. "Finish your lips, girl, you're good to go."

I leaned into the mirror to finish my lips, but not for Crack. A quick glance out the side window showed me Rex had gone inside. I said, "I'm an artist, a clown artist. It's about art, not sex."

"It's about money, and ego. Don't kid yourself."

It was about Rex at the moment and, yes, Rex and me, we needed money. I gave my burnt hair a fluff.

"Listen, I'm not asking you to blow the guy, just spend a little time. He's a fetishist, and there's cash in it, no joke."

"No sex?" I said. "I don't believe it for a minute."

"No sex and big cash." Crack drew an X across the front of her striped tank top. "Cross my heart, or whatever God gave me in place of a heart." Her voice boomed. She blocked my exit. I was a rabbit in a pen, a raccoon in a trap. "For the guy, it's the same as sex just having his fetish catered to."

"Like, how big?" I said.

"How big what? It's not like I checked out the guy's goods— he hasn't ponied up the bills yet." She hooked her thumbs under the armholes of her tank top and gave a snap.

"I don't want to see his goods," I said. "I mean, how big's the cash? What kind of money?" The more fast money I made, the sooner I'd surprise Rex, impress him with a bankroll, and the sooner we'd start our life together.

I needed to get Rex out of the neighborhood before he found out more than he wanted to know—or more than I wanted him to know.

Crack said, "I tell you, the guy's giving money away. We'll get one rate up front, get him to buy a few drinks, then renegotiate scratch as the night goes on... No lie, Sniff. What's this about?" She poked a finger into the scorched mound of the Pendulous Breasts.

I shrugged. "That? I call it the Juicy Caboosey Show. Still working it out." The outfit needed a few patches after the fire.

"Well, hey, why save it for the opera?" she said. "The thing is, there's no money in art, but there's an art to making money and it's in my blood. In yours too, I'd say, with the Caboose Suit. You just ain't actualized yet. Stick with me, I'll show you how."

If it was enough money, it could be my last gig with Crack. I'd cut her loose. "OK," I said. "But those are the rules: no sex, and a big paycheck." Then right away I changed my mind. Who was I kidding? A clown date was all about sex. They always were. I said, "No, I can't do it. I don't do dates. I have to draw the line..." I said, "Never, never, never."

I was an artist.

Crack said, "Listen, it's an easy deal. I'm cutting you in, and I'll say it frank here—you got one thing I ain't got, and that's natural good clown looks. Guys like it." She said, "So you know those old buildings at the edge of King's Row?"

The Ruins? Our Ruins. A private place made public, or perhaps a public place made private in my mind and memories. "Sure."

"Cool," she said. "Meet us there tomorrow night, nine o'clock. He's got a big green van."

A big green van, at The Ruins. And nothing would ruin them more than a cheap clown date in the place of my grand romance. I wavered: "I can't do it, Crack."

"It's easy. Just look sexy, play it up, something like you got on now, maybe. Oh, shit," Crack said. "I hate to be the hair-bringer of bad tidings, but…"

"Harbinger," I said. My dress fell off one shoulder. I pulled it into place.

"Who?" Crack asked. She ducked behind the open ambulance door, and looked through the frosted, cross-marked window.

I said, "You said the hair-bringer. It's harbinger."

"Harbinger's the hairbringer?"

"No, you'd be the harbinger. Harbinger of bad tidings."

"I don't know about that, but what I'm getting at is, bad news—a cop, at six o'clock, heading our way. We'll talk later." She hid beside the open door.

I stepped out of the van, one bare foot at a time, and a pile of clothes followed, stuck to my hot skin. My knees were numb from kneeling. Tucked beside Crack, I peered around the side of the open back door. It was Jerrod, urine funnel in front of him like a white plastic shield. He turned where the sidewalk met Herman's crumbling cement walkway and went right up to Herman's house. That was the last straw.

"I know that guy," I said. I had to stop him. "I'll do the gig."

I needed the cash, to get life moving again. There was no more time to waste as a trapped rabbit. Berkeley, here we come.

He was about to knock on the door. How could I insist I wasn't dating cops if Jerrod asked for me by my clown name? "Jerrod."

He dropped his hand and turned, looked surprised, flashed a smile and sauntered over. Crack and I were kids in costume playing in the street, the ambulance our toy box. Jerrod tapped a light *hello* on the side of the ambulance. It sang like a bell.

"You must be Harbinger," Crack said. She tipped her hat. "And I must be going. See you later, Sniff. Good luck." She ducked out.

Jerrod said, "Who's your friend?" He pointed toward Crack's fleeing, striped back.

I took the urine funnel and threw it over my shoulder into the mess of props. "Jerrod, what're you doing coming around here? It's not O K with my housemates."

"Well, last I checked this was a city street. As a cop, it's my job to hit the streets." He showed me his open hands, Mr. Innocent. "Besides, you left your halo in the car. Thought I'd bring it by."

"I'm serious. You can't knock on my door, carry my stuff around..." I picked up a handful of fallen scarves, an errant feather boa.

"So they didn't kick you out..." With a palm to the doorjamb, he leaned into the ambulance, took a look around. "You got a great setup right here. Who needs the house?" He picked up my purple satin cape and swung it over his shoulders. Superman.

I reached to take the cape back, moved in close just as he handed it over, and our fingers brushed. Sparked. Silently greeted. I pulled my hand back, bundled the cape, looked away. I didn't tell him that I already lived on the street, slept in the ambulance, broke a vagrancy law every night. Instead I said, "I'm in a tenuous situation here. Your presence? It doesn't help."

Jerrod said, "Sniff, you've got to recognize it—you're not in jail."

Not yet, I thought.

"You can choose your own friends."

Fast, I said. "It's the cop thing."

He said, "I'm not always a cop. Right now, I'm off duty." He reached to fumble with his badge.

I kept an eye on the house and folded a long scarf into tiny squares. "You're still in uniform, and even if you weren't…"

Jerrod watched me work. He said, "What about you—are you working now, or just favoring the clown wear?"

I hoisted the fallen shoulder strap of my big red clown dress. "Doesn't matter, I'm still a clown, same as you're still a cop, on the job or off. And clowns, cops…We're from opposite sides of the tracks."

Jerrod said, "Sniffles, if it's what you want—and not just what your friends want—then fine. I'll walk the other side of the street, but you could stand to look past the costume, the police work…When I see you in clown clothes I know there's more." He nodded toward the house. "That's got to be worth something."

"Of course it is, but… Just go on. Walk your beat. There's nothing to see here, right?"

"Except you," he said.

The front door of Herman's swung open. Rex stepped out. Rex! My savior. This was my chance to clear things up, maybe introduce the two of them, make it known who was my man.

"Rex!" I called. Rex, my king, took one look at Jerrod, and his whole body jumped. His shoulders tightened. Even his curls tightened. With a fast step backward, he went inside and slammed the door.

Rex was scared?

Jerrod didn't flinch, but stayed strong and steady. "See that?" he said. "Still think you're the only outsider on the block? I know what it's like to walk Baloneytown in costume all day. I get the stares. People run. Hide. They drop their plastic whatever-that-is." He tapped the urine-collection funnel. "Or else they come at me with expectations. Either way, let's just say I don't get many dates …"

He said, "People don't see me as a guy, doing my job. They see the job." He pulled a loose thread on my oversized dress. "I understand more than you think."

Inside, Herman's shadow moved past the living room window. Sun hit the glass. The orange curtain gave a flutter, and my heart did the same. Rex was hiding, peering out, watching me talk to a cop.

Rex, rendered audience.

Over Jerrod's shoulder the orange curtain dropped, as though a play had just ended, an act over. Rex's act. The one I was meant to star in. I didn't want it to be over! Rex and me, we had a whole show ahead of us, a life. Jerrod touched my arm. I held my breath.

21.

Granulation and Ruination

SO I'D DO ONE INNOCENT CLOWN DATE FOR THE MONEY. No sex. Then I'd top off my savings, follow Rex to Berkeley, and move into the art-clown life happily ever after. The date, Crack, and corporate clowndom would melt into the gentle fog of a bad dream.

In the Ruins the van loomed in the dark like a rocky cliff, the precipice I'd soon throw myself over. I wore the top half of the patched Caboosey suit under the red sequined dress. It was a quick patch job with electrical tape, for the occasion. I stepped one teetering, clown-style Manolo Blahnik knockoff into the loose sand of the open lot. The Pendulous Breasts jiggled. The van door slid open and Crack tumbled out, a bottle in hand, as dust danced in the twilight.

"Here she is!" Crack called. "Our clown lady of the evening."

"I'm not a *clown of the evening*," I whispered, maybe only to myself. "I'm an artist," I said louder, to the open lot, as though to convince the world. Then I tripped on a piece of rebar, snagged my dress, caught myself with a hand to a cinder block, and skinned my burned palm.

"Yes," Crack said. "Our artiste, star of the show!"

Behind her, a bouquet of pale blond hair cut into the moonlight; a man climbed from the back of the van.

I straightened up, stood and brushed off as Crack came forward, took me by the hand. She passed me the bottle. The bottle was hot at the neck from her clutch. Freixenet.

"Meet your date, Rich Johnson." She waved a hand. "Rich,

meet Juicy Caboosey." She slapped me on the rear, hard enough to knock me forward and toss champagne from the bottle's mouth in a moonlit gush.

"Hello there, Juicy!" His voice was low. His suit was nice, well-cut and dark.

"Rich?" I said. "That's his name, or his tax statement?"

He laughed. "A regular Mae West, just what I ordered."

Ordered. I didn't like the sound of that.

"To you, that's his name," Crack said back, fast. She gave me a wink, clown sign language for *Don't Ask*.

The man had a narrow chin, ruddy cheeks, and eyes that were too vacant. He seemed familiar, like I'd seen his pompadour and ruddy cheeks before. "I know you, don't I?"

He chuckled again, nervous this time. "Strangers is better," he said, and tugged on his shirt cuffs.

Of course—coulrophiles always preferred the anonymous thing.

Crack whispered, "Don't blow it, Sniffers." She wrapped her arms around my neck, gave me a smooch on the cheek like some kind of staged lesbo clown moment, and it was all an act until she hissed in my ear, "Play it right, in twenty minutes it's over and you'll be the richest joke in Baloneytown. No kidding."

She laughed loud and fake, like our powwow was one big party. One big lie. Rich looked over his shoulder, gave me a profile view of his long nose, sharp chin, and then the flash of teeth, and in that flash I remembered exactly where I'd seen him—the hallway, outside the Chaplin gig. Old Blondie. He'd done his hair differently. And at the street fair, the day I fainted, hanging around with another pompadour altogether. He wore his hair like a costume, but it was the same guy. This was no generic clown date, it was personal. I folded my arms across my chest, held the bottle of grocery-store bubbly against my hip. Crack took my hands, as though to loosen me up.

She whispered, "Plan to be a party pooper or a party trooper? We've only got room for troopers around here. I need you on board." She straightened my dress. Plumped my fake cleavage.

With her face close to mine, I whispered back, "Why didn't you tell me?"

"Tell you what, Clownster?" She reached for the warm champagne.

"You set me up. We know this guy—he's practically a stalker."

"We don't know him. He's a date. You're dating, right?" She turned away. I followed her toward the van. A second, shorter man spilled out the open van door, his hair pressed tightly to his head like a stocking cap, then I saw it was a stocking cap. Crack reached for his hand. She'd take the little guy, and leave me with Mr. Blonde and Blow-dried.

I wasn't ready to pair off yet. "Can we talk?" I asked her.

Crack looked to Rich, his hair bright and pale as a streetlight. She looked back to me. "You and me," she asked, "or, like, talk as part of the show?"

A date wasn't a show in my book. I said, "You and me, alone."

Blondie shrugged, gave the go-ahead. Crack and I walked into the dark.

I said, "I can't do it, Crack. It's too hookerish."

She said, "It's a piece of cake. Let him do all the work. All he wants is a brush with fantasy, maybe to cop a feel of your plastic hair. These guys, they're a dime a dozen and simple as flapjacks, no joke."

"But why this one? He's seen our shows. I don't want to be in his high beams."

Crack shook her head. "He's been to our gigs, so what? He likes what you put out."

"Put out?" I said. I felt the blood drain from my face.

"What you offer, I mean. You don't have to put out."

My mouth was dry; my mind broke out in a rash of panic. "Feels like I'm cheating on Rex. It's not good. I love Rex, and he trusts me." What I didn't say was that it felt like I was cheating on art too. Cheating myself.

Crack laughed then, and not her bitter or fake laugh, but a deep belly laugh, loud and for real. "Oh shit," she said. "You're still hung up on Rex? And we thought Matey was the sadomasochist in the group..."

"Hung up?" I said. "We're in love."

She said, "Sheesh... Good old sexy Rexie back in town, and you're his puppet all over again. Don't think Rex hasn't had his share of clown dates."

My heart was a knotted balloon then, a stopped watch. "What do you mean?"

She said, "That old rubber-chicken routine? It's a classic. Hell, even I fell for it way back when." She slapped an arm over my shoulders. "How do you think he paid for that fleet of unicycles?"

"What are you saying?" Her arm was heavy across my back. I tried to shake her off, the way I wanted to shake off new information, the possible truth.

"Don't be shocked, little Sniff. You make too big a deal of it." With a gentle pressure she steered me left, and then left again, and we made a U-turn until we walked toward the van. The men were outside tipping bottles back. Crack said, "Get in the game, give it a good play. If you don't want to do it again we won't. My word."

I was numb. Rex and the rubber-chicken routine? What did she mean? Plucky. Plucky the chicken, who was even now in my pink shoulder bag. How many clowns had Plucky been with?

"Call the shots on the date," Crack whispered. "Do what you're comfortable with, and no more." She dropped her arm from my shoulders. "I got the down payment, but set your own prices as you go, and make sure you get cash before it's over."

I teetered in my oversized heels, across chunks of broken concrete.

"You get the clubhouse. We'll find our own space." Crack grabbed the short man by one of his thick hands. I watched their backs as they climbed over a pile of broken joists, then disappeared into the dark.

"Come on in," Rich Johnson said from the dark cave of the van.

I was there to do a job—not a hand job, not a blow job, but the same logic applied: the faster we got started, the sooner it'd be over. I hitched up my dress. Sequins fell and glinted against the ground, caught in construction debris. I took his hand. His palm was damp. In one big step, I launched myself into the back of the van. He reached to close the door behind me. I intercepted with my elbow.

"Like a tab, let's keep it open, right?" A quick exit route.

He shrugged. "It's your show." I liked the sound of that. My show. Then he said, "Besides, there's nobody out here. Just you and me. And I thought clowns didn't talk."

He put a hand up as though to cover my mouth and winked. That I didn't like, but it was part of the fetish: muteness, not mutiny.

He spit out the side door and popped the cork on another bottle of cheap champagne. The cork hit the side of the van like a bullet. I ducked. My ears rang. He sat hunched, a vulture, on a narrow, cramped wooden bench that was attached to one curved wall inside the van. He patted the plank beside him.

I crouched on the wheel well. He held a plastic champagne glass my way, pulled it back and tipped it toward his lips, then raised his eyebrows in his own little act meant to be a question: did I drink?

I fanned my hands in front of the Pendulous Breasts and pushed the air away, a flutter of sign language to say *no no no*. The breasts crowded my knees.

He dropped the plastic glass, took a swig off the bottle, wiped his mouth with the back of his hand, and murmured, "Juggle something." He rolled an old beer bottle toward me.

I didn't reach for the bottle, but dug in my bag for juggling balls, then chicken-walked toward the open door and dropped a foot outside.

Rich snagged me by the dress. "Ho-no! The act stays onstage."

The dress stretched like a bungee cord; sequins sprang like fireworks while I hovered between the fresh breeze and fetid air.

I pointed at the ceiling, a pidgin version of clown sign language: too low to juggle.

"Let's see," he said. He pulled me deeper into the dark corner of the van, wrapped his arms around me, and slid up close behind. We were both on our knees, against the matted carpet. Something on the floor cut into my kneecap. "I want to feel your jugs while you juggle," he said, and his breath was a death wheeze. "Get it? Jugs and juggling? I always think of that. Since I was a boy at the circus." He ran a hand over the Pendulous Breasts.

He had me in a tight squeeze. I tossed one ball, tried to lunge for it but couldn't move. The ball hit the side of the van, rolled, then nested in a carpeted corner.

He hiked up my skirts. I tried to wriggle out of his arms.

"Why the resistance? I've got money." With one arm still around me, he pulled a wallet from his pocket. The wallet flipped open. He shook it like a kid pretending the wallet was a seagull, and the gull dropped bills. He laughed as dollars drifted.

He undid his belt and his pants fell all too willingly down around his knees. Rich whispered, "Feel my big balloon dog." His breath was murky with the smoke of old pot and soured champagne. He rubbed himself against my thighs. I fell forward under the pressure of his weight, onto my hands on the loose bills scattered on the dirty carpet. "Feel it?"

I could feel it. I nodded, and broke a rule as I said out loud, "Is that a big balloon dog, or a whoopee cushion? Maybe someone forgot to inflate—"

He said, "Hey—*sh sh sh*. Just give it to me, Juicy," and he rubbed himself against my underwear. He twisted my Pendulous Breast nipple, except it wasn't a nipple. It was electrical tape that came off in his hand, and the scorched threads gave in. Sand rained down.

He liked it! He said, "The lactating clown act! My lucky day. Lucky, lucky luck."

Under my breath I said, "More like granulating."

He grunted and thrust, and said, lucky, lucky, lucky. All that separated us was one thin panty line, my cotton underwear, and I was so glad for that thin line as the final line I wouldn't cross. Lucky, lucky… He slid his fingers inside my underwear.

He crossed the line.

All I could think of was escape. I didn't want his little roll of nickels in my pocketbook. He moaned, sweaty, fingers prodding. My skin was up against Rich's skin, and he felt like a rubber chicken, and made me think of bitter blood and feathers barely plucked. The closer to his skin I got the more I thought of dimestore buffet lines, processed ham and margarine and all the fake food I wished I'd never eaten. Rich was a squealing ham sandwich, a spoiled fake milk trick. And whose fault was this—mine, or society's? Kafka's or the cockroach's, the audience's or the director's? I was the only one there; I couldn't go on with the date. I caught Rich Johnson by surprise and threw him off. Ta da! I scrambled, and fell out the side of the van.

Voilà!

"Juicy," Rich said. "Don't go. Not like that." He lunged. We wrestled on the dusty ground, over broken cement. The sequins in my dress were tiny claws.

I said, "I'm done. I can't do it."

He sat up. I rolled away, brushed myself off. We were both breathing hard—maybe for different reasons. He ran a few fingers through his high pompadour. He looked tired, a little puffy-eyed, older than he'd been only minutes before. He said, "Look, you, I'm in this for the fun. Helps cut the tension of a big work-week. Like the ad says, a good time. No joke. But if you're not with me—at least let me pay up."

Paying is half the fetish for some of these guys.

He grabbed a handful of bills from the van floor; three spotlights swung over the area. Like the opening to a big top three-ring hoopla, lights circled and danced, made shadows against the fallen walls until they found their way to all point to the same place: Blondie and me. Front and center, main ring, playing to an audience of cops.

Money fluttered like the drift of confetti.

"Stay right where you are," a voice boomed across the Ruins.

One remaining Pendulous Breast hung out like a Cyclops. The other was a drained sack.

"Nobody move!" the voice said. "This is an arrest."

Rich put his hands up like he knew the ropes. I followed his lead. We squinted into the glare. Cops came over the edge of a low, broken wall. One stumbled.

"Jerrod?" I said, hopeful, nervous, in need of a safety net. There was no answer, no Jerrod. No friendly officer waiting in the wings.

THE CHARGES: SOLICITING SEX, SEX IN A PUBLIC PLACE, trespassing, indecent exposure, and no proper ID.

Down at the station, I said, "Indecent exposure? These boobs are fake."

A woman cop, filling out forms, said "Many are. Doesn't make 'em legal."

I pulled my sweaty clown ID from inside my bra. The stack of family photos fluttered out, and there were my parents. I grabbed for the photo fast and tucked it back against my skin, didn't want my folks to see me at the cop station. I pushed the clown ID across the desk. Nobody would touch it.

"State-sponsored ID," one cop said. "Put that joke away, cupcake."

I said, "I'm not a hooker, I'm a union-registered, dues-paying clown. The ID proves it."

The woman writing up the paperwork said, "Clown, hooker—are the two mutually exclusive or redundant?"

"Or oxymoronic," I said. "Ever think of that?"

Somebody snickered, in the sidelines. The woman cop said,

"O K. Say you're not a hooker. What's the story, just all dressed up with no place to show? Lonely and looking good?"

Another cop, passing through, said, "So how come clown whores make so much money?" He face was blotched and red, his ears big. His neck…well, he had no neck. After a moment's dramatic pause, complete with wheeze and whistle, he said, "A trick up every sleeve. Ha!"

I said, "You're about as funny as a cry for help."

"My pleasure." He went back to huffing and puffing his way across the room.

I said, "This is prejudice. You don't like clowns, I'm a clown, and I'm getting the shaft."

Another cop leaned in close. He said, "Righto…We don't like clowns. We don't have to. We put up with a lot a trouble from clowns around this precinct."

I asked, "Where's Crack?" She'd been in the Ruins too, on her own paid date.

The cops looked up from their paperwork shuffle. Eyebrows raised. A few met each other's glances. One guy said, "Come again—what're you looking for?"

I said, "Crack. My boss."

They all laughed, together, leaving me adrift in a sea of heads tipped back, hair tossed, flabby chins. A woman tried to catch her breath long enough to say, "So what's your official title, 'Crack Whore'?" She broke herself up again.

The fat man with the circus jokes said, "First crack whore we've seen that admits it up front."

"I'm not a crack whore! I'm a clown. I work for Crack, my agent."

They laughed harder. "That's rich, that's rich. Will work for crack. You got a sign proclaiming that?"

I said, "Speaking of Rich, where's he?" They'd taken him down a hall. For all I could tell, they let him out a back door. The money was gone, confiscated as "evidence" or spent to buy his freedom.

"A clown crack whore," the woman said. "We don't get many of those through here." She shook her head.

I said, "It's not a crime to be a clown."

"Ah, Jerry! Get a load of this one," the woman called out.

Jerrod walked through the room, hands full of manila files, with a giant peanut-butter cookie on top of the stack. When he saw me he looked twice, tripped against a trash can, and did a stumbling dance. The cookie slid across his files, dropped, and broke.

"Shit." He ran a hand over his forehead.

"Check this out," a cop called.

"I'm busy," Jerrod said, straightened up and kept going. Crumbs lay in a circle on the floor, a mini crime scene.

"Jerr," the woman cop called after him. "You OK?"

He didn't look back.

WHEN I COULD, I CALLED REX. REX WOULD BAIL ME OUT. He'd know I was innocent. We'd get the charges reduced in court—I didn't need Jerrod's help. They left me in a holding cell big as my mudroom, only air-conditioned, with a cot and a view of the hallway. It was good as any room at the YMCA.

After forever Jerrod came by. He cleared his throat. Nervous and jumpy, he said, "Well, I want to apologize. I was wrong… It was presumptuous, to think I understood anything about where you're coming from."

I said, "What do you mean?"

He said, "I thought you were different."

I was different. "This is not me, not here." I pointed to the floor beneath my big clown high heels.

He looked into my eyes. I took a breath. We both knew the question left unasked: if this wasn't me, who was I? He touched my hand where my fingers rested around the bars. I pulled my hand away, didn't want to touch anybody.

"Society?" he said.

I didn't answer.

He said, "I can't get you out of here. Couldn't if I wanted to. Maybe if I'd been first to the scene..."

"That's all right, I know." With Jerrod's help, it'd definitely look like I was dating cops. "Just do your job. That's all I was doing, was mine."

Jerrod said, "They have twelve-step groups for all the compulsions. The addictions..."

"It's not a compulsion! I'm an artist. I wasn't doing anything—"

He said. "I've heard a few different ideas about art...conceptual stuff...self-expression, sexuality—"

"I'm a performing artist!"

"Performance?" he said, and looked at me straight on. A big question.

I said, "Not some kind of sex art. Not that kind of performance."

He said, "You might consider this as an addiction, and like any addiction it's out of control, running your life."

"Addicted to clowning?" I asked.

He said, "Addicted to making poor choices, putting yourself in a bad way."

I said, "Come on, you can't hang a clown without a trial. I've got it under control, it was just a little slipup."

"Ever feel like it's easier to act the part of a person than to just let yourself be one?"

"I'm not sure I know the difference."

"Ah," he said. "Right. Well, that explains a few things. For me, most times, I know what I should do as a cop, what I'm supposed to do. Same as if I had a script. But once in a while I don't want to be the cop in the picture. I want to drop the act, break scene...be a civilian, a citizen, a bozo...The deal is, you're building a record," Jerrod said. "Same as the rest of Baloneytown. I'd like to believe that you've got a handle on your actions, you know I would, but here, now, booked on solicitation, caught half-naked outside a van, in an empty lot with a known john...it makes it hard for me to give you the benefit of the doubt."

He had all the details.

"You read my file," I said softly.

He nodded, looked down, and his lashes danced over his tired skin.

I said, "Sheesh. With a write-up like that, how can I even hope you'll see my side of it?"

He shrugged. "If it helps, I hear the conviction in your voice. That's one thing."

"Conviction," I said. "How about acquittal? That's what I want to hear. Acquittal in my voice and everyone else's."

I still had big plans, plans to make myself into somebody special, talented and altruistic. "Once I patch this up, maybe it's time for me to skedaddle, get serious, join a real circus or Clowns Without Borders or go—"

"Or time to quit running away," Jerrod said, and offered a hint of a smile. "Your friend the landlord hasn't pressed charges, so that's good." He touched one of my fingers again, ran a calloused thumb over my skin. "Life is so short. People waste it. I see it every day on the streets. You don't want to get stuck in Baloneytown on parole."

After a minute he said, "'Man is what he believes.'"

"What about women?" I asked. "And clowns."

He sighed. "I'd say the same goes, all around. It's a quote, from Chekhov. I like to believe in the essential goodness of human nature. And I'd believe in you, if you'd give me half a reason."

This time, I didn't pull my hand away.

22.

Bailing, Bailing...; or, Kafka is Mine!

REX WALKED LIKE I WAS A STRAY DOG HE WANTED TO shake. My long-toed, pointy, clown high heels clattered on the pavement as I tried to match his pace. With Rex giving me the icy treatment, ours was a long, hostile walk through a short town. Out of sight of the cop station, finally he looked back over his shoulder and said, "Shit, I try to stay away from the slammer, Nita."

I said, "Not a big deal. We're still doing O K. A little glitch." I waved it off with one hand. I wanted to hug Rex, to hold him, make him stop walking. I almost caught up to him, then reached for his elbow. He swerved away and shook out his arms. He seemed loose after the station. Maybe too loose. He wouldn't catch my eye. I said, "Dahlink. Are you stoned?"

He looked over his shoulder again, like somebody might be coming for him. Then he looked me up and down, in my ripped dress, as I tried to match his fast clip with my one good Caboosey boob jostling. He said, "Enough to take the edge off. Wouldn't hit the pig farm any other way."

Myself, I wouldn't go to the cop station any way but sober.

"Nita, what's happened anyway? I'm gone for three weeks, come back, I've seen you two days. First you're at the tavern for breakfast and now you're a hooker, busted, and ask if *I'm* stoned, like that's the glitch in the gig." He shook his head.

"I'm not a hooker," I said, and linked one finger through his belt loop to pull myself close to him.

He reached a hand to his pocket. His elbow pushed against

my chest. "Then what's this about?" He came up with a piece of paper, folded up small, and started unfolding it, still walking fast. I let go of the belt loop. My heart sank. "Trixie, Twinkie, and Bubbles!"

I snatched the paper from Rex's hand.

"Where'd you get this?" I unfolded the page the rest of the way. It was a picture of me, between Crack and Matey, clown shirt unbuttoned low, red hair lacquered. Matey's hand grabbed my boob. Crack kneeled on the floor in her fishnets, lips pouted.

Compromising clown porn.

"Clown Union Hall. The place is plastered with 'em. And it's not art." He spit on the ground. "Maybe that's what tipped the pigs off, huh?"

"Just wait, Rex. We need to talk. I can't talk when you're walking so fast." He kept going. I said, "I was working a clown gig, like a birthday party or a corporate deal, only smaller, that's all. A private show. One-on-one."

"A private show," he said, and scoffed as though I'd claimed to be joining a convent, working on a cure for cancer, raising Chaplin from the dead. "Go ahead, con yourself, but don't bullshit me, Nita."

"It's true," I said. "What I thought was—"

Rex cut me off. He said, "I'll tell you what's true. I'm busting my ass in California to set up our future and you're a hooker, and a drunk."

"But Crack said—"

"The truth is you're out of control."

I said, "We need money to get—"

"You've lost your way as an artist, Nita. You're getting nowhere. I can't keep doing this."

"This?" The icy hand of Dread fingered my insides, knotted my spleen, my gut. My heart. "Doing what?"

He waved a long arm my direction and said, "Supporting you. Encouraging you, trying to set an example. Hoping you'll make a clown of yourself." He started walking fast again.

I ran alongside him. "I thought we were supporting each other, Rex. That's why I gave you the money for Clown College. Why I've been working hard to make more." I put a hand out to stop him from walking, to hug him, to talk to each other. I said, "Crack said you've been on clown dates before too. She said that's how you paid for—"

"Oh, bull," he said.

"—the unicycles. Is it?" I wanted to see in his bleary eyes.

He looked away and said, "Crack? How reliable is Crack?"

"Is it true?"

Then he glared. "I bail your ass out, and you interrogate me." He stomped up ahead.

I trotted behind.

I said, "She knew about the rubber-chicken sex thing, the jokes. Plucky."

He didn't answer.

"Rex, tell me. Have you done clown dates?"

He bit off the end of my sentence when he snapped, "Don't make this about me. I'm not the bad guy here. I'm not the one fresh out of the slammer, posing for porn."

Then he added, "I'm not the one dating cops."

Dating cops. So Rex had talked to Herman. I said, "I'm not dating him!" How many times could I defend myself?

"Him?" Rex said, and smiled a thin lizard smile. "Who is 'him,' exactly, that you're not dating?"

"Anyone. I'm not dating anyone, except you." I tried again to touch Rex, to find the comfort of our bodies. He shook me off, stepped away.

"Is it the cop I saw you with out front?"

There was no good answer. I said, "While we're on it—what about you and Crack? How'd she know about the rubber-chicken sex jokes? I thought that was our thing, private." I grabbed his arm, and this time got a good hold.

He sneered. There was no love in the way he looked at me. None.

"Tell me," I said. "Is love just an act with you? A big show?"

He turned on the sidewalk, stared at me. He said, "Sheesh, chill, O K? Listen, babe, you've got problems. I care about you, and you're a mess. But I've got bigger things on my playbill than your messed-up tricks. Even the cop doesn't matter, 'cause I take the long view, and my big deal right now is Clown College, whether you're on board or not. I've got the scholarship gig in less than a week. That gives me five days to put together some award-winning shit." He put his big hands on my shoulders, pulled me close. He ran one hand over my burnt hair. "We're wasting our creative juices, arguing." His voice was soft. The sneer was gone. Was this an apology?

"I don't want to fight either." I leaned into his chest, and breathed his skin through his shirt. He ran his hand over my hair. I was a kitten, ready to purr.

He said, "What I could really, really use is your help, with the application."

I'd helped him before as a test audience and a prop, a sidekick, and a judge. "You can do it, Rex," I said. "You're a show-stopper."

He said, "Nita, you don't get it. Sure, I can do the club thing, wow the drunks and underage druggies. A little fire, a handstand, the one-wheeled bike tricks… "

"You can wow anybody."

"This is different. It's for… culture. For older people. Real people, at the Cultural Center. There's a lot at stake, you know? I want to make it, to be one of the Community Arts Advancement scholars. The money would mean something, but I'm after the recognition. Nita, it's been fifteen years of stage shows, talking myself up, always proving and promoting. Now, an Emmett Kelly Award… that'd do the talking for me."

We'd had variations on this conversation before. I was the audience, there to give prompts. I said, "So, what're you going to do? I can help, any help you need. We've got all kinds of resources." I held on to his elbow and felt a rush of love.

He let go, started walking again. He said, "First, you have to pay me back that bail money."

I trotted along at his heels. "Of course. I always pay you back ... But didn't I just give you that money to go to San Francisco? For Clown College, all that?"

He whipped his head around, looked at me, then looked away again. The edge was back in his voice when he said, "I didn't plan on spending it to bail you out."

"All right, all right, so I'll pay you back my own money. No reason to be uptight." Again I took his elbow, laced my fingers around his arm, and held on. I said, "I can make more money."

He said, "Don't whine like I'm your pimp, it's just that I need that cash. If I didn't need it, I wouldn't've taken it in the first place. But listen, there's another way you can help me. I'm working on this thing, Kafka's 'Metamorphosis' ..."

I stopped fast, and his elbow tugged against my folded-together hands. He jerked away. I said, "'The Metamorphosis'? Rex, that's ... That's my thing. I've been working on my 'Metamorphosis' sketch for years. You've watched me develop it—watched me practice the transformation into vermin on my back, seen me work out the surrealist confusion, the naturalist horror. The modernist angst."

He said, "Sure, I know you're into it, but mine'll be different. In this one, it's like the guy's job is as an office executive ..."

In my version, the woman was an office assistant. I never did think big enough.

"... and he turns into a snake instead of a bug. It's hilarious, and it's sad. It's really something."

"Turns into a snake?" I said. Somebody had turned into a snake, right there in front of my eyes. I felt a wave of nausea.

"I think mine's pure, undiscovered genius," he said. "Besides, if mine's different, or the same, what're you worried about—you're not using it. It's just an idea. Ideas are a dime a dozen."

My throat was tight, my head a scream of swarming bees. I couldn't believe my ears. I staggered, clutched my one fake breast.

The rash of panic in my brain broke into all-out cerebral hives. I said, "I am using it. I work on it all the time. I just can't get it into production, because I'm trying to make a living. Trying to pay your way to Clown College."

He laughed. "Looks like you're making a pretty fast living to me." He shook his head. "Those johns need Kafka?"

"I'm not a hooker," I said again. "There's just not the same fast cash in Kafka as there is in the corporate work. Not yet, not until I get ahead."

"Get ahead, or give it? And since when is whoring corporate?"

If Jerrod was right, if clowning was my addiction, then this—not jail—was as low as I could sink; watching my gilded savior, Rex, tarnish. His brilliance was nothing, not even his own. Actually, this round? The ideas were mine. "Rex, you haven't even read Kafka."

He said, "I've seen you practice the skit like a hundred times, right? And you just said you'd help. Give me a little more of the structure then."

If I went along with him, I'd be an enabler, a participant in my own defeat. "There's all kinds of material, pick something else. Pick, like, *Pride and Prejudice,* or *Romeo and Juliet. One Hundred Years of Solitude.* Anything, O K? Kafka's my deal."

He said, "No need to be possessive. We've got enough to go around. We're doing O K, you said so yourself."

"Sure, but I was feeling a surge of love for you then. Hopeful." I'd been noting his humanity, not his greed.

He shrugged. Smiled. "You'll feel another." He was so confident!

"Rex, could you just please lay off my material, until I get it together?"

He said, "Nita, cultivate some professionalism. You don't have the rights to Kafka. Just because I haven't read the dude doesn't mean I can't do my own thing with it. You know what Gold-digger the Great said—'Cheap clowns scrounge, great clowns steal.'"

"Sure, Rex. I've heard the phrase, but I don't subscribe to it," I said. "Great clowns have a little integrity, I'd say. What about the Clown Commandments?"

He stopped walking then, stood on the sidewalk, and blocked my way. "So, what're you saying—I bail you out, and you won't help with the most important act of my career? This is the thing that's going to get me past the club circuit."

"You bailed me out with my own money, and I'll pay it back. I didn't sell the Kafka sketch."

"Jesus," he said. "That was our money when you gave it to me. Knock off the bullshit generosity next time."

"It's not bullshit generosity," I said. "I wish you weren't stoned right now. You're impossible. You make it impossible."

Rex laughed then, a mean, sharp snort. "Impossible? You want to talk impossible? This is all bullshit, babe. You want to think you're not a hooker, just a clown on a private date. Think you're an artist, working a new car lot? I'll tell you something— that's not art. It's just a story you're making up. Maybe the same story you'd tell our baby, if we still had a baby. Mommy's not a hooker, she's a corporate party girl. No wonder the kid bailed. Christ, maybe the thing's lucky you dumped it."

I stopped fast. My boob swung forward with momentum, then slapped against my real boob underneath, a thump to the heart. "What're you saying? Like the miscarriage was my fault?" I held my torn dress like a sari wrapped around me. He shrugged.

"You haven't exactly been leading a healthy lifestyle, have you?"

I crouched on the sidewalk. It was either that or fall over. The bees, the bees! I could barely hear. "I can't believe you'd say that." I whispered, "You're blaming me."

"Well, it wasn't my fault." He towered over me. His pants billowed in the night air. "My part worked out just fine."

I couldn't stand up. My eyes watered, my chin trembled. Since when was a miscarriage about blame? That was so like Rex, to make it adversarial. I said, "Where were you, Rex? When I was bleeding? I called you, needed to hear your voice. You never called back."

Rex rolled his eyes. He said, "I called you back."

"Once. After it was over. Way late." I stood up. Put a hand to my head. I said, "And now your big concern is that you want 'your' money back?" I used my fingers to make quotation marks in the air. It was a jab—Rex hated the quotation mark gesture. He turned away. We were almost to Herman's. "That money I gave you? I'll give it back, right now." I kicked off the high heels and ran the last block to the ambulance.

"Don't be melodramatic," he said behind me.

"Don't be an idea thief," I yelled back. I flung open the ambulance doors, hitched up my big skirts, and climbed in. I wiped tears from my eyes. The ceramic Rex-head stared from a dark corner with empty eyes, with that slight smile—Rex, immortalized as stoned and trying not to get a hard-on.

I put the head under my arm and climbed back out. "Who's the whore now, Mr. Galore? Come get your cash, if that's what you care about."

I pulled the pair of socks from the bottom of the clay head, threw the socks back in the ambulance and took out a fistful of dollars. "Does that keep you from stealing Kafka?"

He walked on past, to Herman's. "Jesus, Nita. You're so over-the-top."

I said, "Take it. I don't want to be in debt to you." I followed, and pressed the money up against him.

"That's great." He pointed at the bust under my arm. "You keep your slut money in my head. What's that, irony? Art and ideas, sex, money and commerce. That's so, so like you." He brushed me away with one big hand.

"What, you're too big for money now?" As I sidestepped his brush-off, barefoot, I teetered. The heavy ceramic head slipped in my hands. Rex's head smashed on Herman's sidewalk. Dollars scattered like spent tickets.

"Shit. Pick that up, would you?" Rex said. "Someone's going to hit us up, or think we're doing a drug deal."

Nadia-Italia's laugh screeched from the darkened porch like a bad gag gift. I wiped my eyes again and said, "It's your money. You pick it up."

"Whatever. Forget it." Rex kept going up onto the porch. He said, "Guess I'm on my own." He was a king, head held high. He was a prince, a dog, a man I didn't even know, and he didn't look back as our future, my hours spent in clown wage-slavery, rustled like garbage in the gutter.

23.

Harsh Medicine; or, My Strabat

REX COULD DO WHAT HE WANTED, BUT WHEN A BALONEY-
town wild child swooped out of the dark and nabbed a twenty, I
chased the kid off, got down on my knees, and picked up the cash.
Let Nadia-Italia laugh, but no way would I watch the fruits of my
clowndom drift like yesterday's lottery tabs. My bad leg whined
with the motion. Rex triggered Herman's floodlight and made
himself the star of a one-man show. His curls caught the high beam,
his muscles were sculpted with shadows.

Nadia-Italia, still hidden in the dark, said, "Hey, superstar,
how's 'bout a smoke." She giggled. Stoned. Rex's dream audience.
Three little pigtails poked up where she slumped on the couch.

Rex stopped to dig through his pockets.

He said, "How 'bout a trade. A little more of that smoke you
got for a few of these," and shook a cigarette out of the pack.

I tried to ignore their production. "Jee-zus," Italia said.
"Check this shit out." She giggled again. I looked up then.

"This shit," as she called it, was Chance, on the porch.
Chance sat up and begged for nothing, looking at nobody.
She stood up and did her soon-to-be famous hula dance, pawed
the air, and bounced left and right.

Nadia-Italia snorted and laughed and said, "Hey, baby,
Momma's got your treats!"

Momma? Chance wobbled toward Italia's outstretched hand.

"Munchies," Italia said. "Yummy." Chance ran in a mad
scramble, the length of the porch and back.

Chance, my drug-sniffing canine, so easily swayed!

I said, "You're feeding my dog pot?"

"She got into the stash," Italia slurred. "Her party habit."

"You do that on purpose..."

Rex said, "You're always the victim, aren't you? It's not about Chance, it's about you. Feeding your dog pot. It's about your Kafka trip, your little dream."

"Look at her, Rex." Chance was goggle-eyed. Nadia-Italia wasn't much better off and let her own head loll against the split fat couch. "It's not about me." I left the busted bust of Rex on the sidewalk, shoved dollars into my prop bag. I said, "This is what I put up with. She's trying to kill our baby."

"Our baby?" Rex said, and paused. "I don't think she's the one—"

"Our dog!" I wanted to scream. It felt good to scream. He knew what I meant.

He said, "You overreact. I'm beat. I can't take it anymore, Nita." He went in the house.

"Rex?" I called after him.

He was out of sight by the time he called back, "We'll talk in the morning."

Morning? That was hours away. Forever. I'd waited so long for Rex to come home, but he felt no urgency. Nadia-Italia followed Rex, said, "Cha-cha, clownster," and pulled the front door closed.

Rex as I knew him—high artist, Clown God—wouldn't waste time as an idea thief. Chance smacked dry lips. We needed hydrogen peroxide, pronto-presto. I walked barefoot to where my clown shoes lay like discarded party favors. Chance watched invisible angels in the night sky, head bobbing and loose.

At the Lucky Trucker Motel and Sundries I carried her into the store. "No dog in here," the man at the register said. "No dog, no dog!" He flung one arm out like a wing.

A bottle of hydrogen peroxide waited on a dusty shelf. I

ducked, snagged the bottle. There was a line at the register. I waved the peroxide. "Just this. One thing."

"No dog," he said again, "you wait in line." The man's teeth were a mix of gold and yellow.

"My dog is dying. Look." I held Chance up like a puppet, the store our puppet theater. A strand of drool found its way to the floor.

Two scrawny men and a woman with shaking, veined hands all laughed. A man with a mullet and a quart of beer said, "Nice act, stooge, take it to Nashville." He put his money on the counter. Even an old woman who watched TV in the corner, who never spoke any language at all, even she laughed.

I held my ripped dress closer and cradled Chance. "It's serious!" They laughed harder.

And that laugh echoed what I felt inside as more real than my blood, my heartbeat: that I was a joke. In protest I said, "It's not a joke." But the laugh only grew. And who laughed the loudest? A hooker in a torn red dress at the back of the line, naturally. My doppelgänger. Each minute, I sank a little deeper into Baloneytown.

There was my face in the aluminum rim of the hot-foods incubator, around jo-jos and chicken. I was reflected in the glass of the Coke cooler and the grease-smeared deli case, all powdery makeup, black liner, and big red lips, the face of a clown hooker right out of an old-time jail-time act. My one Caboosey boob hung free.

The doppelgänger said, "Tha' poodle part a your show?"

The only show was my life, and it was a bomb. The only routine was the daily one. I'd been in clown costume so long, I wasn't an artist. I was a freak. My hands were shaking and I couldn't blink. I felt as though I were falling, a high-wire dive, safety ropes unfurling and unraveling left and right, loose and looped. This is a strabat: an aerialist's finale, when all could be lost.

There was nobody to be my net, to close the curtains, to

know me without the makeup. Rex saw me as a muse in the worst way—a place to steal material.

Mr. Galore.

I couldn't think of his name without love. But Rex, as I saw him, was a big projection: I wanted the artist's life and thought I'd found it on the blank screen of his painted face.

My name is Sniffles, and I'm a clownaholic...

Man is what he believes. All I knew was: Christian clowns, hookers, coulrophiles, and the fetishized silence of mime—I was bigger than the roles.

In the Lucky Trucker I took a tip from Jerrod and said, "Just because I'm a clown doesn't mean I have to put up with abuse." I picked up a box of travel-sized baby wipes.

"Still have to wait in line, though," a drunk, wobbling woman hiccuped. Her hair was spun asbestos, her nose a withered apple. She spoke from experience.

Baloneytown was crowded with worn-out clowns, good intentions, and bad choices. The mistakes were easy and I'd made them all, sure, but the Lucky Trucker vaudeville team testified to Matey's truth: S & M and clowning dovetailed into one and the same.

And the lives? Dog years.

Yes, I should've waited in line at the Lucky Trucker, and I would have waited if Chance weren't digesting Herman's pot as I stood there. I slid a bill on the counter next to the Turkey Jerky, and way overpaid in the hope that the dollars made up for my rudeness. Out in front, by the overflowing trash can and broken pay phone, I tipped Chance's head back. She took her medicine, a harsh cure for an easy mistake, and as she foamed at the mouth I tried to come up with a cure for my own mistakes aplenty.

Chance's steps were sloppy as we started back to the ambulance. She vomited white foam laced with dabs of pot like green sprinkles on snowy cupcakes. I opened the box of baby wipes, ran one over my cheek, and wiped makeup away. I tucked the used wipe in my bra and got out another. One swipe at a time, I cleaned up my act.

Near Herman's, there was a fast glint and flicker of a UFO, and just as quickly the UFO crashed in a scatter of broken glass. Herman's voice came out of the dark: "Fuck."

A shadow ran, the soft pad of tennis shoes. I matched Chance's tipsy stride. From somewhere, the ice-cream truck song started up in fast gear. It was either a late night sweet tooth emergency or a giveaway of a getaway car. Nearer, I saw Herman, soaking wet in the street on the ground, surrounded by glass, a hand to his head.

"Ah," I said. "Another bashing? I thought clowns were the only fools targeted on the street."

Herman muttered, "Never should've diversified... " Chance waddled and vomited, weaving and slow. Herman said, "You know this is about...your piss...harassment." His forehead sported a goose egg.

Like his bad deal was my fault? I said, "Drugs, urine, and ice cream all in one vehicle—a regular Baloneytown variety store." I kicked a piece of mason jar glass. "It cut your head, Hermes. And God, it reeks."

He pulled his fingers away, squinted at the blood. I reached inside my bunched-up dress to unfasten the boob bib, the only thing more battered than Herman looked at the moment. I slipped the top over my head, and when I let go the single Pendulous Breast fell to the ground.

"We've got to get you out of the street before a car comes. You can rest in the ambulance. Put your arm over my back." I bent to pick him up. As I brushed against him, pee seeped onto my dress.

"No." He climbed to his feet. I offered a shoulder. He said, "If I'm going...to die..." He had to catch his breath. "I want to be ...not in a clown-bulance."

"You're not going to die."

"Not yet, anyway." Like a cowboy into the sunset Herman staggered toward the glow of the porch light.

I stayed where he left me, in the dark, outside that circle of light, and listened to the ice-cream truck ramble far away with a sound tiny as a music box, oddly optimistic, almost cheerful. The sidewalk was dotted with Chance's pot-laced vomit, each tuft white and reflective as the moon, marking the path I'd walked like Hansel and Gretel's bread crumbs, except in my story every dollop was a single-sized serving of pot soufflé laced with incriminating evidence. If the cops traced the path to Herman's grow operation, we'd be cited with distributing a controlled substance through dog puke.

We? Yes. It was Herman's operation, but the lot of us would go down. It'd be the Big Bust, starring Herman, front and center. I'd be a bit player blinking into the footlights. Then, *voilà*! Curtains! The co-op would fall into a Baloneytown real estate deal: confiscated, put up for silent auction, and sold back to B-town Barons for chump change. We'd all be in stripes. Not the fun-loving stripes of clowns, Pixy Stix, and barber poles, but the state-issued stripes of convicts.

In short, the house, the yard, us—we'd all go to pot.

I saw something move behind a window upstairs, Herman or Natalia. They, my friends, were hucksters, drug dealers, and bullies. But in that world of defeatism I was the jester, the fall guy, the rubber chicken. I was the one who put on face paint and shades, limping in one big shoe.

I was the one who'd accepted a tiny free room in the back of the house from an ex-boyfriend on the verge of arrest. Who chose to wait while Rex spent my money in another town. What kind of life was that?

Chance and I went back to our cabin in the ambulance.

I kneeled in front of the EMT chair, in front of the mirror on the medicine cabinet, and wiped the rest of the makeup away. My skin was raw, pink and new. The ambulance had a single round light in the middle of the ceiling. The light cast long shadows under my nose, ears, eyes, and chin, and in the shadows I was young and I was a crone, in the exact same moment. That's it, I thought: life is short. The only value of wasted time is knowledge.

Clown dates and corporate gigs weren't the answer. Maybe money wasn't the answer. I needed to remember who I'd been back before I came to live in makeup, before I devoted myself to Rex, a vague future and a badly dressed present.

I'd start over, with the clothes on my back. Well, I'd take a few more clothes, out of the sea of fabric in the back of the ambulance. Why not? And then I'd take my lovely, half-trained, left-handed, purebred schipperke. I couldn't leave Chance—no, I'd take my Chance and my chances both. And I had the money I'd saved for Rex's career at Clown College, in stacks of twenties.

Behind the medicine chest, separating the front from the back seats, there were two sliding Plexiglas windows. With the flat of my palm, I slid one window open. I leaned through, reached a long, thin arm, and pulled up the lock on the driver's side door.

I got out of the back of the ambulance and went around to the front, to sit in the driver's seat. Rex always drove, though the ambulance was at least as much mine as it was his—like everything, we bought it with corporate clowning money. Whoring money, if you saw it that way. I flipped down the sun visor. A set of keys fell to my lap.

So I had clothes and my dog and money, and I had the ambulance, that portable home, our mobile circus full of storage compartments, complete with shades on the windows and a bed in back. And then I had myself, my health, more or less, Kafka and da Vinci and all the big ideas.

What was I waiting for?

The streets of Baloneytown were dark and empty. I drove slow and easy down the same roads I'd walked a hundred times. Driving, I rode a little higher off the ground, and all the old storefronts and empty lots seemed suddenly so close together, the neighborhood incredibly small. To live here, to stay, would be to consign myself to the life of a moth banging against a window-pane; there was a whole world just outside.

I'd take time out of costume, try to learn to merge the roles—beauty and art, comedy and sex—until I could make myself whole again.

I passed Hoagies and Stogies. At one side of the bar the little dusty red and white checkered curtains were parted, creating a tiny stage. Inside, as though on stage, a man sat at a small table near the window under the red and blue of a beer light. His shoulders were hunched, head bowed over a newspaper. He had a hoagie on an open wrapper in a woven straw plate on the table. I pulled to the curb. The man turned a page. He wiped his mouth on a napkin. Put the napkin down and crumpled it against his palm.

I'd recognize those hunched shoulders anywhere: it was Jerrod, out of uniform. Alone, he looked so serious, and human. A vulnerable cop.

I turned off the idling ambulance. When I went in the bar Mad Addie, behind the counter, barely gave a glance. She didn't tap her *No Clowns* sign or flick cigarillo ash. I walked to Jerrod's table.

I was at his elbow before Jerrod looked up.

Then he was startled. "Can I help you?"

And I felt calm. I felt calm for the first time since ... since ... since the night I'd kissed Jerrod. Even my heart felt fine, relaxed. I thought about what the Buddhists said, that when you meet your soul mate you'll be at ease. Not agitated or nervous. Not the way I felt around Rex Galore. With a steady voice, an easy breath, I said, "I don't need any help."

It was true. I didn't need help for the first time in ages.

At the sound of my voice, Jerrod blinked, maybe startled, then smiled, and closed his paper. He pushed the paper wrapper with his sandwich on it an inch farther away. "Sniffles?"

I said, "Nita."

He said, "You need a ...?"

Then I laughed. "No, that's my name. Really, I don't need anything." I didn't.

He pulled a chair over, gave it a pat. I took a seat. He said, "I didn't recognize you right off. You threw me."

"That's O K. I don't recognize myself, just now." In the guise of myself, I was somebody else, somebody I hadn't been in years. And as the great clown question goes, if that's me in the mirror, then who am I? I was new, unmasked.

It was a fine, though dangerous, way to walk through the world: accountable.

If life were a Chaplin film the frame I lived in would've closed like an aperture at this moment, shrunk to a small circle or maybe even a heart shape, until it was just Jerrod and me, our faces lit, ready to live happily ever after. Ah, zounds! If only it were that simple. Instead, we sat under the flickering beer light on our separate chairs, close together but apart, cop and clown, clown and cop, out of costume though still a little guarded and a little exposed, as though the cop and the clown were there in both of us. I kept breathing, and had to hold on, to relax, to teach myself new tricks. The bartender slid a glass of beer on the table. I took a sip.

Jerrod, half-shy, held back a smile. He said, "Well, I couldn't have picked you out of a lineup, after all."

I wiped a bit of beer from my lip, then said, "That's O K. Maybe you'll never have to."

Hawthorne Books & Literary Arts
Portland, Oregon

Current Titles

At Hawthorne Books, we're serious about literature. We suspected that good writers were being ignored and cast aside as a result of consolidation in the publishing industry, and in 2001 we decided to find these writers and give them a voice. We publish American literary fiction and narrative non-fiction, although we won't turn down a good international title if we find one. All of our books are published as affordable original trade paperbacks, but feature details not typically found even in casebound titles from bigger houses: acid-free papers; sewn bindings which will not crack; heavy, laminated covers with French flaps and built-in bookmarks. You can probably buy Hawthorne Books wherever you buy books, or from our Web site (*hawthornebooks.com*) postpaid* and for a substantial discount. If you like to read, we think you'll enjoy our books. If you like to write – well, send us something. We're always looking.

* Free postage available only for orders shipped within the United States. Sorry about that.

Core: A Romance
Kassten Alonso

Fiction / 208pp / $12.95 / 0-9716915-7-6

This intense and compact novel crackles with obsession, betrayal, and madness. As the narrator becomes fixated on his best friend's girlfriend, his precarious hold on sanity deteriorates into delusion and violence in this twenty-first-century retelling of the classic myth of Hades and Persephone.

FINALIST, 2005 OREGON BOOK AWARD

"Jump through this Gothic stained-glass window and you are in for some serious investigation of darkness and all of its deadly sins. But take heart, brave traveler, the adventure will prove thrilling."
Tom Spanbauer Author of *Now is the Hour*

501 Minutes to Christ
Poe Ballantine

Essays / 174pp / $13.95 / 0-9766311-9-9

This collection of personal essays ranges from Ballantine's diabolical plan to punch John Irving in the nose during a literary festival, to the tale of how after years of sacrifice and persistence, Ballantine finally secured a contract with a major publisher for a short story collection that never came to fruition.

TITLE STORY INCLUDED
IN THE BEST AMERICAN ESSAYS 2006

"My soul yearns to know this most entangled enigma. I confess to Thee, O Lord, that I really have no idea what Poe Ballantine is talking about."
St. Augustine

Decline of the Lawrence Welk Empire
Poe Ballantine

Fiction / 376pp / $15.95 / 0-9 66311-1-3

Edgar Donahoe is back for another misadventure, this time in the Caribbean. When he becomes involved with his best friend's girl and is stalked by murderous island native Chollie Legion, even Cinnamon Jim, the medicine man, is no help—it takes a hurricane to blow Edgar out of the mess.

"This second novel ... initially conjures images of *Lord of the Flies*, but then you would have to add about ten years to the protagonists' ages and make them sex-crazed, gold-seeking alcoholics."
Library Journal

God Clobbers Us All
Poe Ballantine

Fiction / 196pp / $15.95 / 0-9716915-4-1

Set against a decaying San Diego rest home in the 1970s, *God Clobbers Us All* is the shimmering, hysterical, melancholy account of eighteen-year-old surfer-boy/orderly Edgar Donahoe, who struggles with romance, death, friendship, and an ill-advised affair with the wife of a maladjusted war veteran.

"Calmer than Bukowski, less portentous than Kerouac, more hopeful than West, Poe Ballantine may not be sitting at the table of his mentors, but perhaps he deserves his own after all."
San Diego Union-Tribune

Things I Like About America
Poe Ballantine

Essays / 266pp / $12.95 / 0-9716915-1-7

These risky personal essays are populated with odd jobs, eccentric characters, boarding houses, buses, and beer. Written with piercing intimacy and self-effacing humor, they take us on a Greyhound journey through small-town America and explore what it means to be human.

"Part social commentary, part collective biography, this guided tour may not be comfortable, but one thing's for sure: You will be at home."
Willamette Week

WINNER, 2005 LANGUM PRIZE FOR HISTORICAL FICTION

Madison House
Peter Donahue

Fiction / 528pp / $16.95 / 0-9766311-0-5

This novel chronicles Victorian Seattle's explosive transformation from frontier outpost to metropolis. Maddie Ingram, owner of Madison House, and her quirky and endearing boarders find their lives linked when the city decides to regrade Denny Hill and the fate of their home hangs in the balance.

"Peter Donahue seems to have a map of old Seattle in his head... And all future attempts in its historical vein will be made in light of this book."
David Guterson Author of *Snow Falling on Cedars*

Clown Girl   Introduction by Chuck Palahniuk
Monica Drake

Fiction / 298pp / $15.95 / 0-9766311-5-6

Clown Girl lives in Baloneytown, a neighborhood
so run-down that drugs, balloon animals, and even
rubber chickens contribute to the local currency.
Using clown life to illuminate a struggle between
integrity and economic reality, this novel examines
issues of class, gender, economics, and prejudice.

"The pace of [this] narrative is methamphetamine-frantic, as Drake
drills down past the face paint and into Nita's core ... There is a lot
more going on here than just clowning around."
Publishers Weekly

So Late, So Soon
D'Arcy Fallon

Memoir / 224pp / $15.95 / 0-9716915-3-3

An irreverent, fly-on-the-wall view of the Lighthouse
Ranch, a Christian commune the eighteen-year-
old hitchhiker D'Arcy Fallon called home for three
years in the mid-1970s, when life's questions over-
whelmed her and reconciling her family past with
her future seemed impossible.

"What would draw an otherwise independent woman to a life of
menial labor and subservience? Fallon's answer is both an inside
look at '70s commune life and a funny, poignant coming of age."
Judy Blunt   Author of *Breaking Clean*

September 11: West Coast Writers
Approach Ground Zero   Edited by Jeff Meyers

Essays / 266pp / $16.95 / 0-9716915-0-9

The events of September 11, 2001, their repercussions,
and our varied responses to them inspired this
collection. By history and geographic distance, the
West Coast has developed a community different
from the East; ultimately shared interests bridge the
distinctions in provocative and heartening ways.

"*September 11: West Coast Writers Approach Ground Zero* deserves
attention. This book has some highly thoughtful contributions
that should be read with care on both coasts, and even in between."
San Francisco Chronicle

Dastgah: Diary of a Headtrip
Mark Mordue

Travel Memoir / 316pp / $15.95 / 0-9716915-6-8

A world trip that ranges from a Rolling Stones concert in Istanbul to meetings with mullahs and junkies in Teheran, from a cricket match in Calcutta to an S&M bar in New York, as Mark Mordue explores countries most Americans never see, as well as issues of world citizenship in the twenty-first century.

"Mordue has elevated *Dastgah* beyond the realms of the traditional travelogue by sharing not only what he learned about cultures he visited but also his brutally honest self-discoveries."
Elle

FINALIST, 2006 OREGON BOOK AWARD

The Cantor's Daughter
Scott Nadelson

Fiction / 280pp / $15.95 / 0-9766311-2-1

Sympathetic, heartbreaking, and funny, these stories—capturing people in critical moments of transition—reveal our fragile emotional bonds and the fears that often cause those bonds to falter or fail.

"These beautifully crafted stories are populated by Jewish suburbanites living in New Jersey, but ethnicity doesn't play too large a role here. Rather, it is the humanity of the characters and our empathy for them that bind us to their plights."
Austin Chronicle

WINNER: 2004 OREGON BOOK AWARD; 2005 GLCA NEW WRITERS AWARD

Saving Stanley: The Brickman Stories
Scott Nadelson

Ficion / 230pp / $15.95 / 0-9716915-2-5

These interrelated short stories are graceful, vivid narratives that bring into sudden focus the spirit and the stubborn resilience of the Brickmans, a Jewish family of four living in suburban New Jersey. This fierce collection provides an unblinking examination of family life and the human instinct for attachment.

"Focusing on small decisions and subtle shifts, *Saving Stanley* closely examines the frayed ties that bind. With a fly-on-the-wall sensibility and a keen sense for dramatic restraint, Nadelson is ... both a promising writer and an apt documentarian."
Willamette Week

Seaview Introduction by Robert Coover
Toby Olson
Fiction / 316pp / $15.95 / 0-9766311-6-4

This novel follows a golf hustler and his dying wife across an American wasteland. Trying to return the woman to her childhood home on Cape Cod, the pair are accompanied by a mysterious Pima Indian activist and shadowed by a vengeful drug dealer to the novel's apocalypse on the Seaview Links.

WINNER, 1983 PEN/FAULKNER AWARD

"Even a remarkable dreamer of nightmares like Nathanael West might have been hard-pressed to top the finale ... Unlike any other recent American novel in the freshness of its approach and vision."
The New York Times Book Review

The Well and the Mine
Gin Phillips
Fiction / $15.95 / 0-9766311-7-2

In 1931 Carbon Hill, Alabama, a small coal-mining town, nine-year-old Tess Moore watches a woman shove the cover off the family well and toss in a baby without a word. The apparent murder forces the family to face the darker side of their community and attempt to understand the motivations of their family and friends. Most townspeople don't have enough money for a newspaper and backbreaking work keeps them busy from dawn until well after dusk. But next to the daily toil of hard work are the lingering pleasures of sweet tea, feather beds, and lightning bugs.

Leaving Brooklyn Introduction by Ursula Hegi
Lynne Sharon Schwartz
Fiction / 168pp / $12.95 / 0-9766311-4-8

An injury at birth left fifteen-year-old Audrey with a wandering eye and her own way of seeing; her relationship with a Manhattan eye doctor exposes her to the sexual rites of adulthood in this startling and wonderfully rich novel, which raises the themes of innocence and escape to transcendent heights.

"Stunning. Coming of age is seldom registered as disarmingly as it is in *Leaving Brooklyn*."
New York Times Book Review

Faraway Places   Introduction by A.M. Homes
Tom Spanbauer

Fiction / $14.95 / 0-9766311-8-0

This novel marks the end of childhood for Jake Weber and the beginning of trouble for his family. An innocent swim ends with something far beyond anyone's expectations: Jake witnesses a brutal murder and is forced to keep quiet, even as the woman's lover is falsely accused.

"Forceful and moving ... Spanbauer tells his short, brutal story with delicacy and deep respect for place and character."
Publishers Weekly

FINALIST, 2005 OREGON BOOK AWARD

The Greening of Ben Brown
Michael Strelow

Fiction / 272pp / $15.95 / 0-9716915-8-4

Ben Brown becomes a citizen of East Leven, Oregon after he recovers from an electrocution that has turned him green. He befriends eighteen-year-old Andrew James and together they unearth a chemical-spill cover-up that forces the town to confront its demons and its citizens to choose sides.

"Strelow resonates as both poet and storyteller. [He] lovingly invokes ... a blend of fable, social realism, wry wisdom, and irreverence that brings to mind Ken Kesey, Tom Robbins, and the best elements of a low-key mystery."
The Oregonian

WINNER, 1987 PEN/FAULKNER AWARD

Soldiers in Hiding   Introduced by Wole Soyinka
Richard Wiley

Fiction / 194pp / $14.95 / 0-9766311-3-X

Teddy Maki is a Japanese American jazz musician trapped in Tokyo with his friend, Jimmy Yakamoto, both of whom are drafted into the Japanese army after Pearl Harbor. Thirty years later, Maki is a big star on Japanese TV and wrestling with the guilt over Jimmy's death that he's been carrying since the war.

"Wonderful ... Original ... Terrific ... Haunting ... Reading *Soldiers in Hiding* is like watching a man on a high wire!"
The New York Times